THE SPIRITUAL QUIXOTE

THE SPIRITUAL QUIXOTE

OR, THE SUMMER'S RAMBLE OF
MR GEOFFRY WILDGOOSE

Richard Graves

NONSUCH

First published 1772
Copyright © in this edition Nonsuch Publishing, 2007

Nonsuch Publishing
Cirencester Road, Chalford, Stroud, Gloucestershire, GL6 8PE

Nonsuch Publishing (Ireland)
73 Lower Leeson Street, Dublin 2, Ireland

www.nonsuch-publishing.com

Nonsuch Publishing is an imprint of NPI Media Group

For comments or suggestions, please email the editor of this series at:
classics@tempus-publishing.com

British Library Cataloguing in Publication Data:
A catalogue record for this book is available from the British Library.

ISBN 978 1 84588 600 4

Typesetting and origination by NPI Media Group
Printed in Great Britain

CONTENTS

INTRODUCTION TO THE MODERN EDITION

THE TERM 'QUIXOTISM' CAME ABOUT as a direct result of Spanish author Miguel de Cervantes' early comic novel *Don Quixote*, first published in Spain in 1605. The protagonist, Alonso Quixano, is a country gentleman who has read so many stories of chivalry that he descends into fantasy and becomes convinced he is a knight-errant. Together with his earthy squire, Sancho Panza, the self-created 'Don Quixote de la Mancha' sets out in search of adventure.

Based on the amusing and absurd traits of Cervantes' protagonist, the quality of quixotism has since been used to describe a person or an act that becomes ludicrously caught up in the romance of noble deeds and the pursuit of unattainable goals. It describes an over-zealous and impulsive idealism that takes little account of practicality—the very quality that leads Don Quixote in his infamous attempt to fight the windmills that have, in his own imaginary world, been transformed into powerful and threatening giants.

By the mid-seventeenth century the word 'quixote', and its clear reference to Don Quixote's romantic idealism, had already found its way into the vocabulary of the more learned English scholars. In 1644 the poet John Cleveland wrote in his book *The character of a London diurnall* about:

> the Quixotes of this Age that fight with the Wind-mills of their owne Heads.

Throughout the seventeenth and eighteenth centuries more writers were to adopt the ideas behind Cervantes' picaresque novel by introducing characters of their own, whose over-idealism consequently blinded them to the absurdity of their elaborate and ambitious pursuits. Richard Graves' *The Spiritual Quixote*, first published in two volumes in 1772, is one such example.

There are numerous parallels between the two novels, not only in their introduction of the hapless quixote figure, but in their simultaneously comic and affectionate treatment of social attitude, behaviour and convention. As Don Quixote sets out in pursuit of adventure, so Graves' protagonist, Geoffry Wildgoose, sets out, each accompanied by his trusty companion, Sancho Panza and Jeremiah Tugwell respectively. Each protagonist then enters into a series of adventures before ultimately acknowledging his own far-reached ideals and modestly accepting defeat in his original pursuits.

The novels differ, however, in their individual creation of the quixote figure. Graves, although clearly basing his protagonist on that of Cervantes' *Don Quixote*, puts an innovative spin on the Spanish original by making Wildgoose a pursuer of exclusively *religious* goals.

The young squire, conceiving a pique against Mr Powel, the parson of his parish, who had got the better of him in a theological discussion, betakes himself to the systematic study of Methodist and Puritanical literature. He embraces its doctrines with rigorous ardour, stimulated by a perusal of the journals of the historical figures Wesley and Whitfield, and makes it his goal to right the wrongs of every living soul. With good intentions based on a dubious idealism, Wildgoose sets out, on foot, to reform the world—not through knight-errantry, but by preaching the principles of Methodist teaching with a view to converting sinners all over England. His attendant, Tugwell, is a shrewd individual, and a great lover of good cheer. Not a chapter passes by without some mention of his hearty relish of creature comforts. Despite meeting with considerable opposition, Wildgoose remains resolute in his own ability to spread the word, lecturing relentlessly against sin in the slow but sure path to New Birth through the power of faith.

The leading idea in the mind of Wildgoose is the conversion of souls: that is his first object, in every company and under all circumstances. Unsurprisingly, the leading idea in the mind of his fellow-traveller is a perpetual hankering after good food and good ale. Forever denouncing Tugwell's incessant hunt for sustenance, Wildgoose's over-zealous sermons are highly hypocritical as he, too—supposedly for the good of their Christian cause—gives in to the pressures of hunger and fatigue at every available opportunity. Along the way, a love interest also comes to divide Wildgoose's attention from the concerns of the spiritual man, and he is continually engaged in a conflict between the flesh and the spirit; a conflict which, eventually, gets the better of him in a wonderful take on the comic romance plot. As expected by all but himself, his field preaching proves to be far less successful than his zeal had inspired him to suppose, and he finally relinquishes his scheme and returns to the society of his family, re-embracing the doctrines and discipline of the Church into which he had, originally, been baptised.

In addition to its adherence to the picaresque sub-genre, *The Spiritual Quixote* can also be seen as a lively religious satire, directed against the extravagances of Methodism shortly after its revival in England. As Graves' novel demonstrates, it was a denomination particularly popular with the lower and working classes—hence Tugwell's initial enthusiasm in his neighbour's ambitious ideals—due to its enthusiastic preaching and dynamic presentation of doctrine, the actual *content* and therefore importance of which undoubtedly remained incomprehensible to most of them.

Methodism originated in the early eighteenth century, predominantly under the evangelical teaching of John Wesley, and was quickly spread through vigorous missionary activity. In one of his sermons, Wesley skilfully appealed to his audience by placing their interests above his own:

I am no longer my own but yours. Put me to what you will, rank me with whom you will; put me to doing, put me to suffering; let me be employed for you or laid aside for you, exalted for you or brought low for you; let me be full, let me be empty, let me have all things, let me have nothing; I freely and wholeheartedly yield all things to your pleasure and disposal.

The preachers of the day were notorious for their over-zealous sermons, and as such were often accused of fanaticism. Many members of the established Anglican Church—of which Richard Graves (1715–1804) was himself a respected clergyman—grew to fear the new doctrines promulgated by the Methodists and, in particular, the way in which the forceful nature of their sermons might have the ability to sway weak-minded individuals. Theophilus Evans, an early critic of the movement, even went so far as to say that:

the natural tendency of their behaviour, in voice and gesture and horrid expressions, is to make people mad.

Likewise, in one of his prints, William Hogarth attacked Methodists as 'enthusiasts' full of 'Credulity, Superstition and Fanaticism'.

Although Graves can be seen to ridicule the followers of Methodism in *The Spiritual Quixote*, it is important to note that he always maintained a certain respect for genuine piety. Furthermore, the attack on Methodism by no means comes to dominate the novel—its attraction also lies in the accounts of the social life and entertainments of the time, the ways of travellers and the customs of rustics and inn-keepers. In the words of writer William Alfred Jones (1857):

It is full of adventure and reflection, a fair picture of the manners of the day, and the current fashionable follies of the time.

BOOK I

I

THE EDUCATION AND JUVENILE PURSUITS OF MR WILDGOOSE

IN A SEQUESTERED VILLAGE, WHOSE Gothic spire (though hardly discernible in a map of the world) makes a picturesque appearance under the Cotswold hills, the family of the Wildgooses had been settled for many generations. The only surviving heir to their freehold estate, which, next to that of the 'squire, was the most considerable in the parish, was Mr Geoffry Wildgoose, the subject of the following history. They had another son, indeed, who died in his infancy; and also a daughter: but as she married young, contrary to her parents' approbation, and became the careful mother of many children, she, for that reason, made but a small figure in the annals of the family.

Mr Geoffry Wildgoose received the first rudiments of his education at a little free-school by the side of the church-yard; from whence he was removed, at a proper age, to a considerable grammar school: and having, by the time he was seventeen, gained as much classical knowledge as is usually taught in those seminaries, the master greatly extolled his parts and genius. His father, therefore, whose veneration for learning rose in proportion to his own want of it, thinking his son might augment his fortune by some learned profession, sent him to finish his studies in the university of Oxford. Young Wildgoose applied himself to the sciences with great assiduity. And, though he had been prevailed on to make one or two excursions to London, and had taken a glimpse of the fashionable world: had seen Quin in his meridian at Drury-lane, and Garrick in his dawn at Goodman's-fields: had shown his face at the Bedford coffee-house, and even eat a jelly with Betty Careless★ in Covent-garden; notwithstanding these youthful sallies, young Wildgoose went through the business of the college with diligence and regularity. And having in his person and behaviour something naturally agreeable, an openness of countenance and a simplicity of manners, he gained the

★ *Carlesis! ah! nostris et fleta et flenda camoenis.* Meret. Brit.

love and esteem of his acquaintance, which were pretty numerous, and of the genteeler sort of young people in the university. But, soon after he had been created senior soph, by the solemn imposition of Aristole upon this head (which solemnity he made a pretence for drawing upon the old gentleman for ten guineas extraordinary,) and when he was just aspiring to the high dignity and, honourable privileges of a bachelor in arts, he was recalled to his native seat by the death of his father.

Old Mr Wildgoose had always shown a great affection for his son. But the necessary expences of a university education appearing to him the height of extravagance, according to the opinion he now entertained of his son Geoffry, he was afraid his estate would be squandered away the moment he was laid in his grave. Besides, as it had been freed from a considerable encumbrance by Mrs Wildgoose's fortune, who was the daughter of a wealthy clergyman, and as it had been greatly augmented by her good economy and his own frugality, he left a great part of his fortune in Mrs Wildgoose's power. As Mr Geoffry, however, was the only son, and was conscious of being the darling of his mother, this circumstance gave him no kind of uneasiness. And though his father had intended him for some learned profession (as was observed,) yet, being now his own master; and the natural aversion which most young people have to confinement, falling in with his mother's inclination to keep her son always with her; he dwelt at home for some years; a comfort to his mother in her decline of life, a conversable companion to the neighbouring gentlemen, an oracle amongst the farmers, and a wag amongst the gossips at every christening and festival entertainment.

Mr Wildgoose's chief employment was, to manage that part of his mother's estate which she kept in her hands, to the best advantage. This, however, with the assistance of an old servant, gave him little trouble, and left him at liberty to amuse himself, either in company or in the common recreations of the country; or, what was more to his taste, in reading history, poetry, and, in short, most of the best authors in the English language. He frequently walked out, indeed, with his greyhound, or with his spaniel and gun; but the one was rather for a companion, and the other for show, than for any great pleasure which he took either in coursing or shooting. In this obscurity Mr Wildgoose had probably spent his life, and joined the undistinguished list of his deceased ancestors, but for the following contemptible incident.

II

A DISPUTE WITH THE VICAR

Christmas being still observed amongst the lower sort of people as a solemn festival, Wildgoose had been invited by a substantial farmer, at that season, to spend a sociable evening with Mr Powel, the vicar of the parish, and other company. Mr Wildgoose, though a sensible man, used frequently to entertain his illiterate companions, and excite their admiration, with some academical paradoxes; and was fond of exhibiting his dexterity in managing an argument, on the most trifling occasions, in all the forms of mood and figure, agreeably to the rules. In the course of this evening's conversation there arose a dispute between Wildgoose and the vicar, in which, according to the letter of the law, Wildgoose, perhaps, had the right side of the question.

There had lately been a new window-tax imposed, which, amongst the middling sort of people, was a frequent subject of complaint. Wildgoose, it seems, since his retreat into the country, had been improving the old mansion-house, by opening a glass-door into the garden. The question was, whether this door ought to be taxed as a window or not, as the overseer, supported by the vicar, seemed to think it ought. Wildgoose insisted upon it, that, however a set of country justices (who seldom were great logicians) might determine, a door was not a window; that it was essentially distinguished from it, by its name, its structure, its use, and what not.

The vicar, instead of answering him merely in a serious way, turned his reasoning into ridicule, with some humour, and, perhaps, with some solidity. He said, that as a glass door conveyed light, it answered the end of a widow, and ought to be taxed as such: that its being used as a door, did not destroy the use of it as a window; and, that the name of a thing did not alter its nature. In short, says the vicar, you may as well argue, that a pudding and a dumpling are essentially distinguished, as that a glass door and a glass window are so.

As a pun or a ludicrous expression has frequently more weight with the vulgar than the most solid argument, the doctor by his raillery turned the laugh against his antagonist, and put him to an awkward silence. The conversation, however, was soon changed, and the company continued their mirth and good humour. But this defeat sunk deeper into Wildgoose's bosom than one would easily imagine, and was attended with considerable consequences, which greatly affected the future conduct of his life.

III

THE SERIOUS CONSEQUENCES OF IT

Some of the most important events in history, if traced to their original, have sprung from the most trifling causes. The murder of Caesar in the capitol was chiefly owing to his not rising from his seat, when the senate tendered him some particular honours. The negociations with the pope for dissolving Henry the Eighth's marriage (which brought on the Reformation) are said to have been interrupted by the Earl of Wiltshire's dog biting his holiness's toe, when he put it out to be kissed by that ambassador: and, not to multiply instances in so plain a case, the duchess of Marlborough's spilling a bason of water on Mrs Masham's gown, in Queen Anne's reign, brought in the Tory ministry, and gave a new turn to the affairs of Europe.

Thus, to descend from these heroic examples, the greatest revolution in Mr Wildgoose's life sprung from a frivolous dispute, in which he was apparently so slenderly interested.

To account for his resentment on this occasion, however, we must observe, that every man acts a kind of subaltern part in conversation; and he who is an inferior or a common man in one company, may

be a captain, or a leading orator in another. There are few persons of
so mean a capacity, or so despicable accomplishments, as not to have
a circle of acquaintance who reverence their opinions, and amongst
whom they are heard with attention, and utter their decisions with a
kind of oracular authority. This was the case with Mr Wildgoose. In
company with any of the neighbouring gentlemen, his superiors, he
was modest, and patient of contradiction; but in an assembly of yeomen
he was in his glory, in his very kingdom. By ridiculing his opinions,
therefore, and diminishing his consequence amongst his own subjects,
Mr Powel was guilty of a kind of high treason, which Wildgoose could
not easily forgive.

Time, however, might have worn off this unreasonable disgust against
the vicar, if Mr Wildgoose had not gone to church the next Sunday,
whilst the impression was strong upon his imagination. He had always
been remarkably decent in his behaviour at the public worship, and not
only made his responses with an audible voice, but generally, leaning
over the pew, accompanied the minister through both the lessons, with
a Latin Bible, which he had brought with him from the university. At
the same time, however, Mr Geoffry was shrewdly suspected to have
been guilty of some slight offences against the rules of chastity, with his
mother's maid. And though, in general, he might not be worse than his
neighbours, yet he probably did not surpass them so much in his private
character, as he did in his external deportment at church.

Now it happened unfortunately, that the doctor was haranguing that
day upon the sin of hypocrisy; which, one would think, is a subject
the least liable to a particular application by the hypocrite himself;
for what knave or debauchee would be encumbered with the mask
of piety, unless he flattered himself that it concealed his real character,
and screened him from the attacks of public censure? It is to be feared,
however, that Mr Wildgoose was conscious to himself of some slight
failings, inconsistent with his sanctified appearance, and was too nearly
concerned in the subject of the parson's discourse, not to make a
particular application: and whether he suspected Mr Powel to have
pried into his secrets, or whether, as he was piqued against the vicar, he
thought the resentment was mutual; whatever was the cause, he from

that time avoided his company, and determined for the future to absent himself entirely from church.

As he could not, without exposing his weakness, give any reasons for this alteration in his conduct, he by degrees grew shy of the rest of his acquaintance, and sunk insensibly into a gloomy, unaccountable kind of misanthropy. Mrs Wildgoose, who was fond of her son, became very uneasy on his account, but could not guess at the cause of his malady. She was always pressing him to go more abroad, and visit his neighbours. Nay, she got Mr Powel, the vicar, himself (who was really a good-natured man, and, with his wife, often drank tea at Mrs Wildgoose's) to talk to her son on the subject. Mr Geoffry pleaded lowness of spirits, and a disrelish for company; and said, with some sullenness, that he chose to be alone. In short, he found out so many excuses from time to time, that at last it was looked upon as his way, his humour, to be always alone; and Mrs Wildgoose desisted from her maternal expostulation.

IV

MR WILDGOOSE ENTERS UPON A NEW COURSE OF STUDIES

Buttered toast for breakfast now became unseasonable, and gave way to sage and bread and butter. Lamb and sallad ceased to be a Sunday's dinner or part of the second course, and was an obvious dish at every table. The parson of F—field★ no longer threw his oyster-shell into the street, ambitiously luxurious! but supped in his garden upon codlins and cream, or a bit of soft cheese and a cucumber. In other words, the spring was far advanced when Mr Wildgoose was, one day, sitting in his old-fashioned parlour; and, in an indolent posture, ruminating upon such trifles as usually employ a disgusted mind: the windows were shaded

---

★ On the Bath road.

with an over-grown laurel, and the solemn vibrations of an old clock
from its sable trunk, with the distant sound of a doleful ditty which the
servant whistled as he was digging in the garden, concurred to increase
his melancholy.

He roll'd his eyes, that witness'd huge dismay,

and surveyed over and over again every picture, and every part of the
hereditary furniture of the mansion-house, which had been so familiar
to his eyes from his very infancy. At last, he happened to fix them on
an old forlorn quarto, that lay upon a lofty shelf, covered with dust, and
tinged with smoke an inch within the margin. Something prompted him
to look into it, which, starting from his elbow chair, he immediately put
in execution. He found it to contain a miscellaneous collection of godly
discourses, upon predestination, election and reprobation, justification by
faith, grace and freewill, and the like controverted points of divinity, the
productions of those self-taught teachers and self-called pastors of the
church, in the time of Cromwell's usurpation. As his usual studies had
been very insipid to him, since he was become thus a prey to melancholy,
and out of humour with himself, the vicar, and all the neighbourhood,
this crude trash happened to suit Mr Geoffry's vitiated palate; espcially as
these writings abounded with bitter invectives against the regular clergy,
and the established church; and with sentences of reprobation upon all
mankind, except a few choice spirits called the elect.

Mr Wildgoose read over this curious volume in an indolent manner,
which rather amused than pleased him, and bewildered rather than
instructed him. He was so far from being cloyed, however, with this
crabbed food, that he found his appetite increase by indulgence; and
recollecting that there was a closet in the house, which had been locked
up ever since the death of his grandmother, who was a rigid Non-
conformist, thither he instantly resorts, and finds it stored with a variety
of authors of the same stamp; some Presbyterian, some Independent,
some Anabaptist, some Fifth-monarchy men; the works of that swarm
of sectaries in the last century; all differing somewhat in their principles,
but all agreeing in their inveteracy against the church of England.

This was no unpleasant food for Wildgoose's disorder; for, having conceived so great a prejudice against the vicar of the parish, he gladly embraced any system that seemed to thwart his usual doctrine. In short, in half a year's time he had gone through the whole library of godly discourses; the *Marrow of Divinity, Crumbs of Comfort,* and *Honey-combs for the Elect, The Spiritual Eye-salves and Cordials for the Saints,* and *Shoves for heavy-ars'd Christians;*★ and was forced at last to take up with an old tattered folio of Foxe's Martyrology, and another of Master Clark's *Lives of famous Men*; amongst others, that of Mr Carter of Norwich, who, the history informs us, was a mighty lover of Norfolk-dumplings.

V

ADOPTS A NEW SYSTEM OF RELIGION

The puritanical principles which he had thus imbibed, prepared Mr Wildgoose to relish the doctrines of the Methodists, which began, about this time, to spread in every corner of the kingdom: and he was much pleased with the journals of their proceedings, two or three of which he had accidentally met with, and which made no slight impression on his imagination. Such a multifarious body of divinity, indeed, quite unsettled Mr Geoffry's mind, and filled his head with such a farraginous medley of opinions as almost turned his brain. It produced at least, to speak candidly of the matter, that sort of phrenzy which we ascribe to enthusiasts in music, poetry, or painting, or in any other art or science; whose imaginations are so entirely possessed by those ideas, as to make them talk and act like madmen, in the sober eye of merely rational people.

But to complete poor Geoffry's religious phrenzy, some straggling itinerant had lately penetrated into that neighbourhood, and held forth

---

★ A very good book of old Baxter's.

once or twice a-week at a market-town a few miles from the village where Wildgoose lived. These nocturnal meetings he now frequently attended; at first without his mother's knowledge, or that of any of his neighbours; and when she discovered it, by his frequent absence, she thought it more prudent to connive at his whimsies, than aggravate them by opposition.

A pious inclination to retail those doctrines which he had heard at those meetings, as well as the natural propensity which men have to propagate their own opinions, concurring with the prejudice which Mr Wildgoose had conceived against the parson of the parish, strongly urged him to give vent to that fund of spiritual knowledge, which, like the volatile bee, he had been the whole summer in gleaning from those flowers of rhetoric, and from those flourishing orators above-mentioned.

He would now and then venture to defend the cause of the Methodists before his mother; but she would never hear him with patience on the subject. She said, if the clergy would but do their duty, as her poor father did, and as the canons of the church required, there would be no necessity for these extraordinary proceedings: and if they neglected their duty, complaint should be made to their lawful superiors. Her own father, she said, was a very good man: and, whatever little show of piety these upstart preachers might raise amongst their followers by the novelty of the thing, she was sure her father did more real good in his sphere, by a regular discharge of his duty in an extensive parish: that he instructed the ignorant, and reproved the vicious; that he catechised the children, visited the sick, and (as far as his circumstances would permit) relieved the poor; and that not only his own parish, but the whole neighbourhood, were the better for his instructions and his example, to this day.

As Mrs Wildgoose was so zealous an advocate for the church, Mr Geoffry forbore to display his sentiments any farther in her presence, though he took an opportunity, now and then, of privately insinuating his notions into the maid, who, being young, was more attentive and more pliant than the man whom age and habit had rendered stubborn and averse to speculation. In other respects, as Wildgoose had long since deserted his old companions amongst the credible part of the neighbourhood, he was under a necessity, at present, of keeping silence from (what he thought) such good words, though it was no small pain and grief to him.

VI

PRELIMINARIES WITH THE FASTIDIOUS READER

Mr Wildgoose, being impatient of any longer confinement, began, after some time, to creep out in the dusk of the evening, and join the sober assembly of labourers and mechanics under an old elm, at the cottage gate of an honest, sociable cobbler, where the news of the parish, or the weather of the ensuing day, the badness of the times, or the scarcity of money, and other matters of general concern, were adjusted with great wisdom and penetration.

As Jeremiah Tugwell (which was the name of this cobbler) will bear a considerable part in this history, the polite reader will not be offended with a slight sketch of his person and character.

Here, however, it may be necessary, once for all, to settle preliminaries with such readers, as are possessed with the modern *tapino-phoby*, or dread of every thing that is low, either in writing or in conversation. For as people in high life are less prone to that excess of zeal or religious enthusiasm, which gave occasion to the following tale, than people in a less elevated sphere, the author could not, consistently with probability, introduce him so frequently amongst the former as amongst the latter.

I have sometimes been tempted to think, however, that high and low are by no means necessarily confined to the different ranks and stations in life; and have even suspected (though I do not presume to have penetrated into the very *sanctum sanctorum* of high life) that there may be as much low wit and as many practical jokes going on over a bottle of burgundy at the Star and Garter, or at Arthur's, as over a pot of porter at the Robin Hood society. It seems at least probable, that as we sometimes find very low wit employed upon the highest subjects, so there is room for high humour (if the author had abilities) upon the lowest subjects.

If the reader, however, has otherwise determined it; if he is of opinion that every representation of nature that does not relate to the great world is to be exploded as contemptible stuff, he will certainly repent of having read thus far; and I would exhort him, by all means, to return in peace to his card assembly, or to his chocolate-house, and pursue so low a subject no further.

For the sake, however, of the less critical customer, the fat, sleek-headed guest, who, like a prudent traveller in a stage-coach, instead of affecting to be more squeamish than his companions, is resolved to be pleased with whatever is set before him, we will proceed in our narration.

VII

What sort of man Jeremiah Tugwell was

Come! then, thou goddess Fame, if haply thou canst steal a moment from high life; from trumpeting forth the praises of the great artist of the golden boot in Berkeley-square,* and I do not blasphemously invoke thy power to record the humbler virtues of a rural craftsman, come to my aid! and bestow one blast in honour of the fidelity, courage, wit, and humour, of the renowned Jeremiah Tugwell.

Jeremiah Tugwell then, or Tagwell, or Tackwell (for learning having been at a low ebb in the family, the orthography is somewhat dubious;

---

* On a sign there, a painter had copied Roubiliac's figure of Fame on the wing; in her right hand exalting a golden boot, with a trumpet in the left, sounding forth the praises of the illustrious boot-maker.

nay, a conceited fellow in the village, who pretended to etymology, said it ought to have been written Tugwool, and that wool was put for sheep, and sheep for mutton (by a synecdoche:) so that the true meaning of the name, according to his conceit, was Tug-mutton. But I value at a nut-shell these fanciful etymologies, which endeavour to elicit a significative meaning from every family name, the originals of which are infinitely uncertain; and our conjectures about them are often as far from the truth as the interpretation of dreams by an old midwife).★

Tugwell, then, was a thickset little fellow, near fifty, but of a strong constitution and hale complexion: and though time and accidents had made considerable depredations on his person, had turned the colour of his bushy locks, had made bald the crown of his head, and robbed him of most of his grinders, yet these strokes of time had only given him a more picturesque appearance; and one solitary tooth in his upper mandible, when any thing excited his mirth, gave an inexpressibly droll and joyous air to his physiognomy.

As to his character, Jerry had a tolerable share of natural sense; but having somewhat of a speculative turn, and being fond of books, he too much disregarded the common maxims of prudence, and passed amongst his more provident, though really less sagacious, neighbours, for a half-witted fellow. By which means, though Jerry was really a tolerable hand, a more popular operator having started up, he had lost most of his custom as a shoe-maker, and was dwindled into a mere mender of shoes or what is vulgarly called, a cobbler. He still worked for Mrs Wildgoose's family, however, who had always made it a point of conscience, not wantonly to change their tradesmen from any imaginary want of skill in an old man, whose honesty and desire to oblige them were unquestionable.

Though Jerry was fond of books, it was chiefly those of the fabulous kind, which dealt in the marvellous and the romantic. As he did not trouble himself about the niceties of chronology or geography, Jerry

---

★ A learned antiquary insists upon it, that Tugwell is a corruption of
  Toghill near Bath, and Toghill of the Oakhill, being a wood of oaks,
  where the Druids went in search of the sacred Misleto.

was particularly fond of the Seven Champions of Christendom, who
are said by the historian to have sprung up soon after the destruction of
Troy; that is, about some thousand years before Christ was born; and one
of them to have ridden on horseback from Sicily, through Cappadocia,
Tartary, the Island of Cyprus, &c. the direct road to Jerusalem. Tugwell
was possessed also of the old edition of Mandeville's Travels, who is
the author alluded to by Shakespeare, as speaking of antres vast and
deserts idle, and of men whose heads do grow beneath their shoulders.
Jerry delighted to talk of Prester John, of the Holy-land, and of the
wandering Jew, that cursed shoemaker, who thrust Our Saviour out
of the judgment-hall; for which he is condemned to a vagabond life,
till Christ comes in judgment; whose real existence★ Jerry as firmly
believed as any part of the Gospel.

He had also some smattering in astronomy, though he had not yet
embraced the Newtonian system: he could point out Charles's wain
and the polar star, and could give as good an account of the northern
lights as most other philosophers; yet Jerry strenuously denied their
appearance in England before the beheading of the rebel lords, in the
year fifteen.

For, as to his political principles, Tugwell was suspected, like some of
his neighbours, to be strongly attached to the Stuart family; though this
attachment seemed to have no other foundation, than a compassion
for the distressed; and never showed itself but in a harmless pun once a
year, in wearing a sprig of rue and thyme on the eleventh of June (the
accession of his late majesty,) as the tenth was honoured with a white
rose.

As for Jerry's moral character, his justice, temperance, and fortitude,
they will sufficiently appear in the course of this history.

Tugwell had no family but his wife Dorothy, his dog Snap, and a tabby
cat. His only son Joseph, having violated the chastity of the justice's
maid (who was known to be common to all men,) rather than marry
her, listed for a soldier; and was supposed to be dead in America.

★ Matthew Paris, no contemptible historian, mentions his being
  frequently seen in the East, about 400 years ago.

Jerry and his spouse were more equally yoked than Jobson and Nell in the farce; though in the present instance, the female prerogative rather preponderated; by a proper exercise of which, notwithstanding his censorious neighbours thought Jerry cursedly hen-pecked, Dorothy contrived to convince him, that he had the best wife in Christendom.

VIII

SKETCH OF MR WILDGOOSE'S THEOLOGICAL SYSTEMS

No more of Jeremiah Tugwell! for heaven's sake, says the delicate reader, whose patience has hitherto been unexhausted. I shall only add, therefore, that as Tugwell's name was liable to puns, and capable of significant applications, so the situation of his stall, within view of the street, exposed him to the familiar salutation of those who passed by. And, as every one had something to say to Jerry, so Jerry had something to say to every one: and this gave a sort of petulant dicacity to his repartees, by no means agreeable to the natural civility of his disposition.

The reader will observe likewise, that Tugwell's profound knowledge of books had infected his language; which was frequently interlarded with hard words, not always applied or pronounced with the utmost propriety.

Such, then, were the circumstances, person, and character of Jeremiah Tugwell, at whose cottage-gate Mr Wildgoose made the first essay towards propagating the doctrines which he had lately adopted.

He took occasion first to lament the great decay of Christian piety (which with regard to his present audience, was probably a complaint but too justly founded.) He then began to insinuate, that the present doctrine and discipline of the church were the chief causes of this degeneracy: that, for his part, he had attended the public worship, as others did, merely because it was the custom of the country; but that he had always found it a tedious piece of lip-labour, without the least edification: that as for the parson's preaching, it might serve just to keep up some little appearance of religion amongst us, and perhaps might prevent some people from being quite so bad as they would otherwise be; but could never reform one sinner, nor 'make men wise unto salvation.' Besides, says he, if we could live a good moral life, and practise all the good works which the doctor so earnestly recommends, all this would be little to the purpose. Faith in Christ, says he, is all in all. We must be clothed with the splendid robes of his righteousness, instead of the 'filthy rags of our own works.' In short, continues Wildgoose, we must be assured, that we are in the number of the elect, and have the seal of adoption (the impression of which, he hinted, none but a few choice spirits like himself were acquainted with,) and if our name were thus once up (according to his doctrine,) we might lie a-bed, and give ourselves no further trouble.

With this, and a great deal more to the same purpose, Mr Geoffry entertained his little circle under the great elm at Tugwell's gate: and though they were not capable of distinguishing nicely between his doctrine and what they heard at church; yet being delivered to them in a more familiar manner, and by a new teacher, and in a new place, it made a considerable impression upon them, and brought them punctually the next evening to their usual rendezvous. But, as the report of Mr Wildgoose's appearing amongst them soon increased the number of this little assembly, and also as the evenings began now to be pretty cool, he thought it proper to adjourn to Tugwell's chimney-corner. Besides, Mr Wildgoose was sufficiently sensible of the difference between mere talking, and preaching in a fanatical manner. Where nothing was intended but informing the understanding, the former alone might answer the end; but where the passions were to be moved and the affections engaged, a more vehement action (approaching to gesticulation,) a greater earnestness, and more impassioned tone of voice, were to be made use of: which an orator upon a level with the crowd, and in the open street, could by no means exert to the best advantage.

IX

He commences orator

Mr Wildgoose, therefore, now borrowed a stool of Dame Tugwell, and exalting himself above his audience, harangued them in the true Gospel tone and style of address. To shew them the necessity of the new birth and of a divine faith, he began to describe, in heightened colours, the universal depravity of human nature. He confessed, that for his part, he had violated every precept of the moral law, as contained in the ten commandments. And, in the heat of his oratory (with eyes, fixed and foaming mouth,) he insisted upon it, that he had blasphemed God, and cursed the king: that he had dishonoured his father and his mother: that he had murdered his brother.—Here the company stared, as it was well known, that he never had but one brother; who died of the chin-cough.—He declared, that he had defiled his neighbour's wife; that he had robbed upon the high-way—Stop! stop! master, (cries Tugwell, who could hold no longer) why sure you are beside yourself—I believe your worship is as honest a gentleman as any in the county—

Ah! Jerry, replies Wildgoose (correcting himself) I have not, perhaps, been actually guilty of those enormous transgressions: but every unregenerate man is daily guilty of them virtually, as we say; inasmuch, as he has the seeds of corruption in his heart: and it is only by the grace of God, that he is restrained from putting them in execution.

In this style Mr Wildgoose usually addressed his little audience; and though he had really a classical taste, and, on common subjects, an elegance of expression, yet by confining himself so long to the puritanical writings above mentioned, and those of the methodists, he had strongly imbibed their manner: and his language on religious topics abounded with that strange jargon of those pious people, which chiefly consists in applying the quaint Hebraisms of the Old Testament, and the peculiar expressions of the primitive apostles, to their own situations, and every trifling occurrence of modern life.

Thus, in allusion to the sacred unction, he would tell them, that God anointed (that is, greased) the wheels of his soul; and blasphemously makes him act as a surgeon and apothecary, 'purging him with hysop, healing his putrid sores, and binding up his broken bones.' Sometimes God is a Grub-street writer, and writes bitter things against him. And he always speaks of himself, as an apostle and evangelist; that few could resist the power with which he spoke;★ and that 'he spake as one having authority, and not as the scribes,' that is, common country parsons.

As Mr Geoffry was sometimes rather prolix in his discourses, Tugwell would put him in mind, that talking was dry work. He, therefore, frequently enforced his arguments with a flagon of good ale from his mother's cellar, which afforded great comfort to his thirsty audience, cemented their friendship, and contributed not a little to convince them, that they were in 'the right way.' And to keep Dame Tugwell in good-humour (who was sovereign in that mansion,) and to make her some recompense for the use of her house, Mr Geoffry ordered her to come daily to his mother's kitchen; where, together with her broth or pot-liquor, he contrived to slip something more substantial into Dorothy's pipkin.

X

A PECULIAR SPECIES OF ECCLESIASTICAL DISCIPLINE

By this kind of management, Mr Wildgoose's audience greatly increased, and became almost as numerous as Mr Powel's, the vicar's, at church. For though Mr Powel did his duty in the parish with sufficient care, there was a peculiarity in his conduct, which made him many secret enemies, and which deserves to be recorded.

Mr Powel was a man of great benevolence; but being a Cambro-Briton, (of the Ap-hoels of Brecknockshire) he was subject to a national impetuosity of temper; and being endued with great bodily strength and proportionable courage, if any of his parishioners were notoriously

---

★ *Journal*, p. 108.

guilty of swearing, drinking, or any other scandalous vice, he would address them in this manner: Look you, my friends, your drunkenness and profaneness are an open insult upon the laws of that great King whom I have the honour to serve, and an affront to me who bear his commission. As I have often admonished you, therefore, against swearing and drinking, and you still persist in the same course, I give you fair warning once more, that the next time I hear or see anything of this kind, I will drub you most confoundedly. This method had so good an effect, that as they knew he had strength and courage to put his threats in execution, he was very seldom under any necessity of doing so.

Those, however, who were thus kept in awe, though they could not but reverence Mr Powel's character, rather feared than loved him, and were glad to listen to any doctrine which they thought was in opposition to the vicar's. But to return from this digression.

XI

MR WILDGOOSE TAKES AN EXTRAORDINARY RESOLUTION

By haranguing so frequently upon the same topicks, Mr Wildgoose began to talk very fluently: and from attending to the applauses of his little audience, and observing the effect of his oratory upon them, he began to entertain no mean opinion of his own eloquence, and to aspire after a more extensive fame. Nay, he thought himself false to his trust, thus to bury 'his talent in a napkin,' to hide his 'candle under a bushel,' and not let his 'light shine before men,' for the benefit of his fellow-creatures.

Besides, from the accounts of God's dealings with several of his saints, particularly with John Bunyan, who, in his youth, had been greatly addicted to the diabolical diversions of ringing bells, dancing at may-poles, and other profane amusements (as he himself informs us,) yet in his advanced age, was thought worthy, for his pious labours in God's vineyard, to be sent to Newgate; from perusing these I say, and the Acts of our modern Apostles, contained in their Journals above mentioned, Mr Wildgoose was ambitious of emulating their spiritual adventures, and even burnt with zeal to imitate them in their sufferings, and wished for nothing so much as to be persecuted for the sake of his religion. The suffering for one's opinions gives a man an air of consequence in his own eyes; as it supposes him to think for himself, and to be distinguished from the herd of mankind, who live and die unregarded, content with the hereditary notions of their unthinking ancestors.

Mr Geoffry Wildgoose, therefore, having no longer any pleasure in the society of his more creditable neighbours, nor in his wonted amusements, since his fancy became entirely possessed with these enthusiastic ideas, determined to leave the management of his mother's estate to their old servant Stephen, and, like a true Spiritual Quixote, to abandon his dwelling: and, in imitation of Mr Whitfield and his associates, to use his earnest endeavours, to revive the practice of primitive piety and the doctrines of the Reformation, by turning missionary, and publishing his religious notions in every part of the kingdom.

BOOK II

I

ORIGINAL OF METHODISM.
MR WILDGOOSE'S RESOLUTION
TO VISIT THE SOCIETY AT BRISTOL

WHEN THE LEARNED HUMPHRY PRIDEAUX (as the story goes) offered his *Life of Mahomet* to the bookseller, he was desired to leave the copy with him a few days, for his perusal. The bookseller, who had not the learning or taste of a modern artist, having consulted with his learned garreteers, who were highly pleased with the performance, told the doctor at his return: Well, Mr What's-your-name, says he, I have perused your manuscript; I do not know what to say to it: I believe I shall venture to print it: the thing is well enough, but—I could wish there were a little more humour in it.

Now though the courteous reader should be as fond of humour, as this facetious bookseller was; yet if, in travelling through a flat country, he should now and then meet with a picturesque prospect, sometimes with a bit of galloping ground, and sometimes with a droll object upon the road, he must patiently submit to jog on some parts of the way without any thing to entertain or amuse; for such probably will be the fate of the gentle reader of this various history.

About this time the sect of the methodists (as was before observed) began to spread into most parts of the nation; though, perhaps, it is doing them too much credit, and at the same time an act of injustice, to call them a sect; as I know of no new opinions which they maintain, except that of the lawfulness of preaching without a legal call; and of assembling in conventicles or in the open fields, in direct opposition to the laws of the land.

A late writer* does Mr Whitfield the honour of being the first author of methodism, whom he also calls a fellow of Pembroke college in Oxford. But as Mr Whitfield disclaims all worldly grandeur, and with great humility assures us, that like the blessed Founder of our religion,

---

* *Historical Review of the Transactions of Europe.*

he was born at an inn;* so, like him, I am persuaded, he will confess, that 'he came not to be ministered unto, but to minister:' for he was really a servitor, and not a fellow of that learned society. Neither was Mr Whitfield concerned in the first institution of methodism, though he has since made so shining a figure amongst them; for, some years† before he came to the university, Mr John Wesley, fellow of Lincoln college, his brother Charles, a student of Christchurch, Mr Clayton, of Brazen-nose, and two or three more young gentlemen, with a very laudable intention, agreed to spend two or three evenings in a week together, in reading history or other entertaining and instructive books, instead of drinking, which, at that time, was too much in vogue among the young people of the university. The Sunday evenings they appropriated to religious authors, which soon convinced them of the great neglect of practical religion in that place, as well as in other parts of the kingdom. In consequence of these convictions they formed themselves into a little society, and raised a small fund for charitable uses; to relieve the necessitous, buy medicines for the sick, and to disperse books amongst the ignorant. They agreed also to go occasionally and visit the prisoners in the castle, who, at that time, were much neglected: and, that they might have the more leisure for these charitable offices, without breaking in too much upon the business of their colleges, they were obliged to fix stated hours for these employments, and their other religious exercises; to which they were directed by Mr Nelson's *Practice of Devotion.* This strict regularity and methodical conduct, after some time, acquired them the name of methodists; though not without allusion probably to an ancient school of physians of that denomination.

---

* *Vide* God's Dealings with Mr Whitfield. There is nothing so ridiculous, or rather profane, which pious writers will not say for the sake of a witty allusion. Thus the learned bishop Taylor says, that Christ was born at the sign of the Star in Bethlehem.

"Born at an inn,
    A star the sign—"

† About the year 1730.

Mr Wesley, however, I am convinced, had no thoughts at that time of separating from the established church (the most essential of whose doctrines he has generally adhered to), much less of robbing the community of so many useful mechanics; who, with a view of raising themselves above their fellow-plebeians, without any other apparatus than a long cravat, and a demure pertness of countenance, together with a little common-place jargon (picked up at their weekly assemblies), forsake their lawful callings, and commence reformers and teachers of their brethren. But 'the beginning of strife is as the letting out of water;' and if one man may break through the established order of society, another has the same right to do it; which must end at last in utter confusion.

These people then had several societies at this time in London, Bristol, and in most of the considerable towns in England but as Bristol was the nearest to the place of Mr Wildgoose's habitation, and he saw by the newspapers, that Mr Whitfield at this time made that his principal residence, he resolved to visit the society in that city, and confer with them upon the subject of the cause in which he was now a volunteer; and to take instructions for the better discharge of the mission, to which he flattered himself he had a divine call.

II

COMMUNICATES HIS INTENTIONS TO JERRY TUGWELL

Mr Wildgoose, having determined to go on a pilgrimage to Bristol, after some deliberation, communicated his intentions to his foresaid honest neighbour, Jeremiah Tugwell, but under a strict injunction of the greatest secrecy: and, as he thought it would be more agreeable to have a companion in his travels, finding him alone in his stall, he began to sound Jerry upon that subject.

Mr Wildgoose esteemed Tugwell, and Tugwell fancied himself a true convert to his religious system for, hearing him harangue so often upon the same subject, Jerry had learned, whenever Mr Wildgoose talked to him upon that head, to echo back most of his expressions with an appearance of a sincere conviction. If Mr Wildgoose lamented the sad decay of Christian piety, Tugwell would shake his head, and clinch it with a more vehement exclamation against the wickedness of the age. If Wildgoose asserted the preference of faith to works, Yes, yes, cries Jerry, faith's all; our good works are no better than 'filthy rags,' in the sight of God.

And as Jerry's passions were naturally tame and moderate, he was not often guilty either of swearing or drinking; the most common foibles of men in his rank of life.

As to the former, however, Jerry might rather be called a Demi-juror, than a Non-juror; as, instead of the usual profane execrations, he would content himself with some softening modifications of them. Instead of the shocking exclamation of G-d damn you! Jerry would use, G-d mend you, or convert you! Instead of Od's blood, od's wounds, or Pox take you, Jerry was content with Odsbodikins, odszounterkins, pock-i-cat take you, and the like: and even these castrated imprecations Jerry seldom used, even in the paroxysms of his wrath, without a decent *salvo*; as, God forgive me for swearing, or I was going to say, and the like.—Which, however, answered the purpose of venting his rage, and at the same time secured him from the imputation of impiety and profaneness.

As to drinking, Tugwell's greatest temptation was from the Angel, in his neighbourhood: I mean, the sign of the Angel, where he longed to be tippling with the sociable part of his acquaintance; but as there is no law in England against the wife's wearing that emblem of sovereignty, the breeches, Dorothy kept the cash, and by that means kept Jerry within tolerable bounds, unless when he could secrete a tester for some bye-job; on which occasions he would sometimes elope and take his fill. But, since Mr Wildgoose had made use of his cottage for their nightly assemblies, this supplied the place of other less innocent amusements: so that Tugwell flattered himself he was a true convert to religion; that he had made a great progress in the road to heaven, and was qualified to teach others the way.

But to prepare Tugwell for a proper assistant in his mission, Mr Wildgoose took this opportunity of examining him upon some of the distinguishing doctrines which he had of late been inculcating.

Wildgoose asked Jerry, therefore, whether he had a true sense of his fallen condition, and that he was a wicked sinner, and had broken every commandment of the moral law? for unless he was convinced of sin, he said, he could not hope for pardon.

Tell me, therefore, Jerry, says Wildgoose, have you ever broke the first or second commandment, or have you ever been guilty of worshipping idols?—*Idols!* says Jerry, why yes to be sure, I have been very *idle* sometimes, that's *sartain*; especially at Christmas and Whitsuntide; and *sich* good times, as one may say!—Pshaw, says Wildgoose; you mistake me, Jerry; I mean, did you ever worship more gods than one, or any false gods, as the Jews and heathens did?—Oh! says Jerry; what! Bel and the dragon, and Nebuchadnezzar, and *sich* like: no, no! thank God, I never *troubles* my head about them. I says my prayers, and *worships* the Father; the Son, and the Holy Ghost; but there is no great harm in that; for they are all the same, as a body may say.

Well, Jerry, but you may have been guilty of idolatry, by setting up idols in your heart, and loving any thing more than God.

Ah! says Jerry, God forgive me! to be sure, I formerly loved nine-pins and cudgel-playing, better than going to church and saying my prayers.—Well then, Jerry, thou hast broken the first and second commandment. Now for the third;

Didst thou never take the name of God in vain?

No, says Jerry, I hope not. God be friends, I never was guilty of that—though to be sure, when a body is in a passion, a body may use a bad word now and then, such as, pock-i-cat take you, ods-bobs, odsbodikins, and the like—but there is no harm in that—

Why, says Wildgoose, if you think them bad words, there is harm in them, and they are very wicked; and if you do not, they are very ridiculous. Do you know, Jerry, that many of those words are corruptions, either of the most tremendous oaths, or of the most shocking execrations? Pock-i-cat take you, is only a corruption of The pox of God take you! Odsbobs, as you call it, means, As sure as God's above us! and Zounterkins, which you frequently use, is a construction of God's wounds, and is a most shocking oath, as swearing by the precious wounds of our Redeemer. In short, Jerry, the only way to avoid the guilt of profane swearing, is to use the greatest simplicity of speech; to let your Yea be yea, and your Nay nay, as our great Master directs.

Tugwell stared at this exposition of his unmeaning gibberish; but Wildgoose proceeded in his examination.

In the next place, Jerry, have you never profaned the sabbath, by doing your ordinary work on the Lord's day?

No, says Jerry, except paring turnips now and then, and boiling the pot; which we han't time to do always on working days—and I remember I once sat up till Sunday morning, to finish a pair of shoes against Easter.

Well, Jerry, continued Wildgoose, If I were to examine you through the whole decalogue, I am afraid there is not one of the moral precepts but what thou hast transgressed, either in thought, word, or deed: for, as the tenth commandment is intended to guard against the breach of the rest, if you have not actually been guilty, you may intentionally, even by coveting your neighbour's house, your neighbour's wife, or any thing that is his.

Nay, says Jerry, as for coveting my neighbour's wife, nobody can accuse me of that; for, thank God, I have the best wife in England.

Just as Jerry was saying this, Dorothy, who had listened for some time, and did not hear the noise of the hammer, called out with no very harmonious voice, Why don't you mind your work? Don't you know those shoes must all be finished against Whitsunday?

The dread of Dorothy's displeasure, therefore, put a stop to Mr Wildgoose's scrutiny, for the present; and so they parted.

As Jerry then had no family to provide for, but his wife Dorothy, who could support herself by her own industry, and, as he suspected, had already made a purse for herself, he wanted but little persuasion to come into Mr Wildgoose's proposal; especially as the course of his studies had given him a romantic turn, and a strong inclination for travelling; although his situation in life had never permitted him to indulge that propensity. Besides, as Jerry made a sort of merit of accompanying Mr Wildgoose, he did not doubt but he would, some time or other, recompense him for his trouble. Tugwell, therefore, told Mr Wildgoose, that he should be very proud to bear him company, if he was resolved to go. But, please your worship—Jerry was here going to propose some artful scruples, which will be related in the next chapter.

III

JERRY'S AFFECTED SCRUPLES

Tugwell assured Mr Wildgoose he should be very proud to accompany him to the land's end, if occasion were; for that he always loved travelling. But master, says he, what must we do for money to pay for our lodgings, and to provide necessaries upon the road? for as madam is not to know of our going, belike your worship's purse will soon be *dis*hausted.—Oh! as for that, says Mr Wildgoose, you may make yourself easy—The labourer is worthy of his hire. Those to whom we impart our spiritual things, will abundantly supply us with those carnal conveniences which you are so anxious about: at least, Providence will infallibly provide for those that rely upon him; and I have as good security for the necessaries of life, in God's promises, as if I had millions in the Bank of England.

Was not Elijah fed as well by ravens, dost thou think, as he would have been from the king's table? and did not he sleep as sweetly under a juniper tree, as he would have done upon a bed of state?—Yes, yes, says Jerry, that is very true, but then that was in the holy land, where belike it is much warmer than it is in this country: and then, mayhap, there were no inns nor ale-houses in those days; nor any thing to be got for love or money, in the wilderness where Elijah travelled; so that he was obliged to trust to Providence, as a body may say—

However, folks were not so hard-hearted in those days; but were more given to *hostility* than they are now.—Hospitality, I suppose you mean, says Wildgoose.—Well, well, that is all one, replies Tugwell; but I am no Oxford scholar, that's *sartain*; which was all that Jerry thought requisite to make him as wise as his master—But howsomever, now-a-days, if a poor man does but ask for a cup of drink upon the road, he's taken for a thief or a *bugabond*. Instead of giving a man any thing to eat, they will only give one good advice; Why don't you get to your own parish? says one; Why don't you work? says another, and not beg? Here are so many idle fellows about the country, says another. And then it's good luck, if the house-dog be not set upon one, and one gets off without a torn skirt! I should like well enough to travel amongst your Turks and *Hometans* (as Thomas Coryat, the Somersetshire man, did), where a man may lay down his knapsack in an evening, and lodge in a sort of alms-house or *carry-fancy*, as the book calls it, and nobody ask any questions; but there's no travelling in a Christian country without a little money in one's pocket.

Well, says Wildgoose, if that be all, I could take money enough to provide us necessaries upon the road. But I greatly question, whether it be lawful for a preacher of the gospel to take any thought for the things of this life. The first apostles, you know, were forbid to take, 'either purse or scrip, or to have two coats a-piece.' Well, says Tugwell, I believe we shall have but one coat between us, as your worship will hardly walk in a great-coat this summer time, and mine is but a waistcoat, and make the best of it!—Why, I suppose, the only intention of those particular expressions, replies Wildgoose, is, that we should not distrust Providence—but should give good christians an opportunity of displaying their charity and benevolence.

Well, but master, continues Tugwell, what must we do for clean linen, as a body may say? for your worship belike has been used to shift you twice a week; and I most commonly puts on a clean neckcloth every Sunday, and sometimes a clean shirt. Now I have thought (if so be it is not contrary to scripture) to take my wallet over my shoulder; and, that would hold some clean linen, and a crust of bread and cheese sometimes; for we may happen to lose our way upon Cotswold, and that's but a heathenish sort of a country at best—

Why, to be sure, Jerry, replies Mr Wildgoose, we ought to take all prudent means for our subsistence, and not expect Providence to feed and clothe us by a constant miracle, as he did the children of Israel in the wilderness.—No, no, says Tugwell, to be sure, their meat dropt into their mouths, as a body may say; and their shoes never waxed old in their forty years' travel; and yet I believe they trampt it on foot all the way.

Well, says Wildgoose, I do not recollect, that either Mr Wesley or Mr Whitfield ever make any mention, in their journals, that they took either money or clean shirts with them, nor whether they thought it lawful or unlawful to use any precaution of this kind. But, let me see, you have got a brown jug at home, I think, Jerry; have you not?—That I have, master; and it will hold two quarts, good measure.—Well, well! you must know then, that Mr Whitfield and his friends have revived a custom of deciding doubtful points, by lot. He does not tell us, indeed, the manner of doing this; but I know, the method amongst the ancients was to write down the two questions upon scraps of paper, and shake them in an urn or pitcher, and leave the determination to Providence.—Why, says Jerry, if that be all, one may put those same papers into an old hat; or why cannot one toss up a halfpenny; heads or tails, as boys do: but then, methinks, it may happen wrong sometimes; and what is lawful at one time may be unlawful at another, just as it turns up trump.—Why, you must observe, Jerry, this method is only to determine particular facts, or, whether one should act so or so, on any particular occasion; and this sure we may leave to the decision of Providence.

But, however, Jerry, without any more dispute on the matter, we may be sure of this, that whilst we are honestly employed in promoting the glory of God, and the good of mankind, he will never suffer us to want what is necessary for our support. 'Seek ye first the kingdom of God, and his righteousness, and all other necessary things shall be added unto you.' A text of scripture, how absurdly soever applied, was always decisive with Tugwell: and he was now worked up to a pitch of Spiritual Quixotism, and grew impatient to set out; and begged Mr Wildgoose to name a day for their departure towards Bristol.

Wildgoose told him, that as Whitsuntide was at hand, and that great irregularities were practised amongst the common people upon those festivals, at wakes and revels, and other ungodly meetings; particularly at a heathenish assembly of that kind, on the Cotswold-hills, called Dover's Meeting,★ he had thoughts of making that in their road to Bristol.— Ah! says Tugwell, I have been many a time at Dover's Meeting, and won a hat there, at cudgel-playing, when I was a young man; and they say there is to be good sport there this year.—Ah! Jerry, replies Wildgoose, dost thou call that sport, where so many poor souls are devoted to destruction, by drinking, swearing, and all kinds of debauchery? These wakes or revels are the devil's strong-holds, whence he issues forth, and takes captive the poor deluded people at his pleasure. However, I am determined to bear my testimony against them, by preaching to our brethren, and warning them of their danger, 'whether they will hear, or whether they will forbear:' and so, we'll resolve to set out next Thursday morning, which I think is the day when that meeting is always held.

Tugwell said he would be ready to attend his worship at break of day, if he could give Dorothy the slip. But, says he, there is another thing, which I had forgot; how does your worship design to travel; on foot or on horseback?—Why, Jerry, says Wildgoose, didst thou ever hear that apostles ever rode on horseback? No, St Peter himself never thought of any such thing (much less of riding in a coach or post-chaise, as many of his successors have done), but performed all his journeys on foot, as I intend to do.—Well, well, master, says Tugwell, I do not speak upon my own account; for I never have been on horseback since I was twelve years old, when I used to ride the 'squire's horses to water sometimes, along with old Thomas Heartwell, the coachman.

Well, master Geoffry, I will be ready to attend your worship on foot or on horseback, by land or by sea, whenever you please: and so they parted for the present; each to make what little preparations he thought necessary for such an expedition.

★ This was a meeting of great renown in the last century, revived by one Captain Dover, for wrestling, back-sword, and other athletic exercises; and celebrated in verse by the Pindars of Oxford and Cambridge.

IV
Essay on Quixotism

Though the profession of chivalry has been exhibited to us, by Cervantes, as an object of ridicule, we must not imagine that it was in itself, and in its original, really ridiculous. Knight-errantry took its rise from true heroism, and the most generous principles of honour and public spirit. The most celebrated heroes of antiquity were in reality knights-errant; who wandered about to subdue monsters, or, to deliver men from oppression; to protect the innocent, or chastise the insolent; and, in short, to redress those grievances which were not sufficiently provided against by established laws, in the ruder ages of the world.

The absurdity which we laugh at in the celebrated Don Quixote is, his attempting to revive that profession, when the more perfect regulations of civil society had rendered it not only unnecessary, but unlawful.

By poring incessantly over the legendary tales of romance, his ideas of things were so strangely perverted, and his imagination possessed with such frantic notions, that he thought himself obliged in honour to sally forth and submit to voluntary hardships, in quest of adventures which he was not likely to meet with, and to redress grievances which no longer existed; or in which, under a regular government, he had no right to interfere.

Thus he not only mistook windmills for giants, and a harmless flock of sheep for an army of Pagans, but challenged an honest farmer to mortal combat for correcting his own servant, and set at liberty some prisoners, who by legal authority had been condemned to the galleys.

The like absurd imagination had possessed our Spiritual Quixote. There was a time when Providence, for wise reasons, thought fit to delegate men invested with extraordinary powers, to publish some important truths to mankind; to warn them of approaching calamities; to combat the superstitious opinions, or to reform the immoral practices which had prevailed in the world to an enormous degree.

In this sense, patriarchs and prophets, apostles and evangelists, and even St Paul himself, might be styled Spiritual Knights-errant; though they had divine commissions to take the profession upon them, for the most important ends.

And even our primitive reformers had both reason and scripture so evidently on their side; and the errors of popery were become so flagrant and intolerable, that they seemed justified in breaking through the restraints of human establishments, by the palpable necessity of the occasion.

But our modern itinerant reformers, by the mere force of imagination, have conjured up the powers of darkness in an enlightened age. They are acting in defiance of human laws, without any apparent necessity, or any divine commission. They are planting the gospel in a Christian country; they are combating the shadow of popery, where the protestant religion is established; and declaiming against good works, in an age which they usually represent as abounding in every evil work.

But there is another species, or rather a slighter degree of Quixotism, which proceeds merely from the mimetic disposition of mankind, and is, perhaps, more common in the world than is generally imagined; what I mean is, a desire of imitating any great personage whom we read of in history, in their dress, their manner of life, their most indifferent actions, or their most trifling peculiarities; especially of those who, by living in some distant age of the world, have acquired a kind of venerable heroism to their character, and there are few people, I believe, so severely rational, as not to have some slight tincture of this harmless frailty, or, as the wise men of the world would call it, this ridiculous affectation.

Indeed, life itself would be insipid; nor could human nature support itself upon merely rational pleasures, did not fancy enlarge our sphere of enjoyment, not only by giving an additional gloss to the most substantial objects, but also by stamping an imaginary value upon the most trifling which, by that means, whilst the novelty lasts, frequently become the source of the most exquisite delight.

I remember a gentleman of the house of commons, a man of great learning and fine taste, who, having been particularly conversant in the English history and antiquities, and whose fondness for the paintings of Vandyke had given him a relish for the dress of our ancient nobility, indulged himself, when at his country-seat, in the humour of wearing shoe-strings, instead of shoe-buckles, and a collar band, instead of a neck-cloth; and in several other antiquated customs, which he would gravely defend by arguments of convenience and propriety.

I also knew a man in the university, who, having read at how great a price the earthen lamp of Epictetus was sold after his death, and flattering himself that the implements of his lucubrations might be valued as curiosities by posterity, determined to renounce the use of candles as a modern invention, and, like that philosopher, to study by a lamp; which, to his utter confusion, he happened to overturn, and spilled a considerable quantity of oil upon a handsome folio, which he had borrowed of his tutor.

Nay, a whimsical gentleman within my memory, took it into his head, that instead of a night-cap, he would sleep, like the ancient heroes, in an iron helmet, which adorned his hall; till one night it unfortunately fell off his head, and demolished his chamber-pot.

Thus Mr Wildgoose; in imitation of our primitive reformers, and those other worthies in the frontispieces of those books of the last century with which he had been lately conversant, who wore their own hair according to the fashion of the times; that he might resemble those venerable men, even in his external appearance, Mr Wildgoose, I say, since his retreat from the world had suffered his own hair to grow for some months. Though, perhaps, there might also be something of convenience in this at first, to avoid the impertinence of his officious barber, who, whilst he was working the lather into his stubbed hair, would take upon him to insinuate some sociable advice into his patient, which was more irksome to Mr Wildgoose in his present gloomy situation, even than the rough instruments and heavy hand of this rustical operator. This alone, therefore, would have been a sufficient reason for his omitting to be shaved, and nourishing his own hair, which, though it was now thick enough to keep him warm, yet as it did not extend below his ears, he made but an uncouth appearance to those who had been used to see him in a decent periwig. But to proceed in our story.

V

MR WILDGOOSE AND HIS FRIEND TUGWELL SALLY FORTH IN QUEST OF SPIRITUAL ADVENTURES

Early on Thursday morning then, in the Whitsun-week, Mr Geoffry Wildgoose forsook his downy bed; and rejecting that artificial covering of his head, called a peruke, just smoothed his locks with his fingers, put on a plain blue coat, with a black plush waistcoat and breeches, and with a few guineas in his pocket, issued forth in quest of spiritual adventures.

The harmless red-breast, with his solitary note, began to break in upon the stillness of the dawn, and, from the sweet-briar that grew round the lattice, to interrupt the gentle slumbers of Jeremiah Tugwell, when Mr Wildgoose arrived under his window, and, by the signal agreed upon, summoned him to the place of rendezvous. Jerry soon appeared at the cottage gate, in his short jerkin (being somewhat between a coat and a waistcoat), his jelly-bag linen cap upon his head, with his oaken staff under his arm, and his wallet on his shoulder.

Wildgoose delivered to him a couple of shirts, a small Bible, and two or three pious manuals, which were to be the companions of his pilgrimage. Tugwell, however, who was a happy composition of flesh and spirit, having some regard to the body as well as the soul, had the precaution which Wildgoose wanted, to thrust privately into his wallet a good luncheon of brown bread, and some Gloucestershire cheese; which clandestine conduct it is not recorded that Wildgoose ever thought proper to resent.

The sun had hardly appeared above the horizon, when the two pilgrims turned their backs upon their native village, making what speed they could towards the Cotswold-hills, to avoid meeting any of their neighbours, whose curiosity might retard them in their progress.

In about two hours they reached the brow of the hill, when Mr Wildgoose making a halt to take breath, looked round upon the country below them. The sun had now begun to exhale the dews of

the morning, which, being thinly dispersed through the air, gave a
charming freshness to every object that rose to their view. There was an
extensive prospect of the rich vale of Evesham, bounded at a distance
by the Malvern hills. The towers and spires, which rose amongst the
tufted trees, were strongly illuminated by the sloping rays of the sun;
and the whole scene was enlivened by the music of the birds, the
responsive notes of the thrushes from the neighbouring hawthorns,
and the thrilling strains of the skylark, who, as she soared towards the
heavens, seemed to be chanting forth her matins to the great Creator
of the universe.

  Wildgoose was touched with a kind of sympathy; and a ray of true
devotion darting into his soul, he broke out in the words of Milton,
with whom he had been much conversant—

> These are thy glorious works, Parent of good,
> Almighty! Thine this universal frame,
> Thus wondrous fair; Thyself how wondrous then?
> Unspeakable! Who sitt'st above these heavens,
> To us invisible, or dimly seen
> In these thy lowest works; yet these declare
> Thy goodness beyond thought, and power divine.

After a little pause, Jerry, says he (addressing himself to Tugwell,) I
am always charmed with this fine prospect, though I have viewed it
so many hundred times.—Yes, says Jerry, who was slipped behind his
master, one may see—a number of miles here—that's *sartain*.—I don't
think the beauty of a prospect depends upon the number of miles one
may see, says Wildgoose, but upon the number and distinctness of the
objects, and the richness of the country.—Why, yes, says Tugwell, to be
sure—the vale—is rich land—and most of it—worth forty shilling an
acre—but then—it's plaguy dirty—in the winter—

  As Tugwell was going on, Mr Wildgoose turned about, and found
that the breaks in his speech were owing to the regular whiffs which
he took at his pipe: for whilst Wildgoose was engaged in contemplation
and soliloquy, Jerry had been employed in striking fire to some touch-

wood, which he always carried in his tobacco-box for that purpose; and had just lighted, and was puffing, with violent efforts, his short pipe. Ah! Jerry, says Wildgoose, I find thou art not yet weaned from the vanities of this world—Thou art not content with the heavenly manna of meditation, but still lusteth after the garlic and flesh-pots of Egypt. Why, then, master Wildgoose, is it any sin to take a harmless pipe of tobacco? I don't think smoking now and then is contrary either to the law or the gospel.—Jerry, says Wildgoose, I don't think smoking tobacco absolutely sinful; for to the good all things are good, if it be received with thanksgiving.—Then belike one ought to say grace, over a pipe of tobacco? says Jerry.—I don't say that, replies Wildgoose, but I'll venture to say, that one ought not to take any sort of pleasure, for which one cannot return God thanks. In short, Jerry, I am afraid thou hast got such a habit of tickling thy palate with something strong, that thou canst not easily do without it; for which reason thou oughtest to break it off at once.—Jerry, who was a little nettled at being interrupted in what he thought so innocent an enjoyment, cried out, Well, well, I *loves* a pipe; and, thank God, can afford to buy an halfpenny-worth of tobacco; and I would not leave it off if the bishop himself, or even Mr Whitfield, were to preach against it. In short, master, if smoking a dry pipe be a sin, God send us some good liquor! which is all that I'll say about the matter.

Wildgoose shook his head, and began to fear that Tugwell was only half a convert; but thought it was best not to exasperate his fellow-traveller, or discourage him by too much severity at their first setting out; he, therefore, dropped the dispute, and trudged on at a round rate for some time.

VI

TUGWELL MEETS WITH
A PERILOUS ADVENTURE

The two friends now proceeded on their journey. Mr Wildgoose occasionally inculcating some wholesome doctrine into his disciple, and Tugwell fumigating the air with the incense of his tobacco.

They had travelled near two miles without any occurrence worth recording: when, on a sudden, they heard at a distance the cheerful cry of a pack of hounds, accompanied with the music of French-horns. As they trudged on, the sound approached still nearer and nearer, and at last they were surprised with the appearance, not of four or five foxhunters, as might be expected, but of fourscore or a hundred horsemen upon full speed. The case was, Lord B—— of Nottinghamshire had taken a seat upon the Cotswold-hills, for buck-hunting; and had that morning turned out a fine stag, which the hounds had pursued with great eagerness, and probably over-run the scent; for, coming to a wall, they were now at a stand, and gave the whole company an opportunity of coming to a rendezvous.

I have observed there is hardly a man amongst the vulgar people but affects to be a sportsman, and that would not think it as great a disgrace to be thought a coward, or deficient in courage, as void of taste, or ignorant of the terms peculiar to the manly exercise of hunting.

Accordingly Tugwell, though his sedentary occupation had permitted him to be but little conversant with field sports, or the pleasures of the chase, yet was ambitious of being thought a sportsman; and seeing the dogs at a stand, lagged behind Mr Wildgoose (who walked on, wrapped in meditation) to wait the event. At last, in the midst of a furzebrake, Tugwell spied the head of some animal; which his imagination immediately represented as the branching horns of the stag: and now, fired with ambition, and making sure of the applauses of the whole field, Jerry waved his hat over his head, and with the utmost vociferation, in the fox hunters' language, cries out, Tallio! Tallio! Tallio!* The huntsman

---

* Quasi, Tail-oho!

understood him, and immediately drew off the dogs towards his bawling monitor, when, to his great vexation and Tugwell's utter confusion, up starts a swinging jack-ass, whose long ears Jerry mistook for the horns of the stag. The jack-ass, with his hideous braying, put to flight the huntsman's courser; who, however, was wheeling round to reward Tugwell for his intelligence, with the discipline of a horse-whip: and many of the gentlemen being now come up, and disappointed of their sport, and suspecting that Jerry had done it out of fun, were surrounding him in great wrath, and threatened to be the death of him. Poor Tugwell threw himself upon his knees, and with one hand flourishing his staff to guard his head; he extended the other to sue for mercy; but expected every moment to fall a sacrifice to the rage of the vociferous stag-hunters. At last, one of the gentlemen, who saw these affairs in a less important light, turned it off with a joke, and dismissed him in the polite phrase (being a mixture of real compassion and affected profaneness—) D-mn the fellow; let the poor devil go about his business.

Tugwell took them at their word, and gathering up his steps with great agility, and without looking behind him, soon joined his friend Wildgoose; who, wrapped in contemplation, was advanced a considerable way before him, having not given the least attention to what was going on; but upon Jerry's relating to him his danger, and his escape from it, Wildgoose immediately started from his reverie, and in the first transports of his zeal for his friend, was determined to attack these sons of Nimrod with the thunder of his eloquence. But, luckily for them, they were by this time gone off many furlongs, in pursuit of their game, and out of the reach of Wildgoose's rebukes.

He, therefore, contented himself with sending a pious ejaculation after them, and with reprimanding Tugwell for his officious impertinence; recommending to him a more simple and uniform conduct for the future, and not to entangle himself again in the vain amusements of a carnal and wicked generation.

VII

THE NATURAL EFFECTS
OF HUNGER AND FATIGUE

The two pilgrims had now almost reached the plain called Dover's-hill, where the revel was to be held; but as the sport did not begin till the afternoon and the sun now began to wax troublesome, Jerry proposed resting under an oak, that cast an inviting shade near the side of a wall; and opening his wallet, he produced a large fragment of a brown loaf, and cheese in proportion, the reviving odour of which put Wildgoose in mind of his breakfast; for hitherto he had not bestowed a thought upon that article, nor on the means of procuring it.

Now, master, quoth Tugwell, if we had trusted to Providence, and I had not brought some bread and cheese in my wallet, what would your worship have done for a breakfast?—Hold thy profane tongue! replies Wildgoose; this is not a difficulty which requires the interposition of Providence. But whenever that is the case, I am certain of his assistance: and God often makes those his instruments to bring about his gracious designs, who intend nothing but their own pleasure, as I suppose thou didst, Jerry, in bringing thy bread and cheese in thy wallet.

After making a hearty, though dry breakfast (for his precaution did not extend so far as to provide drink as well as food,) Jerry's spirits having been exhausted by his early rising, long walk, and the consternation he had been in from the huntsman's whip; he threw himself at length upon the turf, and was soon got into a world of his own, snoring most profoundly.

Mr Wildgoose at first pulled out one of his little manuals, and began to read; but he being likewise a little fatigued, soon yielded to the demands of nature, and followed his fellow-traveller's example: where we shall leave them to their repose a little, whilst we inquire what effect their departure had upon Mrs Wildgoose and Dame Tugwell, whom they left at home.

VIII

CHARACTER OF MRS TUGWELL.
AND THE PERPLEXITY OCCASIONED BY MR
WILDGOOSE'S AND TUGWELL'S ELOPEMENT

Mrs Wildgoose was a woman that wore a white hood—and breakfasted upon sage-tea—which particularities, and the principles that gave rise to them, were the distinguishing strokes of her character: for in every instance, Mrs Wildgoose (like a sensible woman) preferred convenience to show, and always sacrificed any present pleasure to the future ease and happiness of her life. Accordingly, in contempt of modern fashions, and to guard against the tooth-ache, she continued in the venerable sarsenet hood, which was the mark of gentility in the days of her youth; and she drank sage-tea rather than indulge herself in the delicious flavour of hyson or congo, at the expense of her health; which she found affected by that more agreeable beverage.

Mrs Wildgoose had a truly maternal fondness for her son, and was disappointed in not having him as a constant companion at her meals, and her hours of leisure from her domestic business. But as she was sensible that he was at present under a wrong influence, she forbore to exasperate his malady by opposition or teazing expostulations. She was no stranger (as we observed) to her son's frequenting Tugwell's house, to the company he kept there, nor to the manner in which he entertained them,—had heard of his attending the methodist's meeting at ——, and had frequently consulted with Mr Powel the vicar on that subject. But though she was afraid this religious cast of mind was rather the effect of melancholy than of any rational conviction; yet she thought it was the most innocent turn his disorder could take, the dram-bottle or other vicious indulgences being too frequently the sad refuge of such unsociable mortals in their solitudes. And as his motions had of late been so very irregular—and he frequently walked out at the garden-gate very early into the fields with his grey-hound, and breakfasted at his own hours, she took no notice of his absence this particular morning.

But Dame Tugwell, though Jerry had been often as early as this at the labours of the strap, and was frequently whistling and singing, to the disturbance of his neighbours, before sun-rising—yet she regularly summoned him at eight o'clock, from his little stall near the house, to partake with her of a warm breakfast; but not finding him this morning at his station, if I may use that expression for want of a better, she had made diligent inquiry amongst her neighbours without success. At last, it came into her head, that Mr Wildgoose and he had been more frequently together of late, than they ever used to be before. She, without much hesitation, therefore, repairs to Mrs Wildgoose's, to inquire if he had been there this morning. Upon being answered in the negative, and also informed that Mr Wildgoose had not been seen that day, though it was now much later than he had ever been absent before, both she and Mrs Wildgoose began to be greatly alarmed—I will be hanged now, says Dame Tugwell, if these two have not some *figary*, in their brain; I have observed his worship and our Jerry always whispering and laying their heads together of late; and whenever I came near them, they were as mute as a fish forsooth. For my part, I never liked all this preaching and praying: there is no occasion for it—is there now, Madam Wildgoose? If a body does but keep one's church, and does one's best to live, and pays every one his own, I do not see what else is required of us. (This she said as knowing Mrs Wildgoose's opinion of the matter). But what crotchet can be got into their heads now? continued Dorothy. Master Wildgoose has been so *malancolly* of late, to be sure he would not go to such a place as Dover's meeting; for, else, our Jerry has been talking of the *sport* there two or three times within this day or two—but what should Jerry do there now, unless he puts in for the silver spoon that is to be grinned for? However, I shall hear of him, if he is thereabout—and I will lock up his best waistcoat for the future—and make him know, he shall not run about spending his money at this rate without my leave.

Mrs Wildgoose, as soon as the volubility of Dame Tugwell would permit, desired her to make herself easy about her husband; that, if he was gone with her son, she would pay him for his trouble, and be answerable for his coming to any harm.—No, God forbid! quoth Dorothy, for I am but a poor helpless woman, you know, madam, since my poor Joseph went for a soldier, and now if my husband leave me too, what will become of me? Times are so hard, and money so scarce—and I can earn but one poor eighteenpence a week—and that is but a small matter to keep a body, you know, madam.—Dorothy was running on, like the flier of a jack, when Mrs Wildgoose desired her to be pacified, ordered her some victuals, and left her.

When Mrs Wildgoose was alone, however, she began to be very seriously alarmed for her son. She could not possibly guess what project he was engaged in. She was at first inclined to send her old servant to Dover's-hill, which Dame Tugwell had mentioned, that she might be satisfied whether he were gone thither or not, but immediately rejected that design, as she was convinced young Wildgoose, in his present state of mind, would not appear at a public meeting of that kind.

Whilst she was in this perplexity, Mr Powel, the clergyman of the parish came in, as he frequently did in the morning; who being informed of the affair, immediately said, he should not be at all surprised to hear that Mr Geoffry was gone somewhere or other after these methodists; for he was well ascured, he had been preaching up their puritanical notions amongst his neighbours for this half year, that he had lent two or three of their journals about the parish, and had frequently attended an itinerant preacher at ——, though it had been kept a secret from Mrs Wildgoose. I have often had a mind to talk to Mr Geoffry on this subject, continued the vicar,—but you know, madam, he has of late avoided me, and, indeed, there is no reasoning with people—who refer you to their own inward feelings, which you can no more deny than they can prove; and who take for sacred the wild suggestions of their own fancy.

Mrs Wildgoose knew what Mr Powel said to be very true, and could not tell what to think of the matter—but as her son's conduct had for some time been so unaccountable, she thought it in vain to form any conjectures about it, so waited with patience for his return; which she expected every hour. But in that poor Mrs Wildgoose was greatly disappointed.

IX

PROCEED TOWARD DOVER'S-HILL REVEL

The two fellow-travellers were left, under a spreading oak, taking a comfortable nap together. Wildgoose's high spirits, however, would not suffer him to doze long: but having roused his companion, they were now moving on toward the scene of action, refreshed from the fatigue of the morning; which refreshment proved by no means unseasonable in the sequel.

Mr Wildgoose, being intent upon his adventurous undertaking, that of preaching for the first time to a mob of holiday clowns at a revel, moved on in profound silence. And though he did not think any premeditation necessary, as he depended upon some supernatural power to give him utterance—yet he could not forbear anticipating, in some measure, the incidents which he should probably meet with, on this occasion—nor avoid recollecting how ingeniously Mr Whitfield spiritualized every circumstance attending his ministration.

Thus when he was to preach from the starting-post at Northampton, for instance, he took occasion to speak home to their souls, concerning our spiritual race.* And from the windmill at Bedford—He exhorted them not to be carried about by every *wind* of doctrine; and the like. So Wildgoose was devising with himself how to allegorize the different athletic exercises, which were usually practised on these occasions, and apply them to the best advantage.

To the wrestlers, he intended to preach up the necessity of *struggling* against flesh and blood, against the world and the devil, and also frequently to wrestle with God in prayer; as Mr Whitfield so often did.

The cudgel-players, he thought, he might aptly enough exhort to *bruise* and *break the head* of that old red serpent the devil, as St Austin calls him, and to *guard* themselves against every *attack* of their spiritual antagonists—and the like.

---

* Continuation of Whitfield's *Journal,* p.106, &c.

They proceeded, therefore, in silent meditation for some time, till at length Tugwell took the liberty to expostulate a little with his master upon the subject. Please your worship, says he, I have been thinking about this same preachment of ours, which we are now going about—since we are almost got to the place, methinks my heart begins to fail me a little. To be sure, it does one's heart good to hear your worship preach—and talk about justification—and *prestination* and *reperbation*, and—and—generation, and *sich* like—in our chimney corner—in an evening; for then, as one may say, we have nothing else to do, and nobody to contradict us. But here, when folks are got together—to make merry; that is, to break heads—and to kick shins, and *sich* as that, methinks, they will hardly have time to hear us preach; and mayhap, they may only laugh at us, for talking about religion at *sich* a time as this—or belike may pelt us with dirt or horse-dung—and *sich* as that.

Ah! Jerry, says Wildgoose, have not I told thee, how Mr Whitfield has preached to twenty thousand people at a time, upon Kennington Comnon—where, as he assures us himself,★ he was frequently attended by fourscore coaches, and numbers of horses; and yet all was hushed, the moment he began to speak—their hearts were melted; they would have plucked out their eyes, and have given them to him; they crowded about him, hugged, and were even eager to salute him.† But be that as it may, Jerry, I am determined to discharge my duty, and should think myself happy to suffer in so glorious a cause.—The true saints have often most ardently thirsted after contumelies, derision, and other instances of persecution.—Well, well! master, God's will be done! says Tugwell; I did but speak—not that I am afraid of any one, for my part, nor would not turn my back to the best man in Glo'stershire. Well, do not be too confident, neither, Jerry; remember the violent professions of St Peter; and yet he was found deficient in the time of danger.—We must trust in the Lord, and take the sword of the spirit; but if we confide to our own strength, and to *carnal* weapons, we may find ourselves deserted in the day of temptation.

★ *Vide Journal.*
† *Journal.*

X

WILDGOOSE'S FIRST HARANGUE

They now approached the place of rendezvous, where the revel was held, which was a large plain on the Cotswold-hills. Their ears were saluted with a confused noise of drums, trumpets, and whistle-pipes; not those martial sounds, however, which are heard in the field of battle, but such as those harmless instruments emit, with which children amuse themselves in a country fair. There was a great number of swains in their holiday clothes, with their belts and silk handkerchiefs; and nymphs in straw hats and tawdry ribbands, flaunting, ogling, and coquetting, in their rustic way; with as much alacrity, as any of the gay flutterers in the Mall.

A ring was formed about the wrestlers and cudgel-players, by the substantial farmers on their long-tailed steeds, and two or three forlorn coaches sauntering about with their vapourish possessors; who crept from their neighbouring seats—to contemplate the humours of these awkward rustics, and waste an hour of their tedious month in the *country*, where, as a great★ modern observes, *small matters serve* for *amusement*.

Wildgoose and his friend Jerry, making but a small figure in this humorous assembly, were at a loss how to draw the attention of the multitude. As they had made a dry breakfast, and had drunk nothing the whole day, Jerry asked his master, Whether it were any sin, to call for a pint of ale, at *sich* a time as this? So with Wildgoose's consent, they went to one of the booths, and were refreshing themselves with the aforesaid potation, when the company began to divide; and proclamation was made, that a holland shift, which was adorned with ribbands, and displayed on a pole, was going to be run for, and six young women began to exhibit themselves before the whole assembly, in a dress hardly reconcileable to the rules of decency.

Nice people have been observed to have the grossest ideas; and, perhaps, such chaste men have the most unchaste conceptions of things.

★ *Life of C. Cibber.*

Be that as it will, Wildgoose no sooner perceived that mysterious veil of modesty, the holland smock, thus rudely exposed to public view, and these young women prepared to engage in so loose a diversion, than he perceived his wonted zeal revive; and mounting upon an inverted hamper, near the booth, he beckoned to the mob, crying out,

For Christ's sake, my Christian brethren, if you have any regard to the health of your souls, desist from these anti-christian, these more than paganish recreations, which are poison, and listen to my words!

The people, seeing a man of a tolerable appearance thus exalted above the crowd, and preparing to harangue, began to stare, and to inquire of each other what he would be at! As they heard imperfectly the word *health*, and more words of a medicinal tendency, the prevailing opinion was, that a mountebank was going to dispense his medicines, for the benefit of mankind; and Tugwell's wallet was supposed to contain the sovereign packet of the learned doctor. Mr Wildgoose, however, soon undeceived them, by addressing the crowd, in the apostolical style; though he had not yet acquired the true *bon ton* or gospel lingo of Mr Whitfield and his associates.

Men, brethren, and fellow-christians! You are here assembled to keep holiday! that is, to sacrifice to the devil; to perform the most agreeable service, which you could possibly devise, to that enemy of mankind.

This festival is called Whitsuntide, and was appointed to commemorate the most solemn event recorded in the annals of our religion; namely, the effusion of the Holy Spirit upon the primitive apostles. But instead of being filled with the Holy Spirit, as the apostles were, you are filling yourselves with spirituous liquors and strong drink; with the spirits of geneva, with English spirits, and foreign spirits, and what not!

Oh! my brethren, consider what you are about; is this renouncing the devil and all his works? Is this despising the pomps and vanities of this wicked world? and resisting the sinful lusts of the flesh? The very purpose and intent of this ungodly meeting is directly opposite to your most solemn vow at your baptism. Instead of guarding yourselves against the attacks of your spiritual adversary, instead of bruising the head of that old serpent, the devil; you are breaking one another's heads with cudgels and quarter-staffs; instead of wrestling against flesh and blood, you are wrestling with and supplanting one another. So far from remounting the pomps and vanities of this wicked world, you are running for holland smocks, and making provision for the lusts of the flesh.

Ah! my dear country-women, you that are so solicitous for these terrestrial garments, these garments spotted by the flesh! let me beseech you to labour, after the celestial robes, the spiritual decorations and saint-like ornaments of piety, meekness, and chastity; and not to set your hearts upon such profane trappings as pink ribbands and holland smocks.

Indeed, what use will you make of these tawdry shifts, should you gain the prize! I blush to answer such a question. They may *make* a poor *shift*, like the fig-leaves of Eve, to cover the nakedness of your bodies, as our good works clothe nakedness of our souls. But unless you are clothed with a better righteousness than your own, you will hereafter be stripped bare, and be exposed to the derision of men and angels—

From the secret connection which this subject had with generation, Mr Wildgoose was insensibly sliding into the nature of regeneration, and the newbirth; and was going to explain some of the most mysterious doctrines of Christianity to these unruly disciples, when a good orthodox publican, thinking his craft was in danger, cried out, Odzounterkins! lift up the smock! come, my maids! stand ready for the sport!

He was seconded by a shrewd young carter, with a silk handkerchief about his neck, who could not but laugh at the familiarity of Wildgoose's comparisons; and thinking also that this harangue would spoil the diversion, which they were now intent upon, he threw the rind of an orange at the orator's head. Another levelled a piece of horse-dung, with an unlucky dexterity, exactly into Tugwell's mouth as he stood listening with a conceited attention to his master's eloquence. Their example was followed by a great part of the company; who, as Jerry had foretold, began to bombard them so furiously with clods of dirt and horse-dung, that Mr Wildgoose was soon forced to dismount from the top of his hamper and one of them, tilting up the form on which Tugwell was exalted, laid him sprawling in the moisture occasioned by the staling of horses, or spilling of the liquor; where he lay wallowing for some time, being sainted with several bumps and jostles in contrary directions, which prevented his emerging from the slippery soil.

In short, Wildgoose thought it advisable to preserve himself for a more favourable opportunity, wherefore, lifting up and disengaging his fellow-labourer, they drew off from the field of battle, amidst the loud scoffs and exulting shouts of the unthinking multitude; Wildgoose only expressing his compassion for them, by a significant shake of the head, and crying out, Poor souls! they know not what they do; and Jerry, when he was got pretty well out of their reach, bawled out, Ay, ay! *parsecute* on *parsecute* on—*parsecute*—*parsecute*! You have the best of it in this world, but we shall be even with you in the next.

Thus unsuccessfully ended Wildgoose's first effort towards reforming the world; which, however, so far from discouraging him, only excited his zeal; and he thought himself extremely happy in being counted worthy even of so slight a persecution; and desired Jerry not to be disheartened, for that they should meet with better success, when God should think fit to incline the hearts of his people to listen to their admonitions.

Tugwell, who was a little disconcerted by the bad success of their first attempt, answered, that he did not doubt but God would bring every thing about in his own good time; but, says he, perhaps the time is not yet come. And having a great desire; though he did not care to speak out, to return to his own chimney-corner, he said, Suppose, master, we were to go and try first what we can do with the men in the vale: and now, I don't think there was any body at Dover's-hill that knew us; for I did not see one soul of our town, and I know they are all busy in hay-harvest; so that we might slip home again at night, and nobody be ever the wiser.

Why, Jerry, says Wildgoose, with some warmth, dost thou think me such an apostate? what! to turn back, as soon as I have put my hand to the plough? No, Jerry, you may do as you please; but I will this night make the best of my way towards Gloucester, where Mr Whitfield was born, and first preached the word, and I make no doubt but I shall there find a little flock at least ready to receive me.

This gentle rebuke had its effect upon Jerry, and he found his spirit of travelling begin to revive. He told his master, therefore, he scorned to

forsake him and said, when he had washed his face, which was a little
sullied by his fall, he should not value what had happened of a rush.
But, adds he, if it were to do again, I would have had one bout with the
cowardly dog who tilted up the form.

Wildgoose exhorted his friend to christian patience, and to return
good for evil; and so they trudged on for some miles, without any
other adventure.

XI

Armigerorum Laudes;
or, a Panegyric on Esquires,
both ancient and modern

Whose house is that, said I, to some labourers on the London road,
with a little cupola on the top, and an enormous length of Chinese
rails before it?—Squire Shapely's, the Londoner's, says one of the
labourers.—Yes, says another, with an arch leer, he was a London taylor;
but has got a little money, and has built a fine house; and is now a justice
o'peace, and a 'squire.—Such is the style and title, taste and economy, of
your London esquire.

A country 'squire is a gentleman in a remote province, who resides
constantly at the mansion-house of his ancestors, which he keeps in
tolerable repair—makes a new pair of gates, and builds a summer-house
at the corner of his garden. Relying upon his silver spurs and a tight
boot, he makes one attempt towards gaining a rich heiress; but not
succeeding, he marries his maid, gets an heir to his estate, dies, and is
forgotten.

He visits the metropolis once in his life-time; and takes up his quarters
at the Ram in Smithfield—goes to visit his old aunt, from whom he
has great expectations; who, for the credit of the family, makes him put
on a sword, which gets between his legs, and almost oversets him. He,
therefore, walks through Fleet-street in his boots; a sharper jostles him

into the kennel—another snatches his whip from under his arm, under pretence of revenging the affront, and makes clear off with it—gives five and six-pence for a pair of buck-skin gloves, double stitched; returns into the country, with a terrible idea of the extravagance and tricks of the town—and, though a constant dupe to the knavish cunning of his tenants, and the exorbitant gains of a country shop-keeper, detests every thing that bears the name of London, except, the London Evening-post, and the London carrier, that brings him down a barrel of oysters at Christmas. Now this sort of man is your country esquire.★

From these instances, I infer, that esquires are of various kinds, and that an esquire, in the modern sense of the word, is a being, in his definition, his existence, and his economy, totally distinct from the 'squires of antiquity. The race of 'squires, whose utility to the word in general, and to us diminutive authors in particular, I wish to celebrate, were, in their original, *armigeri*, or *scutiferi*; that is, armour-bearers to some ancient heroes; and from thence transferred into modern tales and romances, in which every knight has his esquire. Such was Automedon to Achilles, the faithful Achates to Æneas, Sancho Panza to Don Quixote, and Ralpho to Hudibras—Now, as the 'squires of the heroic ages performed these inferior offices of life, which were beneath the dignity of the hero himself; drove his chariot, bridled his horse, or ran on errands, and the like; so in mock heroics, or familiar romance, the 'squire is frequently the vehicle of low humour, or the subject of such practical jokes, as would too much degrade the solemnity of the knight-errant himself. Thus Sancha Panza is tossed in a blanket, whilst good epic rib-roastings, and heroic knocks on the pate, are reserved for the noble don, his master.

And as poetry and romance is, or ought to be, an imitation of real life, the like subordination of character is frequently to be met with in company, and the conversation of the world. An esquire, in this view, is a gentleman of an easy submissive temper, of moderate appetites, and patient of injuries; who acts an under-part in life, and serves as a kind of shield—to protect, or a foil to set off, the principal character.

★ A character now almost forgotten in England.

Every person of any distinction is accordingly surrounded by his proper satellites or attendants of this kind. My lord has his dangler, who secures him a proper deference amongst strangers, by setting the example himself. The bishop has his chaplain, who, at put or all-fours, lets his lordship name the trump. Nay, every 'squire, in the modern sense of the word has a 'squire in the ancient sense, who attends him on all occasions, in the shape of a hunting parson, a nominal captain, or a pacific lawyer; who shields him from the vehemence of his brother justice's wit, or acts the dwarf in understanding, whenever his worship is disposed to shine or to be witty himself, or explains his jokes, or defends his paradoxes, as the occasion happens to require.

I might proceed to show the same convenient subordination of character, in every rank of life; but this would be too great a digression from my purpose, which was, only to show the utility of this race of men in works of this kind; and to entreat the reader to consider the 'squire as a lawful representative of the knight, or rather as a *merry andrew*, to our spiritual *quack*; and that if Tugwell is not only witty in himself, but the cause that wit is in other men (as Falstaff says)—if he utters a facetious thing, or receives a kick on the breech, let it be placed to account, as so much wit and humour in the author, which he could with the same ease, though not with the same propriety, have transferred to Wildgoose himself, his principal character.

But to proceed in our history.

XII

WILDGOOSE'S HOSPITABLE RECEPTION AT THE HOUSE OF AN ORTHODOX CLERGYMAN, AND THE EVENT OF A DISPUTE BETWEEN THEM

The two pilgrims had now proceeded near seven miles from the place of their luckless achievement; Wildgoose rejoicing that he was counted

worthy to suffer for religion (as he thought it,) and Tugwell consoling
himself with the hopes of better success for the future; when they
arrived at an obscure village on the side of the hills, a little before sunset. They were directed to a neat public-house, by a small sign—whose
device it required some skill in hieroglyphics to decipher. The painter
had probably intended it for the Red Lion; but some ambiguity, which
arose from an injudicious mixture of the lights and shades, gave it rather
the appearance of a shoulder of mutton. When they entered the house,
they found it pre-occupied by a very sober party; consisting of an
exciseman, a grazier, the parson of the parish, and a mole-catcher.

Mr Wildgoose inquired of the landlord, whether he could furnish
them with a bed? Instead of answering his question, the landlord,
according to custom, asked him, which way they were travelling? This
not being to the present purpose, Wildgoose desired an answer to his
first question. Mine host told him, theirs was but a bye-place, and no
great thoroughfare, and that they had seldom any body lay there; but,
however, when his dame came home (which she certainly would do
before midnight, as she was only gone to a merry-making in the next
parish,) he would see about it, and he did not doubt but they could
contrive to lodge them; though, says he, we have but one room, where
I and my wife lie, but then we have two beds in it. Well, but what will
you please to drink, sir, continued my landlord.

Our travellers being a little disconcerted at this account of my
host's accommodations, Wildgoose inquired, How far it was to
Gloucester?—To Gloucester, sir? Why you are out of your way to
Gloucester; but, *howsomever*, we call it twelve miles, and I believe it is
pretty good measure, do not you think it is, master Pottle? This was
the name of the honest clergyman, to whom mine host appealed, by
way of commencing a conversation between him and the travellers;
as talking together is generally an introduction to drinking together,
which it was his interest to promote: but Mr Pottle being conscious of
the impropriety of his present situation, and that he must appear in a
low light to a stranger of a tolerable figure, as Wildgoose was, affected
to have no connection with the company, but to be employed in some
useful meditation. Instead of regarding my landlord's appeal, therefore,

he assumed all the dignity he was possessed of, inflated his cheeks, and puffed out whole volumes of smoke, which being reverberated by the low roof, he soon filled the house with the fumes of his tobacco.

As the doctor did not vouchsafe them an answer, Wildgoose had now given his attention to a common subject of dispute, which was carrying on between the grazier and the exciseman—the former of whom had asserted, that if a man happened to buy a horse which was touched in the wind, or had any other concealed defect, it was no harm to put him off again, without discovering his faults.—As this dispute bore some relation to the precepts of religion, and seemed to concern Wildgoose, who had taken upon him the office of reforming pernicious principles and corrupt practices, he could not forbear interposing and having been formerly a smart logician (as was observed in the beginning of this history,) after expressing his concern, that such a practice should bear a dispute in a christian country; he said, that most controversies were perplexed for want of settling precisely the question in debate, and keeping strictly to the terms. He begged leave, therefore, to reduce the dispute to the following argument,* or syllogistical form, as it is called:

> All cheating is sinful:
> The putting off an unsound horse for a sound one is cheating; therefore,
> The putting off an unsound horse for a sound one is certainly sinful.

Here the doctor, taking the pipe from his mouth, could not forbear putting in his verdict. Oh! ho! sir, says he, I find you have been bred at the university. *Negatur minor:* I deny your second proposition, that of putting off an unsound horse *in a fair,* is properly cheating, in the *popular* sense of the word.—Look you there now, says Wildgoose, this is the common method of disputing; you beg the question, and have also changed the terms of the proposition upon us, and put words into the

---

* Though they despise human learning, those that have had a learned education are fond enough of displaying it.

premises which have nothing to do with the conclusion. If we were to be governed by popular opinions and popular practices, we should soon have no more honesty amongst us than we have religion.—Religion! says Pottle; why, to be sure, it is a very profligate age that we live in, and the world is over-run with infidelity, heresy, and enthusiasm; and the church never was in so much danger from atheists and sectaries as at this day.

Sir, says Wildgoose, I apprehend the church's greatest danger is from the careless lives and degenerate principles of its own members.— Come, come, replies Pottle, we will not dispute about religion in this place; and, as I am afraid my landlord cannot very commodiously lodge you, rather than you should be distressed, you shall be welcome to such a bed as I can give you at my house.

Though Wildgoose recollected what had passed between him and the parson of his own parish, and was a little apprehensive of being involved in some controversy with a person whose professions would probably lead him to combat his present opinions, and discourage him from the undertaking in which he was now engaged, yet he could not refuse so kind an offer, especially as it was now too late for them to think of going farther that night. He, therefore, thanked the doctor for his great civility, and, attended by his trusty friend, accompanied him to the parsonage-house.

As they were going out of the house, my landlord's curiosity prompted him to whisper Tugwell, and ask him, Whether he and his fellow-traveller did not deal in corks? Or, perhaps, says he, in a low voice, you have some *run* goods in your wallet to dispose of.—No, no, replied Tugwell, my master is no such person as you take him for; he is a gentleman that is heir to three or four hundred pounds a year, and scorns to sell any thing. But no matter for that, I shall not tell our private matters to every fool that asks me. No, no, I understand travelling, better than that comes to.

XIII

WHAT HAPPENED AT THE PARSON'S HABITATION

Mr Pottle had now brought his two guests to his own house, and, sending Tugwell into the kitchen, took Wildgoose into a tolerably neat parlour. His elbow-chair stood ready for his reception, and his Tunbridge-ware tobacco-dish, with some scraps of paper folded up for the use of his pipe, were placed upon the table. There were several old newspapers lying in the window, and a single picture of Cardinal Fleury hung over the chimney-piece.

Mr Pottle was a hale man, of about five and fifty; was a bachelor; and all his domestics were an elderly housekeeper and a man-servant about his own age. His character will sufficiently appear from the evening's conversation.

Pottle had a cloth laid for himself and Mr Wildgoose, who eat pretty heartily of a cold shoulder of mutton and cucumbers; and Tugwell was very happy in the kitchen, with a jug of good liquor, and the remains of what came out of the parlour.

After supper Pottle filled his pipe, and began to beat about and investigate what scheme Mr Wildgoose was engaged in; what was his business at Gloucester, and how he came to travel on foot. As Wildgoose despaired of converting a man of his years and profession, whose principles were probably settled for life, he was at first a little upon the reserve; and evaded the hints Pottle had thrown out in regard to the intention of his journey.

Pottle then began to make some apology for being seen in an ale-house, and, that his guest might not suspect it was his usual custom, he said, as the parsonage-house was so far from the church, he had gone thither to wait for the funeral of a poor man, that died three miles off, in a hamlet belonging to his parish. But, says he, they know my method; that if they do not come by six o'clock, I would sooner leave the corpse in the church-yard all night than bury it; and so, I suppose, they have deferred it till to-morrow.

Why, replies Wildgoose, I believe the poor country people are very troublesome upon these occasions; but their ignorance is rather to be pitied than blamed. They fancy it a mark of respect to their deceased friends, to keep them above ground as long as possible.—Yes, says Pottle, and don't care what inconvenience they put us to, for the sake of their ridiculous humour, which *can* be of no service to the dead.—Why, to be sure, says Wildgoose, it is of no great consequence what becomes of the *bodies* of the deceased: but yet, I think, one should condescend a little to the scruples, and even to the weaknesses of our brethren in indifferent things, especially if our doing otherwise may probably prejudice them against us, and prevent our being of service to them in their more important concerns. I own, if I were a clergyman, I should consider myself, in some measure, as the servant of the public; and think myself obliged to bear with their humours, in some degree, rather than forfeit the good opinion of my parishioners.

Sir, replies Pottle, with some warmth, whatever opinion a parcel of ignorant country bumpkins may have of me, I'll never submit to their unreasonable prejudices and superstitions. A pack of rascals! the more you humour them, the more they will impose upon you. If they have any thing to complain of, let them complain to the bishop; but I'll do my duty as to the *cure of souls*, and let them go and be hang'd!

Pray, sir, says Wildgoose, (if I may take the freedom) what do you mean by the cure of souls? By the cure of souls? Why,—I mean, burying the dead—baptising children, and marrying—and—and—reading prayers, and preaching—and the like.—Why, as to burying, and marrying, replies Wildgoose; those functions seem rather to belong to the care of the body than to the cure of souls: and as for preaching (though I don't doubt, sir, but your doctrine is an exception) yet, from what I have observed from the generality of preaching, whatever becomes of our souls, christianity cannot long subsist amongst us, unless it should please God to send some better labourers into his vineyard.

Upon this Pottle flew into a perilous passion; took the pipe from his mouth, started up from his chair, and advancing towards Wildgoose, Sir, says he, what! do you affront me in my own house? I am afraid you are a presbyterian, or what is worse, one of these methodists, that ramble about the country, unsettling people's minds, and prejudicing them against their proper pastors—a pack of rascals! who are a reproach to toleration. But s-s-s-sir, says he,—Though Pottle was eloquent enough in his pulpit, where nobody contradicted him, yet, having naturally some impediment in his speech, it showed itself upon the least opposition. Being, therefore, in great wrath with Wildgoose, his choler almost choaked him, and he could hardly utter his indignation intelligibly. But, cocking up his tobacco stopper on his little finger—I'd have you to know, sir, says he, the ch-ch-ch-church has po-po-power—I say, the ch-church has po-power to pu-pu-pu-punish such r-r-r-rascals—I say, the ch-ch-church has po-power—just as he was uttering these words, and was retreating backwards from Wildgoose, who was got up to pacify him, he happened to tread in a smoaking-box, filled with leaves, and fell flat upon his back—bawling out and reiterating, The church has power, so loud, and in so angry a tone, that Pottle's man (who, together with his housekeeper and Tugwell, came to listen) threw open the parlour door; and, seeing Wildgoose standing over his master (whose wig was tumbled off in the fall,) and endeavouring to assist him in getting up; the man mistook his intention, and imagined it was the posture of a triumphant combatant. He, therefore, runs up to him, and with great violence gave Wildgoose a blow under the left jaw. Tugwell, seeing his master thus rudely treated, attacks Pottle's man in his turn. The old housekeeper fell upon Tugwell, tooth and nail, crying out, in an exalted key, I thought they were a couple of *casuistical*, *tyrannical* rascals; and would not have had my master harbour such vagabonds. After filling his belly with the best in the house, to knock a gentleman down! a *dis-gratitude*, *villantry* fellow!

The housekeeper's voice, being a sort of unison to the barking of a dog, alarmed an old spaniel that lay sleeping in the chimney corner, who began yelping round the combatants with great fierceness; and completed the tumultuous uproar.

Pottle, however, had now raised himself, and with Wildgoose, was endeavouring to part Tugwell and his man Jonathan, who were the only parties that continued the fray. Pottle also explained the affair to the old housekeeper; told her, the stranger was in no fault as to his fall;

but, says he, I am afraid we have taken a couple of wolves in sheeps' clothing into our house.

Wildgoose, likewise, perceiving he had forfeited the good opinion of his host, could not bear the thoughts of remaining all night under his roof. He, therefore, bade Tugwell follow him, and making the best apology the circumstances would bear, to Mr Pottle, for the trouble he had occasioned in his family, and, thanking him for his kind entertainment, marched out of the house, without any interruption from his reverend host.

XIV

Night-thoughts:
of ghosts and goblins.
They meet with an uncommon adventure

The character and conduct of this very orthodox divine contributed not a little to convince Mr Wildgoose of the necessity of some reformation in the church, and confirmed him in his resolution of prosecuting with all diligence his romantic undertaking.

The moon shining very bright, and there being but little night at that time of the year, the two pilgrims pursued their journey, taking the first road they could find which pointed towards Gloucester. They had travelled near a mile, and were now got into a very dark lane, by the side of a wood, that led down the hill on which the village stood. The gloominess of the scene, and the stillness of the night, in a strange place, raised in Tugwell some ideas of terror, which (notwithstanding his personal valour in rencounters and at fist-i-cuffs) he had in his youth being greatly subject to: and though he pretended now to be above these childish fears, yet he stuck very close to his master, and, with an affected bravery, began to fish out Wildgoose's opinion about ghosts and apparitions.

Some folks now, quoth Jerry, would be almost afraid to walk by themselves in such a dark lane, at this time of night: but I don't suppose there is any *sich* thing as spirits now-a-days—do you think there are, Master Wildgoose?—Any such thing as spirits, Jerry? Why, I believe there are no more walk by night than there are by day; and I am partly of the same opinion with a great man*, who says, That goblins and spirits have really no more to do with darkness than with light; and accounts for our terror on these occasions from what he calls 'the association of ideas.'—Yes, yes, says Tugwell, I remember the *sociation* in the time of the rebellion: our squire would not *sociate*.—No, no, Jerry, what I mean is the joining things together in our fancy; so that when a child is told by his nurse, of ghosts appearing by night, he shall never be able to separate the notion of spirits from that of darkness, as long as he lives.

But though this may account for that particular kind of terror, yet certainly the sense of our being off our guard, when alone in the dark, and ignorant what enemies we may be exposed to, must necessarily make us apprehensive of danger upon those occasions. So that, let a man have never so clear a head to separate ideas, yet I think it almost impossible to be equally calm and easy in darkness and solitude, as we are in the open day-light.

Tugwell was as still as a mouse during this discourse of Wildgoose, though he did not understand a word that was said.

As for there being any such thing as spirits in one sense, continued Wildgoose, no one that is not an atheist can deny this; but though, perhaps, before the times of christianity, Providence might think it necessary more frequently to interpose, by permitting the visible appearance of superior beings upon important occasions; and though I am convinced the devil has still as real an influence over the souls of men as he had then, yet you may take it for granted, Jerry, that every story which you ever heard of their visible appearance, is an imposture, and, if more nearly inquired into, may be accounted for from natural means; taking its rise either from the interested designs or terrified imaginations of wicked or weak people.—I myself remember, when I first went to the university, I lived in a large chamber, hung with green baize; the bed was placed in a sort of recess,

---

* Mr Locke.

separated from the dining-room by two large folding doors, which were thrown open when I went to bed, to make it more airy. I happened once to wake about midnight, and it being star-light, saw, on the farther side of the room, a tall figure in white, near six feet high. It seemed to have a square cap upon its shoulders, but was without a head.—Lord have mercy upon us! says Tugwell, laying hold of Wildgoose's skirt; yes, without a head! So my grandmother used to say, that ghosts commonly do appear without a head.—Well, continues Wildgoose, though I used to laugh at things of this kind, I could not account for this dreadful phenomenon. The more I stared at it, the more I was convinced it was something real. After laying some time, and mustering up my courage, I leaped out of bed, determined to unravel the mystery—when lo! I embraced in my arms a white surplice, which a scholar of the house, having left in my room after evening prayers; had hung upon a brass peg, over which I had suspended my square cap, such as they wear in the university.—Yes, yes, your *trenchard* caps, I have heard of them, says Tugwell.

Thus I am convinced would every story of apparitions have ended, says Wildgoose, if the scared spectator had had resolution enough to examine it, to the bottom.—

Why, to be sure, says Tugwell, apparitions are not so common now-a-days as they were in former times; but I remember when I was a boy, father had been to fetch the midwife upon your grandfather's mare, old Whitefoot. She was as good a servant, as ever wept upon four legs. Your grandfather bought her of old Simon Perkins: Well, says Wildgoose, proceed with your tale.—It was a very dark night, continues Jerry, and father was riding by a lone uninhabited house, at the end of a close lane, as his may be, when he saw strange lights in every window; and when he came into the middle of the lane, vast balls of fire rolled along under his horse's feet and then the squire's lady, who died in childbed, drove along in her coach and six, with her child in her arms; and—and—the coachman (it is *sartain* true) the coachman was without a head—and—. As Jerry was going on with his terrible story, bounce came his foot against something, and down he tumbled a-se over head, bawling out, Lord have mercy upon me! I have tumbled over a coffin! Blockhead! cries Wildgoose, why, thou wilt talk so long about ghosts, till thou art frightened at thy own shadow. Jerry, however, (strange as it was,) happened to be in the right; and the reader will easily guess at the cause of such a shocking indecency: it was the very corpse which Parson Pottle had been waiting for, of a poor man who died at the extremity of his parish, and his surviving friends, willing to take a decent leave of the deceased, had continued drinking till after six o'clock, when bringing him to the bottom of this hill, and recollecting that Mr Pottle would certainly not perform the last office that night, they had left the coffin there, to the terror of poor Tugwell, and the astonishment of his friend.★

They were now come into the open plain again, and travelled a good pace till towards break of day, and Tugwell pretended to know by the course of the stars, that it was near three o'clock; and, as his zeal was not quite so active as his master's, he began to complain of fatigue and want of sleep. They therefore made towards a barn, a little out of the road, which being locked they were forced to repose themselves upon some straw under a shed, where, however, they slept soundly for some hours; and, rising greatly refreshed about eight o'clock, proceeded on their journey; Jerry, according to custom, reminding his master to lay in a good breakfast at the first public-house upon the road.

XV

THE EVENT OF WILDGOOSE'S SECOND HARANGUE

In the afternoon, when they were got within a few miles of Gloucester, at a genteel house near the end of a village, they saw almost the whole parish assembled in the court, to see a set of morris-dancers, who, this holiday-time, dressed up in bells and ribbands, were performing for the entertainment of the family, and some company that had dined there. Wildgoose thought this a proper opportunity of displaying his

---

★ *N.B.* A real fact.

eloquence, and communicated his intention to his fellow-traveller: but he, having not so soon forgot the ill success of their yesterday's adventure, would have dissuaded Wildgoose from making a second attempt at so unseasonable a juncture; and said, moreover, that for his part he loved to see people merry at *sich* a time as this; but Wildgoose soon silenced his scruples, and, he being by this time sufficiently convinced of his master's obstinacy, immediately got amongst the morris-dancers, and acquainted them of his intention. As they were no strangers to itinerant orators in that country, they suspended their diversion for a while, and got round the preacher, who by this time was mounted upon some steps, and began to hold forth with great vehemence, against all festival amusements, as contrary to the serious spirit of the gospel and particularly against those irregularities which were practised at revels and Whitsun-ales. This doctrine, being rather ill-timed, was not much relished by a great part of the audience, who soon began to be impatient of the interruption which was given to their entertainment.

Those who are acquainted with this sort of *morris-dance*★ (which is still practised in several parts of England) must know, that they are usually attended with one character called the tom fool, who, like the clown in the pantomime, seems to be a burlesque upon all the rest. His fool's cap has a fox's tail depending like a ramillie wig; and, instead of the small bells which the others wear on their legs, he has a great sheep-bell hung to his back-side.

Whilst the company, therefore, were all attentive to the preacher, this buffoon contrived to slip the fool's cap upon Tugwell's head, and to fix the sheepbell to his rump: which Jerry no sooner perceived, than his choler arose, and spitting in his hands and clenching his fists, he gave the tom-fool a swinging blow in the face. The fool, having more wit than courage, endeavoured to escape amongst the crowd. Tugwell pursued him in great rage, with the sheep-bell at his tail, the ridiculous sound of which forming a sort of contrast to the wrath in Jerry's countenance, caused a great deal of loud mirth amongst the company.

★ A corruption of Morisco dance, probably introduced from Spain, by John of Gaunt.

Wildgoose, now finding it to no purpose to continue his harangue, assisted in extricating Tugwell from the throng, who had now formed a ring round him and the jack-pudding; and reprimanding him for his want of christian meekness, he bade him follow him, and shake off the dust from his feet, according to the language of our modern apostles, when they would decently extricate themselves from any uncommon difficulty. They now, therefore, pursued their journey without any farther molestation.

Wildgoose told Jerry, they had hitherto, indeed, met with but unchristian-like usage; but comforted him with the assurance of meeting with a more friendly reception when they should arrive at the Bell at Gloucester (where Mr Whitfield was born;) for, says he, where a true gospel-spirit prevails, the genuine fruits of it are peace, joy, brotherly love, and christian charity. Jerry replied, that a cup of good ale would be the greatest joy to him at present, for that he was very dry. Wildgoose, however, would not take the hint, nor stop till they arrived (early in the evening) at the ancient city of Gloucester.

BOOK III

I

Mr Wildgoose's reception at the Bell at Gloucester, the birth place of Mr Whitfield

It had been the custom of Mr Wildgoose, in any little excursions which he had formerly made, whenever he came into any city or considerable town, to inquire (like other travellers) into the trade and manufactures of the place, or what curiosities of art or nature were worthy of a stranger's notice. But, in the present situation of his mind, he had lost all relish for things of that kind: instead, therefore, of making any observation upon the situation, buildings, or antiquities of Gloucester, or being in the least struck with the beauty of its cathedral, and the remarkable lightness of its gothic tower, Mr Wildgoose considered it in no other light than as the birth-place of Mr Whitfield; and immediately inquired for the Bell Inn.

When they arrived under the gate-way, the travellers addressed themselves to a waiter (who was carrying a dish of Scotch-collops into a parlour across the court,) and asked, whether they could have any lodgings there. He, surveying them with a contemptuous air, did not vouchsafe them an answer.

They then applied to a sort of scullion, who was doing some drudgery near the kitchen. She, seeing two people about her own level, as she thought, spoke to the cook, who, after some muttering expostulations, went to her mistress behind the bar, and asked her, Whether she would lodge two foot passengers? Mrs Whitfield, being engaged with company, rose up with some reluctance, and came to the window of the bar, where spying two such dusty figures, her usual politeness to strangers forsook her—Hey-day, quoth she, lodgings, indeed! yes, to be sure; because 'Squire Fielding, forsooth, in that romancing book of his, pretends that Tom Jones was harboured here, we shall be pestered with all the trampers that pass the road!

Wildgoose was thunderstruck at this unchristian-like reception; but Tugwell, who, on the first appearance of so fine a lady, had stood with his hat off, now replaced it on his head, and, repeating her words, trampers, indeed!—I would have you to know, says he, his worship could have rode upon as good a gelding as any one in the county, and could have mounted me too, for that matter, if it were not more like good christians to travel on foot: but I thought folks that keep an ale-house were obliged to take in all comers.—Keep an ale-house! you saucy jackanapes! says Mrs Whitfield, who had not much christian meekness—you have mistaken the house; you should have gone to the Bird in Hand, in Tripe-lane. There, perhaps, you would find rest for travellers, such as you.—Well, well, dame, says Tugwell, there's no harm done; if you won't lodge us; I suppose there are others that will, and be glad of our custom. Trampers, indeed! I think Mr Whitfield might have preached you into better manners.

II

Procure a lodging

The two pilgrims were a little disconcerted at this mortifying reception, and at a loss how to proceed; and though Wildgoose had of late affected to despise all worldly distinctions, and to make light of external respect, the consequence of them; yet he was a little shocked at this unforeseen effect of his voluntary humiliation, and almost began to wish that he had travelled in a manner more suitable to his station in life.

As they were deliberating what course to take, Wildgoose espied a barber's pole; and reflecting that perhaps Mrs Whitfield, being ignorant of his enlightened heart, might be scandalized at the frouzy appearance of the outward man, resolved to get rid of his beard, have his hair refreshed, and his cravat a little decently adjusted. He, therefore, entered the shop, where the case was quite reversed. The honest barber, whose less affluent circumstances inspired more gentle manners, and made him civil to the meanest customer, received them with great affability, and apparent benevolence; and, with a voluble tongue, as he was preparing his razor, ran over the heat of the weather, dustiness of the roads, and other general topics, which those artists have ready at hand, for the entertainment of their customers, and to divert their attention from the pain which often attends the operation under the most skilful performer.

Whilst Wildgoose was doing penance under the instrument of this ingenious tonsor, he took the opportunity of consulting him about a lodging for himself and fellow-traveller; and informed him what treatment he had met with at the Bell. This Tugwell confirmed, with some expressions of resentment, assuring the barber that his master could afford to pay for whatever he called for, and did not want to spunge upon any one. We know the custom at such houses, continues he: 'tis touch pot, touch penny—we only want money's worth for our money.

The barber, encouraged by these overtures of familiarity, took the liberty in his turn to inquire which way they came, whither they were travelling, what stay they should make at Gloucester, and, if he might be so bold, what branch of business Mr Wildgoose was engaged in. Wildgoose, from the fulness of his heart, soon let the barber into the nature of his calling, and that he intended to employ the talent of preaching, which had been intrusted to him, for the good of the poor inhabitants of that city. The barber replied, that Mr Whitfield, to be sure, had preached there frequently with good success, and had left a few scattered disciples amongst them; but, says he, the shoemaker's wife often goes in ragged shoes.—That is an old saying, and a true one, to my knowledge, cries Tugwell.—Well, says the barber, I was going to observe, that although there had been a society begun here by Mr Whitfield, yet since he went to Georgia, and has been in so great request in London, Bristol, and other parts of England, the people of Gloucester are not much the better for having had so great a prophet born amongst them.

As for lodgings, continued the barber, our house is large enough for that matter, though it is a little out of repair—and, as I have a wife and a family of children, we are a little straightened for beds: however, perhaps my wife will endeavour to accommodate you.—Wildgoose replied, that he was very easily accommodated in that respect, for he had determined not to pamper the flesh, and would submit to any hardships for the good of his brethren. But, says he, what must we do for a room to assemble in?—Why, as for that, returned the barber, we have a sort of old dining-room, which will exactly suit your purpose, though there is no furniture in it, but a few broken chairs and an old cider-cask or two, which will not be much in the way. In short, the barber informed his wife of the affair, who having peeped at them through the kitchen door, and formed an opinion of them no ways injurious to their honesty, they soon came to an agreement; and the two pilgrims took up their residence at this friendly barber's.

III

AT GLOUCESTER

The barber's shop in a country town has been, time out of mind, the grand office of intelligence; partly from the leisure and loquacity of that race of men, and partly (as was hinted before) from the peculiar nature of the connection which is formed between the agent and the patient, during the act of shaving, in which nothing but news or other general topics can prudently be the subject of their conversation. The arrival of a stranger, therefore, of so extraordinary a character as that of Mr Wildgoose, could not long be a secret amongst the lower class of plebeians, especially as the barber, in order to bring more custom to his shop, took care to let every one know, that a stranger of good fortune was to hold forth there that very evening, for so Wildgoose had determined, if he could raise any thing of an audience, being impatient to impart some spiritual advice to his poor countrymen; whom, notwithstanding the residence of their good bishop, dean, and a whole college of learned prebends amongst them, he considered as sheep not having a shepherd.

He was attended the first night only by a few mean persons, who either came accidentally to the shop, or who had been invited by the barber's wife from amongst her nearest neighbours. But the fame of this extraordinary preacher being spread abroad, by each of these, in their several circles of acquaintance, before the next evening it had reached the remotest parts of the city, and had brought together not only the straggling disciples of Mr Whitfield, but also the idle and the curious of every denomination, most of whom bestowed no small encomiums upon the youthful orator. This success encouraged Wildgoose to make a longer stay in Gloucester, than he had at first intended; so that in a week's time it became a sort of fashion to hear him; and he was attended by people of all ranks and degrees—from the sauntering old batchelor and antiquated virgin, who lived upon their annuities and their card-money, to the penniless porter who ran on errands, and the second-hand sempstress, who got her bread by reconciling old tags and making pin-cushions.

Let a man preach like an angel in his own church, as Mr Wesley justly observes, no one regards him; but as soon as one comes unto them, and says, Lo! yonder is a man preaching upon a mountain! the multitude flocks out to hear him. It is the uncommonness of the thing, says he, that especially recommends field-preaching.

The same may be said with regard to Mr Wildgoose's success in his conventicle at Gloucester. If the sexton had given out on a Saturday night, that a stranger was to preach the next day at the cathedral, it might perhaps have brought those to church who happened not to have upon their hands any more agreeable Sunday's amusements; but when it was proclaimed that a traveller was to preach at the barber's, upon a cider-cask, leaning over the top of an old cheese-press (which was all the pulpit which the barber's lumber-room could supply), immediately the house was crowded with attendants from every quarter of the city.

But it must be remembered, likewise, that Mr Wildgoose, notwithstanding the present uncouth appearance of his short hair, had something naturally agreeable in his countenance, and also a very musical tone of voice; and though, in the vehemence of his harangues, he had a wildness in his looks, proceeding from the enthusiastic zeal which possessed his imagination, yet that very circumstance gave a more pathetic force to his eloquence: and he himself appearing so much in earnest and affected with the subject, it had a proportionable effect upon his audience.

He usually began his discourse with lamenting the universal corruption of mankind, and with a lively representation of the dreadful consequences to be apprehended from the justice of God; and instead of speaking of hell and damnation in the refined terms and elegant circumlocutions of modern divines (as a place not proper to be mentioned to a polite audience), he ran, perhaps, into the contrary extreme, by too gross and minute a detail of particulars: which, however, though it might render his descriptions more ridiculous than terrible to sensible people, yet it had its effect upon the bulk of his audience, and engaged their most earnest attention.

When he had sufficiently terrified them by the denunciation of eternal torments, he shifted the scene, and melted them into tears by the tenderest descriptions of the mercy and compassion of God, and the fondest expressions of love from the great Shepherd of their souls.

And having been so deeply read in the puritanical writings of the last century, and their lineal descendants, the methodists of these times, he had thoroughly imbibed their manner and style of eloquence, which consists chiefly in a figurative application of the most luscious expressions and sensual ideas of spiritual subjects, and which have been observed frequently to captivate the hearts of the most profligate, and lull them into a strong persuasion, at least, that they have received lively foretastes of the joys of heaven, when they have really been soothing their fancies with the luxurious recollection of their former sensual indulgences.

Thus did Mr Wildgoose adapt his metaphors to the various characters and failings of his different hearers. For the lewd and lascivious, he abounded with amorous expressions, and talked much in the nuptial style.—Their souls were espoused to Christ: he shall carry the dear lambs in his bosom, and entertain them with sweet kisses from his lily lips—more sweet than the sweet-smelling myrrh:* he shall embrace them, and fill them with ravishing delights. This sort of language particularly charmed the female devotees.

For the thirsty soul and luxurious epicure, he had streams of joy, and rivers of pleasure; feasts of fat things—milk, honey, marrow, and fatness;

---

* Whitfield's *Sermons*.

and all the most savoury ideas, to express the comforts of a spiritual life.

To the covetous and ambitious, he talked of nothing but of hidden treasures; gold, silver, jewels, and precious stones; kingdoms, crowns, and sceptres; and every thing that could captivate a worldly imagination.★

In short, by this soothing eloquence, and the earnestness of his manner, Wildgoose softened those hearts, which for some years had resisted the admonitions of friends, and the suggestions of conscience; and made many converts to religion; at least he made them so as long as the brightness of those similes continued to glow in their imaginations. But, their affections only being moved; and their understandings not enlightened, nor their reason convinced, too many of them soon relapsed into their former dissolute courses.

There was a buxom widow, however, amongst his disciples; who, enjoying a handsome house only for her widowhood, and being, therefore, cut off from *iteration* of *nuptials*, had allowed herself some variety in her amours; but she was now touched to the quick, and determined for the future to keep constant to a half-pay officer, who lodged in her first floor.

And a drunken pettifogger, who had been engaged in several dirty litigations, resolved hereafter to be more sober in his conduct; and also, never to undertake any litigious suit, unless he were sure of being well paid for his trouble.

Nay, an inveterate miser felt such a lively compulsion, that he formed, upon the spot, a solemn resolution to distribute amongst the poor all his old clothes, which had been hoarded in his wardrobe from the very days of his courtship; and so far persevered in his charitable design, as to give away, the very next morning, an old waistcoat, that was too little for him; and two pair of shoes, that pinched his corns; and even added a codicil to his will, by which he ordered a suspicious moidore, which had been refused by his banker, to be given in charity on the day of his funeral.

★ Though these kinds of expression are used in scripture, in compliance with the carnal notions of the Jews, and have affected their common language—yet on moral subjects, I think, they have but an uncouth effect.

IV

HIS POPULARITY INCREASES

The fame of Mr Wildgoose's eloquence being thus spread through the city, Mrs Whitfield was amongst the first whose curiosity led them to make part of his audience. She soon discovered him and his fellow-labourer to be the individual *trampers* whom she had treated with so little ceremony at the Bell; and finding they were bound on a pilgrimage to her brother-in-law and the society at Bristol, she took an opportunity of making some apology for her incivility, and told Wildgoose, that as he could have but indifferent accommodations at his present lodgings, he was very welcome to a bed at the Bell, whilst he stayed in Gloucester. But though Mr Wildgoose was ready enough to overlook the personal slight which had been put upon him, he thought there was something meritorious in his present state of humiliation. He, therefore, thanked Mrs Whitfield for her kindness, but chose to continue where he was.

One evening, when Wildgoose was deeply engaged in haranguing to a full house, an ordinary fellow, in a silver-laced hat, came into the room; and, squeezing through the crowd, gave a letter to one of the company, who handed it to Tugwell, who was sitting on the head of a cask under his master, and officiated as a sort of clerk. He watched his opportunity till Wildgoose made a pause, and then presented the letter. As soon as he began to look on the direction, the man who brought it (who was no other than the Gloucester Journal-man) calls out, Read it, master, read it; it brings you some news of your poor mother. Wildgoose, renouncing all family connections, and disregarding whatever concerned himself, stretched out his hand, and cried out, Behold my mother, my sister, and my brother! And immediately went on with his discourse.

The case was, that although there were none of their towns-men at his first preachment on Dover's hill; yet there were many that knew him by sight, notwithstanding he was disguised in his own hair, and the story had soon spread to Mrs Wildgoose's ears. The odd turn which her son's melancholy had taken, we may be sure, must greatly affect a fond parent;

and it had really thrown Mrs Wildgoose into a fit of sickness. Mr Powel, therefore, the vicar of the parish, having been informed by the Journal-man, that an itinerant preacher of some fortune, as was given out, had been showing off at Gloucester, soon guessed, from the description of him and his attendant, that it was his good neighbour Mr Wildgoose; and so dispatched a letter by him, on his return, to acquaint Wildgoose with the effect his extravagant whim had had upon his worthy mother: but enthusiasm is deaf to the calls of nature; nay, esteems it meritorious to trample upon all the relative duties of life. Men of this cast think nothing of any importance, but what corresponds with the chimerical notions which have possessed their fancies.

Wildgoose, therefore, paid no other regard to the doctor's intelligence, than writing a short letter to his mother, in which he expressed his concern for her illness; but said, he was not at his own disposal, and could not in conscience live in carnal ease and security, when the spiritual harvest was so great, and the true labourers so few. In short, says he, in conclusion, woe be unto me if I preach not the gospel.

V

WILDGOOSE'S SUCCESS WITH THE LADIES

> If chance some blooming nypmh, with locks of gold,
> The brilliant lustre sparkling in her eye,
> Shading her lovely cheeks with hat of straw,
> Or silken bonnet green of glossy hue,
> Enters the shop of learned bibliopole,
> That vends his ware at Tunbridge or at Bath,
> Retailing modern trash to saunt'ring beaux—

Should any of my amiable country-women, I say, smit with the love of novelty, carry home this trifling volume from some circulating library, and throwing herself negligently upon her settee or sofa, or even on the

feet of her truckle bed—have patience to attend two such odd fellows
thus far, she will probably be disgusted that she has not been entertained
with a single love tale, which are generally looked upon as essential to
works of this kind, and not only make a principal part of every episode,
but are usually interwoven with the body of the fable. But I would
have them consider the peculiar character of our hero, which is not,
at first sight, at all friendly to the softer passions. If they can prevail
on themselves, however, to attend him a few pages farther, they may,
perhaps, discover some slight symptoms of an affection, not entirely of
the seraphic or platonic kind.

There was amongst Mr Wildgoose's female votaries, one Mrs Sarsenet,
a milliner, who, notwithstanding she supported an infirm mother and
a lame sister by her industry, yet from the severity of Mr Wildgoose's
doctrine, had conceived some scruples about the innocence, or even
the lawfulness, of her profession. She, therefore, desired Mr Wildgoose
to drink a dish of tea with her, and took that opportunity of consulting
him as a casuit upon the subject. Upon considering the affair with some
deliberation, Wildgoose told her, that although some branches of the
trade, as it was often practised, might *accidentally* promote vice, yet as
some part of the female dress was not only *decent*, but even necessary in
this cold climate; and as the trade had not *directly* any bad tendency, he
could not look upon it as absolutely sinful. However, says he, it greatly
concerns you not to countenance the ladies that deal with you in any
vain ornaments or wanton attire; but to discourage any thing of that
kind, even against your own interest, as mush as you decently can. The
reader will find in the sequel, that Mrs Sarsenet carried this doctrine
rather to an extreme, and to the prejudice of her temporal interest and
that of her family.

We must not imagine, however, that this grave matron was a proper
object of desire to a religious enthusiast. There was with this milliner
a young lady, who seemed not to be in the capacity of an apprentice,
but rather as some friend upon a visit to Mrs Sarsenet, and who had
something in her manner and appearance above her present situation. A
nice critic might, perhaps, dispute her title to the character of a perfect
beauty; but she had a sprightliness in her air, and a piercing brilliancy

in her eyes, which, joined to the gloss of youth, could not fail to attract the particular regard of Mr Wildgoose, and made him very assiduous in directing his pious precepts to so fair a disciple. Whenever he said any thing to which he expected a particular attention, he applied himself to Miss Townsend, by a kind of instinct, for her approbation. But though this young nymph seemed well enough pleased when Mr Wildgoose talked to her upon indifferent subjects, she was inclined rather to disapprove of, and even to rally, the severity of many of his opinions. Nay, in one of his visits, which he repeated pretty often, she took upon her to ask Wildgoose, how he could be so cruel, as not to visit his poor mother, who, she found, was ill and desired to see him for, says she, with a sigh and down-cast look, Heaven will never prosper disrespect to a parent. Miss Townsend's earnestness upon this subject excited Wildgoose's curiosity; and, with a more gallant air than usual, he desired to know why she looked so very dismal upon the occasion. After a little pause and a few blushes, she replied, that the greatest misfortune of her life, and her present unhappy situation, was owing to her disrespect to a worthy, and, in general, a very kind father.—Pray, what misfortunes can so young a lady as you are have experienced? says Wildgoose, for you don't seem yet to be above sixteen! Miss Townsend seemed in confusion at having discovered so much of her own affairs; but Mrs Sarsenet told her, she need not be afraid of talking freely to so good a man as Mr Wildgoose, who would never make any wrong use of her confidence, and might probably give her some spiritual consolation, which would make her more easy under this little calamity, which her own indiscretion, or rather *my folly*, says she, has brought upon you.

Mr Wildgoose, wishing it might be in his power to give her any assistance, and entreating her to gratify his impatience to be acquainted with her story, Miss Townsend dropped a tear, then, pulling up her spirits, gave the following account of herself.

VI

The history of Miss Townsend

My father (as Mrs Sarsenet knows) has a small estate on the borders of
——shire, where he now lives.—No, says Mrs Sarsenet, I know that Mr
Townsend has a very *considerable* estate, which has been in the family
for many generations. Well, says Miss Townsend, I don't know what it is,
but ——shire is my native place. My poor mother has been dead about
a twelvemonth, to my inexpressible misfortune, and that of the whole
family. She left behind her me and two sisters; one a few years older, the
other considerably younger than myself. Whilst my mother lived we saw
a great deal of genteel company; and she took care to have us instructed
at home in all the usual accomplishments of our sex. But soon after her
death my father sent us all three (though two of us were almost grown
up, and my eldest sister capable of managing his house), to a country
boarding-school, to the astonishment of the whole neighbourhood. We
soon found, however, that my father's intention was, to make way for
another housekeeper, to whom he had taken an unaccountable fancy.
This was an Irish-woman, whom I shall call the widow Townsend; as
she came into the neighbourhood about half a year before my mother's
death, in the character of an officer's wife, one Captain Townsend, who
had made a small fortune in America, and called himself a relation of
ours; but he dying soon after, this woman took lodgings in a small
market town, at a little distance from my father's; and, as she did not
appear to be left in very affluent circumstances, she made no scruple,
I believe, of undertaking the management of my father's family, in the
capacity of a housekeeper.

The widow Townsend, as I said, is an Irish-woman, and about forty;
not handsome, but has something in her manner which attracts the
regard of the gentlemen, as much as it disgusts the generality of our sex.
My poor mother (as Mrs Sarsenet well knows) could never bear her. She
is a woman of no sort of conversation, and yet my father now makes a
constant companion of her; and we have no reason to doubt, that, after
a decent time, he will make her our step-mother; in which case, though

I should think it my duty to show her all the respect which is due to my father's wife, yet at present I own I could not bring my stubborn heart to submit with tolerable decency to the many mortifications I daily met with from a woman in her situation.

For you must know, at Christmas last, my father thought it proper to permit my eldest sister and me to leave school, and return home again; as it must appear to every one, that we were banished for no other reason than to make way for a woman in her ambiguous situation. Though I believe she had another view in having my sister at home, which I will explain to you hereafter.

The widow Townsend affected at first to treat us with great civility, and even apparent affection; and used great art to make us rest satisfied under the authority which she had acquired. She indulged us in several little instances and articles of finery, in which I believe my own mother would have thought it improper to have gratified us. These things won my sister's heart, and it would be affectation in me to say that I was not pleased with my gold watch and other trinkets, which she had persuaded my father to procure us. But still I could not bear to be obliged to a woman whom I considered as having an improper influence over my father, for what I imagined I might reasonably have expected, from the great affection he had formerly shown me in particular; in whose favour I flattered myself he had always discovered some little partiality.

For my father, you must know, was always a very bookish, and is, I believe, a very learned man; and is reckoned a great antiquary and virtuoso. I flattered myself, therefore, that he was particularly pleased with the taste I discovered for reading, preferably to every other amusement; to humour which taste he himself had contributed, by turning me loose into one corner of his library, which contained a collection of books made by an old maiden aunt of ours, and consisted of Dryden's *Plays*, and all the dramatical works of the last age; novels; and romances of every kind.

I am afraid, then, says Wildgoose, you had not many religious books put into your hands by your good father?

No, says Miss Townsend, but I had a few by my good mother, which I made a point of reading every Sunday; such as *Tillotson's Sermons*, the *Whole Duty of Man,* and the like.

Why, replies Wildgoose, you might as well have read the *Seven Champions*, or *Jack the Giant-killer*, as either the *Whole Duty of Man*, or Tillotson, who knew no more of Christianity than Mahomet.★

Well, says Miss Townsend, I am not a judge of those things, but will go, on with my story.

VII

MISS TOWNSEND'S STORY CONTINUED

My taste for reading, continued Miss Townsend, not only rendered me the object of my sister's jealousy (who never looked in a book), but made me less agreeable to the widow Townsend; and has been, I am afraid, the principal cause of my present unhappy situation.

For this woman, you must know, though she affects to be a great economist, yet, like most of the Irish ladies, is never completely happy, but at the card-table; and as I was unpolite, or rather impolitic enough constantly to declare my aversion to cards, this gave her frequent occasions to represent me to my father, as one that regarded nothing but my own gratification, which, she said, was a very bad symptom in a young person: and what is surprising, she had brought my father, who was formerly never easy out of his study, to make one at quadrille or piquet, every evening; and my sister, who had rather do any thing than read, or work at her needle, was always happy in being of the party.

The widow Townsend having so far succeeded as to make my father less pleased with my favourite amusements, as it was her interest to have no rival in his affection, she began, by degrees, farther to insinuate, that it would be much more to my credit, if I would apply more carefully to my needle, in which article she represented me very defective, and even hinted, that another year's schooling would be greatly to my advantage; though Mrs Sarsenet, I believe, is far from making any

---

★ Whitfield's *Journals*.

complaint of that kind. In short, my father began by degrees not only to reprimand me, whenever he found me with a book in my hand, but daily discovered, on every occasion, less fondness for me than he had formerly shown. This encouraged Mrs Townsend to treat me with less ceremony; and as for my sister, she not only became reserved to me, in order to recommend herself more effectually to our gouvernante, but began to consider me as a troublesome rival in another affair, which I will now explain to you.

My sister, you must know, had a very considerable fortune (near seven thousand pounds) left her by a great-aunt, independently of my father; and this she will have in her own power the day she is eighteen; which will be within these six weeks. This, I am inclined to think, was Mrs Townsend's chief motive for bringing her brother (one Captain Mahony, as she calls him) into the neighbourhood, and introducing him into our family, where he comes almost every day, and frequently stays there for a week together: he is a lieutenant, I believe, in a marching regiment, though upon half-pay. He is about thirty, a tolerably good person, and dresses very genteelly, but conceited and ignorant. Yet, as we had seldom any other gentleman came to the house (nor indeed, much company of any kind since this woman has been there), this coxcomb contrived to make some impression, I believe, upon my sister's heart: and because he would sometimes condescend to direct his nonsense to me (either to conceal his design upon my sister, or to raise her jealousy), she by degrees began to consider me as her rival, and of course as an obstacle to her wishes, and to treat me accordingly.

In short, this behaviour of my sister, the insults I daily met with from the widow Townsend, and the coldness with which my dear father began to treat me, made my situation at home extremely disagreeable.

But completely to ruin me in the widow Townsend's good opinion, and of course in my father's favour, was a friendly letter which I happened to receive from my good Mrs Sarsenet here, who, having a particular regard for my late mother (they having been schoolfellows at Chelsea), and hearing that this woman, to whom she knew my poor mother had a particular dislike, was come to keep my father's house, she had written to me upon the subject, and, with more honesty than prudence, perhaps, had declared her real sentiments of the matter; which letter the widow Townsend, I believe, by my sister's means, unluckily got a sight of, and from that time grew so inveterate against me, that, presuming upon the influence she had over my father, she insisted upon my being sent to school again with my little sister Quintilla, or somewhere out of the house, otherwise she herself was determined to leave him.

VIII

THE STORY CONTINUED

Being now continually exposed to the widow Townsend's forbidding looks and reproaches, as also to the neglect of my dear father, and the ill-natured treatment of my sister, who would not suffer me quietly to enjoy the only relief which I sought, that of reading alone in my closet; but above all, the expectation of being sent to school again, at my age—all these things put together provoked me beyond all patience.

My romances furnished me with innumerable instances of this kind of domestic persecution, which generally terminated in the elopement of the innocent sufferer, her unexpected success in life, and her triumphant return.

In short, I had a high idea of the grandeur and politeness of London, and saw several instances even of the lower sort of people, who, having been sent for by rich relations or taken into good services, came down more polite and entirely different sort of creatures from those which I generally conversed with.

I last month, therefore, formed a most romantic scheme, for seeing the world, and going to London by myself. In order to this, I determined to get to Oxford, and out from thence in the stage-coach, and endeavour to find out a particular friend and distant relation of my mamma's, who I knew lodged somewhere in Westminster; and who had spent a good part of the last summer before my mother's death with us in the country, and used frequently to invite me to London; or if I should not find her out, having twenty guineas given me at different times by a god-mother, in my own possession, I thought with economy, I could subsist for some time, and had some vague ideas of introducing myself into good company, or, perhaps, even of making my fortune, as other distressed or persecuted damsels had done.

As I had no confidante in my own family, I communicated my intentions to a woman in the neighbourhood, who had been my mother's maid, and was now married to a man, who in my mother's time, had been our coachman: both of them were favourites of my mother's, and of course not so to the widow Townsend. The poor woman at first dissuaded me from pursuing so strange a resolution, but when she found me bent upon it, and knew how disagreeably I lived at home, the man consented to carry me behind him (on a horse which he kept to let) the next night to Oxford, as I had desired, without considering the probable consequences of so imprudent a step.

As my sister was engaged almost every evening at cards with my father and the widow Townsend, I took those opportunities at least of sitting up in my closet to read, and my sister frequently went to bed without making any inquiries after me; so that I easily eluded any immediate search, and escaped to the house appointed.

Not to trouble you with too many particulars; having packed up a handsome brocaded suit of clothes, two silk night-gowns, with some pretty good linen and my money, I got safe with my luggage to Oxford, and met with a place in the coach, which set out the next morning for London.

IX

THE STORY CONTINUED

There was amongst the passengers a well-looking elderly gentleman, of good fortune (as I had reason to think), by his generous behaviour to me, and by a genteel footman behind the coach. He was a little surprised, I believe, at the first sight of so young a person, tolerably well dressed, and of going a journey quite alone. He, by degrees, began to sift out my situation in life, and what expedition I was now engaged in. His humanity, and a desire to serve me, rather than mere curiosity, seemed to be the motives for his inquiries. When we came to dinner, and I happened to be left alone with him, I soon communicated my whimsical project to this gentleman. He was vastly surprised, and expressed great concern both for me and for my father, whom he found to be almost the only person that I was sorry to have left behind me.

He asked me, how I could think of supporting myself for a time in so expensive a place as London was. I told him the state of my finances, and that, if I could not find out my mother's friend in Westminster, I proposed lodging in some cheap part of the suburbs. He smiled at my simplicity, and began to describe to me the extreme danger such a young person, as I was, exposed myself to in so romantic an enterprise; the wickedness of the world in general, and of the town in particular; and, in short, ventured to foretel my inevitable ruin; which he painted in such strong colours, that I burst into tears, and begged him to advise what method to pursue. What, says he, madam? why as soon as we arrive in town, give me leave to take another place for you, the next day, in this same coach, and return to your friends in the country. I was a little staggered at this proposal, and could not bear the thoughts of exposing myself to the resentment of my father, the insults of Mrs Townsend, and the ridicule of my sister.—But when we came to London, and saw the vast hurry and extent of that metropolis, my heart began to fail me, and, in the evening especially, when we reached the inn in Holborn, and the gentleman had bid them send the chamber-maid to show me to my bed-chamber, in came a bold ill-looking fellow, who called himself the chamberlain. There, madam, says the old gentleman, you see who is to wait on you to bed to-night, and to lace your stays in the morning: this is the attendance which a young lady must generally expect at the inns in London.

I was now struck with all the horrors of my situation, and, therefore, told the gentleman, I should gladly accept of his kind offer, and would beg him to take a place for me against the next morning; which he very politely did, and insisted upon treating me with the earnest which he had paid for the coach. I was ashamed to accept of such a favour from a stranger, but he desired me to say no more about it. I took my leave of him that evening, without being able to discover his name; though I found, by several circumstances, that he lived in Herefordshire.

X

THE STORY CONTINUED

Being thoroughly fatigued with my journey, I slept soundly till the morning, when I was called, I suppose, by the chamberlain; but was so drowsy, that I knew not what answer I gave him, when he told me the passengers were all in the coach, and just setting out. However, he insisted upon it afterwards, that I said, I could not get up, if they went without me. In short, about nine o'clock I was awaked by the mistress of the house, who having heard I was a very young woman, without any attendants, came to satisfy her curiosity, and to inquire into my intentions. The woman was civil enough; and when I expressed my surprise at the coach's being gone without me, and my distress what course to take, she said, as I was come to London merely out of curiosity, and was now obliged to stay till the next coaches went out, she would show me something of the town, if I would give her leave.

I told her I had a relation in Westminster whom I would now try to find out. She asked me what street her house was in?—She has no house, says I; but I know she lodges somewhere in Westminster; and, as she is a lady of a large acquaintance, though small fortune, I dare say I shall easily find her out. The woman laughed at my ignorance of the town, and said I might as well look for a needle in a bundle of hay.

She then took me down to breakfast with her behind the bar, where I spent most part of that day, she not being at leisure to attend me abroad. In the afternoon a neighbour of hers, who had a small house in one of the adjacent courts, came to drink tea with her. The woman of the house being frequently called away into the bar, I was left alone with Mrs Skelton (which was the name of the other woman). After inquiring into my motives for coming to London, and finding I had no friends or acquaintance there, she offered to take me to her house, as a boarder, and to bring me acquainted with every thing that was worth seeing in London. To reconcile me to her proposal, she soon discovered that she was my country-woman, and said she had relations in that part of England. In short, I was so well pleased with the apparent friendship of this woman; and, for the reasons above-mentioned, found so little inclination to return to my friends in the country, that I began to be very well pleased with the coach's going without me, and leaving me in London.

I then acquainted the woman at the inn with Mrs Skelton's offer. She said I could not lodge with a better sort of woman; that she had known her for some years, and she was a clever, sensible person, and kept the best of company, ranking herself, I suppose, in that number. I, therefore, paid my bill at the inn, took my leave of the mistress of the house; and accompanied Mrs Skelton to her house.

I am now astonished at my simplicity, but was quite ignorant of the world; and, indeed, after my first imprudent step, what other scheme could I pursue? I soon found, however, that the world in reality was very different from what it appeared in poetry and romance.

XI

THE STORY CONTINUED

Mrs Skelton affected to have taken a great liking to me, and the next morning performed her promise of showing me the town. That she might do this in the most compendious manner, the first place she took me to was the top of St Paul's, where, indeed, I was struck with astonishment at the appearance of that vast metropolis.

After dragging me on to the Tower, she made me take a coach to bring us back to Holborn. By the way, however, she stopped at a milliner's near St Paul's, and equipped me with what she thought a more fashionable cap, and other things which she thought necessary, but without putting me to any great expence. When we came home she helped me to adjust my dress according to her own taste, and told me, the gentleman who lodged in her first floor would dine with us. He is a gentleman of very large fortune, I assure you, says she, and perhaps may fall in love with you. He is rather too old for you, continued she, but I know several young ladies who would be very happy in such an opportunity of setting their caps at him, I can tell you.

Well, at dinner this fine gentleman appeared, dressed in blue and gold. He seemed to be about fifty, and was agreeable enough in his person; but what gave me a sort of liking to him was, that he put me much in mind of my own father. Nay, finding how entirely unacquainted I was with the town, he very kindly cautioned me against the artifices of the people I should probably meet with; and told me if I made any stay in London he would introduce me to some of the female part of his own family.

The next morning Mr Blackman (which was the gentleman's name) breakfasted with us, and though he was engaged to dine with some gentlemen of Lincoln's-inn, he said he hoped to be at home again with us in the evening. At the same time he told Mrs Skelton, that there was a very good play to be acted that night, and asked her if she did not intend to go? She pretended to make a scruple of leaving me alone; on purpose, I suppose, to give him an opportunity of offering each of us tickets for the play, which he immediately did.

Accordingly to the play we went, and sat in one of the side galleries. There happened to sit next to us a young lady most splendidly dressed, who, I found, was an acquaintance of Mrs Skelton's. She talked a great deal, and even in the most interesting parts of the play, and seemed to ridicule every thing that was grave or decent. She was particularly merry upon a country gentleman and his wife, as we judged them to be, who sat together in one of the side boxes, and said, it was astonishing to her how any woman could think of burying herself with a husband in the country, to sit nodding at each other whole winter evenings, on each side of the parlour fire, with nothing to amuse them but a formal visit once a week from some unfashionable creatures like themselves. In short, says she, I'd rather be a mistress to a tradesman in town, than the wife of any country squire in England. I was greatly shocked, instead of being diverted, with this lady's conversation, and began to wish myself in some other place; but I was highly offended at hearing Mrs Skelton ask her, when she should have the honour of seeing her in Holborn? To which she answered, she would do herself that honour very soon.

When we returned from the play, we found an elegant supper ordered from the tavern, by the old gentleman, who was waiting for us with great patience in the parlour. After supper Mr Blackman and Mrs Skelton drank several glasses together, and the latter would have forced me to pledge them; but Mr Blackman desired I would drink no more than was quite agreeable to me, as probably I had never been used to any thing strong. In short, as there was something of a paternal fondness in the behaviour of Mr Blackman, so it inspired me with sentiments of quite a filial love and respect and I lived near a fortnight in the house quite agreeably; Mr Blackman and Mrs Skelton treating me like a daughter for whom they had a great affection, always contriving something to amuse and entertain me.

XII

THE STORY CONTINUED

One morning Mrs Skelton asked me whether I should like to take a voyage by water; for, said she, I want to make a visit to an acquaintance as far as Chelsea. We shall have another lady and gentleman of our party, which will be more agreeable, and lessen the expense of our voyage. I told her I should be very glad of such a jaunt, as I had never been upon the river, and was very fond of water. She wished Mr Blackman could go with us; but, said she, he has so many grand acquaintance it is hardly probable that he will be disengaged. Upon her mentioning it to him at breakfast, however, he replied that he would meet us, if possible, about twelve o'clock at the water side.

When we came to the place appointed, I was surprised to see not only Mr Blackman; but the lady whom we had met at the play, attended by another gentleman. He was a genteel, or rather a showy man, of about forty. He addressed us with an air of familiarity, and affectation of gaiety, which to me was very disgusting; though he was what some people would reckon a cheerful companion and handsome man.

Mr Blackman had provided a covered boat, and furnished it with biscuits, almonds and raisins, and a bottle of white wine; the former, I suppose, for mine, and the latter for Mrs Skelton's entertainment. As the other lady and gentleman, whom I took to be husband and wife, were very fond of each other, Mr Blackman was particular in his behaviour to me, and took a great deal of pains to gain my attention to every thing which he said. But nothing attracted my notice so much as the fine prospect on each side of the river, which he pointed out to me, and explained; from the grand dome of St Paul's to the venerable Gothic piles of Westminster Abbey and the palace of Lambeth, with the rural objects which present themselves gradually till we reached the noble hospital of Chelsea, whither we were bound.

When we arrived at the end of our voyage, Mr Blackman went immediately out of the boat, and said he would bespeak a room for us at a little sort of tavern close to the water: for I soon found that this visit of Mrs Skelton's was only a pretence; and that we were to dine at this house, at these gentlemen's expense.

There was something in this which did not quite please me: but my inexperience, or rather my entire ignorance of the arts of mankind, prevented me from suspecting any ill design. After dinner Mrs Skelton said, she would just step a door or two farther, to call upon her friend, with whom she had some particular business; and charged Mr Blackman to take care of her daughter, as she affected to call me.

Soon after Mrs Skelton was gone, the other gentleman and lady said, they would take a walk in the garden, and return to us immediately. I stared, a little; but as they were strangers to me, and I had no inclination to cultivate an intimacy with the lady, I made no overtures to accompany her; especially as I supposed them to be man and wife: and as I had never seen any thing in Mr Blackman's behaviour at all exceptionable, I was not uneasy at being left alone with him.

After they had been gone a few minutes, I went up to the window, which had a fine prospect of the Thames; and Mr Blackman following me, opened a door near the window, and told me, I might have a better prospect in the next room—

Here Miss Townsend blushed, and made a pause, then turned pale and seemed unwilling to proceed in her story. Mrs Sarsenet, who had heard it more than once, made an excuse for her, but desired she would go on, otherwise Mr Wildgoose might suspect she had been guilty of something which she had reason to be ashamed of.

That I have, says Miss Townsend, of the whole series of my folly; though, I thank God, I have nothing to accuse myself of, but my unparalleled indiscretion. However, I have great reason to be thankful to Providence, for preserving me from the probable effects of it.

Why, says Wildgoose, Providence rarely deserts us, even in those misfortunes which are the consequences of our own inadvertency, if we humbly apply for assistance, and sincerely endeavour to retrieve any false step as soon as we become sensible of it, and do not presumptuously persist in a wrong course of action, against the suggestions of his Holy Spirit.

But come, madam, I must beg to hear the sequel of this adventure, since you have interested me in your escape from the critical situation in which you have described yourself at the window, where you were left alone with this fine gentleman.

XIII

THE STORY CONTINUED

Well, sir, Mr Blackman came up to me, as I told you, and opened a door near the window, and told me there was a better prospect from that room. Seeing it was a bed-chamber, I started back; but he laid hold on my arm, and pulled me in by force, and shut the door.

I had read in poetry of fawns and satyrs; in romances of discourteous knights and savages; but had no conception that a man of so respectable an appearance, in a brigadier wig and grave habit, that looked more like a justice of peace or high sheriff, than a debauched rake, could be guilty of any rudeness or indecent behaviour.

I cried out with all my force, and said, I would sooner die than remain with him alone. I struggled, and at last got to the sash, but found it was screwed down. I continued calling out with great violence, and made all the noise I could, but to no purpose. This vile man continued his detestable importunity and I despaired of any assistance—when I was providentially relieved by a pretty loud rapping at the outer door. Upon his opening it, the waiter introduced a very genteel modest-looking woman, and a pretty girl about ten years old. On seeing me and Mr Blackman, who were both strangers to her, she drew back, and made an apology for her mistake. The waiter told us, the lady had inquired for one Mr Andrews; and insisted upon it that he came with the company in our boat.

Mr Blackman reprimanded him for his impertinent intrusion; but I begged of him to inform me where the other gentleman and ladies were; and upon my going out upon the staircase, I met Mrs Skelton coming up. I complained of her leaving me alone with Mr Blackman, and told her how brutishly he had behaved. She affected great surprise and indignation; and, upon coming into the room, Lord! says she, Mr Blackman, I did not think you could be guilty of any thing so rude to this young lady! Why, sure your love for her, which you mentioned, has turned your head; but I will never suffer her to be injured whilst she is under my protection.

Thus this vile woman endeavoured to persuade me that she was unconcerned in his villany; but I began to have a very bad opinion of her, and to wish myself out of her hands.

Though the fright I had been in raised my courage, yet I now found my spirits flag to such a degree, that I was hardly kept from fainting; but a little water, which Mrs Skelton gave me, soon brought me to myself again.

Mr Blackman pretended he was only in jest, and was sorry he had frightened me; and hoped I would forgive him an innocent frolic. But how monstrous is vice, especially in an elderly man! This gentleman, whom I had before regarded with a filial love and esteem, I could not now behold without detestation. Age ought in general to be treated with so much reverence and respect, that I do not love to hear the two words *old villain* or *old fool* united; yet I could not separate the ideas inn my mind whenever I beheld this man for the future. But as I was determined to make my escape the first opportunity, I dissembled my resentment as well as I could, and returned with Mr Blackman, and Mrs Skelton, leaving the rest of the company to themselves.

The gentleman and the lady that came with us never returned after they left the room. But, as we were going out of the house, we heard a great disturbance in a parlour below stairs; and, by what I could collect, the lady who came so providentially to my relief, was the real wife of that other gentleman who had been of our party; and having long suspected her husband's connection with the creature whom we had met at the play, had, by means of a faithful servant, traced out his intended jaunt for this particular day; and with more passion, perhaps, than prudence, came to reproach him with his conduct: and, in order to make the greater impression upon him, had taken her eldest daughter to be witness to his imprudence; who, I afterwards found, was squandering away upon this strumpet a good fortune, which his unhappy wife had brought him, and with which he had hitherto carried on a genteel trade in the city.

XIV

THE STORY CONTINUED

In the evening when I was going to bed, I asked the maid who assisted me to undress, what sort of a man that was who lodged in the first floor. She seemed at first a little reserved; but upon my giving some hints of his rude behaviour, she smiled, and shook her head, as if she knew more than she dared to express.

When I told her I was determined to quit my lodgings, if not the town of London, the next day, she asked me where my clothes were?

I replied, in the chest of drawers; but upon looking there; I found they were removed into Mrs Skelton's room; and the maid whispered to me, that I should find some difficulty in getting at them.—Lord, said I, and there's the little leather trunk gone, in which is the chief part of my money! The girl then told me, I had better say nothing about removing the next day; but, says she, if you are determined to go, your things are in a dark press in my mistress's room, and I will watch my opportunity some time to-morrow to get your little trunk at least: if not your clothes; and will myself accompany you the next night following; for I live here little better than a slave. But my mistress owes me a quarter's wages, which, however, I don't regard; for I am determined to go and live in the country again; where I was born.

But, for God's sake, madam, continues she, don't let my mistress know what I have said; for she would contrive, right or wrong, to send me to Bridewell. I assured her of my secrecy; which promise it was so much my interest to observe.

Having met with a sort of friend and confidante, I was a little easier in my mind, and resolved to behave with cheerfulness the next day, the better to conceal my intended escape.

In the afternoon the lady who sat next us at the play, and had been of our party to Chelsea, came to drink tea with us. On her affecting an astonishment at our returning without them, Mrs Skelton, with unparalleled assurance, told her, that the poor young lady which she had taken under her protection (meaning me) was terribly frightened yesterday, by a gentleman that offered some rudeness to her. She began to rally me most unmercifully, and said it was a sign that I came lately out of the country; for that those things must be expected to happen to such a fine girl as I was (so she chose to express herself,) if I went much into the polite world. But, child, says she, I would make the most of my charms, and get a good settlement, as I have done, and then you would never wish to see the country again.

As she ran on in this style, she took occasion to adjust a diamond *solitaire* which she wore, and displayed to the best advantage three or four handsome rings. But I was not so ignorant as to be dazzled by such splendid trifles, or not to despise the creature who, I had reason to believe, had purchased these by the sacrifice of her virtue and innocence.

XV

THE STORY CONTINUED

Well, continued Miss Townsend, at length night came, and the maid informed me, she had secured all my things, except one silk night gown, which her mistress had not hung up with the rest, and she did not care to search after, for fear of being discovered. I told her I should be glad to leave that, as some recompense for near a fortnight's board; for, however wicked Mrs Skelton's intentions might be, I could not bear to be guilty of any act of injustice, that I was not obliged to for my own preservation.

We were forced to wait till near two o'clock, before the maid had seen her mistress, and Mr Blackman safe to bed; for after he came home they sat up for near an hour, in close debate; and the maid assured me, they were laying some other plot for my destruction.

When we came down to the street door, the maid, shaking her head, Ah! says she, it is as I feared—the key is gone. I was thunder-struck at this news; but she said she knew a trick worth two of that; and bidding me follow her, we came down into the kitchen, from which she opened a door into the area (as I think they call it;) and, bringing a pair of steps, which were made use of about the kitchen, we clambered up to the balustrades, and got into the court, narrowly escaping the watch who had just cried, past two o'clock. In short, after several frights and alarms, we got clear of the town; and, about sun-rising, found ourselves beyond Hammersmith, I think, upon the western road.

As my dress was rather too good for a foot-passenger, the girl proposed to rest that day, in some house near the road, to prevent suspicion; and so take our chance of some carriage that might pass by.

I had hitherto been under much anxiety, for fear of being pursued, though I was not conscious of having injured any one, that I had no time to reflect, or to form any scheme, so complied with the girl's proposal. Accordingly we stopped at a little public-house where we reposed ourselves, and spent the remainder of that day, not without a mixture of joy and anxiety.

Whilst we were here the maid let me into the true character of Mrs Skelton; who, I found, made a practice of seducing young people; and that the fine lady, whom we had met at the play, was an unhappy creature who had been drawn in to prostitute her youth and beauty to Mr Blackman, for Mrs Skelton's advantage; though she was now kept by that tradesman, who (as has been mentioned) had almost ruined himself to support her extravagance: that the gentleman, who lodged with her was really a man of good family, and considerable fortune, but who spent it all in the gratification of his own humour and vicious appetites; dividing his whole life between his tavern companions and his mistresses, with a variety of whom this vile woman was well paid for supplying him. So that I found I had great reason to bless myself for this escape.

Wildgoose said, that Providence, for wise ends, permitted such monsters to fulfil the measure of their iniquities; but that they ought to be punished, he thought, by human laws: that a double tax, however, would be the least return, such useless wretches could make to the public, for the protection they enjoyed.

XVI
THE STORY CONTINUED

Well, continues Miss Townsend, we lay the next night at the same house; but the people, I suppose, entertaining no very favourable opinion of our characters, took care to lodge us over a little room distinct from the rest of the family.

As we had no sleep the preceding night, we went early to bed,—and I never waked till seven o'clock the next morning, when to my surprise,

I missed my bedfellow; and also, upon looking round the room, I found she had eased me of a good part of my luggage, particularly my little trunk which contained my money, and the silk night-gown in which I had escaped.—My brocaded suit of clothes, however, and one silk and another cotton night-gown were left me; and I luckily had four guineas and some silver, and my watch, in my pockets; which, according to custom, I had laid under my pillow.

I had now seen enough of the world to satisfy my curiosity; and had paid dear for about ten days' experience. The loss of my clothes and money was the least of my misfortune. I had certainly forfeited my father's favour; should expose myself to the ridicule and reproaches of my sister and Mrs Townsend, and probably to the censures of the whole neighbourhood, if I ventured thither. To go back to town, where I had not one friend or acquaintance that I knew where to find, was to run into inevitable destruction. I immediately determined, therefore, to find out my good friend Mrs Sarsenet here; whom having been an old school-fellow likewise of my mamma's (though by the misfortunes of her family in less affluent circumstances,) and having been for a month at our house about two years since, and showed a particular fondness for me, I considered as the only friend I could apply to in my present distress; though I am now sensible it has given the widow Townsend a handle for irritating my father still more against me, on account of the letter, which I before mentioned she had seen, in which Mrs Sarsenet expressed herself with some freedom in regard to Mrs Townsend's character. In short, having inquired whether any carriage went that road to Gloucester, I was informed, that a Gloucester waggon would pass by the house that day, which it accordingly did; and, meeting with an elderly woman and her daughter, who were travelling into some part of Wales by the same conveyance, I took my place; and got safe to Mrs Sarsenet, without any disagreeable event.

XVII

THE STORY CONCLUDED

Mrs Sarsenet, was kind enough to write to my father, and acquaint him with the whole progress of my rash adventure; and to assure him, that I was thoroughly sensible of my folly; and that I was desirous to throw myself at his feet; and ask his forgiveness.

I wrote at the same time to the poor woman who had assisted me in my flight, to know what effect my elopement had had on my poor father.—She wrote me word, that he was almost distracted at the first news of it; that it made a great disturbance in the family, as was naturally to be expected; but that the widow Townsend found means to pacify my father, by some false suggestion or other; and my sister had persuaded them that I was certainly gone to a relation of ours near Warwick (as I had really talked about them to my sister;) and that my father's first journey in quest of me was thither: but not getting any intelligence of me there, somebody told him, that I had been seen two or three times of late at the coachman's house above-mentioned. Upon which he went, and threatened to send them both to gaol, unless they discovered where they had concealed me. Having extorted the secret from them, he went immediately to Oxford, (where I had taken coach,) and traced me to the inn in London; but the woman there being afraid, I suppose, to discover into what hands she had recommended me, my father went to Mrs Calvert's (the lady in Westminster whom I wished to find out,) and not hearing any thing of me, was returned into the country, where he was quite melancholy, till he received Mrs Sarsenet's letter.—What effect that had upon him, we are yet to learn; but as it is now above a fortnight since he must have received it, I am afraid the widow Townsend will not permit him to make any farther inquiries after me: so here I am, an exile from home, and an encumbrance to poor Mrs Sarsenet; and I do not know what return it will ever be in my power to make for the trouble I have given her. To this, Mrs Sarsenet made a complaisant reply, which the author cannot recollect.

XVIII

THE EFFECTS OF
MISS TOWNSEND'S NARRATION

It is a vulgar maxim, that a pretty woman should rather be seen than heard: and, indeed, when a fair lady seems to talk merely for the sake of talking, or with a direct intention to attract admirers, she seldom prepossesses a stranger in her favour; but as Miss Townsend's story had interested Wildgoose sufficiently to raise his compassion, there is an easy transition from pity to love; and it is far from certain that he did not begin to feel something of that mere human passion for this young lady. But being desirous of acting in character, he observed, that to be sure nothing but a prior obligation which we are under to obey our heavenly Father can justify our disobedience to an earthly parent: and although he by no means approved of Miss Townsend's leaving her father upon so slight a provocation, yet as Providence frequently produces good out of evil, and makes even our indiscretions concur with his gracious design of promoting our felicity, perhaps, madam, says he, you may be directed hither to receive instruction, in the way of salvation, even from the meanest of God's servants; and I may, perhaps, be made a happy instrument of your *conversion*.

Miss Townsend, though a well-disposed girl, did not much relish Wildgoose's enthusiastic notions, or nice distinctions in divinity: but, as his person was very agreeable, and they had learned from Tugwell that he was heir to a pretty good fortune, she had conceived no contemptible opinion of him; and listened with great attention whenever he talked upon common subjects.

I would not insinuate that Miss Townsend was of a mercenary temper, for she really was not: but though fortune alone, where the person is disagreeable has seldom any considerable influence over the affections of a young girl; yet, I believe, in conjunction with other circumstances, it operates insensibly upon their fancies, and contributes to make the person possessed of it more agreeable than he would otherwise appear; as the want of fortune frequently prevents their seeing those perfections in a man which he is really possessed of.

Miss Townsend, however, instead of answering Wildgoose in a serious way, turned the discourse, and began rallying him upon his external appearance. Lord! Mr Wildgoose, says she, what makes you go about in that frightful hair of yours? I wonder you do not wear a wig, as other gentlemen do.—Madam, replies Wildgoose, I should be sorry if any part of my dress were to prejudice any one against me, much less would I willingly raise a disgust in so pretty a lady against my person. But pray, madam, why don't you like my hair?—Oh! frightful! says she, 'tis so *ungenteel*; so *unlike other people*!—Why; as for other people, replies Wildgoose, I should choose to be unlike a great part of the world, in their vain fashions and idle customs: but as to its being *ungenteel*, I am sorry any thing should be thought so that is natural, convenient, and, I think, becoming. If you do not think so, young lady, I am afraid it is owing to mere prejudice, and the force of custom.—Custom! says Miss Townsend, why, custom or fashion is every thing, in regard to dress.—I own it has too great a force, replies Wildgoose; and I dare say, for that reason only, you think this great hoop of yours very *genteel*, and very *becoming*; and yet, in the opinion of many people of the best taste, nothing can be more monstrous, or more unnatural, than hoop-petticoats are; and I dare say we shall live to see these Gothic ornaments banished from the world.*—What! hoops go out of fashion? Lord! what a creature should I be without my hoop!

Well, madam, says Wildgoose, as I should be sorry to differ from you in the least trifle, and not endeavour to comply with every one in matters of indifference, I wish I could bring you, and all mankind, to my way of thinking, in this article of wearing one's own hair; for you must know, the honest barber, where I lodge, had a great dispute with me last night upon that very subject; and almost insisted upon making me a fine flowing white wig, as, he said, he had done for Mr Whitfield; who, he assured me, was of opinion, that nothing contributed more to the conversion of sinners, than a good periwig, as it gave a dignity to our appearance, and prepossessed people in favour of our preaching.

Why, says Mrs Sarsenet, there may be some truth in that observation.

---

* This came to pass a few years after.

Well, continues Wildgoose, it was in vain for me to plead the examples of patriarchs; prophets, apostles, and reformers. The poor barber, for the credit of his trade, said, if there were no wigs in those days, there were certainly barbers, by David's allusion to the chief instrument of their art: 'With lies thou cuttest like a sharp razor.'

Well, says Mrs Sarsenet, who was apt to raise scruples upon the most trifling occasions, but do you really make a serious affair of this? I should be glad to be set right upon the lawfulness of using art about one's person, and especially as to false hair; as many of my customers are as faulty in that respect as the gentlemen; and I believe I sell as many wigs, or *tetes*, as any barber in town.

Wildgoose then, accustomed of late to harangue upon all occasions, proceeded upon this important subject in the following manner.

XIX

A DISSERTATION ON PERIWIGS

The use of false hair, madam, by particular people, for particular reasons, is, I believe, very ancient in the world. Vain persons of both sexes, either to conceal some natural defect, or to improve (as they imagine) their natural charms, have, in all ages, had recourse to these artificial decorations. Xenophon, a Greek writer, mentions the use of them among the Medes; and some commentators are of opinion, that the hair of her head, with which Mary Magdalene wiped our Saviour's feet, was really a *tete*, or a set of false curls, which, she might employ in that manner, to express her detestation of the wanton and dissolute life which she had formerly led. It is certain, however, that these unnatural ornaments were esteemed infamous in those more early times, by all good and sensible people. Julius Caesar, though he is said to have been particularly pleased with the laurels decreed him by the senate, because they concealed the baldness of his temples; yet that great man, I believe, would have been highly offended, if his barber had proposed a set of false curls for that purpose.—Though it is confessed that the emperor Otho, many years after, wore a periwig; as he also is reproached with carrying a looking-glass amongst his baggage in his military expeditions.

The first mention which I remember to be made of periwigs, in our English history, is in the account of Prince Charles and the Duke of Buckingham's appearing in disguise at a ball at Paris, in their way to Madrid;* but that was evidently a masquerade dress, as they wore false beards for the same purpose; which also was done by the players in Shakespeare's time. Wigs were but little if at all used in England till the Restoration of Charles the Second, and then chiefly by persons of distinction. These, indeed, by degrees, were imitated by the beaux and fops of the age; yet it was some time before the fashion extended itself to the graver professions of law, physic, and divinity. But when once it had the sanction of those venerable bodies, it was not long, we may suppose, before it spread amongst all ranks and degrees of men in the nation.

At first, however, some resemblance of nature was observed in these contrivances of art, and a periwig was only a more complete head of hair, suited to the complexion, and fitted as exactly as possible to the forehead and temples of the person who wore it. But of late years any man that has a mind to look more considerable or more wise than his neighbours, goes to a barber's, and purchases fifty shillings-worth of false hair (white, black, or grey) and hangs it upon his head, without the least regard to his complexion, his age, his person, or his station in life: and certainly if an inhabitant of the Cape of Good Hope were to behold the stiff horse-hair buckles, or the tied wigs of our lawyers, physicians, tradesmen, or divines, they would appear as barbarous and extraordinary to them, as the sheep's tripes and chitterlins about the neck of a Hottentot do to us.

Miss Townsend and Mrs Sarsenet forced a smile at Wildgoose's vehemence and far-fetched comparison. But he, correcting himself, went on.

---

* In King James the First's reign.

I am ashamed, says he, to dwell so long upon the absurdity of our modern periwigs, in point of taste: but as Miss Townsend objected to the gentility of my own locks, and as the chief intent, of hair, considered as ornamental, seems to be to give a softness to the features, by rising in an easy manner from the forehead, and falling loosely down upon the parts which it was designed to cover, I own I had rather see the worst head of natural hair, than the most accurate wig that ever adorned a barber's block: and as a good taste in other articles of dress seems to prevail in the world, I should not be surprised to see periwigs again banished from the genteel part of mankind, to our poor labourers and mechanics, to whom it may be sometimes convenient to be freed from the encumbrance of a long or bushy head of hair.

But, continued Wildgoose, I have a particular and more important objection to those supplemental locks, from the bad influence they certainly have upon the moral and religious conduct of too many in this age.

As how? for goodness sake! cries Miss Townsend.

Why, madam, says Wildgoose, perhaps there never was a period that furnished so many instances of unseasonable gaiety, or so great a number of old debauchees, as the age we live in. You yourself have met with one instance, in the short course of your ramble. Now, I have often conceived, how strange soever you may think it, that this was owing in a great measure to the use of periwigs; that is, to the great ease with which the gentlemen of this generation may conceal the effects of old age, and exchange their grey locks for those which are expressive of youth and vigour. It was certainly the kind intention of Providence, to remind us of the approach of age and infirmity, by the several symptoms of wrinkled foreheads, decaying teeth, and grey hairs. Now, when a man of a debauched and dissolute mind is almost worn out in the service of his lusts and sensual appetites, he puts on a fine flowing Adonis or white periwig (and, perhaps, a set of false teeth;) surveys himself in the glass, and immediately forgets his real age; commences beau again in the winter of his days, and, if he cannot prevail on any modest woman to accept of him as a husband, he has probably recourse to some mercenary wretch, who squanders away his money, ruins his health, and exposes him to the ridicule of his very servants and dependants; and, what is worse, to the eternal displeasure of his offended Creator.

Bless me! cries Miss Townsend, why you have given us quite a sermon upon periwigs. I really never apprehended there was so much sin, though there might be a great deal of folly, under the wig of a beau: but you will persuade one to believe that, in a literal sense, the hairs of our head are all *numbered*, and that it is unlawful either to increase or diminish them on any account.

Indeed, I myself was imposed upon by an old gentleman in a solemn wig; and, on the contrary, I heard lately of an old baronet, that fell in love with a young lady of small fortune, at some public place for her beautiful *brown locks*. He married her on a sudden: but was greatly disappointed upon seeing her wig or *tete* the next morning thrown carelessly upon her toilette; and her ladyship appearing at breakfast in very bright *red hair,* which was a colour the old gentleman happened to have a particular aversion to.

Well, madam, replied Wildgoose, then I hope I have almost made you a convert to my opinion, and reconciled you to the natural ornaments of the human face, though you were so lately disgusted at my appearance.— Why, really, says she, whatever may be naturally beautiful, yet custom, as I said before, makes one like or dislike things, as the fashion varies.

But, madam, if painting the face were as much the fashion in England as it is in France, could you think it lawful for a good Christian to comply with such a fashion, or to make use of such meretricious decorations? Lord! says Miss Townsend, you use so many hard words; you may call one names, for aught I know, and we not understand you. But, I think, we have had more than enough upon this foolish subject.

Wildgoose, therefore, made an apology for his impertinence, and took his leave for the present: and, having been now near a fortnight at Gloucester, the next night he made a farewel harangue to his usual audience; appointed Mrs Sarsenet a sort of deaconess, and Mr Keen, the barber, a ruler of the little synagogue, with instructions to assemble the brethren occasionally, and exhort them to perseverance; and left Gloucester the next day, after promising to visit them again in his return from Bristol.

XX

THE FAREWELL-HARANGUE IS ATTENDED WITH A DISASTROUS CIRCUMSTANCE

When Wildgoose came to take his leave of Mrs Sarsenet, she happened to be gone out, and he found nobody in the shop but Miss Townsend. After a short conversation with her on the subject of religion (on which head she never seemed to relish his doctrine,) Wildgoose said, he hoped to have the pleasure of hearing of her sometimes by the hands of Mrs Sarsenet. Miss Townsend answered, she did not know how long she might stay at Gloucester; but, fetching an involuntary sigh, which was immediately succeeded by a blush, she owned she should be always glad to hear of Mr Wildgoose, especially when he was returned to his disconsolate mother. Wildgoose replied, that he had written to his mother, and given her the reasons for his conduct; but must leave it to heaven to dispose of him as it should think fit. Then, taking Miss Townsend's hand, and pressing it to his lips, he took his leave, with a deep sigh, and a very expressive silence.

At Wildgoose's farewell-harangue, there was a piece of fun played off, which, as it was attended with serious consequences to the poor barber, ought not to be here omitted.

Under the same roof with the said artist, and in part of the same ruinous mansion, there dwelt an honest publican, to whose craft the pious conventicle at Mr Keen's was by no means favourable. The publican, therefore, gladly connived at, or rather aided and assisted, an unlucky project of his son and some apprentices, to disturb at least, if not put a stop to, this dangerous assembly. The ancient dining-room, in which they met, had a communication with each part of the house; but the common door had been stopped up, by agreement, for some years. This, however, the lads contrived to open, and from thence, early in the morning, had carefully laid a train of gunpowder by the side of the wall, as far as the tub upon which Tugwell usually seated himself near his master, and at proper intervals had bestowed squibs and crackers, with balls of wild-fire; and into the tub they had conveyed a considerable quantity of that infernal composition.

Having thus laid their plot, they waited with as much impatience for their time of meeting, as Guy Fawkes and his associates did for the meeting of the Parliament on the fifth of November. At length the evening came, and whilst Wildgoose was in the most pathetic part of his discourse, dealing about his judgment of wrath and indignation, fire and brimstone, with great zeal and vehement gesticulations, they set fire to their train, which, corresponding with the heated imaginations of the audience, had its proper effect, and threw them into the utmost consternation. The saints and sinners fled promiscuously, without waiting for the benediction. The tub, on which Tugwell was perched, burst into a thousand pieces, with so loud a report, and such violent force, that if Jerry's prudence, had not prevailed over his fortitude, and prompted him to make his escape amongst the foremost of the company, he would probably have been sent to heaven before his time, in a chariot of fire. A poor decrepit old woman, however, in her crowned hat, who, on account of her deafness, was seated near the preacher, was terribly battered and burnt, by the bursting of the barrel; which of itself was a sufficient reason for Mr Keen's getting a warrant, and carrying the publican before the mayor; who, unless he had found sufficient bail, and given security to indemnify the old woman for her burns and bruises, would have committed him to the Castle. The publican, however, took an opportunity of revenging himself sufficiently upon his pious neighbour; which will be related in its proper place.

BOOK IV

I

SETS OUT FOR BATH

Mr Wildgoose, during his stay at Gloucester, having heard that there was a considerable society of godly people established at Bath, was resolved to visit that place in his way to Bristol: and being likewise informed that there was, at this time, a race at Cirencester, he was inclined to make another effort at one of those public meetings, and attack the devil a second time, in one of his strong-holds; and resolved, therefore, to take his route by that place and Tetbury, and so to Bath.

Accordingly they set out pretty early in the morning, and about eight o'clock reached Birdliphill.

Wildgoose, being a little thoughtful on parting with his Christian brethren; and a sort of melancholy likewise succeeding in his mind to the innocent sprightliness of Miss Townsend, but little conversation passed between the two pilgrims. Tugwell, however, took the liberty to remind his master of his mother's illness, and said it was a little hardhearted in him not to write her a letter, *howsomever*; that he himself should not mind the loss of his son so much, if he could but hear from him now and then, that he might know whether he was alive or not: he hoped, therefore, that Mr Wildgoose would write to madam, and let her know *as how* they should be at home again very speedily. Wildgoose replied, with some degree of peevishness, that he had written to his mother; but as to their returning home again, that was according as Mr Whitfield should dispose of him, and according to the success of his labours in the gospel. In short, says he, hast thou forgot our great Master's declaration, 'Whosoever loves father or mother more than me, is not worthy of me?'—Jerry stood corrected, and so trudged on without farther reply.

They now proceeded for several miles, without meeting with any adventure; and Wildgoose might as well have thought of preaching the gospel in the Deserts of Arabia, as on the Cotswold-hills. He would have been like the preacher, whose discourses generally produced such a solitude in his church, that he was facetiously called; 'the voice of one crying, in the wilderness,' or desert, *Vox clamantis in deserto.*

Indeed, the fame of Cirencester races operated so strongly, that it had drawn every man, woman, and child, for ten miles round, that could either borrow a horse, or walk on foot, into its vortex; so that they did not meet a living creature, unless a London waggon might be called so, upon the high road.

In the afternoon, however, they saw a pompous equipage, with a numerous attendance, come whirling along the road, amidst a cloud of dust. It was a landau, or open coach, with six horses; and four or five out-riders in most flaming liveries. They came upon them so suddenly, that Wildgoose had hardly time to get out of the road; and one of the footmen gave Tugwell a hearty cut with his whip, to quicken his pace and clear the way.

The principal figure in this gay party was a young fellow, whom, on a sudden glance, Wildgoose immediately recollected to have been an intimate acquaintance in the university. He had unexpectedly arrived at an immense fortune; was just married; and was conducting his bride; with some other company, to his country-house in ——shire. He would hardly have reconnoitred Wildgoose, however, in his short hair, and present uncouth appearance, if he had vouchsafed a look upon two such dusty objects as he and his fellow-traveller now were. The whole company consisted of three ladies and two gentlemen, who were laughing and talking in all the gaiety and wanton levity of un-thinking youth. Wildgoose, however, was so far from envying them, that he only lamented their unhappiness, that notwithstanding their splendid appearance and seeming felicity, they had not yet been blessed with the illumination of the Spirit, as he flattered himself he and his humble companion had happily been.

This scene was hardly shifted, when, as a contrast to the splendour of it, they espied a poor tinker and his trull sitting calmly on a shady bank, under a hedge, a little out of the road. Tugwell inquired of the tinker, how far it was to Cirencester. Instead of giving a direct answer to his queation, the tinker told him he would be too late for the sport, for that the horses were to start at three o'clock, and that this was the last day of the race. The first part of this intelligence damped Tugwell's spirits, as the latter made Wildgoose waver in his resolution of going that way. He then asked the tinker, whether there was not a nearer way to Tetbury than through Cirencester?—Yes, says he, by some miles. If you keep the right-hand road at the next turning, it will bring you to a public-house, called Park-corner, where there is good ale and civil usage. As the tinker and his doxy were regaling themselves with a bacon-bone, which they had got at a neighbouring farm-house, it put Tugwell in mind of what he had stored in his wallet; and Wildgoose considering it as an act of humiliation, and that he might probably make a meal and make a convert at the same time, complied with Jerry's request, to join this happy couple, and refresh themselves with what Mrs Whitfield had furnished him at Gloucester, where, besides a substantial slice or two of a round of beef, he had laid in an old French flask, filled with some good ale or strong beer. They, therefore, with a proper apology, took their seat upon the bank; Wildgoose next to the tinker, and Tugwell by his trull.

They were hardly seated when Wildgoose (in his way) asked the tinker, why he chose to lead such an idle, vagabond life, as those of his profession generally did?—Yes, says Tugwell, it is like a travelling cobbler, that goes about, and takes the meat out of the mouth of an honest workman, that is to live by his trade.—Hey! what the devil! says the tinker, the pot calls the kettle black a-se; why I suppose thou art a pedlar, as well as myself; sure all trades must live.—Yes, says Wildgoose, very true; but I wonder any one should choose to live in such an unsettled way, if it is in his power to avoid it.—Aye, says the tinker, but those that cannot live at home must seek their fortune abroad. It is better to pick a bone under a hedge, than to rot in a gaol, as, perhaps, I might have done, if I staid at home.—How so? says Tugwell; What, I suppose you owed money, and had none to pay?—Yes, replied the tinker; I was ruined by a piece of good fortune, or rather by trusting more to the smiles of fortune than to my own industry.—That is no uncommon case, says Wildgoose; but how did that come to pass? To which the tinker replied as in the following chapter.

II

THE TINKER'S TALE

I was settled in a very flourishing trade, as a brazier, in a large town in the west of England, in which I employed a great many hands; and my wife and I lived happily together. A distant relation dying without children, left five thousand pounds betwixt me, my three brothers, and a sister; which one would have thought might easily have been divided between us, without the assistance of a lawyer. But, as we were to pay an old aunt an annuity for her life, of twenty pounds half yearly, this part of the will being *ambitiously* expressed,—*Ambiguously*, I suppose you mean, says Wildgoose—I mean, says the tinker, what the lawyer told us, that it was impossible to know, as the will was worded, whether it meant twenty pounds or forty pounds a year; though every one knew the intention of my kinsman was, to leave her only twenty pounds a year in the whole; and the lawyer that made the will had probably expressed it so, on purpose to make work for the tinker, as the saying is. Well, we were advised to put the affair into Chancery, *in an amicable way*, as they call it; which, as they told us, would be a trifling expence, and would soon be determined. But my sister and one of my brothers dying in the mean time, and leaving children, we were forced to have bills of revivor, I think they call them, one after another; so that by some means or other, we could never get a decree to settle this affair under seven years. When that was done our lawyer told us, the business would now soon be ended; for that there was nothing now to do, but to settle the account before a Master in Chancery, which, one would think, might have been easily done. But we soon found, that not a few years were required to settle an account which any schoolmaster, or indeed, any schoolboy, might have settled in a few hours.

But I should have told you before, that, after a decent mourning for the death of my kinsman, I had invited some of my friends to a tavern, to partake of my joy, for the legacy which he had left me. I also thought it unnecessary to make myself any longer a slave to my business; and the respect with which I found myself treated by the waiters and tapsters at the public-houses which I frequented made me fond of repeating my visits at those places of rendezvous.

My poor wife saw the absurdity of my conduct, and whenever I came home elated with liquor, would reproach me for my folly in no very gentle terms. In short, home began to be disagreeable to me, and I was never easy out of a public-house; so that by neglecting my business, and spending considerable sums at the tavern, by the time our law-suit was ended, I found myself more in debt than the share of my legacy which the law had left me amounted to; for instead of one thousand pounds apiece, it did not turn out above five hundred. Her vexation on this account was the death of my poor wife; and though I held up my head a year or two longer, my landlord at last seized upon my stock for rent, and I was forced to abscond, and leave my three children upon the parish, and to fly my country: and thus, by my own folly, and the iniquity of a court of equity, from a topping tradesman I am become a travelling tinker, at your service.

Though Tugwell had been cramming in his cold beef, during the tinker's narration, yet he shook his head at the conclusion of it, and said that the law was a bottomless pit, as the exciseman used to say.

Wildgoose observed, that those forms of law, which were sometimes so oppressive to individuals, were the greatest security in general, of justice and of property.—That is true, master, says Tugwell, but come, let us drink, and drive away care, quoth Jerry. He then put the flask to his mouth, and tossed off one half of it; then clapping his hand upon the young woman's knee, who was a handsome black girl (black I mean from the sooty contact of her paramour, for naturally she was as fair as the Venus of Corregio)—Tugwell, I say, squeezing her knees with a waggish air, bid the lady pledge him. But the tinker's dog, who lay at his mistress's feet, not approving of Jerry's familiarity, starts up, and snaps at his fingers; in return for which he gave the dog a kick in the guts. This roused the tinker's choler, already provoked at Tugwell's amorous freedom with his doxy, and he gave him a click in the mazard. Tugwell had not been used tamely to receive a kick or a cuff; he, therefore, gave the tinker a rejoinder which would have brought on a regular boxing-match, had not Wildgoose on one side, and Trulla on the other, interposed, and put a stop to farther hostilities. The tinker, however, sacked up his budget, and his companion her bundle, and went growling off, with hearty curses both upon Tugwell and his master, for intruding upon them and interrupting their tranquillity. Such was the event of Wildgoose's benevolent intention of converting this itinerant copper-smith and his female companion, which Tugwell called, casting their pearls before swine; though his own indiscretion alone, and carnal waggery, had defeated his master's purpose, and deprived him of an opportunity of giving them any spiritual instruction.

Our two pilgrims finished their repast, took a short nap to refresh themselves, and then proceeded on their journey, leaving the Cirencester road, and bending their course towards Park-corner: but the shades of night overtook them before they reached their intended quarters.

III

THEIR COMFORTABLE RECEPTION AT PARK-CORNER, NEAR LORD BATHURST'S WOODS

Blessed be the man that first invented warming pans! said an old gentleman with whom I passed the Alps, upon coming to a comfortable inn on mount St Bernard; and blessed be that good christian who first found out chimney-corners, said Tugwell to himself, upon spying the distant light of the inn to which they had been directed. Nothing is more comfortable, continued Jerry, than a pipe of tobacco in a chimney-corner, after wandering about in a dark night and in a strange country, as we have done: and if I can but meet with a bit of soft cheese and a raddish, to close the orifice of the stomach (as the exciseman used to say,) I shall be as happy as the Great Mogul.

Tugwell was consoling himself with these savoury ideas, when, about nine o'clock, they approached Park-corner. But, lo! instead of this snug scene, which Jerry had formed in his imagination, they found the inn so crowded with company from Cirencester races, that they were forced to sit drinking out at the door (it being a warm evening;) and the stables also were so full, that there were near twenty horses standing round the sign-post.

It was in vain for foot passengers to expect any kind of lodgings upon such an occasion; and it was even with difficulty that they got any sort of refreshment. Tugwell began to complain of great fatigue, and to lament their distress; but Wildgoose, attentive to nothing, so much as the conversion of sinners, cried out, in a strain of exultation, Now for it, Jerry! this is an unexpected opportunity! let us take possession of the devil's strong hold; we will make his kingdom shake, I'll warrant you.

Having said this, in the warmth of his zeal, without any more ceremony, he mounted the horse-block contiguous to the sign post, and began to harangue with such vehemence, that he soon drew together all the company about the house; and though some mocked, yet others were very attentive: for, as many of them came at no great distance from Gloucester, they had heard of Wildgoose's fame, and were glad of an opportunity of gratifying their curiosity at so easy a rate.

But, after a little time, some of them began to regret the leaving their pipes and their punchbowls; others were provoked at being interrupted in the midst of their songs and catches, and could not forbear renewing their melody at every period of Wildgoose's discourse; which he perceiving, after some time, addressed them in the apostolical strain: 'If any is merry, let him sing psalms;' and ordered Tugwell to give out the hundredth psalm. But the people of the house, thinking their craft was in danger, and that preaching and singing of psalms interrupted more profitable business, were not much pleased with these proceedings. They connived, therefore, at a proposal of the hostler, who, climbing up the sign-post, which was not much illuminated, discharged a bucket of water upon the heads of the two pilgrims, which raised a great uproar, threw all into confusion, and effectually cooled their devotion.

They were now certainly in very evil plight, almost wet to the skin, and thoroughly tired, nor likely to get any bed, or any comfortable accommodations at Park-corner; and they were assured, there was no other house upon the road nearer than Tetbury, which was six or seven miles. In the midst of this distress, however, a gentleman's servant, in a green coat and black cap, with some dog-couples by his side, having observed that Wildgoose had a watch in his pocket, which he consulted about the hour of the night, and that he had otherwise the appearance of a gentleman, thought he might safely invite him and his companion to his habitation. This was part of an old Gothic building, about a mile within Lord Bathurst's fine woods, which extend for five or six miles to the west of Cirencester, and are cut into glades and avenues, most of which are terminated by towers or spires, or some other striking objects, agreeable to the magnificent taste of that worthy nobleman.

Upon the keeper's offering them such accommodations as his house would afford, the travellers; we may be sure, having no choice, were glad to accept of so unexpected an invitation. They accompanied their honest guide, therefore, who was then going to his castle, together with a groom of my lord's, who had staid out beyond his time, and intended to lie at the house in the wood till the morning.

The gloomy darkness and solemn silence of the woods, through which they were conducted by mere strangers, filled Tugwell with terrible apprehensions, which were greatly aggravated upon their approach to the house, by the loud barkings of some wolf-dogs, pointers, and southern hounds, and the like; which, echoing from the ruinous walls, revived in Tugwell's imagination his danger from the adventure of the buck-hunters; but when they came still nearer, the canking of some Spanish geese, the gobbling of turkeys, and the noise of other uncommon fowls which are kept there, threw poor Jerry into the utmost consternation. He was soon freed from this alarm, however, on being conducted into a cheerful kitchen, where the keeper's wife was expecting the return of her husband by a good fire. Being informed of the distress from which his benevolence had freed the travellers, she received them with tolerable civility; desired them to come to the fire and dry themselves, and entertained them with as much hospitality as their circumstances would allow of.

The keeper had but one spare bed, which Tugwell could not be prevailed upon to partake with his master, so took up his lodgings with the groom in the hay-loft; and Wildgoose, making it a point of conscience not to indulge himself in the softness of a down-bed, when his fellow-labourer fared so coarsely, wrapt himself up in the coverlet, and lay down upon the floor. So, though they were both thoroughly tired, through the complaisance of the one, and the Quixotism of the other, a very good feather-bed remained useless and unoccupied. Wildgoose, however, slept tolerably well on the floor, and Tugwell would have slept better in the hayloft, had not the groom, who chose to lie in his boots and spurs, given Jerry now and then an involuntary titillation.

IV

SPIRITUAL ADVICE

In the morning, as soon as the keeper arose, he prepared them a good breakfast of toast and ale; and, as his wife was dressing a sucking child by the fire, she expressed some concern that Mr Wildgoose had so bad a lodging, and was forced to lie upon the floor all night, as she found he had done. Wildgoose, recollecting Mr Whitfield's method of allegorizing upon such occasions, shook his head, and, turning towards Tugwell, in allusion to the child at the breast, Ah! says he, I sweetly leaned on my Saviour's bosom, and *sucked out* of the *breasts* of his consolation; and I can truly say, the banner of his love was spread over me the whole night.*

The poor woman, a stranger to this pious jargon, stared at him with astonishment, to hear a jolly man, as Wildgoose was, talk of sucking at the breast; which Tugwell observing, and imagining he could explain his master's meaning, Yes, yes, says he, his worship only talks in the way of Christian discourse, look ye! that is, as a body may say, his worship took a good swinging nap, and had a comfortable night's rest. Wildgoose did not reflect upon the improbability of his audience's not comprehending his allegorical meaning, but thought the least he could do, in return for their kindness; was to impart some spiritual advice to his host and family.

---

* Vide *Journals*.

After a few observations, therefore, upon the laudable nature of hospitality, and putting them in mind, that in the primitive times, some had entertained angels, without suspecting any thing of the matter, he proceeded to assure them, that in such cases (as that of Rahab the harlot for instance) it was her *faith*, and not her kindness to the Jewish spies, that was so acceptable to God. In short, says he, though it is a very commendable thing to entertain strangers in distress, as you have done us, yet you must be very cautious not to place the least *merit* in this, or in any other good work which you can possibly perform; for we must be saved by faith alone, without works.

Faith and troth, master, replies the keeper, (little used to religious speculations) I never thought about *merit*, or any such thing. I did as I would be done by. Our ale is but poor, indeed, but such as it is, you are welcome to it as a king; and I don't desire a farthing for my trouble.

However, master, I don't know what you mean by being *saved* without *work*; but I am sure all the *faith* in the world, without *work*, would not *save* me from starving. It is true, continues he, I live in my lord's house here, rent-free; but never a man in the country *works* harder to support his family than I do: and if you choose to taken a turn here in the woods, I will show you some serpentine walks which I *advised* my lord to let me cut out this last week; in which, indeed, the honest man probably took more pride than my lord himself did.

Wildgoose, therefore, having given his hostess half a crown for her trouble (which she did not at all expect from such guests,) took his leave, and accompanied the keeper into the woods.

V

A STRANGER OF A PECULIAR CHARACTER ARRIVES

As the keeper and his guests were in the amphitheatre before the Gothic house, there arrived a tall, elderly gentleman, with his servant, whose curiosity had brought him to see the place. Well, says he to a country fellow, who had been his guide, where are these *turpentine* walks which you told me of? Then, alighting from his horse, and surveying the structure, which represents the ruin of a castle overgrown with ivy; Aye, says he, a very ancient place! Probably one of the *castra cestiva*, or summer camps, of the Romans; some appendage to Cirencester, I suppose, which was one of the *castra hyberna*, or winter stations, of the Roman legions. The Castle itself was probably built during the barons' wars, in the reign of Henry the third, or of King John.—Aha! look ye there now, says the keeper, smiling, so several gentlemen have thought: but, sir, I assure you, it was built by my present lord, but a few years ago; and his lordship used to say; he could have *built* it as *old* again if he had had a mind.—Built by my present lord! cries the gentleman, with a frown, and were there no ruins of a castle here before?—Not that I ever heard of, replies the keeper.—Well, for my part, says the stranger, I don't at all approve of these deceptions, which must necessarily mislead future antiquaries, and introduce great confusion into the English history. I don't wonder, continues the stranger, turning towards Wildgoose, that any gentleman should wish to have his woods or gardens adorned with these venerable Gothic structures, as they strike the imagination with vast pleasure, both by the greatness of the object, and also by giving us a melancholy idea of their past grandeur and magnificence. But for a man to *build a ruin*, or to erect a modern house in the style of our Gothic ancestors, appears to me the same absurdity, and must be attended with the same inconvenience to posterity, as that which many people have of late run into, of having their pictures drawn in the habit of Vandyke; or Sir Peter Lely; or that of our modern mint-masters, of representing our English heroes in Roman armour, and the dresses of antiquity; for though I myself have a great veneration for the Roman customs, yet this foolish practice, I think, destroys one considerable use of pictures and medals, that of conveying to posterity the habits and customs of the age we live in.

I find, sir, says Wildgoose, you are a connoiseur in these things; and I suppose have a taste for antiquities.—Sir, replies the gentleman, I have some little taste that way, and took Cirencester in my road to

Gloucester, not to see the races, I assure you, but to inquire after some of those Roman coins which are found there in great abundance.

As the antiquary was talking, he pulled out his *sudarium*, or pocket handkerchief, to wipe his face, when two or three silver and copper medals, which he had met with at Cirencester, dropped out of his pocket; which he picked up, and began explaining them to Wildgoose and the company; upon which Wildgoose observed, that the study of medals was a curious study; but he could never be convinced of the utility of it.—The *utility* of it, replies the virtuoso, with some vivacity, why as to that, I'll only refer you to Mr Addison's Dialogues upon that subject, to which I think nothing can be added.

But people often run themselves into difficulties, continued he, and lay themselves open to their antagonists, by resting their cause upon a wrong plea; every thing must be proved *useful*, forsooth! whereas I think it sufficient if some things are proved *agreeable* and entertaining. Why has not the imagination or fancy a right to be gratified, as well as the passions or appetites, in a subordinate degree; and under the directions of reason?

If I were to dispute with a Methodist about luxury in food, and about the necessity of fasting and mortification, I should not think myself obliged to prove, that every thing we usually eat was absolutely *necessary* to support life.

Sir, says Wildgoose, interrupting him; I never heard that the Methodists laid any stress upon those legal observances of fasting or distinction of meats, but eat and drank just as other people do.—Probably they may; replies the virtuoso, notwithstanding their mortified pretensions. At least from what I know of their self-denial, they are the last people with whom I would trust a wife or a daughter.

But, however, suppose I were disputing, I say, with any superstitious person, upon the subject of luxury in eating and drinking, I should say, that bread and cheese, for instance, was a hearty, wholesome food; and the staff of life, as the saying is. But I should think it a sufficient defence of the lawfulness of eating cheesecake or custard, by saying that it was *agreeable*. Thus we may say of several arts and sciences; of law, physic, and divinity, that they are necessary for the subsistence of society; but for poetry, painting, sculpture, and the like, I think it enough if they are allowed to be ornamental, and to contribute to the recreation of mankind.

In short, sir, if history, chronology, and several other branches of polite literature, are allowed to be of any use to the world, the knowledge of medals must also be allowed to have its share of merit, as instrumental in illustrating and confirming several particulars in those sciences.

Why, sir, replies Wildgoose, I must confess myself to be one of those who think only one branch of knowledge at all necessary or worth our pursuit; and that is, the knowledge of our fallen state, and of our redemption, as revealed in the Bible.

The antiquary stared at first with some astonishment at Wildgoose's declaration, but soon guessing at his religious turn. Well, says he, to carry the matter still farther then we could not understand the Bible, at least several expressions in it, without the assistance of this study.

The history of the Jews; from the time of the Maccabees to the birth of Christ, was all obscurity and confusion, till Monsieur Vaillant, from a collection of Greek medals, had given the world a complete series of the Syro-Macedonian kings.

And the title of EUERGETES, or benefactor, which is found on the coins of the Antiochus's and the Ptolemy's, very well explains what is meant by the Gentile kings being called *benefactors*; which the commentators, I think, made but bungling work of before.

The tribute-money, with Caesar's image and superscription, was a Roman *penny* or denarius; and the two-pence, which the good Samaritan is supposed to have given the landlord for his care of the wounded traveller, were two of those denarii, or about *fifteen* pence of our money. These things, perhaps, might have been known, from a slight acquaintance with the collateral histories of those times; but still it is a satisfaction to see the very coins which were then current, and which are preserved in the cabinets of the curious.

Ah! says Wildgoose, I want no commentaries, nor any assistance, to understand the Scriptures. When God has once revealed himself to a man, every expression speaks comfort to his soul; and he can *feel* the truth of it, without any teaching or instruction. Neither do I doubt, that although all other helps should be lost, Providence would preserve the knowledge of the Scriptures in his *church* to the world's end. I don't mean the established or *visible* church, which I am afraid has departed from its own doctrines: but the *invisible* church or society of true Christians, by whatever denomination they are distinguished.

As Wildgoose was launching beyond the comprehension of the virtuoso, and they were now come into a beautiful avenue, which terminated upon a *visible* church, the gentleman turned the discourse to the beauty of the prospect; and they being now come near the Tetbury road, Wildgoose took his leave, and, together with his trusty companion, proceeded on his journey to Bath.

VI

SOME ACCOUNT OF THE VIRTUOSO

As soon as they were got out of sight of the antiquary, Tugwell began to open. Od'slife; quoth he, this is a desperate man for the *Romans*—I suppose he's one of your *Papishes*. I never heard of such a whimsical, gentleman since I was born. His *sarvant* says, he almost starved one or two of his children, by breeding them up in the Roman way; for he would never let them eat till sunset; and would never suffer his little boy to wear a hat, because the Romans belike went bare-headed. He makes his children, instead of shoes and stockings, wear leathern buskins, like Joseph and his brethren in the Bible.

And his man says, he would have had the body of his eldest son who died, burnt to ashes, because the Romans did so; but his wife would not consent to it. Nay, he threatens to put his daughters to death if they marry without his consent, as the old Romans, he says, used to do.

His man says, if the gardener happens to dig up a piece of an old cream-pot, he'll lock it up in his cupboard, and call it a piece of Roman crockerware, such as they used to put the ashes of the dead in: and he says, they came ten miles out of their way to see this old castle and other curiosities.

Did you ask where he came from? says Wildgoose. Yes, replies Jerry, 'tis one 'Squire Townsend, and he comes out of ——shire. Wildgoose's heart immediately rose to his mouth, and his colour changed: for he was now convinced it was Miss Townsend's father with whom he had been talking; and he wondered at his own stupidity in not discovering this before.

It instantly occurred to him, that Mr Townsend was going to Gloucester in quest of his daughter, and he fancied he might have said many things to him in her favour, if he had known who he was; though it is ten to one he could have said nothing upon the occasion but what would have been improper, and have done more harm than good.

Though Tugwell, as was observed, had some smattering of history himself, yet, as the antiquary did not touch upon any of those legendary subjects with which Jerry had been chiefly conversant, such as the Travels of Joseph of Arimathea—the History of Glastonbury Thorn—or any romantic accounts of the Holy Land, and the like, he had thought it rather a dry discourse, and beginning to spit sixpences, as his saying was, he gave hints to Mr Wildgoose to stop at the first public-house they should come to. But there was none till they came to Tetbury, where they went into a second-rate inn, for fear of meeting with the same insults which they had received at the Bell at Gloucester.

VII

A HURLEY-BURLEY IN THE MODERN TASTE

Wildgoose having been thoroughly fatigued the preceding day, and not slept very soundly upon the floor at night; having also breakfasted upon toast and ale, which he was not much used to, he found himself drowsy, and somewhat indisposed: he desired, therefore, to go into a back parlour, and getting an arm-chair, took a comfortable nap, whilst Tugwell was smoking his pipe in the chimney corner.

When Wildgoose waked, he desired to have some little matter got ready for his dinner. My landlady had a daughter-in-law, a pretty girl about eighteen, who officiated as waiter, and went into the parlour to lay the cloth. As our preacher always found a particular propensity to exercise his talent on the young and handsome, he could not forbear caterchising this fair maid, as she came backwards and forwards into the room, about the state of her soul. The poor girl, conscious of her ignorance in the principles of religion, blushed, and seemed distressed what answer to make; and having placed the spoon and pepper-box on one side of the table, and the knife and fork in parallel lines on the other, would have made her escape from so disagreeable a persecution. But Wildgoose, finding his rhetoric had not force enough to detain her, laid hold on her apron; and desired her to hear what he had to say, which he assured her was for her good; nay, that nothing could be more so: that it was better than all the beauty in the world, and of more value than thousands of gold and silver: that he himself was the servant of God, and that he should be very happy if he could prevail upon her to love *him* above all things.

Just at that instant, Mrs Tantrum, the landlady, came into the parlour, having both hands filled with Wildgoose's dinner. She herself, though now as coarse as Pontius Pilate's cookmaid, yet having been handsome in her youth, and being still amorously inclined, watched her daughter-in-law with a suspicious, or rather with a jealous eye. Seeing the stranger, therefore, thus engaged about her apron, and hearing the words, beauty, love, gold, and silver, she immediately concluded, that he was in *love* with her *beauty*, and was bribing her with gold and silver to her ruin. Mine hostess then, being equally a stranger to Christian meekness and to delicacy, vented her rage, without much ceremony, first upon Mr Wildgoose. Then, setting down the dishes which she had brought in, and falling foul upon the poor girl with her brawny fists, you saucy slut, says she, have not I charged you, often enough, never to listen to any *foot*-passengers! But to leave the room if ever they pretended to trouble their heads about you? and here you stand with your brazen face—As she was going on scolding, and thumping her daughter's shoulders, Wildgoose thought himself obliged, as he had been the cause of the girl's stay, to explain his motives, and to rescue her from the consequences of it. His interposition, however, would of itself have made Mrs Tantrum more outrageous. But Wildgoose, having rebuked her for her passion with some asperity, and having also in the scuffle unfortunately torn my landlady's gown, this added to her fury, and gave her an opportunity which she wanted, of venting her rage more effectually upon the ill-fated pilgrim.

There is a certain farinaceous composition, which, from its being frequently used by our ancestors as an *extempore* supplement to a scanty dinner, has obtained the appellation of a *hasty-pudding*. It is composed of flour and milk boiled together; and, being spread into a round shallow dish, and interspersed with dabs of butter, and brown sugar fortuitously strewed over it, gives one no bad idea of a map of the sun, spotted about according to the modern hypothesis.

A dish of this wholesome food, smoking hot, mine hostess had brought in one hand, and a plate of bacon and eggs in the other: and upon Wildgoose's presumptuously interposing between her and her daughter (as has been related), Mrs Tantrum's fury was infinitely augmented: and, snatching up the dish; she discharged the hasty pudding full in Wildgoose's face: which, with the oiled butter and melted sugar, ran down to the skirts of his plush waistcoat, and made no very cleanly appearance.

Tugwell, hearing the uproar, was now come into the room; and seeing Mrs Tantrum in the condition of a tigress robbed of her whelps, attempted to lay hold of her arms, and prevent any farther efforts of her fury: but she, snatching up the dish of bacon and eggs, gave Jerry as warm a salute as she had done his master: and one of the poached eggs bursting in his face, and mixing with the greasy contents of the fryingpan, poor Jerry was in a worse plight even than his fellow-traveller.

Mrs Tantrum, having now satiated her fury, came a little to herself again: when, reflecting upon the damage she had probably done herself, if her guests should refuse to pay for the dinner, which, though they had smelt, they had not tasted; and beholding likewise the visible effects of her unbridled passion, in greasing her floor, and making unnecessary work for herself and her servant; she was going to repeat the outrage upon her innocent daughter-in-law: but, the girl had wisely withdrawn till the storm was over. She, therefore, sent the maid to clean the room, and set things to rights again and the travellers, having craved the maid's assistance in cleaning their persons, desired her to bring them the loaf and cheese, and a tankard of ale; with which they endeavoured to console themselves for the loss of the savoury food, by the sight of which they had been so disagreeably tantalized.

VIII

THE MISTRESS OF AN INN NOT EASILY TO BE CONVERTED

When Mrs Tantrum was a little recovered from the violence of her resentment, the daughter-in-law ventured to assure her, that the stranger had not offered to take the least freedom with her; but had only talked to her about Mr Whitfield, and our Saviour Christ, and such sort of discourse. Mr Whitfield! quoth she; I'll be hanged then, says Mrs Tantrum, if it is not one of these Methodists that go about the country. Run, and take away the silver spoon and pepper box! A pack of canting toads! I thought he looked like one of those *hypothetical* rascals. There was one of them at Salisbury, not long ago, married two wives; and another was hanged for sheep-stealing—Run, I say, and take away the pepper-box.

The poor girl said, she did not think the gentleman would *steal* any thing neither, *for all* he talked about *religion*. He did not look like that sort of man, she imagined. Whilst they were thus debating the matter, Wildgoose, and his friend came into the kitchen, to pay the reckoning; and Mrs Tantrum, surveying them more calmly, could not discover any thing very thievish in their physiognomy. So, to make some little amends for the rough usage with which she had treated her guests, she dismissed them with a tolerably decent welcome, and wished them a good journey. Wildgoose returned her compliments with a prayer for her conversion; and told her, that, unless God would give her grace

to subdue her boisterous passions, she could no more relish the joys
of heaven, than a hog or a sow could a clean parlours—Ay! ay! added
Tugwell, thou art a *vessel of wrath*, doomed to perydition.—I a *vessel of
broth*! you pot-gutted rascal! no more than yourself! Marry come up!
what does the fool mean? Sure I know my own business best, says Mrs
Tantrum; then concluded in her own way, that every tub must stand
upon its own bottom.

IX

PURSUE THEIR JOURNEY

Poor Wildgoose was a little chagrined at being suspected of carnal
intentions; but comforted himself with recollecting several of the
chosen saints, who had been thus buffeted by satan, and lain under the
same groundless suspicions. But he would, probably, have been more
shocked, if he had known that he was judged capable of stealing a silver
spoon. These were consequences of his extravagance, which he could
not foresee, and of which he had hitherto no conception. I have often
thought, however, it is happy for us that we do not know the half which
is thought or said of us behind our backs, by the smiling hostess or the
surly hostler, who attends us on our arrival or at our departure from an
inn upon the road.

    Our sturdy pilgrims, having sufficiently refreshed themselves,
proceeded on their journey with great alacrity; and, as it was not yet
past mid-day, pushed on to reach Bath that night. They travelled the
whole afternoon without any incident worthy the notice of a grave
historian. But reaching Lansdown, within a few miles of Bath, toward
sunset, they spied a poor horse, which, being overloaded, was fallen
down, and struggling under his burthen; and very near him two men,
instead of assisting the wretched animal, were scuffling and pummelling
each other without mercy. One of them was a slender, gentleman-like
man, and the other appeared to be a butcher's servant or something

in that style. Wildgoose and his fellow-traveller having interposed and parted the combatants, the butcher began to vent his wrath upon his antagonist, D-mn your blood! says he, who the devil are you? What, can't a man be in a passion, and beat his own horse, for *all* you, and be pox'd to you?

Wildgoose, having rebuked him for his insolence and profaneness, applied his hand to the stern of the horse; who after some further efforts, being roused, the butcher remounted him, rode off; and, instead of thanking Wildgoose for his assistance, calls out, D-mn you all together, for a pack of whores-birds as you are! The gentleman, who had fought the butcher, surveyed him for a moment with great indignation and contempt: then, refreshing himself with a pinch of snuff; There, says he, there goes a true picture of English liberty!—Pray, sir, says Wildgoose, if I may make so free, what was the subject of your altercation? To which he replied in the following manner.

X

A KNIGHT-ERRANT OF A PECULIAR KIND. COMPASSION FOR DUMB CREATURES

You see, sir, says the gentleman, how hard that poor beast is loaded. Now that brute of a fellow, instead of driving the horse before him (as he was probably ordered by his master to do,) had galloped him, loaded as he was, for near a mile along the road, in my sight; when the poor creature happened to trip, and come down with his rider, who began to bang him with that stick about the head with so much fury, that, if I had not interposed, he might probably have killed him upon the spot.—My officiousness, however, only made the fellow change the object of his wrath; for he fell upon me with the same weapon, which, however, I wrested from his hands, and banged him with to some purpose, till, he running in to me, we came to that close engagement from which you parted us.

Wildgoose stood staring at the gentleman with marks of surprise,—My compassion for dumb animals, continued he, is so excessive, that it often makes me quite miserable. Our sympathy and assistance is certainly due, in the first place, to our fellow-creatures of the human species, as they stand in a nearer relation to us, as they hold a superior rank in the works of the creation; but I own, the incapacity of a poor brute creature to utter his distress, and his want of reason to find out the means of relieving it, often plead more powerfully with me, than all the rhetoric of a beggar practised in the art of moving compassion.

Yes, replies Wildgoose, and I think, sir, you have suggested the reason of this; because in the latter case there is often a suspicion of insincerity in the petitioner; whereas in the former instances, undisguised nature, though void of speech, expresses herself in the most emphatical manner. For the same reason, the silent rhetoric of tears, or of bashfulness, is often more pathetic than all the oratorical flourishes in the world: and I dare say, sir, the helpless condition of an *infant* in distress, must affect you still more sensibly than that of any of those dumb creatures for which you express so much concern.

I don't know, replies the gentleman; it certainly ought to do so: but I cannot reason myself out of this strange effeminacy; nor do I recollect any instance of *human* distress, that has given me more pain, than the sight of a poor hare, for instance, almost *run down*, as they call it; to see her squatting behind a hedge, panting and listening, with her ears erect, to the cries of her pursuers, from whom her natural scent, augmented by the perspiration she is thrown into, makes it almost impossible for her to escape.

I entirely agree with Mr Addison, in applauding the humanity of the sultan, who chose rather to cut off the sleeve of his robe, than awake his favourite cat, which was asleep upon it; and I myself, in my walks, have often gone a furlong out of my way, rather than disturb a poor unwieldy ox, that has been lying down and chewing the cud; or than interrupt an innocent lamb that was sucking its anxious dam.

Nay, I have gone so far, as to erect an urn in my garden, as a testimony of my compassion for dumb animals, with the inscription from Ovid's speech of Pythagoras:

Quid meruistis, oyes, placidum pecus—&c.
Quid meruere boves, animal fine fraude dolisque,
Innocuum?

What have ye done, ye flocks, a peaceful race?
Or what the harmless ox, so void of guile,
To merit death?

Why, as for those animals which are fairly slaughtered, without torture, for the support of human life, says Wildgoose, I can easily reconcile myself to their fate; as the pain of death consists, I believe, chiefly in the apprehension: and when it is instantaneous (as in those cases it is, or ought to be) they enjoy themselves, and feel nothing till the stroke arrives; and the moment it does so, the violence of it either deprives them of life, or at least of the sense of pain. Mr Pope has finely described this in his ethic epistles;

The lamb thy riot dooms to bleed to-day,
Had he thy reason would he skip and play?
Pleas'd to the last he crops the flow'ry food,
And licks the hand just rais'd to shed his blood.
Oh! blindness to the future! kindly given,
That each might fill the circle mark'd by Heaven.

Why, doubtless, returns the gentleman, one feels the most for those animals that are tortured and abused: but I think none are more so than the generality of horses and beasts of burden, from a want of sensibility in the reasoning brutes to whose care they are usually intrusted. You saw how little compassion that butcher's lad has shown to his loaded steed; and to see a noble creature start and tremble at the passionate exclamation of a mere Yahoo of a stable boy, who, if he knew his own strength, could drive a dozen men before him, I own equally excites my pity and my indignation. I never meet a string of pack-horses, bending under their loads, but my heart bleeds for the mute sufferers; and I make it a point of conscience to give them the road. Nay, I have, in my own mind, added one more to the curses denounced by Moses against the unmerciful; 'Cursed be he that maketh the pack-horse to go out of his way.'

Here Tugwell could not forbear putting in his verdict. Well, says Jerry, the tailor of our town is the best man for that. He keeps a horse to let; but then he'll never let him to any one, till he has made him promise faithfully, that the poor horse shall stand still *to do his needs*.—The gentleman laughed at Tugwell's instance of compassion. But Wildgoose silencing him with a significant look observed that the good man to be sure was merciful, even to his beast: and it is pity, continued he, that cruelty to those animals cannot be provided against by our laws, as it was in a great measure by the laws of Moses.

Very true, sir, replies the gentleman; and as that cannot well be done in this land of *liberty*, I wish every gentleman would endeavour to supply that defect by discouraging all cruelty of that kind, as far as his power or influence extends; and certainly every parent should be particularly careful to instil principles of mercy and tenderness, to birds, beasts, and insects, into the tender minds of their children. For my part, I profess myself a sort of knight-errant in the cause; and assure you, have met with many such skirmishes as this which you found me engaged in, by interfering where I had no other motive but humanity and compassion.

XI

THE POLITE PHILOSOPHER

The frank disposition of this gentleman, who called himself Graham, encouraged Wildgoose, as they walked along, to communicate something of his own pretensions; and he informed the gentleman, that he himself was a volunteer in the service of his fellow-creatures; and professed to regulate their opinions in a matter of much greater importance than any thing which regarded this life, even the salvation of their immortal souls.

I presume then, says Mr Graham, you are one of these Methodists who have made such a noise in the world. Wildgoose replied, that he might call him by what name he pleased; but what he professed was to preach up true Christianity, and the genuine doctrines of the reformation.

Why, returns Mr Graham, though I have formerly conversed much in the world, I have of late confined myself a great deal to books and meditation, and the investigation of truth; the result of which is, that I cannot reflect with patience upon the many absurd practices and opinions which prevail in the world, and have often been tempted to turn itinerant myself, and sally forth in order to reform mankind, and set them right in various particulars.

When I hear of a father's marrying his daughter against her inclinations; and sacrificing her happiness to her grandeur, I am ready, like the Spanish Don, to challenge him to mortal combat, and rescue the unhappy victim from the power which he abuses.

Though I am not in Parliament, nor am fond of politics, I could not forbear giving the public my advice, in a pamphlet, upon the Militia Act, Triennial Parliaments, and the Necessity of *Sumptuary Laws*.

I have by me also a manuscript, which I call *Litertae Hottentoticce*, or Letters from a beautiful young Hottentot to her Friends at the Cape; giving an account of the many barbarous customs and preposterous opinions which she had observed in our metropolis, during her three years' abode amongst us.

But, sir, you will pardon my freedom when I declare, that of all the opinions which have been the subject of my contemplation, none appears more absurd to me, than that all religion should be made to consist in thinking rightly upon a few abstruse points, which have been controverted ever since the reformation, and about which hardly any two persons think exactly alike. I really believe, when the Methodists first set out (as Providence often brings about salutary ends by irregular means) they did some good, and contributed to rouse the negligent clergy, and to revive practical christianity amongst us. But I'm afraid they have since done no small prejudice to religion, by reviving the cobweb disputes of the last century; and by calling off the minds of men from practice to mere speculation. For, by all the accounts I have heard of late, if a man does but frequent their meetings regularly, express himself properly upon justification, and a few more of their favourite topics, he is immediately ranked amongst the elect, and may live as carelessly as he pleases in other respects; nay, may be guilty of drunkenness, fornication, luxury, and what not. In short, if a man does but *talk* and *look* like a saint, he may, without any reproach, live like a sinner.

Sir, says Wildgoose, whatever the case may be with a few individuals, who call themselves Methodists, you cannot say that any of those irregularities are the *necessary* consequence of their principles.

No, sir, replies the gentleman; but they are the *probable* consequences of their practices; for, by being thus distinguished from their brethren, they begin to look upon themselves as a sort of priviledged persons; and finding so much stress laid upon *thinking* rightly, they begin to be more careless about acting properly; and the original depravity of their nature returning upon them thus unguarded, they are but too prone to relapse into the greatest enormities; which reflection, I am afraid, might be confirmed by too frequent experience; not to mention the tendency which their particular doctrines of *assurance* and *inward feelings* have to make men presumptuous, and to delude them to their own destruction.

Wildgoose was not inclined to continue the dispute with a person who appeared so much prejudiced against his doctrines, and who, indeed, was so full of reflections, made in his solitude, that he would hardly give him leave to put in a word.

As their road, however, lay near a mile the same way they talked upon various subjects; and Wildgoose found, in the course of their conversation, that Mr Graham was quite a polite philosopher; had a competent knowledge of almost every science, had travelled over most parts of Europe, and made many delicate and curious remarks upon the manners and customs of the several people with whom he had conversed.

But what gave a peculiar beauty to his conversation, was the delicacy of his taste, which selected the most agreeable or the most striking circumstances, on every subject; so that his descriptions and narrations never became languid by too minute a detail of uninteresting particulars.

He now lived a very retired life; went sometimes to Bath, as a mere spectator; but, having sequestered himself from the world on a particular occasion, and having had sufficient experience of the selfishness, malignity, and insincerity of the vulgar part of mankind, he confined himself to a few select friends; and by exercise and temperance contrived to pass through the autumn of life with health, cheerfulness, and tranquillity.

Mr Graham was a man of that natural benevolence, that he rather affected the misanthrope than was really such. He invited Wildgoose and his friend, therefore, with great cordiality, to refresh themselves at his hermitage (as he called it,) which he pointed out to them amidst a tuft of lofty oaks, at a little distance, on the descent of the hill. Mr Wildgoose, being impatient to join his christian friends at Bath, would have waved the accepting this invitation; but Tugwell having an habitual thirst upon him at this time of the year, said he should be obliged to the gentleman for a draught of small beer, or a cup of cider.

They, therefore, accompanied him to his habitation.

XII

A SINGULAR MANSION

Mr Graham's house was almost concealed from the road by trees, and was literally founded upon a rock; some craggy parts of which appeared rising upon each side of the house: a clear spring which rose from the bottom of one of them, almost covered with moss, hart's tongue, and other fountain plants, determined the situation.

They entered, by a strong door, into a sort of porch, or vestibule; on one side of which Mr Graham showed them a neat bed-room, about seven feet square; on the other side, a beaufet, and other conveniences about the same dimensions. He them took them into a parlour, elegantly furnished, of about twelve feet square, exclusive of a bow-window, which commanded an extensive prospect over a beautiful valley, terminated by a distant view of the city of Bath and its evirons: and this was apparently the whole house.

Mr Graham, however, took them down a few winding steps, cut out of the rock, to another room under the former, which served him for a kitchen, cellar, and all other accommodations for himself and his maid. She was a middle-aged woman, and was sitting there at work with her needle. But, to prevent all suspicion of her serving him in any other capacity than that of a servant, Mr Graham had pitched upon a deserving person, with one eye, a protuberant shoulder, and one or two more accidental deformities, sufficient to stop the mouth of that infernal fury, scandal herself. A garden, proportioned to the house and its inhabitants, was laid out in a simple taste, and stored with those fruits, flowers, herbs, and plants, which were natural to the climate in which they were to grow.

Mr Graham left Tugwell to drink some cider with his maid Maritornes, and took Mr Wildgoose into his parlour, and offered him a glass of something better—which it is not recorded that Wildgoose refused.

As Mr Graham opened the door of a little closet, or rather niche in the wall, which contained his books and his cordials, Wildgoose could not forbear fixing his eyes upon a small oval picture of a young lady, in a gilt frame, that was fixed in a pannel, within side of the door; which Mr Graham observing, shook his head with a sigh, and said, the lady whom that picture represented had influenced the whole tenour of his life, and was the original cause of his present retreat from the world. Wildgoose, expressing some curiosity on that subject, and himself fetching a sympathetic sigh on having the idea of Miss Townsend revived by the sight of that picture, Mr Graham said his story could not be very interesting to a stranger. But, sir, says he, as I take a sort of melancholy pleasure in recollecting the occurrences of my youth, if you have patience to hear me, I will relate the particulars. He, therefore, began, without more ceremony, in the following manner.

XIII

MR GRAHAM'S STORY

I am a younger brother, of a younger branch, of a noble family; but, partly by my own economy in the former part of my life, and partly by that of my father, I have at present but a slender income, yet sufficient to live very comfortably in my present situation. I was bred at the university, and after that was sent to the temple; and when a young man there, went to make a visit to my sister, who was married to a baronet in the northern part of this county. Here Wildgoose listened with a more earnest attention. During my stay here we were invited to a supper and a ball, at a neighbouring gentleman's, where was a great deal of genteel company. Amongst the rest there was a clergyman's daughter, whom I will call Ophelia, who had the character of a learned lady, and a great wit. She was tolerably handsome, but had a very melancholy air; which, upon inquiry, I found to be the effect of a disappointment in her first love, by the sudden death of a man of fortune, to whom she was upon the verge of being united in marriage. As she thought it a kind of indecorum to mix in the gaiety of the company, though she had been invited with a good-natured intention to divert her melancholy, Ophelia sat by a bow-window in the room; and, as I was always of a studious turn, and not fond of dancing, I chose to keep her company.

We two were of course engaged in a separate conversation. But instead of what is usually meant by a wit, a pert girl who values herself upon saying smart things with a saucy petulance, I found her a young woman of great good sense and delicacy of sentiment, and thoroughly versed in all the best writers in the English language, and even the translations from the classics; upon whose several beauties and defects she passed sentence with a penetration and judgment superior to any one I had ever conversed with.

In short, I was quite charmed with this young lady's conversation, which of course brought on a personal attachment; and I made an errand to her father's the very next day, under a pretence of inquiring after his daughter's health, and how she got home. He was a very learned and a very sensible man, but had very small preferment; and, as he had exerted all his abilities in instructing his daughter, so he had gone to the utmost limits of prudence, in dressing her out rather above her rank. However, they lived in a frugal, though genteel manner; and I was so pleased with my quarters that I stayed all night, with my servant and two horses; and repeated my visits very frequently.

You will imagine, from this account, that I met with a very cordial reception from the young lady; but this was by no means the case. I found her affections still so much attached to their first object, that it was near half a year before I appeared to have made any impression upon her heart. After this, however, we continued an intimacy for above two years; during which time we lived in all the innocent endearments of a mutual fondness, and I was determined to make her my wife.

XIV

MR GRAHAM'S STORY CONTINUED

You will wonder, no doubt, says Mr Graham, what prevented my marrying Ophelia immediately. Why, nothing but my absolute dependence on my mother for my future support. She had a considerable jointure; and, as I was a favourite, she promised to increase my younger brother's fortune by what she could save out of her annual income. I had a considerable legacy left me by a relation; but as I had lived very expensively, I was obliged to make free with the principal, and had almost run through it; so that I had reason to fear my mother's resentment, who, you may suppose, was not at all pleased with this indiscreet engagement: as it not only disappointed her in her hopes of my marrying advantageously in point of fortune, but involved me in a life of indolence quite inconsistent with my study of the law, and making any figure in my profession. She, therefore, made use of every prudent stratagem to break off my attachment to this young creature; in which, alas! she at length succeeded.

While I was in London for a month, at my mother's earnest request, who had a house in town, I received an anonymous letter, full of invectives against the clergyman, his daughter, and, in short, against the whole family. As I was convinced many of them were without foundation, so I had good reason to believe the principal aspersion upon the young lady herself, was entirely so; which was, that she had got a habit of drinking spirituous liquors for her private amusement.

I was greatly shocked at the contents of this letter; but thought it unjust and ungenerous to be influenced in an affair of such importance by a letter of that kind, which was evidently written with a malicious intent.

I immediately, therefore, went down to my sister's, with a design to come to an *eclaircissement* with poor Ophelia, or at least to inspect her conduct more narrowly in the particular alleged; though I confess I was shocked at the want of generosity in such a proceeding with regard to a person, with whom I had had so long an intimacy, without the least reason for such a suspicion. I recollected, indeed, that she would drink two or sometimes three glasses of wine after dinner, without those squeamish airs which some ladies affect. But I have always thought it a good rule in these cases, that a woman, who upon proper occasions, refuses *one* glass in public, will drink *two* or *three* in private.

When I came to Lady ———'s, my sister, I found there a young lady of the neighbourhood, upon week's visit to my sister. She was a young woman of good fortune, and a smart sprightly girl; and one that I might probably have liked well enough, if my affections had not been pre-engaged.

I showed my sister the letter which I had received, at which she affected a great surprise; but added, that she was afraid most of the facts alleged had too good a foundation: and, with regard to the principal accusation with which the young lady was charged, she used so many plausible arguments to convince me of the reality of it, with so many artful insinuations, that I began to waver in my opinion of the matter; and, in short, instead of waiting on Ophelia, as I ought to have done, and as I at first intended, I was prevailed upon only to write her a letter; in which, after some excuses from the imprudence of such an engagement, as my entire dependence on my mother would probably involve as both in indigence and distress, I desired the affair might proceed no farther.

This bare-faced declaration produced such an answer as I had reason to expect from a girl of Ophelia's spirit; whom I had quite teazed into a return of affection, and now very unhandsomely, not to say basely, deserted; so that her resentment, though so well founded, contributed to abate my fondness; and I now thought myself at liberty to attend to the coquetry of Miss ———, whom I shall call Lavinia, upon whom my sister had prevailed to act a part, and to play off her artillery, on purpose to draw me off from my former engagement.

I proceeded so far as frequently to ride out with her alone, attended only by a servant; and she, very maliciously, made me accompany her one day, to dine at a gentleman's house in the village where poor Ophelia lived, and by whose very door we must necessarily pass.

This behaviour, though it probably extinguished the love, yet it so far wrought upon the *honest* pride of Ophelia, that, in a few days, it brought on a fit of distraction, which, in a few months, terminated in her death.

This shocking event of my perfidy awakened my fondness, and alarmed my conscience; and I immediately quitted my sister's house, where the artful Lavinia was still detained, and returned to London. I had been there but a few days, when I received, enclosed in a frank, a large packet, which I found sealed with Ophelia's seal, and the direction in her hand writing. My mother and a younger sister were in the room; the moment I saw the seal and superscription the letter dropped out of my hand, and I almost fainted away in my chair. My mother and sister ran to my assistance, reasoned with me upon my folly, and, by my permission, my sister opened and perused the letter.

The case was this. The cause of my deserting the celebrated Ophelia was not long a secret; and, coming to her ears, though she disdained to vindicate herself to a man who could treat her so ungenerously, yet she had written a long defence of her conduct, and pointed out almost to a demonstration, from what quarter the malicious tale had sprung; and this she had ordered to be delivered to me after her decease.

The person hinted at, as the conductor of this wicked artifice, was Lady
———, my sister; against whom I vented my indignation; and could hardly
preserve the decency due to my mother, for opposing a match upon
which my happiness depended. However, instead of settling again to the
study of the law, I found myself incapable of applying to any thing.

I determined, therefore, by way of diverting my melancholy,
immediately to go abroad, and rambled all over Europe for four or five
years; at the end of which I was recalled by the death of my mother;
which event was rather seasonable, as I was almost reduced to the last
hundred pounds of my own fortune.

I took possession of five thousand pounds, which she left me, and
which brings me in about two hundred pounds a-year. I left the north
of England, where I was born; changed my name, and came and built
this cottage near Bath, where I have lived these ten years, and where I
intend to pass the remainder of my days.

XV

MR GRAHAM'S WAY OF LIFE

When Mr Graham had finished his story, Mr Wildgoose said, he was
unwilling to interrupt him in his narration; but added that an event of
this kind had happened when he was a boy, in almost the next village
to that where he was born; but, as he had often heard the story, the
gentleman's name was ———

Mr Graham changed colour, and said, that was his real name; and
that he was the guilty person.—Well, says Wildgoose, the poor old
gentleman (Ophelia's father) is now very infirm, and, by various
unlucky accidents, in great distress.—Good God! cries Mr Graham, is
he still alive? Why, before I went abroad I had begged leave to erect an
urn to poor Ophelia's memory; and, by the person whom I employed
for that purpose, was then informed that her unhappy father was at the
point of death, of a broken heart.

But my meeting with you, sir, is very providential; and it will be the greatest pleasure to me, to make some atonement for my wickedness, and even the expense I put the family to, by relieving his distress, which I will take the first opportunity of putting in execution.

Wildgoose observed, that Mr Graham's expression of making an atonement for his wickedness, was somewhat exceptionable, as our Saviour had made a sufficient atonement and satisfaction for the sin's of the whole world; and that we should be cautious in ascribing any *merit* to our own good works.

Zounds; sir! says Mr Graham, (who had no patience with such nice distinctions,) you don't think there is any sin in relieving the distressed, upon whatever motive it is done? As for placing any merit in such an action, I should think myself a rogue if I did not do it in the present case; but if so much caution is necessary upon such occasions, a man that happens to tumble into a river or a ditch, may be drowned or suffocated, whilst we are deliberating about the proper motive or state of mind with which we are to pull him out again.

Mr Wildgoose did not think proper to reply to a man of so warm a temper; but observed, by way of changing the discourse, that Mr Graham seemed under a necessity almost of living the life of a hermit, as the dimensions of his habitation would not admit of much company.

Why, says Mr Graham, a life of absolute solitude is a visionary and unnatural state, and can only subsist in poetry and romance. I don't pretend to live upon roots and rock-water, though I can feast upon mutton and potatoes, and a bread pudding: and though I don't love mobs and routs, I would not have you imagine I never entertain any company in my cell; I have two or three friends, of the same simple taste with myself, who, for the sake of varying the scene, frequently eat their morsel with me, when we wait upon ourselves, and limit each other as to the number and variety of the particulars which are to constitute the entertainment.

As to your paltry little esquires, or those who have not sense enough to dispense with the forms of life, or come without a servant to wait behind their chair; puppies; who will drink a bottle or two with you in private, and perhaps not know you in public, I affront them, if ever an impertinent curiosity brings them to my cottage—so that I am seldom troubled with any visitors of that kind.

Neither am I very fond of the company of ladies, out of regard to the memory of poor Ophelia; the recollection of whose excellencies makes the generality of female conversation truly insipid—*Deleo omnes dehinc ex animo mulieres*—I blot from my memory every other woman; those every-day beauties, as Terence calls them, who have nothing but their sex to recommend them.

Mr Wildgoose was a little scandalised at the warmth of temper and appearance of uncharitableness in Mr Graham; though, as was observed before, this misanthropy was rather in speculation than in practice, as he could not treat any one that came to his house without the highest politeness.

Wildgoose, now looking at his watch, Mr Graham said, if he was impatient to get to Bath, he could show him a shorter road over the hill; which he accordingly did: and having pointed out the great road to them again, he left the two pilgrims to pursue their journey.

BOOK V

I

THE TWO PILGRIMS ARRIVE AT BATH

SOME PEOPLE, SAYS AN ITALIAN writer,[*] upon politeness, in the midst of an agreeable conversation are apt to fall asleep. This, says he, with great solemnity, is by no means a genteel custom, as it shows a contempt of our company.

Now, if I might differ from so profound an author, I should rather impute the infirmity of such drowsy people to want of taste, than to a contempt of their company; and if the reader should have taken a nap in the midst of the last chapter, for my own credit I would willingly impute his drowsiness to the same principle. But to proceed.

The setting sun now gilded the summit of the mountains and the tops of the highest towers, when the two pilgrims came within sight of Bath. Upon the first view of that elegant city, Tugwell, who had received all his ideas of grandeur from his bible, and whose head always ran upon what he had read of the Holy Land, observed that Bath seemed to be situated like Jerusalem; according to David's description of it:

As mighty mountains huge and large
Jerusalem about do close.

According to Sternhold and Hopkins' description of it, you mean, says Wildgoose. Well, well, master, that's as our clerk sings it. But I suppose your worship likes the *new diversion* better.—No, says Wildgoose, I like neither of the poetical versions so well as the plain prose.

But, continues Wildgoose, Bath seems huddled so close together, that I should compare it to Jerusalem in another respect, 'Jerusalem is built as a city that is at unity in itself' and yet, perhaps, this little place may be divided into as many parties, and abound as much in scandal, envy, and malice, as London itself.

---

[*] Job. Casce, *de Morum Elegantiâ*.

Wildgoose, however, being vastly struck with the richness of the valley, and the elegance of the buildings, especially of the villas dispersed on the surrounding hills, remarkable for the beauty of their verdure, observed, that, however fruitful the Land of Canaan might be formerly, when inhabited by a populous nation and properly cultivated, yet, by all accounts of modern travellers, the present face of the country, about Jerusalem was not to be compared to the environs of Bath. Though I cannot but wonder, continued he, that any one should doubt the veracity of the sacred writers in their encomiums upon the ancient fertility of that country, which is confirmed by the concurrent testimony of several Pagan authors, yet I am inclined to think it was called 'a land flowing with milk and honey,' partly in opposition to the arable lands of Egypt, and partly in preference to the sandy deserts through which they were to pass in their retreat from thence, neither of which were to be compared to the rich pastures or vine-clad hills of Palestine.

Wildgoose and his friend Tugwell, who were now come into the town, cut but a dusty figure, in comparison with the spruce inhabitants of Bath, which made them desirous of getting under cover as soon as possible: and Tugwell, espying a sign, whose device struck his fancy, exhorted his master to set up his staff there, especially as the house seemed suitable to Mr Wildgoose's appearance in his present voluntary humiliation.

Tugwell was no sooner entered, than he almost mechanically called for a cup of the best. Ah! my lad, says mine host, who was a facetious sort of fellow, thou shalt have it in the turning of a pork griskin. But let's see, what hast thou got in thy wallet? some *run tea*, or some *Welch stockings*? What dost thou deal in? Cry thy trade.—No, no, says Jerry, we don't deal in stockings nor shoes neither; though, for that matter, as good shoes as ever trod the ground have gone through my hands. But no matter for that. I hope God has called me and my master here to a better occupation.

My landlord, not being willing to throw away any longer conversation on such guests, without any further reply, stepped to the tap, drew some ale, and, having blown off the froth, which occupied a third part of the cup, and drunk the travellers' health in another third, he presented the remainder to Tugwell, who had called for it; whilst Jerry was drinking, my landlord surveyed Wildgoose with more attention; and observing in him an air rather above a common pedlar, asked if the gentleman would not please to walk into another room. Tugwell replied, that, to be sure, his worship had not been used to sit in a kitchen; but *howsomever*, my master, says he, scorns to despise a poor *parson*; and is not above keeping company with any good Christian.—Hey, day! good Christian, quoth my landlord; why, we are all good Christians, I hope; but I fancy thou hast left off *mending* of shoes, and art set up for a *mender* of *souls*. I suppose, thou art one of these *Methodites*, or *Mithridates*, or what the devil do you call 'em? Why, sure a gentleman may be a good Christian, without keeping company with all the tag-rags and scrubs in the country.

Then, turning to Wildgoose, having heard Tugwell call him his worship, my landlord went a step further; and, to make amends for his first neglect, Won't your *honour* walk into the parlour? says he, What shall I get your *honour* to eat? This was language which mine host had learned from the footmen, who greatly frequented his house; and who, I have observed, rather than not discover that they have been used to wait upon people of fashion, will bestow those honourable appellations on the lowest of their acquaintance, and even on persons whom they despise.

And here, by the way, I cannot but lament the ridiculous prostitution of titles of distinction amongst the inferior part of mankind in this age. In the glorious days of Queen Elizabeth, *master* was esteemed a very respectful address to any one beneath the dignity of a peer: and even in James the First's reign *your worship* was the highest degree of adulation or respect with which a servant or vassal approached his lord and master whom he served. From the French, I believe, in the last century, we learned to apply the monosyllable sir to any one, whom we considered as greatly our superior. But now, *your honour* is the title universally given to every one that appears in a clean shirt and powdered wig, by the drawer, the chairman, or the shoe-black; who are unwilling to hazard the loss of a customer, by addressing him in a style beneath his real or fancied importance.

In higher life, indeed, where particular titles are appropriated to particular ranks or offices, this confusion has been hitherto avoided.

Our sovereign, the fountain of honour, is at present content with that of *sacred majesty*, one of the lowest attributes of divinity; as our religion does not admit of downright deification. Neither has any one, as yet, been guilty of so presumptuous a piece of flattery, as to bestow the title of *majesty* on any subject whatsoever.

And, as the several orders of our nobility are created by patent, and their titles purchased either by money or merit, it is not usual, amongst that *right honourable* fraternity, to invade each other's property in that respect, or to give the superior titles to those of inferior quality. But amongst the aforesaid lower race of mortals, as the love of false honours increases in proportion to the decrease of real worth; and as the base multitude pay that respect to money which is properly due to merit, it is not easy to say to what a ridiculous extreme this humour may at length be extended; and I should not be surprised, in process of time, to hear a haberdasher saluted with, A coach, your *grace*! or to see a shoe-black importune a walking tailor with, Black your shoes your *majetsty*! But to return to our pilgrims.

II

POPULAR REPORTS SOMETIMES
A LITTLE ERRONEOUS

Mr Wildgoose did not choose to accept of my landlord's invitation of going into a room at present; but asked him, whether there were any of those Methodists, as he meant to call them, in Bath. Are there? says mine host. Yes, I believe there are; enough to turn the heads of all the 'prentices and journeymen in the nation. I am sure, I cannot keep a chambermaid, or a tapster; but the toads must be singing psalms, or preaching to my customers, and be pox'd to 'em, from morning to night. Well, but you should not blame the poor creatures for being too good, says Wildgoose.—Too good! replies my landlord: I don't know that they are any better than other folks. I *loves* a psalm at church, as well as a merry catch over a glass of liquor; but to be singing *sol fas* all day long, in such a house as ours is, I *does not* approve of it, it's *perphane*: its quite *perphane*.

Besides! continues my landlord, without giving Wildgoose room to reply, they are some of the worst people *that is*; there is nothing but whoring and rogueing amongst them. There was one of 'em, at Gloucester, as a gentleman's servant told me that very morning, caught in bed with a milliner's 'prentice but last week; nay, and one of them is in Gloucester gaol at this time, for setting fire to the Cathedral.—Not to the Cathedral, says a footman, who was drinking in the house, but some other church, as this gentleman here told me. D—n thee, says another footman, I did not say, set fire to a church; but to the *little* church, as they call the Methodists' meeting. Wildgoose and Jerry stared at this intelligence; and, after his astonishment would give him leave, Wildgoose assured him that he came from Gloucester but yesterday morning, and that there was not a word of truth in what he had heard. He told him, however, the probable foundation of the latter report, and the story of the gun-powder plot: but concluded with reprimanding him for his credulity; and made some reflections upon the malignity of the world, and the absurdity of those popular stories, which are so freely propagated by the vulgar part of mankind.

III

Landlord alters his tone.
A female saint

My landlord now began to smell a rat; and as it was his business to adapt himself to the taste and principles of his customers, he suddenly changed his tone, and said, that, to be sure, some of the Methodists were good sort of people, for that matter, and did a great deal of good in the world; and were very charitable to the poor; and they *preaches* main well, as they do say; but for my part, continues he, I never was at their meeting.

What part of the town do they meet in, then? says Wildgoose—Why, I don't know; but, here! Deborah, says he to a woman that had been washing in the back kitchen, give the gentleman an account of your little Tabernacle in Avon-street, or where the deuce is it?—Good lack-a-day! quoth Deborah; wiping her hands upon her apron, What! has the gentleman a mind to go and hear our preaching then? Why, to be sure, we have some fine men come amongst us. I am a 'scriber; I can introduce the gentleman any night; I 'scribes three-pence a week. Ah! sir, we have such *soul-searching*★ teachers! such *ravishing*★ ministers! They come *so close to the point*;★ and does so *grapple*★ with the sinner! they probe his sores to the very quick; and *pour in such comfortable balsam*★ and, as Mr Twangdillo told us last night, though it may pain; yet, like physic in the bowels, it pains us to some purpose;★—and, to be sure, as he said, conversion follows conviction, as naturally★ as thread does the needle.—Whilst the good woman was thus retailing her panegyric, she leaned over the chair of a journeyman tailor, who was drinking a penny-pot, and breathed in his face such blasts, so strongly tinctured with gin and Scotch snuff, that the tailor cried out, Why, dame, thou savourest strongly of the *spirit* truly. I fancy thou art a little intoxicated to-night. *Tosticated*! *tosticated*! I scorn your words, cries Deborah. I defy the best man in Bath, to say black is my eye; or that I was ever *consarned* in liquor, since my name was Deborah. *Tosticated*! No; God help me! I have drunk nothing to-day, but a little tea for breakfast, and half a pint of ale at my dinner, except a little still'd water, that my mistress gave me in the morning to keep out the wind! and I am sure there is no harm in that: is there now, Mr Alcock.

Mr Alcock, which was my landlord's name, put a stop to the torrent of her eloquence, by inquiring again the place of their meeting. Which when he had learned, he sent his tapster to show Wildgoose the house, where he was directed to some of the most considerable of the fraternity.

★ All the expressions in one sermon, on redeeming time.

IV

WILDGOOSE ATTENDS A BATH MEETING

When Mr Wildgoose had made himself known, he was surprised to find that his fame had reached Bath before him: for during his residence at Gloucester, several passengers, who had come that road, hearing that a young man of some fortune was commenced Methodist Preacher, had brought the news to Bath, not without enlarging his fortune from four to seven or eight hundred pounds a year.

So that Wildgoose came with the prepossession in his favour, that he was the famous preacher, who made so much noise at Gloucester. The brethren, therefore, were not a little pleased with a convert of so much supposed consequence; and accordingly received him with great cordiality and distinction.

At their next meeting, Wildgoose attended as one of the audience; and both he and Tugwell were greatly delighted with their spiritual hymns, which Deborah had assured them were very melodious. But when the preacher, who that night was neither better nor worse than a journeyman stay-maker, began to display his eloquence, Mr Wildgoose, who had had something of an academical education, could hardly digest the homeliness of his language, or the meanness of his comparisons; and was a little mortified with the apprehension that he himself probably should make no better figure in the rostrum. But being encouraged by some of his friends, who reminded him of the salubrious effects of his preaching at Gloucester, and also of the heinous sin of 'wrapping up his talent in a napkin;' he was prevailed upon to promise, that he would exhibit himself the next evening: which accordingly he did; and displayed his oratory before a crowded audience, with no small approbation and applause.

V

HE HARANGUES ON THE PARADE

Wildgoose's fame began now to be trumpeted forth amongst all ranks of people: and, as he had naturally a good elocution, an harmonious voice, and an agreeable person, he was considered by the society at Bath, as a proper instrument to represent their doctrines to advantage, in an harangue to the company that resorted thither.

Accordingly it was given out, that a young gentleman from Oxford, who had renounced the ease and affluence of a good fortune for the sake of religion, was to preach on the grand parade the next morning.

The greatest charity we can bestow on people of fashion, at a public place, is the furnishing them something new to talk of. A new singer, a new philosopher, a new rope-dancer, or a new preacher, are objects equally amusing to the idle and indolent that frequent Bath. The company, therefore, adjourned from the pump-room to the parade, in eager expectation of seeing and hearing this youthful adventurer.

But Mr Nash, though he himself had greatly reformed and regulated the manners and behaviour of his subjects in the public room; yet, being orthodox in his tenets, and very well content with the present state of religion amongst them, he did not desire any reformation in that article. Having notice, therefore, of this intended preachment, he got ready his band of music, with the addition of two or three French-horns and kettle-drums: and as soon as the orator had exhibited his person on the parade, stretched forth his hand, and, like Paul in the Cartoon, was *in act to speak*, Nash gave the signal for the grand chorus of God save the king. The music struck up; and playing so loyal a piece of music, no one had the hardiness to interrupt them. Nay, a majority of the company were probably pleased with Nash's humour; and it being now breakfast time, the mob was easily dispersed.

Mr Wildgoose's friends, however, would not tamely give up a point of this importance; but took an opportunity that very evening, when the company were going to the rooms, to produce their champion on a sudden, and met with better success.

As Mr Nash had given out that Wildgoose was mad, he made use
of St Paul's words for his text; 'I am not mad, most noble Festus, but
do speak forth the words of soberness and truth.' Wildgoose did not
confine himself, however, to the words of the text; but, as he had
been instructed by the brethren, inveighed with great severity against
luxury in dress, cards, dancing, and all the fashionable diversions of the
place; and even against frequenting the rooms with the most innocent
intentions of recreation and amusement.

As soon as Wildgoose had finished his harangue, which was almost
of an hour's duration, a jolly footman, about the size of one of the
gentlemen in the horse-guards, bustling through the crowd, stretched
out a gigantic fist, and presented the orator a single card. Wildgoose,
who had not of late been much in genteel life,★ could not guess at
the meaning of this ceremony; but imagined it was some joke upon
his invective against *gaming*. The footman, however, with a surly air,
cried out, Read it friend! read it; my lady desires to see you at her
lodgings here on the parade. Wildgoose, then, perusing his billet, read
as follows:

A lady, who is disgusted with the world, desires half an hour's
conversation with Mr Wildgoose, as soon as he is at leisure.

Wildgoose, after a short pause, told the footman he would wait on
the lady immediately. So, as soon as he had given a short answer to
two people, one a fan-painter, the other a butterfly-catcher, who had
consulted him about the lawfulness of their several professions, he
followed the footman to his lady's place of abode.

★ Message Cards had been lately introduced.

VI

A DIGRESSION ON MESSAGE-CARDS

There are few customs generally prevailing in the world, how absurd
soever they may appear, which had not some real propriety or
convenience for their original; but when the fashion is once established
amongst the polite, it descends of course amongst the vulgar; who
blindly imitate it, as such, without any regard to its primitive institution.
Thus, for instance, the conveying messages by a card, was introduced
into the fashionable world, as the readiest expedient against the blunders
and stupidity of ignorant servants and it must be confessed, that, in
some characters and, on some occasions, this practice has not only no
impropriety, but carries with it a genteel air of ease and negligence; and
really saves a great deal of unnecessary trouble, both to the person that
sends, and him that receives the message.

The man of pleasure who transacts his most important concerns in a
coffee-house or a tavern; or the modern lady, the whole sphere of whose
existence is at a drawing-room, can never be supposed without a card
in readiness on every emergency; and, therefore, parties at whist can no
way be more aptly formed, nor messages of compliment more elegantly
conveyed, than by these diminutive tablets, which are generally suited to
the subject, to the genius, and laconic style of the parties concerned.

But, on the other hand, what can be more absurd than this practice
in more serious characters, and on occasions of more solemnity? How
remote from probability is it, that a grave divine, who is continually
inveighing against the vices and follies of the age, should have a pack
of soiled cards in his pocket, ready for his engagements of business or
pleasure? or that a venerable counsellor, who is continually surrounded
with briefs, leases, or acts of parliament, should prefer a trifling card
in transacting business with his client, before a shred of parchment,
or even a scrap of common paper; and I should have kicked my tailor
the other day, for minuting down the dimensions of my sleeves and
pocket-holes upon a card—if I had not luckily recollected that his last
bill was unpaid.

Neither are message-cards proper on *all occasions*, any more than in persons of all characters or professions. It is a known impropriety in a French marquis, who, coming to pay his devotions at the shrine of a saint, whilst his image was gone to the silver-smith to be repaired, left a card for his godship, to acquaint him with his intended visit: and though a certain lady, near St James's, very innocently invited a woman of quality to her rout, by a *whisper* at the communion table; yet, in my humble opinion, she could not so decently have slipped a *card* into her ladyship's hand at so sacred a place as the altar.

Granting, however, the general and unlimited use of this paste-board correspondence, there is yet a propriety to be observed, and many absurdities to be avoided, in the choice of the cards, according to the persons addressed, or the occasions on which we address them.

It is too obvious a hint, and I suppose too trite a piece of adulation to a fine woman, to convey our compliments to her on the queen of hearts: as, on the contrary, it would have been an affront to a late East India governor,★ though he laboured under so groundless a slander, to have inquired after his health by sending him the knave of diamonds. The deuce, or two of clubs, I think, should be appropriated to challenges and duels: and the black aces should be entirely *discarded* in our correspondence with ladies of character; as the nines and tens are at ombre or quadrille.† But these hints are left to be improved by the facetious Mr ——.

My intention was chiefly to observe, that the disgusted lady, mentioned in the last chapter, should have made use of paper with black edges, in a message to Mr Wildgoose, rather than a profane card, which he could not but consider as a diabolical invention, and consequently as intended for an affront to so pious a man. However, he obeyed the summons, as has been related, and attended the lady in her own apartment.

★ This seems to allude to some piece of modern history now forgotten.

† A set of blank cards have since been invented, by which the above absurdities may be avoided.

VII
Tête à Tête

Mr Wildgoose was introduced by the footman into a handsome dining-room, elegantly furnished. The lady received him in a genteel dishabille, sitting, or rather leaning, on a rich sofa, in such a posture as necessarily displayed a handsome foot, somewhat above the instep. She was an agreeable woman, about six and twenty; and though her face was not so exquisitely beautiful as it seemed to have been in her earlier days, yet, being shaded by a chip hat, and receiving a gloss from a white satin nightgown in which she was dressed, she made upon the whole no unpalatable figure.

I would not insinuate, that she had any intention to captivate our hero: yet thus much I believe is certain, that a woman who has once been handsome, and experienced the power of her charms, seldom lays aside the hopes of making conquests, but contracts an habitual fondness for admiration, and would be disappointed in not receiving that incense, even from a man whom she despised.

Mr Wildgoose, however, was at present no despicable object. He was now in his twenty-fifth year. He was well made, and had an agreeable countenance, which his late abstemious way of life had improved, by giving quite a delicacy to his complexion. His hair was of a dark brown; and though it had not received the fashionable frizure, it was grown thick enough to shade his face, and long enough to curl; and his dress, though plain, was tolerably neat and becoming.

In short, though Mrs Booby (which was the name of this lady) really fancied she had occasion for some ghostly advice; yet probably she might not have thought of this ceremony, if she had not liked the person of her casuit; whom she viewed, as he was declaiming, from the window of her apartment.

After bowing to Mr Wildgoose, and desiring him to sit down, she pulled out her fan, and having played it a little in a negligent manner, said, she should make no apology for giving this trouble, as she was convinced, from his character, he would not refuse his advice to any one in affliction.

Wildgoose bowed, and made a proper speech upon the occasion, and she proceeded.

In short, sir, says she, I am sick of the world. But, that you may be a better judge of my situation, I will beg leave to trouble you with a short history of my past life, which will let you into the nature of my present uneasiness.

Wildgoose expressed his earnest desire to give her some spiritual consolation; and Mrs Booby thus began.

VIII

Mrs Booby's story

When I was about nineteen, I came with my mother for the first time to Bath; and whether there was a scarcity of beauty there that season, or whether in my bloom I might not be reckoned tolerably handsome, I don't know. Here Wildgoose bowed again; and, muttering a complaisant speech, Mrs Booby blushed, and went on. Well, sir, as I was going to say, I found myself in great vogue; much caressed by the gentlemen, and in possession of a great number of admirers. Amongst the rest there was a very sober youth, of a good person and a genteel fortune, that was particular in his attachment to me; and, as my mother seemed to have no objection, I encouraged his addresses; and I own he had made some progress towards gaining my affections. But, after about a month's intimate correspondence with Mr Clayton (which was this young man's name), application was made to my old lady by another gentleman, of a much larger fortune, but much older than myself; who offered me a settlement of six hundred pounds a year, and, if required, two hundred pounds a year for what is called pin-money.

My mother was charmed with this proposal, and hoped I would not hesitate a moment in prefering so advantageous an offer to that of the young fellow who had been dangling after me for some time.

I was startled at this speech, and told her I should certainly pay a proper deference to her opinion in an affair of that importance; but, madam, says

I, you know I have encouraged Mr Clayton's addresses, and cannot, in honour, listen to any other proposals. In honour, cries she, a fiddlestick! well, continues she, you may do as you please, I shall not force your inclinations; but whether you accept of Mr Booby's offer or not, I shall insist upon your not admitting that fellow's visits (meaning Mr Clayton's) any more.

This stern prohibition, though it obliged me to alter my external behaviour, could make no alteration in my affection for Mr Clayton. I was denied to him, indeed, the next time he came; but we contrived two or three short interviews at the rooms; and I told him, that although I could not think of disobeying my mother's express commands, I would vow eternal constancy to him; and promise faithfully never to give my hand, much less my heart, to any other.

IX

CONTINUATION OF MRS BOOBY'S STORY

Mr Clayton was now obliged, by some business of consequence, to leave Bath for some time, and was detained near two months in the country. We contrived, however, to carry on a correspondence by letters, in which he lamented how much he suffered by this separation, and how impossible it was for him ever to be happy in my absence. I answered his letters at first with more fondness, perhaps, than it was prudent, or even decent, for any young woman to express, whatever her real sentiments may be; and made the most romantic declarations of preferring retirement and a competence with the person I loved, to the most splendid circumstances with one whom I detested.

The most ardent love, however, may grow cool, by a long separation from its object; for, though a short absence increases, too long a one frequently extinguishes a passion. In short, I am convinced that time and a variety of amusements, must weaken the force even of the sincerest affection.

As my mamma, without mentioning a word of Mr Booby's proposals, was continually representing to my fancy the dazzling images of a splendid equipage, a numerous attendance, and the deference and respect which are usually paid to wealth and affluence; and the like topics which those parents who prefer the grandeur of alliance to the happiness of their children are fond of inculcating; I must own my weakness, and confess, that I began to feel my excessive tenderness for the absent Clayton gradually to wear off; and, in short, I determined, at length, to find out some pretence for breaking off all correspondence with him.

The engagements of lovers are like treaties between princes. The party that is desirous of coming to a rupture is never at a loss for a pretence. In one of his letters, poor Clayton, out of his great fondness, perhaps, had expressed his concern, as naturally he might, lest the constant solicitations to which every woman, who is not absolutely ugly, is exposed in this place, might prove prejudicial to his love, and had even hinted how happy it would make him, if I would not appear in public, more than was necessary to oblige my mamma; who, he knew, was more fond of the rooms, at that time, than I myself was.

This modest request, the consequence probably of the most tender regard, furnished me with the opportunity, which I wanted, of breaking with Clayton. I told him, in my answer, that a woman could never be happy with a man of his suspicious temper; and, if I was to be abridged of the most innocent amusements by a person who could claim not the least right to that power, what must I expect from the authority of a husband of so jealous a disposition? In short, I added, as this engagement was entirely inconsistent with the obedience due to a parent, and the correspondence carried on in defiance of my mother's express prohibition, I desired the affair might proceed no further.

Instead of answering this letter, which greatly alarmed him, Mr Clayton came post to Bath; the news of which, I must confess, staggered my resolution and meeting him the next day by accident, at the house where, by agreement, our letters had been left, I found all my fondness revive at the sight of him; and, instead of exchanging our letters (which, after the receipt of so unaccountable a one from me, he said was the utmost of his expectation), we seemed to have established our correspondence upon a more lasting foundation than ever.

After two or three clandestine interviews, Mr Clayton was again obliged to leave Bath, and we again renewed our literary correspondence. But oh! how little do we know our own hearts! Whether the continual incense of flattery, which I have received from a number of admirers, revived my ambition, or whether mere absence weaned my affections from their object, I began, a second time, to feel a great indifference in regard to Mr Clayton. In short, sir, not to trouble you with too tedious a detail of particulars, I again found a pretence for dropping all farther intercourse with him: and Clayton himself, instead of coming again in person (or, perhaps, thinking me now beneath his regard), only wrote me a defence of his conduct. Such, at least, I guessed to be the contents of his letter; for, with unparalleled insolence, I sent it back unopened. And thus ended our connection.

X

MRS BOOBY'S STORY CONCLUDED. WILDGOOSE'S OPINION OF THE MARRIAGE CONTRACT AND DESCRIPTION OF A BATH LIFE

My mother, perceiving the gloom which appeared in my countenance on Mr Clayton's departure begin now to wear off, and my usual cheerfulness return, gave Mr Booby a hint to renew his addresses. These, at first, I again rejected with great indignation. But, when I perceived, that although my mamma declared against forcing my inclinations, yet that her constant frowns, and perhaps her lasting displeasure, and all the negative discouragements in her power, would be the consequence of my refusal, I began to listen to Mr Booby's proposals: and, after stipulating for a decent time to consider of it, and insisting upon his first offer of two hundred pounds a year, pin-money, I condescended to accept his terms: and in short, our persons were joined together in wedlock, though two such *hearts* could never be united.

Mr Booby, indeed, was not disagreeable in his appearance: and though he was near twenty years older than me; yet, by his manner of dress, in a public place, he concealed what little depredation time had made on his person. But when we had been married near three years, without the consequence which he expected from our union (for he was very desirous of an heir to his estate), he began to lay aside the very desire of pleasing me. And, as he became a sloven, I began to neglect my dress; so that, from being merely indifferent, we soon became thoroughly disagreeable to each other. Every trifle was now made matter of dispute; and we frequently quarrelled *one day*, about what had been the subject of our dispute the day before.

But what rendered Mr Booby completely odious to me, was the high opinion he had conceived of the superiority of his sex; and the arbitrary notions he entertained of the authority of the husband over us poor domestic animals, called wives. In short, Mr Wildgoose, this was a constant subject of debate, and, in fine, the real cause of our separation.

Is Mr Booby then alive? and do you live separate from him?—Why, sir, you shall hear. It was a thing utterly unavoidable; and nothing but an absolute necessity should have forced me to take so imprudent a step. I was driven to it by the most brutal behaviour, as you shall hear.

Mr Booby's family-seat is in the north of England; but, being so remote from Bath (which waters were thought necessary for his health), and a bad sporting country, which is his whole delight, he had taken a hunting seat near the Wiltshire Downs; whither I was banished soon after our marriage: or rather where I was imprisoned, and confined to the conversation of dogs and horses; or, what is worse, mere country 'squires, parsons, and fox-hunters: for there was not above one conversible neighbour within ten miles of us; and that family we rarely saw above once in a quarter.

One day, when Mr Booby returned from hunting, he brought home with him, according to custom, the parson of the parish, and a neighbouring attorney; though he knew that I had invited the only genteel family, which (as I told you) we had in the neighbourhood, to spend the evening with me. As those politer meetings were but rarely indulged me, I usually made a handsome supper; and as our house was a mere box, though I had a dining room to receive my company in on those occasions, yet we were always obliged to sup in the common parlour. As soon, therefore, as we had dined, I desired Mr Booby and his rustic companions to adjourn into a little smoking-room, to take their pipes and their bottles; which he absolutely refused. Upon my pleading a right to the parlour, to entertain my company in, he insisted upon his prerogative of being master in his own house. In short, after many aggravations, I proceeded so far as to tell him, I would rather live in a cottage, than with such a brute as he was; to which he replied, that he would sooner live in a wind-mill, than with such a vixen as I was; and, that he never desired to see my face again. Upon which I threw my hoop-ring in his face; and, having dispatched a card to put off my company, ordered the chariot, and drove immediately to Bath: where I have lived ever since last October.

Now, sir, I should be glad of your opinion whether I have done any thing inconsistent with my duty, or contrary to my marriage-vow, upon this occasion. For you must observe, Mr Wildgoose, nothing but the most *brutal usage* could have forced me to take this step; and you see I was under an *absolute necessity* of acting as I have done. You must mind that, Mr Wildgoose: and then, I am sure, you must pass sentence in my favour, and acquit me of any thing wrong in this affair.

Wildgoose was at first struck dumb with astonishment, and could not tell what answer to make; but, after recovering a little from his confusion, Madam, says he, as you ask my opinion, I am persuaded you expect me to give it you with the utmost sincerity; and my conscience will not permit me to speak what I do not really think: and a good Christian should rather run the risque of appearing unpolite than insincere.

I would by no means, madam, cast the blame entirely upon you; for I think there was no probability that such an alliance as you have described could be productive of any lasting felicity, as it was not founded on a mutual affection; nor, I am afraid, entered into on a religious principle, or in the fear of God. Your affections, you own, were pre-engaged, or at least, having been disappointed in their first object, could not exert their natural force on a second.

Then, I am afraid, madam, you have not sufficiently considered your obligation to *obey* the person to whom you have, by the marriage contract, given up, in some measure, your natural freedom.—Given up my *freedom*! cries Mrs Booby; I'd sooner resign my life!—Give me leave, madam, to explain myself, says Wildgoose. I do not speak of this obligation as founded on the mere words of the marriage ceremony (for all human ordinances are vain and frivolous); but as evidently enjoined by the holy Scripture, and to be deduced from that superiority which nature seems to have given the man over the more delicate sex.

Ay, that's so like my husband now! cries Mrs Booby, turning red, and playing her fan with some vivacity; but you must excuse me, sir, if I cannot allow the *superiority* you plead for.—Well, madam, replies Mr Wildgoose, I will not enter into the dispute about the natural equality of the sexes, which has of late been brought frequently upon the carpet, though the *novelty* of the ladies' claim is, I think, a strong presumption in our favour. But be that as it will, I am clearly of opinion, that in domestic as well as civil government, to prevent continual dissensions and struggles for superiority, there must somewhere be lodged a *dernier resort*, an *arbitrary,* or, to use a softer name, a *sovereign* power: and I am certain that religion, as well as reason, has placed this power in the husband.—Very well, says Mrs Booby, with a contemptuous sneer.—For a proper use of this power, however, continues Wildgoose, the husband is accountable both to the laws of God and of man: and I am convinced, madam, if you could have acknowledged this superior authority in Mr Booby, and had thought it your duty to submit in such trifles as that which was the immediate cause of your separation, you would have been much happier than by your own account you now are. For I believe, as depraved as our nature is, there is no man so brutish, that could bear to tyrannise over a poor helpless creature, who, instead of displaying that masculine ferocity which is too common in the sex, acknowledged her entire dependence upon him for support and protection.—

Support and *protection*, indeed! exclaims Mrs Booby, my pin-money will *support* me, and I scorn his *protection*!—Give me leave, madam, to conclude my argument, says Wildgoose. The very circumstance which you mention has, I am afraid, contributed not a little to bring on that separation which you seem now to repent of: I mean that

monstrous article of modern refinement called pin-money: which, I
perceive, is always uppermost in your thoughts. The allowing a woman
a maintenance, independent of her husband, is not only destroying
that mutual affection which arises from a sense of their interest being
inseparably united, but is also a continual temptation to a woman to fly
out on the slightest dispute; and to despise the authority of a husband,
without whose assistance or support she has it in her power to live in
affluence and splendour. Separate purses between man and wife are as
unnatural as separate beds; which, indeed, one often hears of amongst
people of fashion, where there is no more difficulty in making up *two*
beds than one. But the surest way of preventing such a separation is to
have but one bed to go to; which is most commonly the case with the
happier couples in lower life.

In short, madam, I am inclined to think, the great facility which you
found in exchanging the solitude you complain of, for the gaieties and
pleasures of Bath, was a principal motive of your deserting Mr Booby,
and precipitating yourself into this misfortune; which rash conduct, I
find, now sits so heavy upon your conscience.

Indeed, sir, replied Mrs Booby, starting from a kind of reverie, you
are vastly mistaken. I am more sick of a public place, if possible, than
of my own home; whither, indeed, I have lately had some thoughts of
returning, as I have received several overtures from Mr Booby to that
purpose. The *pleasures* of *Bath*, indeed! No; I detest the place, and could
wish to be banished from it for ever! It is a tedious circle of unmeaning
hurry, anxiety, and fatigue; of fancied enjoyments, and real chagrins:—
to-day one is in vogue, the Lord knows why; to-morrow deserted, and
equally without reason. In the former case one is pestered and distracted
with variety of engagements; in the latter, left a prey to melancholy, and
the disagreeable reflections on the slights we meet with. Such, indeed, is
the spirit of public places. Every one is aspiring after the company of his
superiors, while he despises his equals, and sacrifices the real enjoyment
of friendly conversation to the foolish ambition of being seen in what
is called *good company*. In short, nothing can be more trifling than the
life of a lady, nor more insipid than that of a gentleman, at Bath: the
one is a constant series of flirting and gadding about; the other of

sauntering from place to place, without any scheme or pursuit. Scandal or fashions engross the conversation of the former; the news of the day, the price of fish, the history of the preceding night at the tavern, or savoury anticipations of their next debauch, furnish out the morning entertainment of the latter.

Well, madam, I am glad to hear you speak with so much disgust of this scene of dissipation, which, by all accounts it highly deserves; and I hope it is a good symptom of the new birth. If you are once properly sensible of your own misery, you will soon be glad to take refuge, where only true joys are to be found.

Oh, sir, you do not know half the follies and impertinences of this place. There are some, indeed, who appear more seriously employed, and who pore whole mornings over a game at whist, with the attention and solemnity of mathematicians or privy-counsellors. But one might as well affect tranquillity in a storm or a whirlwind, as enjoyment at a gaming-table. It is exposing oneself continually to the caprice and sport of fortune, and to every boisterous, unsociable, and selfish passion. For my part, though I confess I have been fond of cards, yet they are now my utter aversion; I renounce them for ever and, if I know my own mind, am determined never to touch a card again as long as I live.

Whilst Mrs Booby was making this declaration, and Wildgoose highly applauding her resolution, the footman opened the door, and announced the arrival of Lady Fanny Flurry, who rushed in, tossing her hoop three yards before her. But, seeing so unfashionable a figure as Wildgoose, she started back, and taking him for a shoe-maker, or something in that style, she cried out, Oh! Booby, you are engaged, I see. But Mrs Booby winking upon her, and assuring her she was not; Well, my dear Booby, says Lady Fanny, I only came to bespeak you for a party at quadrille to-night, and shall depend upon your company at the rooms.—Oh! Lady Fanny! name it not, cries Mrs Booby; I have just made a *firm* resolution never to touch another card—after the bad run I had last night. But—your *la'ship* is so obliging there's *no* resisting you— yet, I hate the rooms; and positively I cannot be of your party *there*.— Oh, ho! my dear, replies her ladyship, have you betrayed yourself? What! you are piqued, then, at not being invited to poor Clayton's public breakfast this morning? Come, come! you had the refusal of him; and how can you blame the creature for seeking consolation elsewhere? and really, thirty thousand pounds with a pretty woman, is no unpromising prospect of consolation.

And now the secret was out. The true cause of Mrs Booby's disgust with the world, and of her desiring this conference with a quack preacher, was the arrival of her former lover, Mr Clayton, who, a few years after she had sacrificed him, either to her Mother's importunity or to her own ambition, had married a very agreeable heiress, with thirty thousand pounds, whom he had now, for the first time, brought to Bath, where she made a very brilliant appearance: and Mrs Booby, not having been particularly invited to a public breakfast which Mr Clayton gave that morning; this slight, together with a bad run at cards, had made her *sick of the world*; and to *amuse* herself chiefly, she had had recourse to this spiritual knight-errant. However, she was so well pleased with our hero's company (for, where the peculiarities of his religious system were not concerned, Wildgoose was really very agreeable,) that, notwithstanding his offer to take his leave, Mrs Booby insisted upon his company to tea and coffee, which now made its appearance.

XI

A SCENE IN GENTEEL LIFE.
ENTER MRS BARDOLPH, MISS TRUFLE,
AND MR ROUVILL. THEIR CHARACTERS

The most material difference between keeping good company and bad is, hearing the same things said before a dozen wax lights at the court end of the town, or before a couple of mould candles in the city. This, or something to the same purpose, was remarked by a celebrated genius of the last age. But I am inclined to think, that the honest citizens of our times would suffer by such a comparison; for in that serious part of the metropolis, there are still some remains of the British plainness of speech and manliness of conversation. There, business, politics, news, history, or even religion, are, in their turn, sometimes admitted as interesting subjects of discourse or argumentation. But amongst those choice spirits who have monopolized and appropriated to themselves the style and title of *good company*, one rarely hears any other topics introduced than annals of the whist-table, or anecdotes of the turf, operas, routs, and masquerades; the most trifling relations of the most trifling transactions: and, as Lord Shaftesbury observes of his times, 'If any thing of learning is introduced, it is pedantry; if any thing of morality, it is called preaching.'

In these reflections, however, the good company now introduced is not particularly concerned.

Mrs Booby not having appeared in public that day, was visited by most of the idle and impertinent part of her acquaintance. Amongst the rest there now arrived those two amiable persons, Mrs Bardolph and Mr Rouvill, or (as he was aptly called) Beau Rueful, who were immediately followed by the well-known Miss Trufle,★ with a black spaniel in her arms, and a squirrel in her pocket.

Mrs Bardolph was the wife of a very worthy man; which circumstance, together with the good table which she kept, and her readiness to make one at a party of quadrille, introduced her into a numerous acquaintance amongst people of fashion; of which privilege, however, she made no other use, than that of passing away the time less tediously; of dining and supping agreeably, and of transmitting the insipid occurrences of one family into that of another, the particulars of which her memory enabled her to retain longer than people of more reflection; so that she was a living chronicle of every incident, good, bad, or indifferent, that had befallen her acquaintance for twenty years together.

Of much the same importance was the character of Miss Trufle. She was a woman of family; but had neither fortune, beauty, wit, nor even good-nature to recommend her. Indeed, her person was not only despicably small, but deformed likewise; her understanding of the same dimensions, and her temper as deformed as her person. Yet, under

---

★ Twenty years ago.

all these disadvantages, her rank, and the good company she always appeared in, might haply have captivated some country esquire, who would have thought himself honoured by the alliance, but for that eternal bane to every thing that is amiable, her affectation.

Miss Trufle had two or three sisters who were admired; and from two or three occasional compliments which she had met with on their account, she flattered herself, in downright contradiction to her looking-glass, that she herself had some pretensions to the family features. In consequence of this she nodded her head, was saucy, and said rude things to one's face, and gave herself all the coquettish airs of a celebrated toast; the natural result of which was, that, having lived a virgin to the age of thirty, and now despaired of becoming a mistress of any other sort of family, she had settled her affections on squirrels, monkeys, and lap-dogs, with which, for want of other gallants, she was constantly attended; though they frequently supplied the wags with personal comparisons, not much to Miss Trufle's advantage.

Mr Rouvill, or Beau Rueful, was a young fellow, who, by a strange concurrence of lucky circumstances, with the help of a convenient assurance, and a laced coat, had wriggled himself into tolerable company; and, what is more strange, by boldly criticising every new pamphlet, laughing at every thing serious, and by putting modest people out of countenance, was, by some people esteemed a formidable wit. Nay, what is most strange of all, his profuse expenses having almost dissipated a genteel fortune left him by a relation, he was now commenced fortune-hunter, without any kind of merit, either of person, which corresponded with his nickname, *Rueful*, or of understanding, which was of the lowest standard; or even of birth, which was very mean, he being the son of a grocer in the ancient city of Coventry.

As straws and feathers attract each other on the surface of the water, these three worthy persons, as if linked together by a mutual sympathy, came in a train to Mrs Booby's apartment.

Rueful bowed to Mrs Booby and to Lady Fanny; nodded to Mrs Bardolph, and patted Miss Trufle upon her bare shoulders; but took no more notice of Wildgoose than of the footman that waited, or of the Dutch mastiff, which lay sleeping on a rug in the corner of the room.

Being seated, however, he lolled over the settee, and with the corner of his hat held to his face, asked Mrs Booby, in an audible whisper, who, the devil, she had got there? Mrs Bardolph's curiosity likewise being raised, asked the same question in the same tone, but concealing her face with her fan. Miss Trufle stared in Wildgoose's face; burst into a laugh; then turning to Rueful, asked him, why he did not wear his own hair, which, she heard, was coming much into fashion.

In answer to Rueful's and Mrs Bardolph's questions, Mrs Booby said aloud, that the gentleman was Mr Wildgoose; and she hoped would make them all as good Christians as he was himself. On hearing Wildgoose's name, Mrs Bardolph asked, if he was any relation to the Wildgooses of Wiltshire? Wildgooses of Wiltshire! says Mrs Booby, I know no such family.—What! not Miss Wildgoose, that ran away with her father's butler?——Lord! you mean Miss Gosling.—Bless me! says Mrs Bardolph, so I do: but I am the worst person in the world to remember *names*, (which, however, was no inconsiderable part of her erudition.) Well, Wildgoose or Gosling, they are not much unlike.—No, says Rueful, I suppose they are of the same family, and bear the same arms—a grey goose, *cankant*, *regardant*. Rueful's blazonry was unintelligible to all but himself, and consequently received no applause, but from an affected laugh of his own.

Wildgoose had no very pleasant time of it, whilst the affair of his name and family was adjusting. But his attention was diverted from this conversation by the footman's treading on his toe, as he was handing the coffee to him. Wildgoose begged Mr John's pardon for putting his foot in the way; and moved his chair with no small trepidation. But Mr John, far from being mollified by his submissive behaviour, owed him another good turn; and, in handing his tea to him, did it with so scornful an air, that it flashed plentifully over Wildgoose's plush breeches. Mrs Booby, however, observed the insolence of her servant, and very properly reprimanded him for it; upon which Mr John vouchsafed to wait with a little more dexterity.

Nothing would have kept Lady Fanny so long silent, but the sublime contempt which she had conceived of her company. She had been trifling with her spoon, and cooling her tea with an absent air; and now drank half a dish, emptied the rest into the slop-bason; then, starting up, Lord! says she, what am I about? I am engaged to tea at the rooms this evening; and have a myriad of visits to make before I go thither.—Sir, says she to the footman, please to order my chair.—Then, pulling on her pocket-book, let me see, says she, Lady Loiter, old Lady Shockingphiz, Sir Arthur Lurch; yes, our whist-parties are full for Thursday, Friday, and Saturday evenings. But on Sunday night, Booby, we will expect you for a party at quadrille. Here Wildgoose erected his eyebrows, and fetched a deep sigh, or rather groaned in spirit. But Lady Fanny correcting herself, Bless me! cries she, what do I talk of Sunday? I forget that I am at Bath. That superannuated old creature, Nash, will not let us play on Sunday night—in public. Well, tonight, however, at eight o'clock, I shall depend upon you. Then rising up, and tossing her hoop over Wildgoose's head as she rushed by him, she took her leave with, *Adieu! ma chere Booby; je vous attends, tout à l'heure!*

XII

VARIOUS CHIT-CHAT

After Lady Fanny was gone, Mrs Booby, with no other view than to give Mr Wildgoose an opportunity of saying something, asked him what his opinion was of frequenting the Rooms at Bath, or other public places? Wildgoose replied, that he had had no opportunity of forming any opinion upon that head, from his own experience. But, madam, continues he, as, by all accounts, the chief intent of those assemblies is either gaming, intriguing, or unmeaning dissipation; in short, to prevent our being left a prey to our own thoughts, and seeing our own misery and corruption, I cannot think it advisable, even for people with the best intentions, to countenance, by their example, meetings of this kind.

Well, sir, says Rueful, you may preach as long as you please, but I believe you will hardly prevail upon people of fashion to give up so agreeable an amusement.

Why, sir, replies Wildgoose, from the description which Mrs Booby has just now been giving me of a Bath life, I am so far from thinking it even agreeable, that it appears to me a mere scene of vanity and folly. Pray, madam, continues Wildgoose, did you ever read the *Pilgrim's Progress.*—Ha! ha! ha! cries Rueful, in a horse laugh; I believe we may all have read that, and *Jack the Giant-killer* too, in the nursery.—Well, sir, you may laugh; I now only mention that original author upon a ludicrous occasion, as I think his account of Vanity Fair, seems to be no bad description of the insipid intercourse (to say no worse of it) that usually passes between the thoughtless creatures, at most of those public assemblies.

Well, says Rueful, granting it to be as *insipid* as you please, yet wherever people of distinction agree to assemble, those that would not be out of the world must follow them. Even those that set up for reformers of mankind must frequent those assemblies, if they would do any good amongst them. I will answer for it, St Paul himself, who *became all things to all men*, if he had come to Bath, would have gone to the Rooms; and St Luke, like other physicians, would have frequented the coffee-house.—Very fine! says Miss Trufle, and I suppose you think the four evangelists would have made a party at quadrille! You will make a fine parson, indeed!

Wildgoose was struck with horror at this profane raillery; but Mrs Bardolph, by way of changing the subject, asked Mrs Booby, if she had heard how old Lady Shockingphiz was mortified at the ball last night, or rather at the Pump-room this morning?—No, says Mrs Booby, I have not had a soul come near me to-day, except the present company and Lady Fanny.—Why, says Mrs Bardolph, you know her ladyship's family pride.—Yes, says Mrs Booby; as she has no merit of her own to plead, her ladyship is forced to subsist upon the family fund, and that is pretty well exhausted. She has only one daughter, I think, to keep up the honour of it.—Well, it was for that daughter, says Mrs Bardolph, that she desired Nash to get a partner; who recommended a very genteel young man, and very well dressed; and miss jigged it down, the whole evening, with great alacrity and satisfaction: but this morning, at the Pump-room, the busy Mrs Marrall came, out of breath, to Lady Shockingphiz, and told her, that the young man her daughter danced with was a linen-draper in Cheapside. Indeed! says her ladyship: what does that saucy fellow, Nash, mean by using me thus? and away she trudges, to reprimand him for it. Mr Nash, after some inquiries into the affair, told her ladyship, that, to be sure, the gentleman did deal in linen, but that it was in the *wholesale* way; and that he never *cut* a piece of cloth in his life—Are you sure of that? cries her ladyship: Are you sure he never *cut*, Mr Nash? If the gentleman never cut, why certainly there is no such great matter in it.

Thus her ladyship ran on, till the whole company burst into a loud laugh, both at her ladyship's ridiculous pride, and at the mortification it had deservedly met with.

Well, says Rueful, as Mrs Bardolph has told you how Lady Shockingphiz was mortified this morning, I will tell you how Lord —— was terrified yesterday in the afternoon.

An honest tradesman, who has a handsome wife, was busy in his shop, which is much frequented by the company some parts of the day; but having occasion to go up into his bed-chamber, to his bureau, he saw a very fine *point d'Espagne* laced hat lying upon his wife's toilette; and, upon casting his eye round the room, he espied a man's foot, with a fine stone buckle, peep out from under the bed-curtain; behind which Lord ——, who lodged in the house, was endeavouring to conceal himself. From the confusion his lordship was in, and from several other circumstances, the honest tradesman had now no doubt that an amorous correspondence was carrying on between his lordship and his wife; a glimpse of whom he had just seen, as she slipped down the back stairs, from a closet of communication.

The tradesman, though a man of a tame disposition and mitigated resentment, yet, upon such an occasion, burst forth into a most vehement rage, venting his indignation in a menacing tone, and in the following manner:

My lord! as sure as you are now alive, if ever I catch you in my bed-chamber again, with my wife,—depend upon it, as sure as I have a head upon my body, I will—I will—certainly—throw your laced hat out of the window!

His lordship, though not greatly dismayed at this terrible denunciation, yet determined, for the future, to prosecute his intrigue with greater precaution.

XIII

STORY OF CALOMEL AND LADY RIOT

Mrs Booby now observed that Lady Fanny had looked very grave to-day; one would think, says she, her ladyship had met with some mortification. Rueful remarked that people of rank were always so in mixed company; though, for my part, continues he, I have always found persons of quality the most affable creatures in the world. I remember the first time I spent a week at Lord Grandison's, there was Sir Peter Pierpoint, Jack North, and half a dozen more of us: and I remember I was as free with the young peer the first hour, as I am at this day.—Who suspects you of any *mauvaise honte*, or bashfulness? says Miss Trufle.—I shall never forget a droll accident that happened there, continues Rueful, undaunted by Miss Trufle's hint.—His lordship had a Swiss servant, who pretended to have discovered a new japan, or liquid blacking; and the fellow must needs make the experiment upon our shoes. But, would you believe it? the composition, whatever it was, had contracted the pores of the leather to such a degree, that the next morning we all came hobbling into the room, like so many old gouty fellows.—Lord Grandison was so diverted with the scene, that I thought his lordship would have split his *diaphragm* with laughing.—Why, this was an incident worth recording, truly, says Mrs Booby.

O! now you talk of people of quality, cries Mrs Bardolph, there is Lady Sherwood wants much to have some conversation with this gentleman. She has heard a great character of his piety, and I believe her ladyship is well inclined towards the Methodists: and I can take upon me to assure you, sir, that she would be very glad if you would call on her at her lodgings. Wildgoose replied, he should be very happy in contributing to the conversion of the lowest of his fellow-creatures; and should certainly esteem it an honour to wait on her ladyship, if she desired it.

But here Rueful again interposed, by observing, that persons of distinction often diverted themselves, at Bath, with odd creatures; and that people who did not know the world might easily be drawn in, to make themselves thoroughly ridiculous. Did you never hear how Lady Riot served poor Calomel, an eminent apothecary of this place? Upon the company's answering in the negative, I will tell it you, says Rueful.

Mr Calomel is a very honest man, and an experienced apothecary; but highly absurd in his conversation and manner of address. Lady Riot, who is a woman of humour, has often detained him at her lodgings for her amusement, when his patients wanted his lenient hand for more salutary applications. Calomel was so elated by this distinction, that though he was turned of fifty, he entertained some faint suspicions that his person, as well as his conversation, might have pleased Lady Riot.

Having, therefore, some business in London, last winter, he took it into his head to *call upon* her ladyship, at her house in town, and not finding her at home, he left her ladyship a card, with 'Mr Calomel's compliments to Lady Riot; lets her ladyship know, that he did himself the honour to wait on her ladyship; and that he is to be spoken with at the White Bear, in Piccadilly.'

When her ladyship came home to dinner, at five o'clock, she was highly diverted with Calomel's style of politeness; and, it being her assembly night, she produced his card before the whole company, who, being let into the character of Calomel, voted to send for *him* thither; and *bets* were laid, *pro* and *con*—come or not come—for fifty guineas.

But Lady Riot, to make sure of her point, ordered her coach, and slipping slily out of the room, took Lady Rattle with her, drove to the White Bear, and inquired for Mr Calomel. Calomel being a sober man, and having a *reverend regard* to his health, had retired to his bed-chamber, got into his night-gown and slippers, tied his night cap under his chin, and was just going to his repose, when the drawer brought up the message. Calomel at first said, he supposed they were some naughty women of the town, and he would have nothing to say to them. But upon the drawer's assuring him it was some lady of quality in her own carriage, with a couple of flambeaux, Calomel came down to the door in his dishabille, to reconnoitre them. The moment Lady Riot beheld him, she cries out, My dear Calomel, how do you do? Come, I must have some chat with you: do not stand in the street in your night-cap; step into the coach a moment. Which, having done, the footman, as he had been instructed, clapped to the door: the coach drove immediately to her ladyship's house; where Calomel was produced before thirty card tables, in his night-cap and slippers.

The brilliancy of the assembly, and the wax-lights, a little disconcerted poor Calomel at first; but his vanity soon prevailed over his bashfulness: he mixed with the society, and greatly diverted them with his absurd buffooneries.

To complete the farce, the butler had his cue to mix a soporific with whatever he gave him to drink: and upon Calomel's desiring some Madeira negus, a bason was brought him, properly medicated; which soon began to operate, and before eleven o'clock, Calomel was fast asleep in an elbow-chair. They then rolled him up in his night-gown, like a collar of brawn; and, swathing down his arms with his sash, laid him safely to bed by a fat scullion, where Calomel slept as sweetly as probably he would have done in her ladyship's own bed-chamber.

Well, and how did the poor man get back to his inn, in the morning? says Mrs Bardolph. Nay, says Rueful, I have put him fairly to bed; let him get back in a chair or hackney-coach, or how the devil he pleases. Further this deponent saith not.

XIV

UNIVERSITIES DEFENDED, &C.

Well, says Mrs Booby, to be sure, a mere citizen of Bath is as pedantic a creature, as a mere fellow of a college: is often as proud, has as absurd notions of life, and is as much out of his element, when he gets out of his shop or his lodging house, as the other is out of his own common room.

Yes, rot them! says Rueful; and they get rich by the money we spend here, before they know how to carry their heads, or come into a room.

And yet I know a great many sensible, polite people, says Mrs Booby, amongst the inhabitants of this place.

Why, it would be strange, indeed, replies Rueful, if the great resort of the politest company in Europe did not polish the creatures a little; for I take Bath, as a public place, to be a better school for any young fellow, than all the universities or colleges in the world; and I do not see, but those who have had no other education, appear as well in company, as people who have been plodding at the sciences in a college for seven years together.

Here Wildgoose could not forbear interposing; and observed, that although religion was, he believed, at as low an ebb in the universities as in other parts of the kingdom, notwithstanding the excellence of its institution for that purpose, yet he could not but think them still the chief fountains of erudition.

There is, indeed, says he, a slight tincture of learning, a superficial knowledge, diffused amongst all ranks in this generation. But if there were not some *repositories* for the sciences, and some encouragements, such as those for our professors, to search more deeply into them, than the generality of the world seem disposed to do, I am of opinion the very principles of them would, in time, be lost; and we should again relapse into Gothic ignorance and barbarism.

There may be men of courage that do not wear a red coat, and a gentleman may know how to use a sword, without going into the army, or to stand fire, though not educated in the navy. But still there is a kind of military spirit, peculiar to gentlemen of those professions; a set of traditionary maxims of honour and courage.—Just at this instant Wildgoose started up with the utmost surprise and trepidation, and alarmed the whole company. Rueful burst out into a horse laugh—Mrs Booby cried out, Lord! Miss Trufle, what are you about? The case was, Miss Trufle, who for some time had sat in silent contemplation of her own importance, and playing with her lap-dog, whilst Wildgoose was in the midst of his harangue, had put her squirrel upon his shoulder: the little animal began dancing about, and, fixing his claws in Wildgoose's neck, gave him so smart a pinch, that if he had had the insensibility of a Stoic, or even a Spartan education, he could not have borne it without some emotion of terror or surprise.

When the company had sufficiently laughed at Miss Trufle's wit, and were again composed, Mr Rueful resuming the discourse, said, he did not undervalue a university education, as an old maid rails at matrimony, because he had been denied the sweets of it. Only say, continues he, casting a look of complacency on his own person, that I am more indebted to Bath, and the company of the ladies, for being what I am, than to all the lectures of tutors and professors which I attended in the university.—I dare say you are, Mr Rueful, replies Mrs Booby; and I am sure the figure you make does credit to your education, whatever place had the honour of it.

Upon hearing Rueful's name for the first time, Wildgoose observed his features more narrowly, and asked him, if he was not of such a college in Oxford some years ago; because I remember a person of your name of our college, continues Wildgoose.—That may be, sir, replies Rueful; but I am a Cambridge man.—Well, ladies, continues Rueful, we are very rude in troubling you with our pedantic disputes.—Then pulling out his watch, Pox take it! says he, I was engaged to meet Sir James Townly at seven o'clock, at the coffee-house. Having said this, he started up, and somewhat abruptly took his leave.

The truth was, Rueful had actually been of the same college with Wildgoose, and now very well remembered him; though the alteration which his own hair had made in the one, and the high frizure and laced coat in the other, prevented them at first from recollecting each other's person, especially as there had not been the least acquaintance between them. Notwithstanding the airs which Rueful now gave himself, he had worn a servitor's gown at Oxford, which, upon an accession of fortune, he had exchanged for a fellow commoner's at Cambridge.

As soon as Rueful was gone, the ladies, without the least reserve, spoke of him in such a manner, as convinced Wildgoose that he was the jest of the place; and the evening now drawing on, it was almost time for Wildgoose to attend their religious assembly. He, therefore, took his leave, after Mrs Bardolph had acquainted him with Lady Sherwood's lodgings, whom she desired him to wait upon the next morning, notwithstanding Mr Rueful's discouraging insinuations to the contrary.

When Wildgoose was come down, he saw Rueful walking upon the Parade, not with Sir James Townly, whom he was to meet at the coffee-house, but with elderly virgins, of that homely stamp, who, to view them in a *public place*, seemed formed for no other end than to make a variety in the works of creation, but who, if they would confine themselves within their proper sphere (their own families in the country,) might make tender nurses to their aged parents, exemplary aunts to their young nieces, or charitable assistants to their indigent neighbours, or even shining objects at a country assembly in a remote province; whilst at Bath or Tunbridge they expose themselves to the insolent contempt of youth and beauty, are almost shoved out of polite company, as useless lumber, and are glad to take up with such fellows as Rueful, who was but one remove from the men described by Shakespeare, as fancifully carved out of a cheese-paring after dinner.

XV

TRICKS AMONG SERVANTS.
NEWS FROM MRS SARSENET

Wildgoose, having been sufficiently exhausted with haranguing on the parade, as well as by sitting in form at a ceremonious visit, made part of the audience this evening at the Tabernacle, where a tallow-chandler held forth, and *melted* his flock by the *pathetic force*, and promoted a plentiful consumption of candles, by the tedious *prolixity* of his discourse.

During Mr Wildgoose's visits to Mrs Booby, poor Tugwell had been left to amuse himself at the inn; he met his master, however, at the Tabernacle, from whence they adjourned to their quarters.

As they were going along, Jerry informed his master what a reprobate place they were in—that there was nothing but card-playing, gaming, and swearing, from morning to night, amongst the servants and apprentices that resorted thither. That he heard a footman bragging, how cleverly a friend of his had imposed upon his mistress—That, having had the misfortune to break his leg, he had been confined to the house

for three months: at last his mistress told him it would do him good to
lay up his leg upon a stool, and ride behind her coach, as she went out
for an airing; which accordingly he did. The next morning he goes to
his lady's maid, with a sorrowful countenance, and told her that he had
had a sad misfortune by going behind the coach; that, as he was forced
to lay up his leg, the motion of the coach had shaken six guineas, all
the money he had saved in service, out of his pocket. Upon the maid's
telling the case to her mistress, she very good-naturedly gave him the
money again out of her own pocket. But it happened a little unluckily,
that a few days after, as the maid was in the butcher's shambles, she heard
another servant tell the butcher, that such a footman, which was her
fellow-servant, had lost six guineas such a night, at the gaming-table;
which coming to the mistress's ears, the fellow lost his place by his trick,
and was forced to march off to London.

Wildgoose was shocked at this instance of baseness and villany, and
at the idle character of the house they were in, but said, they should be
only that night at Bath; for that he had observed the two brethren, who
had preached there those two nights, had *preached* almost contradictory
doctrines, and each of them different from that of his own: that he was
determined, therefore, to go to Bristol the next day, and consult Mr
Whitfield, who he did not doubt would resolve all his scruples, and put
him in the true road to salvation.

When they came to their quarters, my landlord asked our hero if
his name was not Wildgoose? To which, when he had answered in the
affirmative, my landlord gave him a letter, which, he said, a gentleman's
servant had brought that afternoon from the Bell at Gloucester, having
been desired to find such a gentleman out; and, upon my describing
your honour, and telling him that you lodged here, he left it with me.

Wildgoose took the letter, which he found was from Mrs Sarsenet,
and read it with great eagerness, in hopes of hearing some news of
Miss Townsend, who, he found, engrossed a considerable share of his
thoughts, and whose sprightly idea none of the fine-dressed ladies at
Bath had power to efface.

Mrs Sarsenet informed him of the state of their little church, under
hers and Mr Keen the barber's auspices and inspection; that she already

foresaw, from one or two instances, some temporal inconveniences to herself, in regard to her trade, from so strict an adherence to her duty; but that she counted all things as dross, in comparison with the love of Christ. She concluded with observing, that there was something mysterious in Miss Townsend's behaviour; that she could not persuade her to attend their meeting since his departure; and that though she seemed seriously enough disposed, and even talked respectfully of Mr Wildgoose, yet she seemed inclined to ridicule his notions of religion. In short, says Mrs Sarsenet, I believe she is rather an enemy to your principles, than to your person.

But the most extraordinary part of her letter was the postscript, in which she informed him, that Miss Townsend's father had come to Gloucester two days after *he* left it; that he had sent for Miss Townsend to the inn, and received her with a mixture of fondness and resentment; that he was angry with her for being with Mrs Sarsenet, and yet had determined nothing about removing her from thence.

This letter, upon the whole, gave Wildgoose rather more pleasure than pain; and he sat down and answered it before he went to bed. He gave them some account of his success at Bath, and of his intention, however, of going to Bristol the next day. He concluded with the warmest expressions of respect to Miss Townsend: whose conversion, he said, he should not cease earnestly to pray for.

XVI

A SERIOUS CONVERSATION
WITH MR RUEFUL

Wildgoose having been kept awake with reflecting on the transactions of the day past, and by the hurry of spirits into which the news of Miss Townsend had thrown him, was but just dressed, when a footman brought him a card, with Lady Sherwood's compliments, who begged the favour of his company to breakfast; for Mrs Bardolph had not failed to visit her ladyship the preceding evening, and to give her a faithful account of what had passed at Mrs Booby's lodgings; and had greatly extolled Mr Wildgoose's person, modest behaviour, and agreeable conversation. Wildgoose, therefore, taking a direction from the footman, promised to wait on her ladyship at the hour appointed.

As he was going a back way into Orange-grove, where Lady Sherwood lodged, he accidentally met with Mr Rueful, in a genteel dishabille. He saluted Mr Wildgoose with a more familiar air than he had assumed at Mrs Booby's, and asked him immediately, whether he was not of such a college in Oxford?—Yes, says Wildgoose.—Why, look you, sir, continues Rueful, you must know I was of that college too; but I thought you asked me last night whether I was at *this time* of Oxford: for you must know, I had a considerable fortune left me by a relation, which enabled me to enter myself a fellow-commoner at Cambridge; and, to be sure, one would not choose to have it mentioned amongst people of fashion, that one had worn a servitor's gown in the university.—I don't imagine, replies Wildgoose, that people of fashion, out of the university, trouble themselves about those things. However, I don't see why a man should be ashamed to have appeared in a situation which was agreeable to his circumstances. There is nothing ridiculous in a small fortune, or even a low birth: but there is in the discovery that we are too anxious to conceal them, and even give the lie to them by our dress and appearance.—Sir, says Rueful, if you knew the honour and happiness of being upon an agreeable footing with people of distinction, you would not scruple a little artifice, to conceal any trifling circumstance that might disgust them, or grudge an expense a little beyond one's income, to enable one to appear in some measure upon a level with them.—Sir, replies Wildgoose, I apprehend, it is neither dress, birth, nor fortune, but *education* and *behaviour*, that puts all gentlemen upon a *level*, even in the opinion of the world.

But, Mr Rueful, let me take the freedom to return the hint which you gave me yesterday, that we may be easily deceived in the civilities which people of distinction show us, and mistake mere politeness for a particular attachment, and by presuming too much upon their plausible behaviour to our faces, expose ourselves to their ridicule behind our backs; and I really believe, Mr Rueful, you would meet with more real respect amongst people of distinction by a more serious, or even religious behaviour, and if you were to turn Methodist, as it is called, than you do now.

Well, I am obliged to you, my dear sir, for your frank advice: and faith, betwixt you and me, though I detest the solemnity of the sacerdotal character, I have at this time some thoughts of exchanging my laced coat for a black one. For, by a parliamentary interest, I have now the offer of a very good living in my own country; which, if I do not succeed in picking up a good fortune this season, I may probably accept of. For you must know, that is another reason for my appearing rather above what I can at present afford; and I had actually almost carried off a merchant's daughter of Bristol, who will be worth twenty thousand pounds. But old square-toes would not part with cash enough down upon the nail: and the devil take me, if I would marry an angel upon the footing of a mere Smithfield bargain.

Wildgoose, though shocked at the libertine airs which Rueful gave himself, could not but smile at the opinion which he entertained of his own person; but said he was obliged to attend Lady Sherwood at ten o'clock. He, therefore, took his leave, and went to her ladyship's lodgings, as he had been directed.

XVII

Lady Sherwood's character and present situation

Lady Sherwood was of an ancient and noble family, and wife to a peer of the realm. She was a woman of fine understanding, though her judgment appeared sometimes almost eclipsed by the brilliancy of her imagination. Her ladyship was now past her bloom; yet in her youth she had been tolerably handsome, and made a splendid appearance in the great world. But her lord, either from some disgust, or from a fondness

for retirement, having early in life withdrawn from the court, Lady
Sherwood had entirely conformed to his humour: and, to amuse herself
in her solitary situation, she had formerly indulged the suggestions of
her fancy, and turned my lord's park into a poetical Arcadia; where
her ladyship and a female companion or two lived almost the whole
summer a mere pastoral life, and ranged about, with their crooks in
their hands, like so many Grecian shepherdesses. Garlands of flowers,
or baskets of fruit, were seen suspended on every beautiful oak, with
rustic pipes, rakes, pitchforks, and other rural implements, disposed
in a picturesque manner, in different parts of the park. Nay, the poor
chaplain was forced to leave his bottle and his pipe, and backgammon
table, with my lord, and even neglect his *pastoral* function, assigned him
by the bishop, to attend her ladyship and her bleating lambkins; and
to sit whole afternoons under a spreading tree, to entertain them with
his flute. For the steward had actually bought her ladyship a score of
sheep at Banbury fair (according to Justice Shallow's expression) for this
romantic purpose.

   The inclemency of the weather, however, in this northern climate
was by no means favourable to these lovely Bœotians. Neither did many
of the pastoral functions suit with the delicacy of a modern woman
of quality. For her ladyship frequently caught the tooth-ache, and was
forced to have recourse to a neighbouring apothecary (a character
seldom introduced in the ancient bucolics;) and one of her companions
met with a terrible accident in the discharge of her office; for having
seized the leg of a large bell-wether with her crook, which was fastened
to her wrist by a blue ribband, the rude unclassical brute struggled with
such force to disengage himself, that he pulled down the poor Pastora,
dragged her some yards, and disfigured her face to such a degree, that
she could not appear again for six weeks; and this put an end to this
extravagant scene in pastoral life.

   Lady Sherwood was now grown tired of the country. But, as she
could not decently go to town against her lord's inclination, considering
the complaisant terms upon which they lived together, the physician,
therefore, had a hint given him, to order her ladyship to Bath for her
health. Not finding that relish, however, in public places which she

had formerly done, when every passion was agreeably flattered by her appearance in them, she grew sick of the world, and began to see, *in a true light*, the emptiness and unsatisfactory nature of all secular enjoyments.

In such a situation it is evident, that nothing but religion could yield any solid conversation. But, as the plain rational scheme of the established religion, which prescribes nothing more than our duty to God, our neighbour, and ourselves, under the sanction of future rewards and punishments, could not satisfy the uncommon genius, and lively fancy of Lady Sherwood, she listened with the same attention to the enthusiastic doctrines of these itinerant preachers, as a person labouring under a hypochondriacal distemper does to the extravagant pretensions of a mountebank; and was glad of this opportunity of conversing with so agreeable an enthusiast as Mrs Bardolph had represented Wildgoose to be.

XVIII

A LEARNED CONVERSATION, NOT ESSENTIAL TO THE STORY

When Mr Wildgoose arrived at the countess's lodgings, he found her attended only by Mrs Bardolph; whose principal plan being to amuse the time between breakfast and dinner, she preferred every place to her own house; and assisted with equal satisfaction, at making a convert, or making a match, at a religious conversation, or at a pool at quadrille.

Lady Sherwood, after a little preliminary chat, opened the congress, by observing the great indifference of the world with regard to religion; and asked Wildgoose, how he could reconcile the present state of Christianity with the pompous descriptions given by the prophets of the kingdom of the Messiah? Our hero was a little surprised at so learned an attack. But, after pausing a moment, answered, that the dispensations of Providence were very mysterious; that, however, God might be supposed to have given the prophets a general view of the kingdom of Christ, from its first establishment to the end of the world; for which reason they generally represent it as in its full lustre.

Well, replies Lady Sherwood, I can only say, that, as far as I have observed, the lives of the generality of Christians are so little better than those of Heathens or Mahometans, that, I confess, it a little puzzles me to account for so strange a phenomenon; and how it comes to pass, that a *divine* institution should answer its end no better.

Why, says Wildgoose, as your ladyship, I dare say, is very well acquainted with ancient history, if you would compare the state of religion and morality in the world for several generations before the coming of Christ, and that of the unconverted Heathens afterwards, with the first three or four centuries of the Christian era, you would find a remarkable difference between them.

I don't imagine the world was worse than it is now, says Lady Sherwood.

I am convinced it was, replies Wildgoose. The Heathens were so utterly void of proper principles, that impurities of every sort were scarce accounted faults among them; nay, most kinds of debauchery were defensible, and even sanctified by their religious system. Exposing of infants, cruelty to slaves, and the sanguinary diversions of gladiators were permitted, and even applauded, by the wisest and politest nations of the world.

But how different a scene of things does Christianity present to us in its primitive state! Its votaries were pious, humble, chaste, and temperate; and their lives were a just comment upon the precepts of their master.

If our religion, therefore, must be judged by its effects, we ought to take it at its first institution, as its earliest were probably its most genuine fruits.

That is but reasonable, to be sure, says Mrs Bardolph, who affected to be very attentive to this learned dissertation.

But, proceeds Wildgoose, such is the degeneracy of our nature, that every effort of Providence for our recovery, in time, loses its force, and becomes ineffectual. It seems necessary, therefore, that the Divine Power should, at different periods, interpose in an extraordinary manner, and give fresh vigour to his own institutions: and accordingly, I am persuaded, that, in the present age, he has poured out an uncommon measure of grace upon his chosen servants Mr Whitfield and Mr Wesley, and their associates; which empowers them to break through the cobweb restraints of human ordinances, and, by seemingly irregular proceedings, to rouse men from their dangerous lethargy, and engage their attention to the pure and genuine doctrines of primitive Christianity.

Sir, says Lady Sherwood, I have a great opinion of Mr Wesley and Mr Whitfield; and, as I hear you are a follower of them, have taken the liberty of desiring this conference with you. But give me leave to ask you, sir, whether those doctrines are not taught in our own church?

Madam, replies Wildgoose, the articles and homilies of our church, as drawn up by our pious reformers, certainly contain those doctrines in their proper sense; but, I am afraid, the present clergy are departed from the most essential of those doctrines, as particularly that of justification by faith alone; and depend more upon their own works, than on the merits of Christ, for their salvation.

I do not know, says Mrs Bardolph. I have often heard that said of late. I own I am a very bad judge of those things; but all the clergy, whom I have happened to hear treat of that subject, have taught me not to rely on my best performances, but to confess myself still an unprofitable servant. In short, continued she, I cannot but think, that, if we practised what we heard at church, we should have a tolerable chance for going to heaven.

Lady Sherwood observed, that she had attended the public worship very regularly for some time, and with a sincere endeavour to know the will of God; but found herself little edified by such formal devotions.

Wildgoose replied, he could not but own, that there were several noble strains of true devotion in our Liturgy; and though people, who went to church with an intention to criticise, might, perhaps, find out some trifling imperfections, yet that, upon the whole, it was an admirable performance. But, continues he, I am afraid the fault is not in the service, but in those who perform it. The most pious sentiments will affect us but little when delivered by the lips of those who appear to have no religion in their hearts; and loll on their elbows, and stare about for objects of amusement, as if their devotions were a fatigue and confinement to them, and they were impatient to return to the pleasures or vanities of the world.

In short, my lady, as things are at present, we must look elsewhere than at church for the means of salvation. For my own part, I must confess myself as yet only in search of the right way, and intend this very day to pay a visit to Mr Whitfield at Bristol; to whom, with your ladyship's permission, I shall communicate your good disposition; whose present uneasiness is, I hope, a promising symptom of the new birth.

Lady Sherwood was going to inform Wildgoose, that she had already frequently conversed both with Mr Whitfield and Mr Wesley, when the servant came and whispered to her ladyship, that Mr —— was below, and desired to know if her ladyship had any commands to London.— Lord! says she, that man teazes me to death; he calls himself my cousin, merely because his grandfather married my great-grandfather's second wife's daughter by a former husband. I wish we could make a convert of him; for I believe he is of no religion at all, and neither loves nor cares for any body but himself. Well, says she to the footman, desire the gentleman to walk up.

When he came, he told Lady Sherwood that he was tired of Bath, and was going the next day to London. She said she had no commands, but told him he had interrupted them in a very agreeable conversation upon religion, and wished he had been there to have heard it.—Religion! says he, I do not want to hear any thing about religion. It serves people to talk and dispute about, but I do not see that any body regulates their actions by their religious principles.—That is, replies Lady Sherwood, because they do not really believe them; they have not a true practical faith in those principles. Faith! cries the gentleman, for my part, I am of Mr Pope's way of thinking in that respect:

> For modes of faith let senseless bigots fight;
> His can't be wrong, whose life is in the right.

I live as well as I can; pay my taxes, and pay my tradesmen; and if I meet with an object of charity, that really moves my compassion, I relieve him. I go to the tavern, indeed, sometimes; but I never drink or eat more than does me good: and though I have no wife of my own, I never invade another's property. In short, I do not see what the best Christian can do more than I do.

Wildgoose was going to interrupt him in his career; but Lady Sherwood calling him by his name, Wildgoose found himself disagreeably affected; though he could not at first recollect upon what occasion he had heard it before. But, after some time, he remembered that was the name of the very gentleman who had endeavoured to seduce Miss Townsend; and, comparing it with his dress (which was the same individual blue and gold she had described,) his square person, his manner of life, but, above all, his system of religion, he had not the least doubt that it was the same man.

Wildgoose was at first inclined to lead him, by some means, to the subject; but reflecting that it could not possibly answer any good end, and being likewise impatient to set out for Bristol, and Mrs Bardolph beginning to gape, and to consult her watch, he took his leave of Lady Sherwood, who charged him with her compliments to Mr Whitfield, and said, she should be glad to see him again, if he returned through Bath.

XIX

LEARNED ACCOUNT OF THE BATH WATERS. MR WILDGOOSE AND HIS FRIEND TAKE THEIR LEAVE OF THAT CITY

When Wildgoose returned to the inn, he found Tugwell just returned from visiting the hot baths; the cause of which surprising phenomenon my landlord, in conjunction with a journeyman apothecary, was endeavouring to explain to honest Jerry. My landlord said, he had heard say, though he did not know it to be certainly so, that the heat of the bath was caused by a constant fire in the bowels of the earth, which had been burning ever since Noah's flood, and would, in time, burn up the whole world, which was to be destroyed by fire.

Fire in the bowels of the earth! says Opifer, the apothecary, with a sneer; thou mayst as well tell me the boiling of thy pot is caused by a fire in the bowels of the earth. No, no; such a constant, regular *ebullition* can never be the effect of a gross *culinary* fire, but is produced by a more latent cause, which we can explain by the operations of *chemistry*. By a chemical process, we can analyze the Bath waters, and reduce them to their simple elements, or *constituent particles*, which are nothing but sulphur and a small quantity of steel.

And that the heat of these waters is caused by their running over *strata*, or beds of steel and sulphur, we can demonstrate by an easy experiment. For if you take an equal quantity of the filings of steel and flowers of sulphur, or what the vulgar call brimstone, and form these into a paste with water, it will produce that fermentation to which the heat of the Bath waters is *indubitably* to be ascribed.

Yes, yes, says Tugwell, the gentleman talks main well, and has made it as plain as the nose in one's face, if one did but understand him.

Wildgoose, who had been present during part of this learned discourse, observed, that the philosophers of this age were not content to make all useful experiments, but had a strange fancy to be creators; and to find out the secret *art*, by which nature performs all her operations. They would not admit any such thing as mysteries in philosophy, any more than in religion; and seemed almost to dispute with Providence his peculiar attributes of omnipotence or unlimited power, as well as unlimited knowledge.

Mr Wildgoose now called for his bill, and was preparing to set out: but though he had been but an indifferent customer, yet there was a secret charm in his serious and religious deportment, which made my landlord desirous of obliging him; he, therefore, gave him a hearty invitation to a fillet of veal, which was roasting at the fire; and, as Tugwell seemed unwilling to travel upon an empty stomach, they made a hearty dinner, paid their reckoning, and set out for Bristol.

BOOK VI

I

WHEN THE TWO PILGRIMS WERE now come into the suburbs of Bath, Tugwell very civilly inquired which was the Bristol road? Follow your nose, and you're a-se will tag after, says a tailor's 'prentice.—You might learn to be more civil to strangers, says Tugwell; for I am sure you live by them.—Not by such strangers as you, replies the 'prentice, who preach against fine clothes and innocent pastimes.— Come, come, master, says Jerry, come along; let us shake off the dust of our feet, for a testimony against them.

An elderly man, however, called out to them, that the way to Bristol was straight forwards at the first turning on the right hand. Though this direction was a little ambiguous, Tugwell was unwilling to hazard a more minute inquiry: they trudged straight along, therefore, without asking any further questions.

Tugwell, being highly disgusted with the insolent behaviour of the Bath people, and expressing himself with some bitterness against them, Wildgoose observed, that the mob of all places were alike, and that he ought not to reflect upon a whole body of people, for the wanton petulance of a few ignorant wretches.

Jerry then asked what my landlord had charged for his supper at Bath. Why, only eight-pence a night, says Wildgoose.—Eight-pence a night! says Jerry; an unconscionable *dis*torting rascal! Why, I will be hanged if I have eat three pennyworth of bread and cheese for supper the three nights that we have been there. I have a good mind to go and make the rogue give me back your worship's money.—No, no, Jerry, these things are customary, and it is best to pay it without making a disturbance. At these houses one pays for lodging, and house-room, and attendance, as well as merely for what one eats and drinks; and I think, upon the whole, we came off very reasonably.

Thus they went on talking near two miles; and, having reached the summit of the hills when it drew towards evening, they came to a place where the roads divided. Mr Wildgoose was inclined to turn to the right, and Tugwell to the left hand; which created a little debate upon the probability of each opinion; but Tugwell, having learned to decide dubious points by lot, threw up a halfpenny, crying out, that heads should determine him to the right, and tails to the left-hand road. Fortune declared for the former; which Jerry, then changing his note, said *must* be the road to Bristol, by the *course* of the country.

While they were yet debating the affair, Tugwell, spying a man in a plain, drab coat, walking soberly at a small distance from the road, calls out, Holloo! master! master! which is the road to Bristol? Whether the gentleman was immersed in thought, or whether he disliked the familiarity of Jerry's compellation, he made no answer. Wildgoose, therefore, advancing a little towards him, repeated the question in a more civilized manner, and asked which of those two was the road to Bristol. Why, neither of them, replied the gentleman; the road you are in would lead you to Wells. Wildgoose was going to crave his assistance, to put him in the right way, when he and the stranger surveying each other with an air of surprise, What, Mr Rivers! cries Wildgoose.—Bless my soul! my friend Wildgoose! replies he; what expedition can you possibly be upon in this part of the world? They then embraced (in the language of romance), or in plain English, took each other by the hand with great cordiality, expressing great joy at this unexpected rencounter; for they had been very intimate in the university, though no sort of intercourse had past between them for six or seven years.

Wildgoose inquired how long he · had been in this country, and whether he was settled any where in the neighbourhood, as he knew him to be originally a north-country man. Mr Rivers told him he had a house within a mile of that place, whither he insisted upon Wildgoose's accompanying him for that night at least, as it was now too late to go to Bristol on foot, if they had not been some miles out of their road. Wildgoose and his companion were well enough pleased with the invitation, in their present circumstances: besides, as Wildgoose recollected that Mr Rivers had in his youth a very religious turn, and that was always uppermost in his thoughts, he immediately conceived some hopes of converting his old friend to his own opinions. As they went along, Mr Wildgoose, at Rivers's request, let him into the nature of his present undertaking; at which his friend expressed some concern, as well as the greatest astonishment: but politely added, that he was glad even of this opportunity of renewing their friendship.

II

DESCRIPTION OF MR RIVERS'S
HOUSE, AND SOME ACCOUNT
OF HIS PRESENT SITUATION

Mr Rivers had now brought his friend Wildgoose, with Tugwell, to the brow of the hill, which overlooked one of those rich valleys in which that part of the country abounds. A gate opened into a wood, through which they descended by a rough, unfrequented road,

> Where the gilt chariot never mark'd the way,

almost to the bottom of the hill. There an old Gothic mansion presented itself, surrounded towards the road by a lofty stone wall, covered with moss, maiden-hair, and other wild plants, enough to puzzle the whole Royal Society, and the indefatigable Dr Hill into the bargain. The house seemed to have been built during the civil wars between the houses of York and Lancaster; but had been *modernized* in Queen Elizabeth's reign, and new glazed and painted for the reception of Mr Rivers.

Rivers knocked at the gate, which being opened by a servant in a russet coat, they now came into an elegant court, where they were regaled with the sight and fragrance of all the flowers of the season. From thence they entered a gloomy old-fashioned hall, but neatly fitted up; the wall covered with maps and chronological tables, above which were a number of cheap prints, representing the customs and habits of the various nations of the world.

Mr Rivers then, showing Tugwell with his wallet the way towards the kitchen, took his friend Wildgoose into a large wainscoted parlour, adorned with some fine prints, a few good paintings, and a bust or two over the chimney: but all his attention was immediately fixed upon Mrs Rivers, to whom his friend introduced him. She was sitting, like the divinity of the place, at the upper end of the room, at her needle, attended by a boy, and a fine girl, about five or six years old. Mrs Rivers received Wildgoose as her husband's friend, with a sweet smile, which, like the sunshine so much admired in the landscapes of Claude Lorraine, diffused an additional cheerfulness over every other object.

Mrs Rivers was about five and twenty, tall, and well-shaped; and though the pleasing cares of a young family had taken off a little of her first bloom, yet had it given such a languishing air to her eyes, and such a delicacy to her complexion, as rather improved than diminished her charms.

Mr Rivers informed her who Mr Wildgoose was, and how accidentally they had met. She made some obliging speech upon the occasion, and then rang the bell for tea; which being over, Mr and Mrs Rivers attended Mr Wildgoose into a garden, which commanded a beautiful, though confined prospect. It was laid out in a romantic taste, with a proper mixture of the *allegro* and the *penseroso*, the cheerful and the gloomy tufts of roses, jasmines, and the most fragrant flowering shrubs, with a serpentine walk of cypresses and laurels, here and there an urn, with suitable inscriptions, and terminated by a rough arch of rock-work, that covered a dripping fountain, were its principal beauties.

After a few turns, Mrs Rivers being summoned by her maid to a consultation about supper, Wildgoose, notwithstanding his religious severity, made some encomiums upon her person and behaviour, and said he was less surprised at his friend's marrying so early in life, than at his good fortune in meeting with so agreeable a woman. He expressed some desire, therefore, to be informed of the particular incidents of Mr Rivers's life since he left the university. Why, says he, though my story has nothing very uncommon in it, yet, as I flatter myself that I have escaped into one of the fortunate islands, from that rock on which the happiness of many a young fellow is totally shipwrecked, I think, as an experienced voyager, I ought to satisfy the curiosity of a friend, and give him all the intelligence in my power, that he may steer the like course with equal success. Then, taking Wildgoose into an alcove, shaded with honeysuckles and sweetbriars, Rivers thus began his narration.

III

THE HISTORY OF MR RIVERS
AND CHARLOTTE WOODVILLE

Soon after you left the university, says Mr Rivers, I was elected fellow of a very worthy society, where I pursued my studies with some regularity, and spent near two years greatly to my satisfaction: but whether the way of life was too sedentary, or too sociable (for I usually spent the day in reading, and the evening in company) whatever was the cause, I found myself, after some time, in a very indifferent state of health. I determined, therefore, during the long vacation, to retire into the country: but as I had neither father nor mother living, and my fellowship obliged me to an occasional residence, I did not care to travel into ———shire, which you know is my native county, and where I had an elder brother, and some near relations, residing; but was recommended by an acquaintance to a pleasant village in ———shire, about twenty miles from Oxford; who also prevailed upon a gentleman farmer, of whom he had some knowledge, to take me as a boarder.

Mr Woodville, which was the farmer's name, was a very worthy, honest man, and had a spirit of generosity far above his situation. He was, indeed, quite a gentleman in his appearance, behaviour, and way of thinking. He was about fifty, and had married for his first wife, a young lady of a genteel family, by whom he had one son and two daughters; but, being afterwards almost a cripple, with a rheumatic gout, he had been persuaded to marry a good motherly sort of woman, beneath his own circumstances, who was glad of the match, though sure to be a nurse, for the sake of providing better for her children by a former husband.

I had here a tolerable apartment, entirely distinct from the rest of the family, which suited with my scheme of prosecuting my studies, and of giving a particular attention to my health, which was the principal end of my retiring from college; having, as you know, little taste for the more robust diversions of the country. But, in this retreat, remote as I was from the intrusion of my former jovial associates, I did not long enjoy an absolute tranquillity.

There are few persons of so phlegmatic a constitution as to content themselves with merely rational pursuits. The passions, the appetites, and the imagination, all lay claim to their respective gratifications. Love particularly is a plant which springs up so naturally in the breasts of young people, that, when I hear one in the heat of youth affect to talk with a stoical indifference of that tender passion, I generally suspect him of indulging it privately, either for an *unworthy*, or at least, for an *improper* object. The latter only was my case; for though an engagement of that kind was highly *improper* in my circumstances, yet the object itself was worthy the love, I might say the ambition, of a prince.

Mr Woodville, as I have said, had two daughters. The elder was about nineteen; and though she had nothing remarkably defective in her features, yet the sour and selfish passions had taken such absolute possession of her countenance, as to render her almost ugly. The younger daughter was hardly fifteen, and as different from the elder as a grace from a fury.

Descriptions of a beloved object are generally heightened, and usually embellished with all the charms which the enraptured imagination is able to give them. Charlotte Woodville, however, was, I think, so near perfection in that respect, that although a severe critic might possibly spy out some trifling defect, yet upon the whole she had so striking an appearance, that few people could behold her without admiration.

She was rather tall than of a middling stature, but every way finely proportioned, and of a natural, easy shape. Her features were neither too large, nor too small; the extremes, in either respect, being, I think, less agreeable. Her eyes had always such a brilliant lustre, that I never knew their real colour. But her hair, which she had in great abundance, was of a bright brown, and gave an inimitably fine shade to her complexion. Her complexion had, at that time, rather the glossy bloom of high health, than that transparent delicacy which is generally the concomitant of too tender a constitution.

But what gave the greatest spirit and force to her external charms, was the beauty of her mind, which was every thing that can be conceived of sweet and amiable. Good nature and good sense, sprightliness, and an artless freedom, the emanations of her charming soul, distinguished themselves in her eyes, and in every feature of her face.

Such was this young creature in her native simplicity, without the least assistance of art, or, indeed, of any other education, than what was to be met with in a country place; and which the loss of a genteel mother, when she was very young, had not suffered to be applied to the utmost advantage.

Sir, says Wildgoose, smiling, you might have spared yourself the trouble, or rather denied yourself the pleasure, of this description; for, in the picture you have drawn, I can easily discover the features of Mrs Rivers, though a few years may have abated, or rather softened the glaring lustre of the colouring. But proceed, my friend, in your narration.

Well, says Rivers, you may suppose a young fellow, though of more philosophy than ever I pretended to, could not be long in the same family without taking particular notice of so lovely an object. But, as any sort of love-engagement would have been highly improper in my circumstances, a discreet person would certainly have checked any tender sentiments, and not have thought of trifling with so young a creature, who, considering my education and future prospects in life, was, in a *prudential* view, beneath my consideration. For, according to the maxims of the world,

> Love's but the frailty of the mind,
> When 'tis not with ambition join'd.

Ah! says Wildgoose, nothing but the love of God can satisfy the *reasonable ambition* of an immortal soul.—Well, replies Rivers, every man to his taste. But to proceed in my story.

IV

MR RIVERS'S AND CHARLOTTE WOODVILLE'S STORY CONTINUED

As I was at that time quite a valetudinarian, and willing also to lose as little time as possible from my studies, I desired to eat at my own hours, and avoided all intercourse with the family as much as I decently could, without the appearance of pride or moroseness. Mrs Woodville kept one maid to do the work within doors, and whose business it was to wait upon me; but as she was often otherwise engaged, the daughters would frequently by turns supply her place. After some time, however, I could not but observe, that the younger was more assiduous in her attendance on me than the elder, which yet I looked upon as accidental, and imputed it either to the good-nature of the one, or the churlish temper of the other. Charlotte Woodville did every thing in so pretty a manner, that although it gave me no small pleasure, yet was it a somewhat painful tax upon my complaisance, which would not suffer me to receive any thing from so fair a hand without some little gallant acknowledgement. The more civility I showed, the more obliging was this fair nymph; so that by degrees as I seemed disappointed whenever any other part of the family attended me, so she grew more kindly officious in her attendance, and,

> Though I call'd another, Charlotte came*

I am convinced, however, that she was utterly void of any design in this, and at present only followed the dictates of her native benevolence and freedom of disposition: though a more powerful motive, I believe, soon took place in her little breast; and *my* indiscretion put matters upon a different footing.

There happened to be a wedding in the village one morning, and curiosity had drawn to church the whole family except the younger daughter, who staid to attend on her father, who was confined to his bed by a fit of the gout. Charlotte came into the parlour, upon some occasion or other, while the bells were ringing upon this jocund occasion. A wedding in a country place sets every girl in the parish to simpering; and, matrimony being an inexhaustible topic of raillery, I happened to joke with Charlotte upon the happiness of the state. She made me some very innocent reply, which, however, tempted me

---

* Prior.

to chuck her under the chin, the lowest degree of dalliance with an inferior. She blushed, and retired with some precipitation, and with such a sweet confusion, that I longed to repeat the freedom; and, begging her to return for a moment, as soon as she came within the door, I caught her round the neck, and snatched a kiss. This increased her surprise, and she again retired with a glow upon her cheeks, which I fancied expressed some indignation; at least it so alarmed her virgin innocence, that I saw her no more that day.

I had now passed the rubicon of discretion.—Yes, says Wildgoose, you had tasted the forbidden fruit. 'The poison of asps is under the lips' of the most innocent of the sex. There is no security against the encroachments of love, but by checking the first emotions of the soul. 'Whoso looketh upon a woman, to lust after her, has committed adultery already with her in his heart.'

You are too severe upon me, replied Rivers; but I will proceed in my narration.

V

THE STORY CONTINUED

I took a walk before dinner; and, upon my return through the hall, where the family generally sat, Charlotte, instead of meeting my eyes with an open, cheerful countenance, looked down with a bashful consciousness, and almost hid her face in her bosom.

My mind was now in such a situation, that if I had believed the freedom which I took had really offended this innocent maid, I should, probably, have entirely desisted, and have pursued the affair no further; but as a little coldness would easily have nipped my passion in the bud, so the slightest encouragement sufficed to keep alive the flame. I cannot omit a trifling circumstance, which I considered in that light.

Being under a kind of regimen as to my diet, I usually supped upon a bason of milk. This the servant brought me that evening accompanied by a plate of wood-strawberries. It being early in the year, I asked her whence they came. She said they were a present to one of her young mistresses. As I had met with so little complaisance from the elder, I easily guessed to whom I was obliged for this favour. This slight instance of her forgiveness, expressed in so pretty a manner, tended but little to the cure of my growing passion.

The next day, in the absence of the maid, Charlotte ventured again into my apartment. I gave her a significant smile, in allusion to what had passed the day before; and, taking her hand, pressed it with some eagerness. She repulsed me in such a manner, as seemed rather to return the compliment than to be displeased with it. In short, though I had no great opinion of my own person, yet I began to flatter myself that I had made some little impression upon Charlotte's tender heart; and, as nothing is a stronger incentive to love than an opinion of its being mutual, this naturally endeared her to me, and made her appear more amiable every time I saw her. In reality, I began to love her extravagantly.

And she more lovely grew, as more belov'd.

Jealousy is often a sign of a little mind and a meanness of spirit; and a jealous *husband* is certainly a ridiculous animal; but a jealous *lover*, I think, deserves the compassion rather than the contempt of his mistress. Suspicion after marriage betrays a want of confidence in her of whose fidelity we are supposed to have received sufficient assurance. But, it is excusable in a lover to be a little apprehensive of the success of his rival, when it would be esteemed a degree of presumption to be too confident of his own preference in her affection and esteem. In short, whatever a woman may think of a jealous lover in other respects, she can have no reason to doubt of the sincerity of his passion.

For my part, I began to be so fond of my little mistress, that I could hardly suffer her to be out of my sight; and, as I thought I had condescended a little in settling my affections, I could not bear with patience the thoughts of a rival; nor, indeed, had I any reason to fear one in her present situation. However, I one evening saw her engaged

in so sprightly a conversation, and laughing with so coquettish an air, as
I fancied, with a young fellow of the neighbourhood, who was talking
to her brother at the door, that it immediately alarmed my jealousy, and
I could not forbear discovering it. I rang the bell with some vehemence,
intending only to put her in mind of me. Instead of sending the maid,
as I expected, she immediately left her company, and came herself. I bid
her send in a glass of water, which, with great good-nature she brought
with her own hands. I had seated myself, sultan-like, in a great chair;
and, lolling in an insolent posture, affected to be engaged in reading, and
with a haughty nod bid her set it down. She was sensible of the insult,
and immediately assuming the dignity of her sex, drew herself up, and
flung out of the room with the air of a countess.

It appeared afterwards, indeed, that the young man, whom I feared as
a rival, was at this time engaged, and upon the brink of being married
to another girl in the neighbourhood; and I was convinced that my
suspicions, with regard to Charlotte, were entirely without the least
foundation. The little quarrels of lovers generally conclude in more
tender reconciliations. Miss Woodville's spirited behaviour on this
occasion, and the explanation which it produced, greatly augmented
our fondness for each other; and this tender intercourse was continued
for some time, without being suspected by any one. I was so happy
in my amour, that I never considered the probable consequences
of so improper an engagement, but rather shut my eyes against any
disagreeable reflections.

As a French writer* observes, 'The most common view that people
have when they commit imprudent actions, is the *possibility* of finding
out always some resource or other:' so I flattered myself with the notion
of being able to recal my affections when I thought it proper; and
imagined I might amuse myself for some time innocently enough, in
so retired a place, without subjecting myself to the censure or remarks
of any one whose opinion I much regarded.

---

* Card. de Retz.

VI
THE STORY CONTINUED

About this time I thought it necessary to visit my friends in Staffordshire, being particularly invited by an old relation, whom you have heard me mention, the little fat clergyman, from whom I have always had some considerable expectations. Though I found myself at present but little inclined to take such a journey, yet I had fixed the day, which was now at hand.

As my interviews with Miss Woodville had hitherto been very transient, and there was no probability of our ever being long together without subjecting ourselves to observation, I made a request to her, in which I was afraid she could not oblige me; and that was, to give me an hour of her company in the evening, after the family were in bed. As Miss Woodville was very young and innocent and entirely ignorant of the arts of our sex, having never had any female friend to caution her against them, she made no scruple of promising me her company, if she could get her sister, who was drowsily enough inclined, to sleep without her; in order to which, she would sit up in her chamber, she said, under pretence of finishing some piece of needlework, which she was very intent upon.

When night came, and the family were retired, I sat myself down with great composure, to wait the event of our assignation. I even took a book, and read, to amuse my impatience, but with as little attention as our candidates for a degree read their wall-lectures, when they expect the beadle every moment with the joyful news that their time is expired. Thus I waited for near two hours, and now quite despaired of my promised happiness, when, unexpectedly, the stillness of the night was agreeably interrupted by a gentle rap at the parlour door. I started up, and opened it with great alacrity. In she came, but with a down-cast look, and sweet blush upon her countenance; and with an apology for the rashness of her conduct, which her native modesty now represented to her in the strongest light.

I told her I had begun to despair of being favoured with her company, and asked her if her sister had any suspicion of her intention.—I believe not, says Charlotte, for she was asleep in five minutes after she was in bed.—Why, then, did you delay my happiness so long? said I. She replied, that upon thinking better of it, she was afraid she had done wrong in promising me, and had more than once resolved not to come down; nay, that she had actually been in bed; but as I talked of going early in the morning, she had not the heart to disappoint me. I acknowledged her goodness, and assured her, she should never repent of the confidence she reposed in me.

I could not but take notice of one particularity in Miss Woodville's conduct on this occasion, which was, that she had taken the pains to put on a clean apron, handkerchief, and ruffles, and adjusted every part of her dress with the nicest exactness; which trifling circumstance convinced me both of the delicacy of her taste, and the purity of her imagination, or rather that she was absolutely void of the least apprehension of any thing contrary to the strictest decency in my behaviour to her.

Nothing can be more insipid, upon repetition, than the conversation of two fond lovers; and it is a sort of profanation to repeat any thing that passes upon those occasions; but, as something very serious ensued from this interview, I cannot forbear mentioning a few trifling particulars. I kept her up pretty late. My journey and the month's absence was the principal subject of our conversation; in the course of which she expressed her apprehension, that there were probably more ladies whom I was fond of in other places.—Oh! what is life without love? said I; to be sure I must have a mistress at every place I go to; half a *dozen* at Oxford, you may suppose. She affected a sort of laugh at the humour of my descriptions, and I imagined took it, as I designed it, merely as unmeaning chit-chat. But, my favourite girl, continued I, is a ——shire lass, the very picture of yourself, a tall, brown beauty, and the best-tempered creature in the world. O! how happy shall I be next Thursday night?

Nothing can equal my astonishment at what now happened. Whilst I was running on in this coxcomical strain, I found her sunk back in her chair, pale as death, without breath or motion, or the least appearance of life. I was shocked, and distressed to the last degree how to proceed. I could not bring myself to alarm the family, and yet had the most terrible apprehensions of what might be the event of this affair.

There was a decanter of water stood on the table, some of which I sprinkled in her face; and, having some spirit of lavender in my pocket, I rubbed her temples with that, and applied some to her nostrils; which, after a few minutes, very happily brought her to herself again.

I cursed my own folly, and assured her, that what I had said was a mere jest; and that there was not a girl in the world for whom I had the least fondness, but herself.

This proof of Miss Woodville's affection for me, you may be sure, endeared her to me extremely; and I parted from her the next morning with the greatest reluctance.

VII

THE STORY CONTINUED

I had proposed being out a month on my journey; but my eager desire to see my fair villager made me shorten my absence, and I returned in less than three weeks.

As I had written to Mr Woodville, and given him notice of my intention, I found every thing in great order for my reception; but was disappointed in not finding Charlotte Woodville ready to welcome me on my arrival. The rest of the family were sitting in their usual apartment. After making my compliments to them, I *affected* to look round, and inquired if some part of the family were not wanting. Mr Woodville looked down with some confusion; but Mrs Woodville, affecting a smile, answered, that their daughter Charlotte was gone to school again for a little time: that, as she discovered a tolerable hand at her needle, they were willing to improve her as much as possible. She will be at home again in the evening, continued she, and then turned the discourse.

I immediately suspected there was some mystery in this, as I had often heard her extolled for her extraordinary skill in needle-work; and was convinced she could not learn much at the place they mentioned, which was at the next village, whither I found she was forced to walk every morning, and return in the evening. Besides, I knew it must be a great mortification to a girl of Charlotte's spirit (who was near fifteen, and very tall of her age), to be sent to such a paltry school, amongst a parcel of children.

I waited with great impatience for the evening, and Charlotte Woodville's return. At last I heard her voice in the next room, which was music to my ears. I immediately ran towards the door, where I could hear every thing that passed. Poor Charlotte, seeing some unusual preparations for supper, inquired into the occasion of them. Oh! says the step-mother, I suppose you can give a shrewd guess. It is for you and your gentleman, I suppose, after we *are in bed*. This spiteful speech of the old lady let me a little into the secret, and soon convinced me that our intimacy was discovered.

As I had imagined, therefore, I should have no other opportunity of seeing or speaking to her that evening, I immediately went out into the room where the family was, under pretence of inquiring how long it was to supper. The moment Charlotte saw me, a blush overspread her cheeks, which was succeeded by a total want of colour. She just courtesied, and welcomed me home; when she was dispatched by the old lady, upon some frivolous pretence or other, into another room; and I saw her no more that evening.

The next morning, however, we found an opportunity of being alone together for a few minutes; when Miss Charlotte informed me of the true situation of our affairs. She said, that her sister, having some suspicion of my affection for her, had feigned herself asleep the night when she came down to me, and had discovered it to her father and mother; that her father had given her a very serious lecture upon the occasion; but that her mother-in-law had been outrageous about it; had talked at first of desiring me to quit my lodgings immediately, to which her father would not consent, he having expressed a great opinion of my honour, and of my innocent intentions. In short, that at last they had come to a determination to send her out to school for the present, till they could think of some other way of disposing of her.

Any one might imagine from this, that Mrs Woodville was a very careful step-mother, and had the true interest of her husband's children greatly at heart. But the reverse of this was really the case. She was what might be called, on the whole, a good sort of woman; but in all second marriages, if there are children on both sides, there must necessarily be separate interests; and a woman who had changed her state with that view, could not be much blamed for consulting chiefly the good of her own offspring. But, in order to do that effectually, another point must be secured; I mean an absolute sovereignty over her husband's affections; which Mrs Woodville seemed to have gained, and of which she was excessively jealous. As Charlotte Woodville then was deservedly a favourite with her father, no wonder that the mother-in-law took every opportunity of lessening her in his esteem, and even desired to wean his affection from the darling of his age. She was pleased, therefore, with this instance of her indiscretion, which she aggravated to the highest degree. She said it confirmed what she had often insinuated to him, that Charlotte was a proud and forward hussy; and insulted him with the prudent behaviour of her elder sister, who, for an obvious reason, had never been guilty of any thing of this kind. Mrs Woodville had really no more regard for the elder daughter than the other; but as Miss Betsy's unhappy temper made her no great favourite with the rest of the family, Mrs Woodville, by a very slender show of kindness, had bribed her to her interest, and employed her as a sort of spy upon her sister; which office she executed with an ill-natured fidelity, not scrupling sometimes, to exceed the bounds of veracity, in order to ingratiate herself with her constituent.

For old Mrs Woodville not only considered her daughter Charlotte as a rival in her husband's affections, but also envied her the probability of so advantageous a match as mine was considered to be, and could not bear the thoughts of her being treated by me with such distinction. She, therefore, took every opportunity of mortifying her; and, in order to lessen her consequence in my eyes, put her upon any servile employment in the family for which she could find a decent excuse. In short, though she contrived to make poor Charlotte's situation (and mine upon her account) as disagreeable as an excessive spleen, joined with absolute power, could do, yet her behaviour had a contrary effect from what she expected, and only the more endeared to me the innocent object of her persecution.

Accordingly, I found my passion for this young creature daily increase; and we continued our intimacy for some time. I had, indeed, indulged my fondness the more freely, as I fancied myself entirely retired from, and unnoticed by, the world; but in this I was greatly mistaken.

VIII
The story continued

It is more difficult for a man to live *incognito* in a country village than in the most populous city. The very precautions that he takes to conceal himself alarm the curiosity of the neighbourhood; and as, in a retired place, small matters serve for amusement, the most trifling incidents soon become the subject of general conversation.

As my regard for Miss Woodville was now no longer a secret in the family, it soon spread through the neighbourhood; and by some means or other the news had been conveyed to my friends in the university. Accordingly, the next time I went thither, I was attacked on all sides, and rallied with great freedom, upon the subject of my amour; nay, one of my more intimate friends, when we were alone together, took upon him, with great seriousness, to expostulate with me about the imprudence of it. He represented the ill consequences of such early engagements, and the inconveniences of settling in life without a proper competency, in such glowing colours, and set the cruelty of involving a young girl that I had an affection for, in the distress of narrow circumstances, in so strong a light; and, in short, he harangued upon these topics so long, that at last I told him, I was resolved to break off all correspondence with her; and, in order to that, to quit my situation in Buckinghamshire as soon as I conveniently could.—Well, then, says my friend, taking me at my word, I will ride over, and settle your affairs there to-morrow morning, and make some excuse for your sudden decampment. Here I found my resolution begin to stagger. Charlotte had taken such possession of my heart, that I could not bear the thoughts of being banished from her for ever. I hastily interrupted my officious counsellor, and told him that my affairs were in such a situation there, that I must necessarily go over, *once more* myself; but, however, that I would, if possible, take some opportunity of breaking off my imprudent engagement. He flew into a violent passion, and immediately gave me up for lost. Then, says he, will this little slut, with one false tear [*una falsa lacrymala quam vix vi expresserit*], undo all that I have been labouring; and, having said this, he left me with an emphatical shake of the head, and a smile, which expressed both indignation and contempt.

However, I returned into Buckinghamshire the next day, full of philosophical reflections, and absolutely determined, as I flattered myself, to regulate with prudence at least, if not to put an end to, this imprudent amour. But it is very difficult to know one's own heart; and, whenever reason prevails over passion, it is more frequently, I believe, to be attributed to the weakness of the one, than to the strength of the other. The moment I saw Miss Woodville, I found my resolution begin to fail me; and though I was weak enough to inform her of what had passed at Oxford, and even of the design I had formed of leaving her for some time, till I had finished my studies, and was in such circumstances as might make it more prudent for us to come together, yet I found my project so inconsistent with the present situation of my heart, and the professions I had hitherto made, that I was heartily ashamed of the figure I must make in this young creature's eyes: and, as an unsuccessful rebellion strengthens the hands of the government, so this temporary defection from my duty helped to rivet my chains; and our interview ended, on my part, with more earnest protestations of future fidelity, and a solemn promise never to forsake her.

IX

THE STORY CONTINUED

Though Miss Woodville and I behaved with great caution and reserve to each other in the family, so as not to give Mrs Woodville an opportunity of any open expostulation with us upon the subject; yet she was so provoked at the success (as she esteemed it) of her daughter-in-law's charms, that with pretended concern for her daughter's reputation, she privately insisted upon Mr Woodville's talking to me upon it, and bringing me to an explanation. He took an occasion one day when I was alone with him, to ask me, with great good-nature, what my friends would say to my love affair? and added, that as he could not give his daughter any considerable fortune, it must be an imprudent match for me, and that she would probably be happier with one in her own station; and therefore he begged I would not trifle with so young a girl, nor perplex her with fruitless expectations.

I replied, that though I was certain I could not be happy without her, yet I was certain, that as I had only a younger brother's fortune, I must make both myself and Miss Woodville unhappy, if we should marry before I was settled in any profession; that, however, as I had a very honourable passion and sincere regard for her, I hoped he would not be uneasy at my continuing the present correspondence with her, till something should happen in my favour, or that I was settled in some way of increasing my fortune; and that then I should prefer his daughter to all the women in the world.

As Mr Woodville was a good-natured, easy man, and I believe had forced himself to make this remonstrance only in compliance with his wife, he was soon answered; and our conversation ended without any peremptory stipulation as to my future behaviour to Charlotte Woodville. Accordingly, we took every opportunity of being alone together, as usual, which so much increased Mrs Woodville's animosity against us both, that I soon found it would be impossible for Charlotte to continue long under the same roof with her step-mother.

Besides, though Miss Woodville had something naturally polite and genteel in her manner, yet I thought it would be highly necessary for her to receive some better instructions in the common accomplishments of the sex, than were to be met with in that very retired situation. After consulting her, therefore, though I found her delicacy a little shocked at the thoughts of being obliged to me for any part of her education; yet, upon setting the affair in a proper light, and representing to her how unlikely it was that her step-mother would suffer her father to be at any extraordinary expense, with a view to forward a match which she seemed so much averse to, Miss Woodville at last submitted to the necessity; and, with her permission, I at first proposed to her father, to send her to a boarding-school, at a large country town, some distance from home: but, after reflecting that London was the fountainhead of politeness, and that she would be there further removed from the speculation of her impertinent neighbours, I determined, with his approbation, to send her thither. He said, that for his part he had an entire confidence in my honourable intentions, and should not scruple to trust his daughter wholly to my care. But, says he, the world will be apt to censure both your conduct and mine, if I suffer her to go from home before I have some security for your marrying her. Besides, continued he, I am certain my wife will not consent to her daughter's taking such an imprudent step upon any other conditions. In this, however, Mr Woodville was mistaken. It had always been his wife's policy to work her own children as much as possible into her husband's favour; and, in order to that, she was continually filling his head with comparisons between their behaviour and that of his own children, which were always injurious to the latter, and had a particular pique, as I have observed, against his daughter Charlotte, as her rival in Mr Woodville's affections. She, therefore, was not at all displeased with the prospect of getting rid of so dangerous a competitor, by her engaging in an adventure of this kind, which she foresaw would probably bring some reflections on her prudence at least, if not entirely ruin her reputation: for that reason, therefore, as also because she found it in vain to oppose an affair in which she saw me now so seriously embarked, she on a sudden altered her behaviour, both to me and to her daughter-in-law.

As to my marrying Miss Woodville immediately, I told her father, that, as I was fellow of a college, though we did not absolutely forswear matrimony, as was a vulgar opinion, when we accepted of a fellowship, yet that a forfeiture of the preferment was the penalty annexed; which I must necessarily submit to, as soon as my marriage became public. As I had therefore some particularly prudent reasons for continuing at college for some time longer, I desired him to dispense with our performing the ceremony; and I would give him any security he should require for fulfilling my engagements as soon as we arrived in London. As he was of an honourable temper himself, he was not apt to be suspicious of others; but, however, could not be brought to acquiesce in such an ambiguous declaration.

X

THE STORY CONTINUED

About this time we had an invitation from Mr Woodville's brother, who farmed a little estate of his own, at a few miles distance, to spend the day with him. The house he lived in was situated in the midst of woods, in a very solitary part of the country. It was a large old mansion house, and had a chapel contiguous to it, in which service was performed once a month. As Mrs Woodville was now upon better terms with me and her daughter, she graciously condescended to accompany us in this little expedition. As the road lay through two or three villages where we were known, this caused some speculation; and it was generally believed in the neighbourhood, that we went thither to be married; and whether Mrs Woodville endeavoured to persuade her husband that we really were so, in order to facilitate our removal, or whatever else was the cause, soon after this, I found him disposed to consent to his daughter's going with me to London.

Accordingly, after a few days' preparation, but without any previous provision for lodgings, or for a place of education to settle my charge in (for I had no friend in town to whom I could communicate a scheme of this kind), I sent to a large town at some distance from Mr Woodville's, and took places in the stage-coach, which set out every day from thence to London.

As poor Charlotte had never been two days together from her father before, who was excessively fond of her, and also in a precarious state of health from very frequent returns of the gout, the parting between them was very affecting; and I believe there was not a servant, or any one of the family, that did not shed tears at her departure: even Mrs Woodville herself behaved with a very decent dissimulation.

Mr Rivers was going on with his story, when the servant let them know that supper was upon the table. Mrs Rivers had furnished out a plain, but elegant supper; and Wildgoose, being happy in the company and friendly conversation of an old acquaintance, forgot a little his usual austerity, and seemed to enjoy himself like a man of this world.

After supper, however, upon Mr Rivers's drinking a health to his *friends* in Gloucestershire, Wildgoose, fetching a deep sigh, Ah! says he, the friendship of this world is enmity with God.—Well, my good friend, says Rivers, not to dispute the propriety of your application, I hope you do not think natural affection, or the regard which one feels for one's relations, is sinful. For my part, I am so far of a different opinion, continued Rivers, that however unsociable I may appear, or however I may renounce the common friendship, or rather impertinence of the world, yet I think the chief happiness of this life was intended by Providence to arise from the exercise of the social affections. In this our present limited state, indeed, it must necessarily be confined within narrow bounds. The pride, malice, and perverseness of too great a part of mankind, arising from the opposition of their several interests, may make it prudent to restrain our connections to a few friends, and almost within one's own family: yet hereafter our benevolence, and consequently our happiness, will be greatly enlarged: and the whole universe will probably converse with the same mutual love and harmony as a single family.

Wildgoose was going to reply, when a little boy, about five years old, with the face of a cherubim, ran into the room, and, leaping up into Mrs Rivers's lap, ran his head into her bosom, by way of asking *her* blessing. She looked down upon him with inexpressible sweetness, and the air of a Madona by Raphael or Corregio; and, having squeezed him to her breast, dismissed him with a thousand kisses. Wildgoose smiled, and owned, that was an unanswerable proof of the happiness arising from natural affection. And Mrs Rivers retiring soon after, Mr Rivers proceeded with his story.

Upon our setting out, as I told you, Mr Woodville sent a trusty domestic with us, to meet the coach at ————, where we lay the first night at an inn which the family always made use of. I committed my charge to the care of the mistress of the house, who, being a widow woman, let Charlotte sleep in her own chamber, and in the morning saw her safe in the stage-coach. I need not trouble you with the particulars of our journey; but suppose us arrived in town about the dusk of the evening, and set down at the Bolt-and-Tun in Fleet-street. Whoever has seen that ancient gloomy hotel (which, however, may have been a magnificent palace before the Reformation), will easily imagine with what horror it must strike a young person who was never before from her father's house in the country. We were taken by a tall masculine creature in petticoats, into a dark back parlour, with one window in it; which, instead of green fields and blooming hedge-rows, which she had been always used to, had no other prospect but into a dusky court, just large enough to contain an old bottle-rack, which faced the window, and bounded our view.

The moment we came into this apartment, O, heavens! cries Miss Woodville, is this London? Well, Mr Rivers, I am entirely under your protection. O, my poor father! and almost fainted away in my arms. I endeavoured to soothe her, by assuring her she should stay but one night in that house; and that the next morning I would look out for some agreeable lodgings; and that she would soon have a different opinion of that grand metropolis.

We were now interrupted by the entrance of a drawer, to know if we called. He surveyed us both with some accuracy; and immediately sent in the chamber-maid, to ask if we must have separate beds. As soon as I had answered her in the affirmative, in comes the mistress of the house; and, after viewing Miss Woodville with an affected indifference, desired to know what we would have for supper. In short, I now began to reflect, which I had hardly suffered myself to do before, in what light the dear object of my sincerest affection must necessarily appear, and was not a little shocked at the reflection. However, I again requested the mistress of the house to get the young lady a safe bed-chamber, which she did in a closet within her own apartment.

The next morning, as soon as we had breakfasted I sallied forth in quest of lodgings. The most retired part of the town that first occurred to me, was St Martin's-lane, where, upon the pavement, I saw a bill up, with a second floor to be let. Upon my rapping at the door, there came out a small middle-aged woman, with a tolerable aspect, who, upon my mentioning my business, entered at once into my schemes, and with apparent benevolence, and great volubility of tongue, told me she had lately had a clergyman's wife, out of ——shire, in just the same circumstances which I had mentioned, and who loved her as if she had been her own mother: that she had two daughters of her own, who would be good companions for the young lady, and went to a dancing-school in the neighbourhood, which would answer my purpose.

In short, we soon came to terms for lodging and boarding; and I brought Miss Woodville thither before dinner, who appeared much pleased with the cheerfulness of the apartment, and I did not doubt but she would be here very agreeably situated.

XII

THE STORY CONTINUED

Well, I had now this young creature entirely in my power, and you might imagine that nothing was wanting to complete my happiness: but, alas! I was conscious to myself that all was not right; and was greatly at a loss how to proceed. There was evidently but one path which I could honourably pursue, and that appeared, upon a superficial view, incompatible with prudence. I had no friend in town that I could consult upon this occasion; nor, indeed, did I care to communicate an affair of this kind to any of my acquaintance.

The next morning, happening to stroll into the Park, by a great accident, or rather by the particular care of Providence (for upon this incident, in a great measure, depended the future ease and comfort of my life), I met an old friend, whom I had not seen for many years. Mr Hammond (which was his name) inquired what brought me to town; to which I made him some evasive answer. But, during our walk, as I knew him to be a man of uncommon sense, a great knowledge of the world, and also of impenetrable secrecy, I soon determined to make him a confidant. I desired him, therefore, to drink tea with me at my lodgings that very afternoon, which he complied with; and as soon as he came, I opened to him my adventure, and prepared him for the appearance of Miss Woodville.

As he knew I was a fellow of a college, and had only a younger brother's fortune; and that such a scheme must be in every light highly imprudent, he began, with great earnestness, to conjure me by all means to put an end to it, begging me to reflect what a concern it would be to my relations, and how probably terminate in my own infelicity. I granted all he suggested; but desired him to consider how far the affair had proceeded: that I had brought a young creature from her friends and from her father, who either believed that we were really married, or at least depended upon my honour to make her my wife.

Miss Woodville now made her appearance, and I observed Mr Hammond seemed vastly struck with her person and figure. However, he spoke very little, but seemed entirely wrapped in thought the whole time she was in the room. When she had made tea for us, and was again retired, Mr Hammond made some short encomiums upon her sweet appearance, her easy and unaffected behaviour, which was so natural to her; then took his leave, and said he would call upon me again the next day.

When he came, after some little pause, Mr Rivers, says he, I have been considering your affair with great deliberation, and though I could have wished you had not engaged in it at all, yet, as things are circumstanced, and as I do not doubt but you really intend to marry Miss Woodville, I do not see how you can possibly avoid the performing your engagements immediately.

Though this was what I earnestly wished, and was sensible it was what I ought in honour to do, yet I own the thoughts of resigning my little preferment, and embarking in the wide world with so young a consort, a little embarrassed me; yet, now I had so prudent and faithful a pilot to direct me, I was glad not to defer my happiness any longer: and he telling me, that he knew a person who was curate in a remote part of the city, and who would perform the ceremony with great secrecy, we determined, with Miss Woodville's leave, to have it done as soon as possible.

Though poor Charlotte had consented, under the sanction of her father's approbation, to put herself entirely under my protection; yet I could not but observe, by an air of dissatisfaction, and several hints that dropped from her, that she was very uneasy in her present situation. You must suppose, therefore, that in such circumstances she could make no objection to my proposal. After some decent scruples, then, she consented to my request, to complete my felicity the very next morning; which was accordingly put in execution: and, it being necessary to acquaint the people of the house with the alteration of our condition, I ordered a handsome dinner, and invited them to a participation: though, by their behaviour afterwards, they affected to believe this no more than a sham wedding; at least they treated Mrs Rivers as if they considered her in no very honourable light.

XIII

THE STORY CONTINUED

After staying a week in town, completely happy in the possession of all that was dear to me, I was obliged to leave my wife, and go down to Oxford.

Whether Mr Hammond considered me in the character of a Spanish husband, or whatever was his motive, he did not offer, nor did I think of asking him, to visit Mrs Rivers in my absence; nor did I acquaint her where he lodged, or give her, as I ought to have done, any direction where to find him, in case of any emergency. Such a precaution, however (as it proved), would have been no more than necessary. I had often been in London before for some months together, and fancied I knew the town tolerably well; but I had no suspicion that about one house in ten, near that part of it, was inhabited by people of none, or rather of abandoned principles.

I had not been ten days in the country before I received a most terrible letter from my wife, informing me, that she was in very bad hands; and conjuring me to come up to town, immediately. I set out, with post-horses, the very next morning, and arrived at her lodgings early in the evening. The woman of the house came to the door; and, upon my inquiry for Mrs Rivers, Why, says she, your lady is gone to bed already. Poor creature, continued she, she is very whimsical, and fancies she is not well. As I knew how healthy Charlotte had always been, I was greatly alarmed. I flew up to her chamber; and, to my great concern, found her in a high fever. Upon inquiring into the cause of her illness, I found it to be as follows.

There lodged in the same house a young gentleman, of a very sober, modest appearance, with whom we spent one or two evenings before I went into the country. He told me he had commanded a man of war in the Mediterranean; and I believe, by several circumstances, that this account of himself was true. Soon after I was gone down, the woman of the house came to Mrs Rivers, and, after some general insinuations, told her, that this Oxford scholar who had brought her to town, would leave her there, and never return any more; that it was a common trick among them; and that she would advise her to make herself as easy as she could. Mrs Rivers, you may be sure, was greatly startled; but her youth and inexperience was, in this case, her consolation: for it could not enter into her imagination, that there was any one in the world so base, or that what this woman told her was true. She proceeded, however, by degrees, to assure my wife, that the young captain was violently in love with her; and, if she would consent to live with him, he would keep her a maid and a footman, buy her much richer clothes, and, in short, take much better care of her than ever I had done; and a great deal more to the same purpose.

The captain himself had frequent opportunities given him of being in company with Mrs Rivers; but, as he always behaved with great modesty and politeness, she was not very uneasy at what the good woman had said to her.

One evening, however, the captain came in to them, and, pretending some particular occasion of rejoicing, said he would treat them with a bowl of arrack punch. At this the landlady of the house affected to be (and probably was) greatly rejoiced, promised how merry they would be, and talked with great glee of the approaching evening.

Mrs Rivers had no suspicion of any design; but was not much disposed to be cheerful, as she began to have a very bad opinion of her company, and of course to be impatient for my return.

The glass went merrily round, with my landlady, her daughters, and two or three neighbours of her own stamp, whom she had invited to partake of their jollity. Mrs Rivers could hardly be prevailed upon to swallow one or two half glasses: but whether it was owing to her not being used to any thing strong, or whether they had contrived to convey any thing intoxicating into her glass, she soon found her head begin to grow giddy; so, without taking leave of her company, she slipped out of the room, and retired to her own apartment. Being apprehensive that they might pursue her, she locked her door; and observing that the bed ran upon castors, she exerted her strength, and placed that against it. She had hardly taken this precaution, when she heard the whole company, like Comus and his Bacchanals, come laughing and shouting, rather than singing, up the stairs, and protesting that they would pluck her out of bed. She was not undressed; but the timidity of her sex, and the particular cause she had to be apprehensive in her situation, almost threw her into hysterics, especially when she heard them thundering at the door and declaring they would break it open. But her greatest danger was from the abandoned part of her own sex; for when the captain perceived, from the tone of her voice, and other circumstances, the excessive fright she was in, he very honourably forced them to desist from their frolic, as mine hostess affected afterwards to call it.

Mrs Rivers was so much alarmed, that she could not close her eyes the whole night; which, together with the pernicious liquor they had forced upon her, made her very ill all the next day.

On Sunday, which was the day following, she was a little recovered; and the two girls, towards the evening, made her take a walk with them into the Park; where she had never been but once before, with me and Mr Hammond.

After walking once round, they came to the canal, and stood some time to observe several people who were feeding the ducks there. This rural amusement attracted Mrs Rivers's attention, and, by recalling to her mind the ease and happiness of her life in the country, soothed her melancholy, and she stood fixed in a sort of reverie; but, on a sudden looking round, she missed her companions, and with great terror and surprise found herself amongst a crowd of strangers. I do not believe she knew so much as the name of the street where she lodged, nor one step of the way that led towards it. She looked wildly round on every side, and her apprehension almost took away her senses; but, in the midst of her distress, she saw a gentleman come bowing and smiling up towards her; and who should this be but the captain! His first appearance, you may suppose, gave her some comfort in her distress, but it immediately occurred to her, that this was a premeditated contrivance between him and the people of the house. The captain conducted her towards the bird-cage walk, and began to inquire seriously into the truth of her story, and whether she was really married to me or not. She told him so many particular circumstances, and with an air of so much simplicity, that he seemed convinced of her sincerity. He then brought her towards the gate at Spring-gardens, which, to Mrs Rivers's great terror, they found to be shut. The captain, however, led her through at the Horse-guards, conducted her safe home, and never tendered her any gallantries afterwards.

These several frights and alarms, however, worked so much upon Mrs Rivers's sensibility, that they brought a return of her indisposition; and she, the next day, wrote the letter which hurried me to town.

I found her in a high fever, as I have related; but the calmness which my return brought to her spirits, and the excellence of her constitution, soon restored her to her usual health; and, after a little fruitless expostulation with the good lady of the house, we immediately shifted our quarters.

I had now fixed upon an elegant lodging, in a neat court, near
———— square; which I was not the less pleased with, when I found
the people of the house were rigid dissenters: for, though the characters
and conduct of the people have seldom much connection with their
religious systems, yet as most of those that dissent from the established
church are supposed to do it upon principle, they have an additional
check upon their behaviour, that they may not discredit the sect to
which they belong; and, as their teachers usually take more particular
care of them on that account, they have generally more appearance of
religion amongst them than the common people who call themselves
of the established church.

Ah! says Wildgoose, with a sigh, it is of little consequence what
church, or what sect we belong to, if we want a true vital faith, and are
not born again of the Spirit.

Well, sir, continued Mr Rivers, I staid a week with my wife at her
new lodging, when I was again obliged to go into the country; but
though the family she was now in had a very sober appearance, yet, as
she had had such bad luck before, I was determined at my return to
fix her as a parlour boarder in a genteel school, not far from the square,
whither she now went every day, for the sake of improving herself
under the several masters that attended there: and I had also given her
directions where to apply to Mr Hammond, in case of any disagreeable
contingency.

I had not been a fortnight in the country before I received a letter,
to my no small surprise, that she had been again obliged to quit her
lodgings, after being again greatly alarmed, though she did not mention
the particulars. When I came to town I found, to my astonishment, the
case to be as follows.

The mistress of the house went very regularly every Sabbath-day to
the meeting. She had not been gone long, the Sunday after I left them,
when Mrs Rivers rang the bell for the maid, to assist her in altering
her dress. After waiting a few minutes, she heard her, as she thought,
come tripping up the stairs; but, to her great amazement, the moment
she entered the door, in came the master of the house. He was a little,
middle-aged man, of a Jewish complexion, with one leg considerably

shorter than the other; and being of a dirty, though one of the genteeler kind of mechanic trades, gave one no bad idea of the poetical Vulcan. His wife, however, being no Venus (like that of the Lemnian god), he was greatly inclined to violate the matrimonial contract.

He told Mrs Rivers, then, that he had a very good hand at lacing stays; and, seeing her without a handkerchief, he offered to take great liberties. She was more provoked than terrified at this despicable gallant; and, bursting from him, ran immediately to the sash, and called out to one Mrs Thomas, (a woman of good family, but small fortune), who lodged upon the first floor across the court, and who, seeing so agreeable a young person left in such indifferent hands, had contrived to get acquainted with her the day after I left her. This spirited proceeding in Mrs Rivers soon put to flight her limping lover; and, upon telling the affair to Mrs Thomas, she assisted her in packing up her things, slipped out, and called a coach; and conveyed her immediately to the boarding-school which I had fixed upon before I went down.

Upon my expostulating with her gallant upon this affair, he said, that happening to go by the dining-room as Mrs Rivers was dressing, he owned it was a great temptation; and, if God had not given him grace, confessed he might have yielded to the force of it; but vowed he had not offered the least incivility. As this wretch was beneath my resentment, and I was desirous of causing as little speculation as possible, I thought it best to pocket the insult, as well as the money, which he voluntarily returned, having a little unconscionably extorted it, for the ensuing week's lodging, though Mrs Rivers was obliged to quit it on account of his ill usage.

You may be apt to wonder what there could be in Mrs Rivers's person or behaviour, that could expose her to so many insults of this kind. You may guess, by what you now see of her, that she must have been a very desirable object, in the bloom of fifteen; which received no small addition by a very cheerful, though innocent behaviour. But I believe it was chiefly owing to the light she must appear in, as my peculiar situation in life required me to affect a privacy; and her prudence and knowledge of my fortune would not permit me to keep her a servant: so that these low people, presuming upon the criminal appearance of our connection, made those attempts, which they would probably have been afraid to have done upon a more favourable supposition.

XIV

THE STORY CONTINUED

Mrs Rivers was now settled in a tolerably agreeable family, where she had an opportunity of improving herself in every polite accomplishment from the best masters, under whose care, in a very short time, she made an incredible progress: and having now equipped herself in a more fashionable manner, and being somewhat improved in her carriage (though she wanted but little addition to her natural gracefulness), she attracted great regard wherever she made her appearance. If she happened to walk the streets, no one passed by her without particular notice; and every young fellow thought her an object worth a second view, and generally pursued her with his eyes till she was out of sight.

Upon her appearing once or twice in the sideboxes, she had several glasses levelled at her from different parts of the theatre; and though two or three fashionable ladies of quality endeavoured to stare her out of countenance, as one *that nobody knew*, yet her conscious innocence, and her natural good sense, which immediately penetrated through the frippery of the milliner, and the tinsel of dress, and saw nothing in those insolent fair ones which gave them any real superiority over herself, prevented her discovering any *mauvaise honte*, or rustic bashfulness: and she was distinguished by nothing but by her attention to the interesting scenes on the stage, from one that had been all her lifetime in public places.

I cannot forbear mentioning an odd kind of distress, which was occasioned by her appearing once in an improper part of the theatre. She went, with the rest of the young ladies, to their dancing-master's benefit, who was very eminent in his way, and the chief dancer on the stage at Drury-lane. Having a very full house, he was obliged to place his scholars in one of the balconies, which, you know, on common nights, are generally occupied by kept mistresses, and people of dubious characters. Her striking figure immediately drew the eyes of all the gentlemen in the pit. Amongst the rest a young man of fortune, one Mr Fitz-Thomas, whose seat was in her father's neighbourhood in the country, and who had frequently dined with me at his house, immediately knew her; and, as he had heard of her leaving the country with me, and was sensible that those sort of elopements too frequently ended in the ruin of such young creatures, it immediately occurred to him, that this was the case with poor Miss Woodville, especially when he saw her in that ignominious part of the play-house. He was a man of uncommon humanity, and began to be excessively concerned, on account of the worthy man her father, and the rest of the family. However, that he might not too rashly take up with such a surmise, he resolved to go round and speak to her; when he was agreeably undeceived, and found, to his great satisfaction, the true cause of her improper situation.

Ah! says Wildgoose, with a sigh, I cannot but think every situation *improper* in that temple of Satan, the play-house: but please to proceed with your story.

Well, continued Mr Rivers, you will think I dwell too much upon Mrs Rivers's personal charms. But, matrimony being usually considered as making a purchase at the expense of our liberty, nothing is more natural than the pride we take in finding our choice approved by the suffrages of the world. I will only trouble you with one instance more.

There was a lady, who had a little daughter in the school, and who was herself a parlour-boarder in the absence of her husband. She and one of the teachers (I know not with what view) dressed themselves out one day, and took Mrs Rivers to the Chapel-Royal at St James's, where, they assured me, a young hero of the highest rank eyed her with his glass the whole time: and, upon their meeting with some difficulty in getting to their chairs, an officer in his regimentals, under pretence of extricating them, inquired very minutely in what part of the town they lodged; in which this lady fancied he had some mysterious view. But, as she was a woman of intrigue herself, she was apt to suspect some deep design in the most indifferent transactions.

The character and behaviour of this lady, indeed, whose name was Mrs Birdlime, rendered Mrs Rivers's situation far less agreeable than it would have been, and was one cause of my removing her sooner than, perhaps, I should otherwise have done. Mrs Birdlime, as I told you, was a parlour boarder; and, as it is usual in that situation to find their own wine, &c. and this lady was very fond of her bottle, she was teazing Mrs Rivers every evening to join with her for a bottle of port, or a bowl of punch; and because she had not politeness enough to trifle away her money for what was disgustful to her, Mrs Birdlime had often reproached her with her *low birth*, and country education.

I had an opportunity one afternoon of drinking tea with this *high-bred* lady; and, after being informed that she was an Oxford woman, and having studied her features with some attention, I soon discovered her to be our old toast, Sally Burrage, an inn-keeper's daughter, who had so long powdered her red locks, and prostituted her face to her father's customers; and, by a judicious mixture of freedom and reserve, had drawn in a genteel young fellow, with a pretty fortune, to marry her; who, partly with a view of improving his income, and partly, perhaps, of being more frequently absent from his doxy, had purchased a commission in a marching regiment, and was now recruiting in the north. Mrs Birdlime, however, contrived to console herself, in her occasional widowhood, sometimes with a cheerful bowl, and sometimes, I am afraid, with less innocent amusements, if one might judge by her conversation and appearance. In short, though I found Mrs Rivers had, at present, almost an aversion to this woman and her way of life, yet as it is very unsafe for the best-disposed young persons to be too familar with vice, I was determined to remove her from hence, as soon as possible.

Upon my mentioning this to the governess, who was a very genteel woman, though elderly and very infirm, she expressed great concern at the thoughts of parting with her; for she assured me, that since Mrs Rivers had been with her, she had not had the least care upon her hands, having found her so prudent and faithful, that, young as she was, she had left the chief management of her domestic affairs to her discretion.

This account of my wife's economy gave me as much pleasure as the vast encomiums she bestowed upon her improvement in dancing, music, and the other superficial accomplishments, since I had now no reason to doubt but she would appear to as much advantage in the capacity of a mistress of a family, as she had hitherto done in every other situation.

XV

THE STORY CONTINUED

Mrs Rivers had, by this time, been near a twelve-month in town, when I received a message one day from a gentleman of distinction, who was then in London, requesting me to bring *Miss Woodville* to spend the day with his lady. This was one Mr Wylmot, whose seat in the country was not many miles distant from Miss Woodville's father's; and who, though much older than myself, from some accidental circumstances, had honoured me with a particular friendship and esteem. Accordingly I took my wife, in the character of Miss Woodville, to dine with them at their lodgings; where she was received with great complacency and politeness.

Upon my being left alone with Mr Wylmot, after complimenting me upon my good choice, he, in a very friendly manner, inquired, in what manner I intended to settle in the world, if I should marry before I was engaged in some profession, as he apprehended, he said, I should be tempted to do. Upon finding myself thus closely attacked by a man whom I knew to be my friend, and with whom I should have been ashamed to trifle; after some hesitation I told him, that we had been already married for some time; and, what was more, that Mrs Rivers, I believed, was pregnant. Why then, says he, with some quickness, do you not own your marriage, and resign your fellowship?—I hardly knew what reply to make to this question; but told him, however, that I intended it very soon, as the time allowed by the college was already expired.—Well, says he, I have nothing to do with your conduct in regard to the college, but, for God's sake, do not run the hazard of exposing yourself to the censure of the world, by keeping your marriage private any longer. Bring Mrs Rivers immediately into the country, and acknowledge her publicly as your wife. Observing me struck silent at this proposal, he very generously proceeded: I see, said he, you are under some difficulty what scheme to pursue.—He then told me, that he had such a particular house at my service, and that he would assist me in furnishing it; and that we should not only be welcome to live there till we could determine upon some better situation, but that he should be very happy in having us for his neighbours.

I was quite oppressed with the generosity of Mr Wylmot's behaviour, not only in offering me so elegant an habitation in so polite a manner, but also his patronage and countenance against the malevolence of the world; for he was a man of such a strict regard to decency, that no one in the neighbourhood would presume to question the rectitude of our conduct, when we were under his protection. I, therefore, gratefully accepted of his proposal; told him I would go to ———, and settle my affairs, resign my fellowship, and bring down Mrs Rivers as soon as possible.—Mr Wylmot said he should go into the country the next day, and, when we came, would send his chariot to meet the stage-coach, and convey us in a more *decent* manner to the place of our abode.

Upon my communicating my intentions to Mrs Rivers, she almost shed tears of joy at the thoughts of returning into the country; for, though she patiently acquiesced in continuing so long in town, as she thought it necessary for her improvement, yet she had often sighed to herself, and sent forth ardent wishes to see her father, her friends, and even her native place again, from which she had never before been absent a week together.

As to her father, old Mrs Woodville, you may suppose, had soon undeceived him with regard to our being married before we left the country; and had taken occasion from thence to aggravate his favourite daughter's imprudence, in consenting to go off in such a manner with an Oxford scholar. Upon my having visited him, therefore, after I had settled Mrs Rivers in London, he had discovered a great anxiety on her

account, and, with tears in his eyes, desired to know when he should
have the pleasure of seeing his daughter again, and when I intended
to fulfil my engagements to her. As I found what made him uneasy, I
gave him sufficient proofs of my having done it already; and assured
him, that she was my wife, and that he should see her again as soon as
was consistent with the end proposed in taking her from home. On his
account, therefore, Mrs Rivers was particularly happy in the thoughts
of returning into that part of the country.

After preparing for our journey, and furnishing ourselves with several
elegant, though trifling articles of furniture, which are apt to occur to
young housekeepers before things of real use or convenience, we set out
from London, accompanied also by our good friend Mr Hammond, and
arrived safe at the place where Mr Wylmot's chariot, with two servants,
met us and conveyed us with no small state to his seat. As I was known
to be a friend of Mr Wylmot's, and considered as a young man, who,
though of small fortune at present, had considerable expectations, we
were received with as much staring and speculation as if we had been
people of more consequence. We staid a few days in Mr Wylmot's house;
and when we were settled in our elegant little mansion, partly out of
respect to him, and partly, I suppose, out of curiosity, we received the
compliments of the neighbouring gentry; and for some time, I believe,
were the subject of no small speculation.

XVI

THE STORY CONTINUED

As every particular of this part of my life is very interesting to me,
continued Mr Rivers, I may probably have been a little tedious in my
narration: I will therefore hasten to a conclusion.

As soon as we were a little settled in our place of residence, Mrs
Rivers was impatient to pay her duty to her father, whither Mr Wylmot
sent a servant to attend us. You can more easily conceive than I can

describe, the tenderness of a meeting between a parent, who doted upon his daughter, and had some reason to fear the event of the journey she had taken, and a daughter, who had never before been absent from so indulgent a father.

Though Mrs Rivers was greatly improved since she left the country, both in her carriage, in her manner, and in the delicacy of her complexion; yet her travelling dress a little obscured her appearance the first night. But the next day (being Sunday) when she came down dressed for church, the whole family were struck dumb with admiration. Mrs Rivers, indeed, wanted no ornaments to set her off, but a full-dress always became her; and she dressed in so good a taste, that it greatly heightened her natural charms.

The fame of Mrs Rivers's beauty and appearance soon spread amongst the neighbouring villages; and some of the young swains, of the best substance who had formerly looked upon themselves as Miss Woodville's equals, began now to curse their folly, in suffering such a prize to be carried off by a mere stranger; nay, some of the most vain and sanguine began to inquire, whether she were yet really married; boasting that they could yet rescue her from the clutches of such a mere milk-sop, as I found they esteemed me. But these conceited rustics had no conception that the improvements in Mrs Rivers's mind would have been a greater obstacle to their ambition than those in her mere outward appearance; for, besides her having read a great deal, and conversed with people above their rank, Mr Hammond, as well as myself, had taken particular pains to cultivate Mrs Rivers's understanding; and by letting her into the real characters of the several persons into whose company she had been introduced, and by giving her a few general maxims for her conduct in life, a girl of her penetration and natural good sense, soon became furnished with a sufficient knowledge of the world: and Mrs Rivers was as quick-sighted in discovering a fool or a coxcomb, as if she had conversed her whole life with what is called *the best company*.

We spent a few days with Mrs Rivers's father, in that complete felicity which sincere friends enjoy after a tedious absence. I soon perceived, however, that the pleasure which Mr Woodville took in his daughter's

company, was fatal to Mrs Woodville's peace of mind; and that she had
been insinuating to her husband, how *proud* his daughter was got; that
she almost disdained to set her foot to the ground; and that nothing
in *their* house seemed good enough for so fine a lady. Though nothing
could be further from the truth than this representation, and though
Mrs Rivers behaved with that sweetness and affability, as to gain almost
the adoration of the whole family, except her step-mother, yet I thought
it best to shorten our visit, and we returned to what we at present
considered as our home, and where for some time we lived extremely
happy.

Mr Wylmot, indeed, took every opportunity of showing us marks
of his esteem, and endeavoured to make every thing as agreeable to
us as possible. Mrs Rivers was invited to partake in every party of
pleasure; and Mr Wylmot and I went frequently whole mornings a-
simpling, which botanical taste was what I alluded to, as the original
of our intimacy; and, in short, Mr and Mrs Wylmot did every thing
with so much delicacy and politeness, that we were not sensible of any
sort of dependance. But yet you may be sure so precarious a situation
could not be entirely satisfactory to any man that was not void of all
consideration or foresight.

I could not bear to reflect upon the light we must probably appear in
to the neighbourhood (who would not long be ignorant of my slender
fortune), to the servants, and, perhaps (though I do not know that it was
so), to some distant relations of that worthy man: for I have observed,
that when a man of fortune has no children (which was the case with
Mr Wylmot), as soon as ever he begins to decline from the meridian
of life, he is marked out by his most remote collateral kindred, as one
that exists merely for their emolument; as a steward who is to manage
and improve his fortune for them or their offspring; that he is generally
beset by mercenary people of that kind, to whom he is accountable for
every act of friendship or generosity; and that they often contrive to
supplant every one who seems to have the least share in his favour or
affection.

But though Mr Wylmot was continually showing us little marks of
his kindness, as has been before mentioned; yet it was in such instances

as were rather convenient to us, than very expensive to himself; and he had too high a sense of justice to his relations, to suffer his generosity to strangers to be any real prejudice to them.

Another reason for our living less agreeably in this situation was, what, perhaps, you would not have imagined, its not being very distant from Mrs Rivers's native place: for, though I am convinced no woman of the noblest birth or highest education could behave with more true politeness or propriety (as was acknowledged by every one that visited us when we first came into the country, and whilst they were pleased with the novelty of the affair), yet I soon found that the humble station of some part of her family, and Mrs Rivers's former situation amongst them, were uppermost in the thoughts of many trifling people of fashion; and that those circumstances were made a pretence, at least, for censuring that behaviour in *her*, which would have been applauded in any other woman. If she dressed genteelly, it was called giving herself airs which did not become *her* of all people; surely a woman of *her* rank had a very good excuse for not following the fashions so very scrupulously. If she happened to omit, or to be mistaken in the minutest particular of ceremony, which was very seldom the case; then, what could be expected from a parson of her education? her behaviour shows what she was; one may always distinguish the true gentle-woman in the most trifling particular. In short, as no people are so sensible of any little slights or indignities as those who find themselves sunk, either by misfortune, or their own misconduct, below the rank which they were born to (and for that reason people of the best breeding are usually more careful not to omit the usual marks of respect to persons in that situation); perhaps, I was more jealous of my little rights in this respect than many people would be, and was less happy in my present situation on that account than I should otherwise have been. Notwithstanding my friend's great goodness and generosity, I was determined to get into some more independent state of life as soon as possible.

XVII

The story continued

You will be surprised, perhaps, my friend Wildgoose, continued Mr Rivers, that, after taking my degrees, and residing so many years in the university, and having had what is called a learned education, I had not pursued one of the learned professions, law, physic, or divinity. But, in the first place, in each of those professions, as well as in higher life, 'ambition should be made of sterner stuff,' as Shakespeare says, than what my constitution consisted of; and I fancied I had substantial arguments against each of them; at least, though I had formerly some inclination to the study of physic, and had made some progress in botany, anatomy, and the other preparatory sciences, yet, by marrying so early in life I had precluded myself (as I imagined) from a sufficient application either to that profession or to the law; for few people will care to trust either their health to a physician, or their fortune to the management of a lawyer, who is not an adept in his profession: and, as to the church, the usual sanctuary of many an idle young fellow, the little progress I afterwards made in divinity, from a wrong plan of study, and an ill-directed application, discouraged me from engaging in so solemn a profession; for though I might be qualified to *read* a sermon once a week to a country congregation, I think it would be much better for the community, if more persons in such circumstances would descend to a more humble sphere of life, rather than (by intruding into a province for which nature, or at least their education, never intended them) to mislead others, by their blunders and ignorance, in the discharge of that sacred function.

Ah! says Wildgoose, it is neither nature nor education, but grace and the call of the Spirit, that can qualify a man for that sacred function.

Why, that may be true, in some measure, says Rivers. A man should not take upon him that office without some inward call from the Holy Spirit: but the most material part of the ministerial call now-a-days seems to be the outward call to a good living; and, if I had not by this match disobliged my good cousin Mr Gregory Griskin, whom you have often heard me mention, I should probably have inherited the advowson of which he is now possessed: but as somebody has taken care to misrepresent my wife to him as a very vain extravagant woman, he will neither see me, nor hear any thing in our favour. I have, therefore, now no prospect of any living; and I do not choose to go into orders, to be a curate all my life-time, and work for about fifteen-pence a day, or twenty-five pounds a year.

XVIII

THE STORY CONCLUDED

Well, sir, continued Mr Rivers, whilst I was in this uncertainty, and undetermined what scheme to pursue, I went to spend a day or two with that Mr Fitz-Thomas, whom I mentioned to you as living in the neighbourhood. I there met another Oxford acquaintance, or rather true friend, who had a good estate in this county where we are now settled. It was Mr Grandison, whom I believe you remember; a near relation to Sir Charles Grandison, who has since made so great a figure in the world, and little inferior to him in the most shining parts of his character.

Upon talking over my precarious situation with my two friends, Mr Grandison said, in a jesting manner, that I must go and take his farm, which was then vacant by the death of an old tenant, and was now upon my friend's hands. Mr Grandison had probably no serious design in this; but, though I was very ignorant of the mystery of modern farming, yet having been so much conversant in the classics, I had conceived a romantic notion of agriculture, with which my taste for botany also had some connection. I was, therefore, agreeably struck with the idea of turning farmer, and began to think seriously of Mr Grandison's random proposal. In short, upon talking the affair over with him more minutely, I found, that, supposing I should not make the most of things, it would yet be no difficult matter to raise the rent which Mr Grandison expected from it; and that, with the interest of my fortune, I might live upon it very comfortably: and, when he found I was really inclined to settle in such a retired way, Mr Grandison seemed pleased with the thoughts of having a tenant, of whom he could upon occasion make a disinterested companion, in that part of the year which he usually spent in the country.

Not to trouble you with any more uninteresting particulars, after consulting with Mrs Rivers and Mr Wylmot, I came down with Mr Grandison to view the premises, which appearing every way agreeable, he gave me a proper security for an uninterrupted possession of my farm, upon paying the old rent, which was a very moderate one; and we soon after left our elegant modern cabinet in ——shire, for this Gothic dwelling where you now find us, and where, by the help of an honest old couple, who live in that cottage behind the elms, and take the chief drudgery of managing the farm off our hands, we pass our time in a manner entirely suitable to our love of ease and retirement. The farm more than furnishes us with all the necessaries of life; and it is incredible, with Mrs Rivers's economy, how small an income supplies us plentifully with all the elegancies which temperance and an unexpensive taste requires.

We are happy in a friendly intercourse with the rector of our parish and his lady, who are sensible, worthy people. We are sometimes invited by people of higher rank in the neighbourhood; but as I am convinced, that, as soon as they have satisfied their curiosity, and displayed their magnificence, there is an end of their civility, I give but few of them that satisfaction.

I converse as little with the generality of my brother farmers; yet, though many of them are people of low cunning, and never speak a word, even about the weather, without some artful design: yet I now and then meet with a great deal of good sense among them, and a plainness and simplicity which is truly valuable wherever it is found.

But my study affords me sufficient relaxation from the business of my farm, which, indeed, employs a considerable part of each day, so that they never hang heavy upon my hands; and I really take as much pleasure in the neatness of my farm, as your grander folks do in their woods and lawns. Nay, I have reconciled myself even to the dirtiest part of my business, and can discover some sort of beauty in a dunghill; which, by reducing the most worthless things in nature into a useful compost, gives me a pleasure similar to that of an artist, who produces order out of confusion; or even that of a painter, who exhibits a pleasing landscape from contemptible materials, and from the confused jumble of various colours upon his pallet. But I begin to be tedious; and will conclude with the poet's triumphant distich,

> I've gain'd the port, and safe at anchor ride;
> Farewel, vain hopes!—let others stem the tide.

Mr Rivers having now brought his narrative to a conclusion; though Wildgoose thought his friend's situation favourable enough to his views of making him a proselyte, and was inclined to give a spiritual turn to the conversation: yet nature now prevailed over grace; and being exhausted with attention, as well as fatigued with his walk, he expressed his drowsiness by a very significant extension of his jaws. Rivers, therefore, waited upon his friend to his apartment, and they retired to rest.

XIX

WILDGOOSE QUESTIONS RIVERS ON RELIGION

Pox take you! I wish you were married and settled in the country! says the Duke of Buckingham to a dog that snapped at him as he walked the street. This his Grace considered as the greatest *curse* he could wish to his greatest enemy. Yet there have been people who have found happiness in a country life, and who have thought even matrimony a *blessing*; and poor Rivers was weak enough to rank himself in that number.

Mr Wildgoose, being waked pretty early by the singing of the birds and the vivacity of his own imagination, was impatient to pursue his journey to Bristol, the place of his destination; and coming down stairs, he found his friend and Mrs Rivers, with their little family, already assembled in the breakfast-room, into which the sun darted his beams through an eastern window. The neatness of the tea-table, the freshness of Mrs Rivers's complexion, and the cheerfulness of her countenance, attended by her little Cupids with their rosy cheeks, revived in Wildgoose, for a moment, his social inclinations; and he began to think but meanly of the present vagabond profession in which he had voluntarily engaged, and could not forbear the tribute of a sigh to the absent Miss Townsend.

After breakfast, however, he thought it his duty to put in a word for God, as his usual expression was, and began to examine his old friend about the state of his religion.

I remember, says he, when we were acquainted at college, you were very piously disposed; and though God had not then awakened me, I could not but admire those who were more religious than myself.

Why, I do not know, replies Rivers, that I was any better than my neighbours. However, I am indebted to a very good, though perhaps an odd man, for what little notion I then had of religion: my good cousin I mean, Mr Gregory Griskin, the little fat Staffordshire clergyman, whom you have often heard me mention, and with whom I lived for some time after the death of my father.

My father, though a very learned and studious man, took but little care of our religious education. I had an old aunt, indeed, who lived with us, after the death of my mother, that used to talk to us upon the subject once a week: but she generally came out of her closet on a Sunday night in such a peevish humour as gave us no very amiable idea of devotion; for, if we did but laugh or talk, she would fall into an outrageous passion, and reproach us with minding nothing that was good. We used to read the *Whole Duty of Man* to her [here Wildgoose shook his head with a contemptuous smile]; and I remember her often inculcating to us what some pious author says of temperance in eating and drinking; that the only end of those natural functions is to preserve life, and that it is even unlawful to propose any pleasure in them. So that I found the most temperate meal I had ever made had been highly sinful; for I always found that the satisfying one's hunger, even with bread and cheese, was necessarily attended with pleasure. Hitherto, therefore, the very mention of religion always damped my enjoyment.

But at my uncle Gregory's I was inured to its severities by an agreeable mixture of mortification and indulgence. There the flesh and spirit seemed to have entered into a very amiable compromise not to invade each other's territories. My cousin Gregory, as no man prayed more, so no man ate better. He was as hearty at his meals as at his devotions. The bell often rang, indeed, three times a day, to summon us to prayers, either in the family, or in the church: but then we immediately adjourned, either to breakfast, to dinner, or to supper; from collects to collations, and from litanies and absolutions to hot rolls in the morning, to tithe-pigs and fat geese at noon, and to raspberries and cream and apple-custards at night; the very recollection of which, at this distance of time, is no unsavoury contemplation.

The good books, however, with which my cousin Gregory supplied me, being better adapted to my taste and to my capacity, gave me the first notions of practical religion; such as, *Bishop Ken's Manual*, the *Great Importance of a Religious Life*, *Nelson's Devotions*, Burkit, and the like plain and sensible writers.

Yet I cannot but confess, that, after I came to the university, by reading the writings of freethinkers, and conversing with dissolute people, I became quite a sceptic in religion, and had hardly any settled opinions at all: but, upon having recourse to my Bible (though I found several things there, which, from the nature of those writings, must necessarily be obscure), yet the essential duties of religion are so strongly delineated, that, I am convinced, nothing is wanting, but an humble mind and an honest heart, to make us understand our duty; and the ordinary assistance of God's Spirit, to enable us to practise it.

Wildgoose began to controvert his friend's opinions; but, finding him rather obstinate, was unwilling to push matters too far at present. He began, therefore, to think of proceeding in his travels, and setting out for Bristol, according to his first intentions.

He had addressed himself once or twice to Mrs Rivers; but Mr Rivers interposing, my good friend, says he, my wife says her prayers, and takes care of her family, and does all the good in her power amongst her poor neighbours; but women, whose affections are employed upon their children, and their attention taken up with domestic concerns, have not time for these nice speculations, in which I find you have of late been so deeply engaged, and which seem to have taken entire possession of your imagination. We will, therefore, drop the subject, if you please, and take a walk in the garden, or try to catch some fish for our dinner. Wildgoose thanked his old friend; but said, he could not possibly accept of his invitation, as he was determined to get to Bristol that evening. He, therefore, took his leave of Mrs Rivers; and, with his fellow-traveller Tugwell, set out upon his expedition, Mr Rivers going with them to direct them into the great road.

XX

COMFORTS OF MATRIMONY

Mr Rivers walked a mile or two with his old friend, to direct him, as I observed, into the great road. Wildgoose could not forbear complimenting him upon the apparent happiness of his situation; and said, he only wanted the one thing needful to complete his felicity.

Mr Rivers replied, that he flattered himself with the notion of being as happy as any one can be in this world. I consider every man, says he, before marriage, as climbing the hill of life. Every step presents him with some new prospect, and flatters him with the hopes of more complete enjoyment. I am now arrived at the summit of the hill, and, I believe, in possession of all the felicity which this world can afford.

At the same time, I have a clear and distinct view down the whole vale of mortality, and can perceive, that there is nothing very exquisite to be expected from it: but, by making the best of every incident, whether fortunate or otherwise, I think a wise man may make the journey tolerably easy through this life, and must wait with patience for more perfect happiness in the next.

Wildgoose made some objection to the inactivity of such a situation for so young a man. To which Rivers answered, that he saw, indeed, some of his acquaintance rising into bishops, generals, admirals, judges, or eminent physicians; but, says he, they have their reward in the splendour and the applause of the world; I have mine in the ease and tranquillity of my life.

Before they parted, Rivers took the liberty, in his turn, to expostulate with his friend on his present romantic undertaking, and said, that although he did not doubt his intention was good, and that the world stood in need of some reformation, yet he could not think, that any private person could be justified in disturbing the peace of society, without some divine commission for that purpose. But reasoning with a man under the influence of any passion, is like endeavouring to stop a wild horse, who becomes more violent from being pursued. The two friends, however, took leave with mutual good wishes. Wildgoose said, he should pray for Mr Rivers's conversion; and Rivers, that it would be a great pleasure to him, to hear that Mr Wildgoose was returned to his disconsolate mother.

XXI

Arrive at Bristol

It was now past the middle of the day, and the weather extremely hot. Tugwell, therefore, interceded with his master, to stop and refresh themselves at a small inn, a few miles short of Bristol; with which request, though impatient to get to his journey's end, Mr Wildgoose thought it expedient to comply. He took himself a very slight refreshment; but desired Jerry to call for what he chose; which having done, and taken his pipe according to custom, Jerry sat down upon a bench, between a Bath postilion and the tapster, and took a comfortable nap. But Wildgoose soon roused him from his tranquil state, and again set out with hasty strides for the great commercial city of Bristol; which he considered, however, in no other light than as the Capernaum, the present residence of that great apostle, Mr Whitfield. Here they arrived about six o'clock in the evening.

As soon as they were got through the city gate into Temple-street, which gives one no very favourable ideas of that opulent city, some boys called after Tugwell who was a few yards behind his master, Ha! Jerry! your humble servant, master Jerry. Before he could express his surprise, another cries out, God ha' mercy Jerry! A third holloos out, Jerry for ever.

As soon as Tugwell could come up to Wildgoose, Odsbobs, cries he, why, master, our name is up; we may lie a-bed; I suppose they have heard of our preaching all over England by this time; the very boys in the street seem to know us, and call us by our names.—Why, replies Wildgoose, I do not suppose it is altogether the fame of our preaching that makes us known here; but I do not doubt that God will send his angel before us, as he did before Mr. Whitfield* in Wales; and wherever we come prepare people for our reception.

Wildgoose was going on in his observations, when Jerry now getting before him, he saw his name, in capital letters, written upon his back, with chalk; which was a piece of waggery of the tapster's, at their last stage, who, having heard his master call him Jerry, while Tugwell took a nap between him and the postilion, as was related, had put that joke upon him. Wildgoose rubbed out the chalk as well as he could, to prevent them from being exposed to unnecessary speculation; and they trudged on towards the heart of the city.

Upon inquiring after a lodging of a sober sort of a tradesman at his door, they were directed down to the Quay; where they met with a tolerable decent apartment, at a gingerbread baker's, on reasonable terms; though they were obliged, by a prudent precaution of their landlady, to pay a week's rent on their taking possession of the premises.

Wildgoose, thinking it now too late to wait on Mr Whitfield that evening, employed it in making proper inquiries after his lodgings, and in giving good advice to the people where he himself lodged; and, after eating a slight supper, retired early to his repose.

---

* Vid. *Journal.*

Book VII

I

MR WILDGOOSE'S INTERVIEW
WITH MR WHITFIELD

ALL THE CIVILIZED NATIONS OF the world had now boiled their tea-kettles, and all the inhabitants of Great Britain, except those of the court-end of the metropolis, were at this instant recruiting their spirits with a comfortable breakfast, when Mr Wildgoose, ever attentive to the great object of his peregrination, summoned his fellow-traveller, Jeremiah Tugwell, from the kitchen chimney-corner, where he had got leave to smoke his morning pipe. Come Jerry, says Wildgoose, up, and be doing; lay aside your pipe, and follow me.

When they were come into the street, Wildgoose told Jerry that he had found out Mr Whitfield's lodgings, which, says he, are but a short walk from this place. But, continued he, that tobacco of thine has a most ungodly savour; thy smell is as the smell of a tippling-house, and will be highly offensive to that holy man, who, I am persuaded, has been watching and praying for some hours, or, perhaps, has been feeding his *five thousands* with the heavenly manna of his eloquence; for my part, I was determined neither to eat nor drink till I had been admitted to commune with him, that I might be the more fit to receive the divine instructions of so great a master.

As Wildgoose was thus expostulating with his friend, they arrived at Mr Whitfield's lodgings; and, upon inquiring for him, they were shown up one pair of stairs by the maid of the house, who, tapping at the door, the two pilgrims were immediately admitted to Mr Whitfield's presence.

Mr Whitfield was sitting in an elbow-chair, in a handsome dining room, dressed in a purple nightgown and velvet cap; and, instead of a Bible or prayer-book, as Wildgoose expected, he had a good bason of chocolate, and a plate of muffins well-buttered, before him.

Wildgoose made a pause at the door, being a little dubious whether they had not mistaken the room; and Tugwell drew back, quite struck with awe at so episcopal a figure. But Mr Whitfield hailed them with a cordial condescension: Come, come in, my dear friends; I am always at leisure to receive my christian brethren. I breakfasted early this morning with some prisoners in Newgate, upon some tea and sea-biscuit; but found my stomach a little empty, and was refreshing myself with a dish of chocolate.

Well, my good friends, continued Mr Whitfield, has God made use of the *foolishness* of my preaching, to convince you of sin, and to bring you to a sense of your fallen condition; Come, my brethren, sit down, and let me know when you were converted, and what symptoms of the new birth you have experienced in your souls.

Ah! sir, replied Wildgoose, we have not yet had the happiness of hearing you preach; but I hope God has, by some other means, vouchsafed to give us some little sense of religion; and we have taken a pretty long journey, to learn from your mouth a more perfect knowledge of this way.

Yes, yes, quoth Tugwell, a little encouraged by Mr Whitfield's condescension, his worship is no novice in these matters himself: he can preach like any bishop, upon occasion, if that were all; but he is come to know how your reverence will please to employ him, and to get a little more of your Gospel lingo, and such like.

This discovery of Wildgoose's intentions was by no means agreeable to Mr Whitfield; for, whether he gloried in the number of his followers, and began to taste the sweets of such distinction, or whether he thought that too great a number of labourers in the vineyard might render the soil less fruitful to himself; however it was, he did not seem inclined to admit any more sharers in the labour;* but began to complain of the great number of divisions already among them; that one was of Paul, and another of Apollos; that brother Wesley had preached another Gospel, entirely contrary to his; in short, that, from that source, strife, envy, wrath, revelling, backbiting, drunkenness, and every evil work, began already to prevail amongst them.†

Well, well, says Tugwell, before Wildgoose could reply, his worship does it only out of love and good-will, as a body may say: we have

---

* Perceived in myself something like envy towards brother H*****.
Journal, p. 6.
† *Journal,* p. 6.

travelled pretty near a hundred miles *a-foot* upon this errand; though, for that matter, Master Wildgoose has as good a gelding in his stable as any gentleman in the county, and can afford to spend his own money, if need be, and does not do it for the lucre of gain.

When Mr Whitfield heard the name of Wildgoose, he immediately recollected the accounts he had received, by letter, from Bath and Gloucester, of this opulent convert; and immediately found himself inclined to receive more favourably Mr Wildgoose's proposals. He thought he might advantageously employ, in some remote province, so creditable a missionary, of whose abilities he had heard no common encomiums. He now, therefore, began to inquire more particularly into the circumstances of his conversion, and what proofs he could give of a ministerial call and qualifications.

Well, brother Wildgoose, says Mr Whitfield, when and where were you converted? when did you first begin to feel the motions of God's Spirit? in what year, what month, what day, and in what manner, did you receive the secret call of the Spirit, to undertake the work of the ministry? What work of grace has God wrought upon your soul? and what symptoms have you felt of the new birth?★

Wildgoose, not being prepared for a scrutiny of this kind, began to stare, and could not readily give an answer to these questions. After a little recollection, however, he said, that several circumstances had contributed to wean him from the vanities of the world; which disposition was confirmed, he said, by hearing one or two Gospel-preachers, but chiefly by reading several good books, and particularly his and Mr Wesley's Journals; whence, from observing the great success God had given to their labours, he found himself inclined to attempt something in the same way.

Here Tugwell could not forbear putting in his verdict. Odsbobs! says he, I believe I understand what the gentleman means by the *new birth*. It is no longer ago than last October, we had been grinding apples, and making cider for Madam Wildgoose, your worship's mother; and all the next day I mortal sick, and troubled with the gripes and belly ache;

★ This was the usual form of examination by the triers in the last century.

and I thought I should have *sounded away*. Old madam gave me some *higry-pigry*; and our Dorothy, who is the best wife in England, would have had me eat some bacon and eggs; but I could not bear the smell of victuals, and I thought I should have died: but at night, as soon as ever your worship began to preach in our chimney-corner, I found comfort; and from that time to this, I have never drunk a drop of cider, nor been at an ale-house, till we came this journey, nor at any merry-making, nor *sich* like, as your worship very well knows.

Wildgoose endeavoured more than once, by winks and nods, to give a check to Tugwell's volubility: but Mr Whitfield desired to hear the particulars, and endeavoured to give the most religious turn that he could to his impertinence. Then addressing himself again to Mr Wildgoose:

Well, sir, says Mr Whitfield, I would have you consider before you put your *hand* to the *plough*, and *compute the costs*; that is, how you can bear the persecutions, the insults, and mockeries, which you must expect to meet with in this arduous undertaking. You must submit to the lowest offices in this *labour of love*; you must pass through *evil report* and *good report*, converse with publicans and sinners, and even with harlots, if there be any prospect of their conversion: and I will consider, continues Mr Whitfield, of the properest method of employing your talents. But, I believe, I shall send you to preach the Gospel to the poor colliers in Stafford and Shropshire, or to the subterraneous inhabitants of the lead-mines, in the Peak of Derbyshire, who are as sheep without a shepherd: though I hope my brother Wesley has, by this time, been amongst them.

Wildgoose replied, he should dispose of him as he thought proper: and Tugwell, who, though he fancied himself another Timothy, yet considered amusement chiefly in his travels, cried out, Odsbobs! I shall like to travel into Derbyshire, and see the wonders of the Peak. There is a hole in the earth, without any bottom to it, as they do say, and a passage into the other world, which they call the Devil's a-se o'Peak.—I do not know what they call it, replies Mr Whitfield; but, by all accounts, the Devil has an extensive property, and great power, over the whole world at present, especially amongst those poor people, whose subterraneous employment cuts them off from all chance of spiritual instruction. But I hope, by the help of my good brother here, and other friends, we shall soon make the Devil's kingdom shake to its very centre.

I am to preach this afternoon, continues Mr Whitfield, to the poor colliers of Kingswood (where, my greatest enemies must confess, I have done considerable service); and, in the evening, to one of our societies in Bristol; to both which places I hope you will accompany me, and behold the wonderful works of God.

Wildgoose said he would with pleasure attend him; but added, as God had so far prospered his journey, as to bring him to the sight of Mr Whitfield, he would trespass no longer upon his time at present than to deliver Lady Sherwood's compliments, as he had promised her ladyship, whom he saw at Bath. Mr Whitfield replied, that that was an elect lady, a star of the first magnitude; and he did not doubt but she would be an instrument, by the influence which her rank and fortune gave her, of promoting the great work which was going to be wrought upon the earth.

Mr Wildgoose then took his leave, promising to attend him with great punctuality, both at his afternoon's and evening's engagement.

II

HEARS MR WHITFIELD AT KINGSWOOD

As soon as they were come into the street, Odsbodikins; cries Tugwell, this is a desperate *familler* gentleman. Methinks he and I could be as good company together as if we had been acquainted these twenty years. But I think he might have offered us a bit of his oven-cake, and a drop of his buttered ale, or whatever it was. But come, master, let us go and get something to eat; you will never be able to hold out as Mr Whitfield does. He seems to like a bit of the good *cretur* as well as other folks.

Ah! Jerry, says Wildgoose, thy thoughts run still upon thy belly and the flesh-pots of Egypt. However, our master does not deny us the use, but the abuse of his good creatures. 'Thou shalt not muzzle thy ox or thy ass, that treadeth out thy corn.' Those that labour most in spiritual things, have the best right to these carnal things, though they do not place their happiness in them.

By the time they came to their lodging, however, their hostess had got a good warm dinner of homely food, the savoury smell of which revived Wildgoose's appetite; so that the natural man getting the better of the spiritual, he sat down with Tugwell and the family, and ate as heartily as the best of them.

The time was now come when they were to attend Mr Whitfield to Kingswood; where, when they arrived after a sultry walk, they found about ten thousand people assembled; the trees and hedges being lined with spectators. There had been a violent storm of thunder and lightning; but this was dispelled by a single ejaculation; and Providence was pleased so visibly to interpose, in causing the weather to clear up just as he began, that Mr Whitfield could not avoid taking notice of it in his discourse to the people, and to hint, that the course of nature had been altered in favour of his harangue. The sun now shone, and all was hushed; and notwithstanding the distance of some part of the audience, they all heard distinctly; for, indeed, the wind was extremely favourable.

Whilst all was thus in a profound calm for near an hour, every one being attentive to the voice of the preacher, on a sudden the skies again grew black, and the assembly was alarmed a second time, by a most tremendous volley of thunder and lightning, and a storm of rain.

A remarkable difference now appeared between the saints and the sinners. Those whom curiosity, or perhaps some less justifiable motive, had brought thither, scampered away with the utmost precipitation, to trees or hedges, or some occasional sheds which had been erected amongst the coal-works, to avoid the impending storm; whilst those who either were, or fancied they were, possessed of true faith, scorned to flinch, or to discover the least regard to their bodies, whilst they were thus refreshing their souls with the heavenly dew of Mr Whitfield's eloquence.

Mr Whitfield now very dexterously shifted his discourse to the present occasion, and observed, that although Providence had, at their first meeting, so miraculously put a stop to the rain; yet he had now, with the same gracious intention, permitted it to rain again, to try the zeal of his audience, and to distinguish his sincere votaries from pretenders and hypocrites; and he did not doubt, but, together with the rain, God would shower down upon them the gracious dew of his blessing, and refresh them with his Spirit. And this compliment many of them thought a sufficient consolation for their being wet to the skin.

The service being now ended, though the storm was over, and the sun shone out, yet a good part of the audience were in such a dripping condition, that it furnished many a pious soul with a good pretence for taking a cordial; and the brandy-bottle and gingerbread were plentifully distributed by the suttlers, that always attended on these occasions.

III

Evening's entertainment

Mr Wildgoose and his friend Tugwell had hardly dried and refreshed themselves after their return from Kingswood, when they were again summoned to attend Mr Whitfield to the nightly meeting at the Tabernacle; where he harangued to a less numerous, yet not a less crowded audience, than that at Kingswood. He usually made choice of a different text at each meeting; but whatever the subject was, it always ended like Cato's speeches in the senate-house, with, *Delenda est Carthago*, 'Down with your good works!' with a denunciation against self-righteousness, and a recommendation of faith alone in its stead, as if virtue were inconsistent with the belief of the Gospel; though, as a great divine★ observes, this doctrine of renouncing their own righteousness has been generally found most agreeable to those who have no righteousness of their own to announce.'

★ Chillingworth.

And now Wildgoose discovered the true secret of making converts. He had often himself had the satisfaction of being followed and applauded for his eloquence; but had reason to suspect, that he rather entertained his audience, than made them real converts to his opinions. His mistake was, that he began at the wrong end. He went the old-fashioned way to work, and was for persuading people to repent of their sins, and reform their lives; to practise the precepts, as well as believe the doctrines of the Gospel; which kind of preaching, though enforced in the most pathetic manner, was not so generally palatable as might be expected.

Mr Whitfield, on the contrary, said little about repentance, but laid all the stress upon faith alone; so that if a man was, or fancied, or even said, that he was possessed of true faith, he was immediately pronounced a convert; and, whether he reformed his life or not, became a saint upon easy terms. By this means chiefly such crowds of colliers and chimney-sweepers were transformed into angels of light, and became entitled to many a comfortable breakfast of buttered-toast and tea with the more wealthy devotees, and helped to increase the fame and popularity of these itinerant reformers; not to mention the many facetious tales with which Mr Whitfield amused his hearers from Joe Miller, and other authors of facetious memory; and the attractions which were found in their psalms and hymns; which, being chiefly set to popular tunes, had the same effect in recommending their doctrines, as the like cause had formerly establishing the fame of the Beggars' Opera.

The meeting being ended, and Mr Whitfield, somewhat fatigued, he took his leave of Mr Wildgoose for that evening, but desired his company to breakfast the next morning, with which Mr Wildgoose punctually complied. Mr Whitfield then told him, he had it revealed to him by the Spirit, that Mr Wildgoose should go towards the north in a few days, and preach to the colliers and lead-miners in those parts; but that he should first give the word of exhortation to their brethren at the several meetings in Bristol, that he might judge of the soundness of his doctrine, and give him any necessary instructions for his future conduct.

Though this was but a proper compliment to so distinguished a convert, and Mr Whitfield was willing to treat his followers with a little variety; yet, as he found some few sparks of jealousy in his own breast, he was desirous of dismissing Wildgoose as soon as he decently could. Mr Whitfield, indeed, had the advantage of him in complexion, and the solemnity of his periwig (and a good periwig, as the barber observed, contributes not a little to the conversion of sinners); yet Wildgoose excelled Whitfield in an expressive countenance, and a more gentleman-like air; not to mention the weight which an opinion of Wildgoose's superior fortune would probably give to his eloquence.

Mr Whitfield, therefore, proposed that Wildgoose should hold forth that very evening at one of their meetings; to which, with a decent reluctance, he consented: which point being settled, Wildgoose took his leave for the rest of the day.

IV

WILDGOOSE MOUNTS THE ROSTRUM. AN UNEXPECTED INCIDENT

In the evening, at the usual hour, the two brethren met at the Tabernacle, and Wildgoose was conducted to the desk by Mr Whitfield himself, where several ladies were already seated (which is a compliment usually paid to persons of any fashion); and they seemed particularly pleased with the genteel, though plain, appearance of this youthful orator.

Mere novelty gives a preacher no small advantage, if there is nothing vilely dull or ungracious in his manner. Wildgoose, however, having several other recommendations, was heard with particular attention and applause; and his fame soon spread universally amongst the saints at Bristol; and he preached almost every evening to more crowded audiences than Mr Whitfield himself.

But his fame was accompanied also with more solid advantages, and introduced him to the acquaintance of two or three wealthy dowagers, and as many handsome wives. Among the rest, he was particularly intimate with Mrs Cullpepper, the young wife of a wealthy alderman of the city of Bristol; who, having no children to amuse her, and finding but few of the comforts of matrimony in the society of an elderly husband, chose to pass two or three evenings in a week at these religious assemblies; in which innocent amusement her spouse gladly indulged her. These pious ladies then thought nothing too good for such good and holy men; so that, with chocolate and rolls for breakfast in the morning, biscuits and sack at noon, with turbot, ducks, and marrow-puddings for dinner, and roasted fowls or partridges for supper at night, Wildgoose passed his time in no unpleasant manner.

After he had been haranguing one evening, with the pretty Mrs Cullpepper (like the angel usually painted at the back of St Matthew) leering over his shoulder; when the meeting was ended, and the crowd began to disperse, he handed her out of the desk, and when they came to the door of the Tabernacle, they found a crowd gathered round two genteel sort of women in travelling dresses, one of whom they said was fallen into an hysteric fit. As this was no uncommon symptom of the new birth, Wildgoose approached to administer some spiritual comfort when the lady should come to herself again; but when that happened, how great was his astonishment to find, that the lady in a swoon was no other than Miss Townsend, for whom Wildgoose had conceived so tender a regard when he was acquainted with her at Gloucester.

Mrs Sarsenet, it seems, under whose protection Miss Townsend had placed herself after her imprudent elopement from her father, had some business at Bristol fair, which began about that time; and Miss Townsend, having a desire to see Bristol (and, perhaps, from some more tender motive), had desired to accompany her in the stage-coach; and, having been awaked early in the morning, fatigued with her journey, and, perhaps, somewhat affected at the sight of Mr Wildgoose's gallantry to Mrs Cullpepper, it was more than her delicate constitution could well support.

Wildgoose, having acknowledged them as his acquaintance, and made a proper apology to Mrs Cullpepper, begged leave to accompany Mrs Sarsenet and Miss Townsend to their inn, where they spent the evening together, in talking over the state of affairs at Gloucester, the adventures of their journey, and such other chit-chat, which, though insipid enough to others, is very interesting to friends who have been any time absent from each other. In short, the evening passed away very agreeably to Wildgoose and to Mrs Sarsenet; and probably, if the truth were known, no less so to the sprightly and amiable Miss Townsend.

V

GLOUCESTER JOURNAL

As Mrs Sarsenet and Miss Townsend staid the next day at Bristol, Wildgoose passed most of the time with them. Mrs Sarsenet informed him, amongst other things, of the persecution which poor Keen, the barber, had undergone from his neighbour at the pot-house, who to be revenged on the barber for taking him before the mayor, had gone privately and paid off a year's rent which he owed his landlord, and arrested him for the money; by which means the poor barber was reduced to the utmost distress. She told him likewise, that she herself had made some enemies, by telling people, in the way of her business, some disagreeable truths; but that she was happy in the slightest persecution for the Gospel's sake.

Miss Townsend also, at Wildgoose's request, related what had passed at her interview with her father, who, he soon found, was the same curious gentleman whom he had accidentally met at Lord Bathurst's house in the wood. My father, says Miss Townsend, sent for me to the Bell Inn, and, upon my knees before him, raised me up, and with great tenderness clasped me in his arms, the involuntary tears trickling down his cheeks. He soon began to chide me, however, as he had too much reason to do, for my unparalleled imprudence; but said he could more easily have forgiven me, if I had not aggravated my crime by taking refuge with my good friend here, Mrs Sarsenet, who, he alleged, had been guilty of so many deliberate affronts to him and Mrs Townsend, in her letters.

Upon my attempting to justify this part of my conduct (as Mrs Sarsenet had been a friend of my mother's, and as I was afraid to return home, where I had been so ill used by Mrs Townsend), he flew into a violent rage, and said, that under the pretence of a great regard for my mother, I showed a great disregard for him; and that it was very saucy and undutiful in me, to take upon me to censure his conduct, or to behave with disrespect to a person who was so useful to him in the management of his family; and, in short, that he could not desire to see me at home again, till I could bring myself to behave with more civility and complaisance to the widow Townsend; but, says he, I will think of some method of disposing of you, for you shall not continue with this woman here, meaning my good Mrs Sarsenet.

He then sent the servant with me to Mrs Sarsenet's, after taking a very cool leave, and bidding me consider of it, and behave better for the future. The servant told me, as we went along, that he believed his master was going into Warwickshire before he returned home; so that I imagine my dear father intends to send me to a very worthy clergyman's, who married a near relation of our's; which, as things now are, would be a situation the most agreeable to my wishes.

Miss Townsend then asked Wildgoose, in her turn, whether he had heard any thing further of his poor mother, who, she was persuaded, must be greatly concerned at his absence; and when he thought of returning into that part of the country Wildgoose replied, that he was soon to go towards the north, and intended to call upon Mrs Sarsenet and his friends at Gloucester; but was afraid it would be too much out of the road to visit his native place; though in this, he added, the dictates of the Spirit must be his guide.

As Mrs Sarsenet and Miss Townsend were to return the following day, Wildgoose took them in the evening to hear Mr Whitfield, though much against Miss Townsend's inclination, who also absolutely refused to go into the desk (whither she was invited), because she saw the same Mrs Cullpepper there, whom we before mentioned as a constant attendant of Mr Wildgoose, and whom she had seen him gallanting out of the desk the night before at the Tabernacle.

Wildgoose took his leave of his two friends that evening, who were to return the next morning in the stage-coach. Yet, when the morning came, he could not forbear another visit to their inn, to take a second leave of the amiable Miss Townsend, which was done with no small degree of tenderness on either side.

VI

TRIUMPHS OF FAITH

After his two friends were gone, Mr Wildgoose went to have another conference with Mr Whitfield, who took him to visit the prisoners in Newgate, and to several other objects of charity; to whom Wildgoose was more liberal than it was prudent for him to be, considering how soon his stock might be exhausted, and how difficult it would be, in his present situation, to recruit it.

Amongst other objects of distress, Wildgoose released from his confinement a journeyman sugar-baker, who had been thrown into prison by his master, out of spite, for being a follower of Mr Whitfield, and for a trifling mistake in his accounts.

Another young fellow was confined (as he assured them) only for writing the name of a country justice to a petition, out of mere charity to a poor farmer, who had suffered great losses by fire.

Mr Wildgoose also bestowed a handsome gratuity upon a poor woman, who had been used to retail gin about the streets, but who pretended to have lost her trade, and to be reduced to poverty, by so many of her customers having been converted by Mr Whitfield. This complaint strongly recommended her to Mr Whitfield's attention, and to Wildgoose's benevolence and liberality.

Mr Whitfield then conducted Wildgoose (by way of curiosity) to several different people, who were great advocates for the right of private judgment, and for the liberty of interpreting Scripture their own way; who looked upon all creeds and confessions of faith as unjust impositions, and as insults upon the freedom of human nature; who were for the independence not only of each congregation on other churches, but of every individual on each other.

In order to pursue their plan the better, these people had given up all secular employment, and did nothing but study the Scriptures from morning till night, the precise literal sense of which they strictly adhered to. There were half a dozen of them, who lived together in one house, and had all things in common (in which was included a community of wives); so that they lay *higgledy-piggledy*, just as it pleased their fancies: they wore each other's shirts and shifts; and it sometimes happened, that the men wore petticoats, and the women wore the breeches; so strictly did they adhere to the letter of the law.

There was one man who had sold all that he had,★ even his very clothes (which, indeed, was only a coat and breeches), and had given it to the poor; so that he himself was become one of that number; for he was quite naked, and forced to subsist upon the charity of his Christian brethren: this, however, he might easily do; for, according to another precept of the Gospel, he thought it necessary to become as a little child, and, like a new-born babe, fed upon nothing but milk, or pap made of the mouldy crusts which were sent him for that purpose. Similar to this was the error of another poor man, who made it a rule to give to every one that asked him; so that having given away all his own money in charity, he now did the same by all that he could extort by begging from good Christians in more affluent circumstances.

These people also shared the benevolence of Mr Wildgoose, though he and Mr Whitfield endeavoured to show them the absurdity of their principles, and the ridiculous consequences which, amongst ignorant people, might arise from thus realizing the metaphors of the Oriental languages. Thus, says Wildgoose, the painter (in Mr Wesley's *History of the Bible*) has drawn one man with a long beam sticking out of his eye, and endeavouring to pull a little straw, or mote, out of his brother's eye. And, although we are commanded 'to build up one another in the faith,' it would make but an odd sort of a picture to see a parcel of Christians turned masons and carpenters, and piling up one another, like so many stocks and stones.

★ Contin. *Journal*, p. 98.

Mr Whitfield said, their principles were too absurd to be criticised. However, as God had once opened their eyes to see part of the truth, he did not doubt but he would perfect his own work, and bring them at last to the true faith.

Mr Whitfield then took Wildgoose into a very dark street, where the houses in the upper storey almost met. Out of the middle of this street they went into a little court, then up a winding staircase, where Mr Whitfield knocked at a chamber-door, which was opened by a little thin man, who desired them to walk in. His apartment was small, but neat enough, having a print of the Crucifixion over the chimney. There were no signs or implements of any art or trade; nor any books but a quarto Bible, which lay open on a table under the window.

Mr Wildgoose, says Whitfield, give me leave to introduce you to a religious curiosity, or rather, if he does not deceive himself, to a miracle of divine grace! Our brother Slender here is a man that has not committed sin these five years.—Hem! cries Slender, lifting up his eyes, and laying his hands upon his breast; nor ever will again, whilst in the body, by the grace of God.—What way of life is master Slender in, then? says Wildgoose.—I am a stay-maker by trade, quoth Slender.— Do not you work at your trade, then? says Wildgoose. No, by the grace of God, answered Slender; for though I was bred to it, I think it an unlawful calling.—Why so? says Wildgoose.—Because it administers to sin, and to the works of the flesh, replied Slender.—I do not see how so necessary a part of the female dress, as a pair of stays, can contribute to sin, says Wildgoose. I should rather think it had a contrary tendency, and might sometimes secure the virtue of the fair sex; at least, as it does not *directly* administer to vice, I can by no means think that of a stay-maker an unlawful calling.

But how does master Slender live, then? continues Wildgoose.— Upon the charity of my friends, and the good providence of God, answered Slender.—I am afraid, then, replies Wildgoose, your whole tenour of life is sinful; as no man has a right to be supported without contributing something to the public stock.

Why, Mr Wildgoose, says Whitfield, I have shown you our brother Slender, rather as a poor soul under the dominion of Satan, than as one whose sentiments I entirely approve of. Our friend has a good heart, but a weak head; for certainly, 'if we say that we have no sin, we deceive ourselves.'—Sir, says Slender, Mr Wesley has given a different interpretation to those words, and applied them to man only in his unregenerate state.—That may be, replies Mr Whitfield; but yet I am afraid, my friend, your present contemplative way of life is really not to be defended, either by reason or Scripture, as it renders you entirely useless to the world, and a burden (though but a *slender* one) to society.

As Slender, however, had told them, that he subsisted upon the charitable contributions of his friends, Wildgoose thought proper (to prevent any suspicion of opposing his opinions from selfish motives) to show him a specimen of his liberality; so gave him something handsome, and took his leave.

VII

THEATRICAL ENTERTAINMENTS.
A NEW PROJECT FOR THEIR REGULATION

Mr Wildgoose, during his stay at Bristol, saw instances enough of the infectious nature of enthusiasm, and what absurdities people frequently run into who have once forsaken the guidance of reason, to have restored a man of his natural good sense to the use of his understanding; but he was so far intoxicated with zeal, as well as with the applause which he gained by his eloquence, that he proceeded with great alacrity and perseverance.

He held forth again in the evening, to a crowded audience, and after the meeting was ended, again supped with Alderman Cullpepper, his fair spouse, and some other company.

The alderman was a good sort of man, who, by his care and frugality in the earlier part of his life, had amassed a considerable fortune. He was much older than his wife; and, having no children (as was observed), could not find sufficient amusement for her at home: he was not displeased, therefore, with her spending two or three evenings in a week in so innocent a way, though he himself was too fond of the pomp of cathedral service, and of appearing at church in his fur-gown, to frequent the Tabernacle of the Methodists.

There supped with them that evening a Scotch officer, one Captain Gordon, who commanded a frigate of war, which lay at that time in King-road, and was soon to sail and join the fleet in the West-Indies. Just as they were sitting down to supper, there came in also a Welsh grocer, who had long been supplied with goods by Mr Cullpepper; and, having been two or three days at Bristol during the fair, had gone that evening, for the first time in his life, to see a play. Being asked how he came to return so soon, and, whether he did not like the play? he said, It was fery goot plaa; they plaad three bouts upon the fiddles, and the harps, and the pipes; but there were some great shentlemen came in, who had some private business to talk of together, and hur thought it was not goot manners to stay any longer.

The case was, poor Taffy (as it has probably happened to other country gentlemen) had mistaken the music before the play for the play itself, and so came away as soon as the actors made their first entry.

This incident, however, introduced a conversation upon that subject, and gave Mr Wildgoose an opportunity of inveighing with great vehemence against plays and theatrical entertainments. He said the stage was a nursery of lewdness and debauchery, and wondered that any play-houses were tolerated in a Christian country. Come, come, says the alderman, I will warrant you, you have been at a play before now. I cannot think there is any great harm in an innocent play. Why, I cannot deny, says Wildgoose, that I have been too often at those entertainments in my youth; but then I deny that there is any such thing as an innocent play. Every play that I have ever read, or seen acted, is a representation of some love-intrigue, or of some base and villainous action, filled with blasphemous rants, profane imprecations, lewd descriptions, or obscene and filthy jests. In short, I look upon the play-house to be as much the house of the devil,* as the church is the house of God; and that it is absolutely unlawful for a Christian to frequent it.

---

* Mr Law's *Christian Perfection*.

Why, says Captain Gordon, I am afraid there is but too much foundation for what the gentleman says; yet I imagine, his inference from it, that all plays are unlawful, is unjust, and proves too much for if a mere representation of vicious or immoral actions (though with a design to expose them, or to deter others from imitating them) be unlawful, how shall we defend the practice of the sacred writers themselves, both of the Old and New Testament, who have recorded many cruel, unjust, and some lewd actions, even of God's peculiar people?—Sir, says Wildgoose, with some warmth, I hope you do not compare the inspired authors of the Holy Bible with our modern scribblers of tragedy or comedy. —No, by no means, replies the captain; I only say, that the sacred writers relate many *tragical*, and, with reverence be it spoken, some *comical* events; but then it is always with a moral or religious intention; whereas, I confess, too many of our modern plays have a very immoral and irreligious intention, which, is a strong argument in favour of what I was going to propose, and what I have often thought would be a very proper regulation.—What is that? says Wildgoose.—Why, says Captain Gordon, as all plays are already subject to the inspection of the lord chamberlain, to prevent any thing offensive to the government from being brought upon the stage; so, to prevent any thing from being exhibited offensive to religion or contrary to good manners, they should likewise be inspected by the bishop of the diocese.—By the bishop! cries Mrs Cullpepper, with some surprise.—By the bishop! quoth Wildgoose, with a significant sneer.—They ought to be entirely prohibited and suppressed.—Why, continues the captain, to be sure those things are at present upon an odd footing in this country. Players, I believe, are considered by your laws as vagabonds; and, I have been told, are excommunicated by some ancient canons of the church, and yet are permitted to stroll about, and corrupt the morals, and introduce a habit of dissipation, in almost every little borough and market-town in England.

Well, well, says the benevolent alderman, all trades must live. I believe, indeed, these plays fill the heads of our 'prentices and young girls with wanton fancies sometimes; but, perhaps, they might spend their time less innocently elsewhere; and young people will have amusements of some kind or other.—Wildgoose was going to reply, but Captain Gordon was now saying gallant things to Mrs Cullpepper, and rallying her taste in preferring the amusements of the Tabernacle to that of the playhouse, and other more fashionable places of dissipation. It must be observed, however, that Mrs Cullpepper seemed more inclined to listen to Wildgoose than to Gordon, which occasioned some little jealousy in the latter (who for some time had been a sort of *cecisbeo* to Mrs Cullpepper,) which was attended with consequences, and precipitated Wildgoose's departure from Bristol.

VIII

A RIDICULOUS DISTRESS.
ADVANTAGES OF THE SACERDOTAL HABIT

The next day, in a conference, Mr Whitfield told Wildgoose, that he would have him be prepared to set out for the north; for that he had frequent invitations, by letter, to visit the brethren amongst the coal-mines in Staffordshire and Shropshire: though he was in hopes that Mr Wesley would take them in his way from that part of England.

But, continues Whitfield, to prepare you for the persecutions which you may expect to meet with from the prince of this world, I would have you undergo some voluntary trials before you leave this city. He then told Wildgoose he should visit the criminals in the condemned hole in Newgate there, and also bear his testimony against one or two places where Mr Whitfield could not go often without giving offence to weak brethren; that is, to a noted gin-shop, which he considered as an emblem of Hell; as also against a house of ill fame, or bawdy-house, as it is called, the mistress of which, he said, had felt some pangs of the new birth, and was not far from the kingdom of heaven. And, indeed, continues Mr Whitfield, I have more hopes of converting publicans and harlots,★ or in modern language, whores and rogues, than those self-righteous Christians, who are usually called *good sort of people.*

★ Vid. *Journal.*

Wildgoose was so zealous to execute any of Mr Whitfield's commands, and had now so much confidence in the force of his own rhetoric, that he would have gone immediately, and have attacked not only Mrs Toddy in her gin-shop, or mother Placket in her bagnio, but even Satan himself, if required, in his infernal abodes. Whitfield, however, advised him to defer it till another day, and to reserve himself for the evening; because he had heard, that several profligate young fellows, drawn by the fame of Wildgoose's eloquence, were to attend the Tabernacle that night: and Providence, he said, often made use of the curiosity, and even the malice, of such poor creatures, for their own conversion. And he could easily imagine, without any shock to his own vanity, that a new preacher might effect what he himself had not been able to do. Wildgoose, therefore, took his leave at present, and went to his own lodgings, to adjust his dress a little, and to wait for the time of assembling in the evening at the Tabernacle.

When Wildgoose came home to his lodging, he was struck with astonishment to see his friend Tugwell decked out with an immense grizzled periwig, instead of his own shock hair and jelly-bag cap; and, in the place of his short jerkin, dressed in a long, full-trimmed, old, black coat. Alderman Cullpepper, it seems, finding how fond his wife was of Wildgoose's company, and seeing Tugwell frequently about the house, thought there was something more decent and creditable in the second-hand finery of a town plebeian, than in the rustic coarseness of a simple clown. He had, therefore, broken through the habitual reluctance which he felt to *parting* with any thing, and equipped Tugwell in that droll manner, out of his magazine of old clothes, of about twenty years standing.

Wildgoose could not forbear smiling at his friend's paradoxical appearance; but, having been used of late to allegorize every event, he was going to make some practical inference from Tugwell's strange metamorphosis, when Jerry cut short his master by pointing out a monstrous chasm which he had spied in Wildgoose's plush breeches, from which two or three inches of his shirt hung dangling down in a most facetious manner. This was a misfortune which Wildgoose could not have foreseen; and as he had no change of raiment, was greatly distressed how to remedy. It could not have happened at a more critical or unfortunate juncture; as in half an hour's time, he was to mount the rostrum. What must be done? There was no precedent of any thing like this recorded in the journals of our modern apostles. Wildgoose could not bear the indecency either of sitting without his breeches, or of admitting a female hand so near his person, in a part so liable to inflammation.

From this awkward distress, however, he was quickly relieved by his trusty 'squire Jeremiah Tugwell; who, amongst the other furniture of his wallet, had had the precaution to pack up a large stocking-needle, and some strong worsted, with which he generously undertook to deliver his master from his perplexity, and with great dexterity levelled his needle at the schism in his master's trowsers.

Tugwell, however, could not forbear, during the operation, to make an obvious reflection in favour of the clerical habit and sacerdotal accoutrements. Ah! master, says he, if your worship now had but a gown and cassock, or could but put on a surplice, like our parson, you might have gone to the Tabernacle without any breeches at all. Adzooks! methinks I almost long to go to our parish-church again, to hear the bells chime on a Sunday, and see the parson walk up to the desk an' it were any bishop; and then turn over the great Bible with such a smack, it does one's heart good to hear him.—Ah! Jerry, says Wildgoose, these are only the outside ornaments, the mere husks of religion, and fit only to be cast before swine; that is, merely to amuse the senses of the vulgar, but afford no real nourishment to the soul. Wildgoose would probably have said a great deal more upon the subject, if, in the midst of his harangue, Tugwell's needle had not slipt a little too deep, and made him cry out with some vehemence, which put a stop to their dialogue.

IX

MODERN PROPHECIES.
EFFECTS OF WILDGOOSE'S ELOQUENCE

It was now time for Mr Wildgoose to be at the Tabernacle. When he came thither, and was going to begin his sermon, Mr Whitfield himself cried out, Let us wrestle in prayer for our dear brother Alderman Pennywise, who lieth at the point of death. He is a chosen vessel; he loveth our nation, and has contributed largely towards building us a synagogue.

As soon as Mr Whitfield's prayer was ended, a journeyman shoemaker, who was a zealous Christian, and himself an occasional preacher, cries out, Hallelujah! we have prevailed; God has given us the alderman's life; it is revealed to me, that the fever has left our brother Pennywise, and he liveth. They then began a hymn of thanksgiving, for the recovery of Alderman Pennywise; but before they had done, one came in and told them, to their great disappointment, that their brother Pennywise was *fallen asleep.*★

Wildgoose now began to harangue with great vehemence; and, as they expected some young fellows to come and make a riot that evening, Wildgoose was determined to exert himself, and if possible, gain their attention.

In order to this, he resolved to imitate Mr Whitfield's lively manner, and facetious similitudes.

He took his text from the book of Ecclesiastes, chapter xi.

'Rejoice, O young man, in thy youth, and walk in the ways of thy heart, and in the sight of thine eyes; but know, that for all these things God will bring thee to judgement.'

As if he had said, go on, young man, and take your swing; go to the tavern, and call for your bottle, and your pipe, and your Welsh-rabbit; entertain yourself with cards and dice, or with a play; then away to mother Douglas's, and regale yourself with a mistress; and, in short, indulge every appetite and passion to the utmost; but, take this along with you, if you do, you will be damned.

Damned! for what? you will say.—Why, not for whoring, or drinking, or gaming; not for cheating, lying, or swearing; no: God Almighty is not so captious, as to quarrel with his creatures for such trifles as these: no; it is for your want of *faith;* it is your infidelity, that you will be damned for.

★ It is well known how frequently these modern prophets have been mistaken in their predictions.

I will tell you a story. A Roman Catholic Gentleman went a partridge-shooting along with a Protestant neighbour of his on a fast-day: they were driven about noon, by a thunder storm, to a little public-house, where they could get nothing to eat but some bacon and eggs. The good Catholic had a tender conscience, and would eat nothing but eggs; the Protestant, his companion, who was one of your *good sort* of people, said, there could be no harm in his eating a bit of bacon with his eggs: that bacon could not be called flesh; that it was no more than a red-herring; it is fish, as one may say. So the Catholic took a bit of bacon with his eggs.

But just as he had put it in his mouth, there came a most tremendous clap of thunder. Upon which, the poor Catholic slipped it down upon his plate again, muttering to himself, What a noise here is about a bit of bacon! He foolishly fancied now the sin was in his eating the bacon. No such matter. It was his want of faith. He had not a proper faith in his own superstitious principles.

I remember, when I was at Oxford, I used to pray seven times a day, and fasted myself to a skeleton. I powdered my wig, and went every month to the sacrament, with the *Companion to the Altar* in my pocket. I might as well have had Ovid's *Epistles* in my pocket. The devil stood laughing behind the church door. The devil loves these formalities. I fancied myself a good christian: and had no conception, that I was as dead as a doornail; that I must be born again to a new life; and that I had no more saving faith than a Jew or a Mahometan.

Thus Wildgoose went on for some time, in the style of Mr Whitfield: but what was natural in the one, was rather ridiculous in the other, and had a contrary effect from what he had apprehended; for there were some youthful scoffers, who at first were a little riotous; yet they were soon overpowered by Wildgoose's eloquence, when he insensibly resumed his own style; and for near a quarter of an hour all was hushed in silence. But, on a sudden, a little girl, who did not seem to be above thirteen years old, cried out from the midst of the crowd, that she was pricked through and through by the power of the word.* This

---

* *Journal*, p.36.

occasioned some confusion; but the people about her checked her zeal, and stopped the poor girl's outcries; when a young fellow near the door, who was half fuddled, cried out, Damn such nonsense! these fellows ought to be whipped at the cart's tail, by G–d! He then threw a piece of an apple at the preacher; and he and his companions, setting up a laugh, rushed out at the door, hollowing and singing. Down with the round heads! damn all preaching and praying, say I.

A fig for the parson, and a fart for the clerk;
Let's put out our candles, and kiss in the dark.

Derry down.

Their rude behaviour, however, roused the fury of the lambs without doors, who began to pelt them with stones and dirt, and soon drove them off the stage.

As the preaching was a little interrupted by this incident, Whitfield took the opportunity to comfort his brother Wildgoose; and observed, that Satan envied their happiness: but, courage! my friend; we shall make his kingdom shake* before we have done with him, I will warrant you. Wildgoose then continued his discourse; and after he had done, he and Mr Whitfield were again invited, by Mrs Cullpepper, to partake of a comfortable supper.

X

EFFUSIONS OF SELF-IMPORTANCE. WILDGOOSE MEETS WITH A REPULSE

Mr Whitfield, having some other engagement upon his hands, withdrew soon after supper; and Mrs Cullpepper retiring to her closet for an hour, the alderman and Mr Wildgoose were left alone, *tete-a-tete*.

---

* *Journal,* p. 50.

Alderman Cullpepper, as was observed, by his industry and his frugality, had made a considerable fortune. And though his ideas were very low, and his soul excessively narrow, yet he had some ambition to get the character of a generous man, if he could obtain it without much expense, or any sensible diminution of his finances.

As the Alderman, therefore was obliged to keep something of a table, he was glad of that sort of submissive companions, who would express some glee at a parsimonious treat, and, content with a glass of wine now and then, would connive at his keeping the bottle on his right hand, and other stratagems of frugality, which he had learned in his less affluent circumstances.

With the same view, he was always recounting acts of munificence, which he had formerly performed; though like the traveller who boasted of the extraordinary leap which he had taken at Rhodes, he chose rather to refer you to witnesses who could attest his generous actions, than repeat them.

The Alderman and Wildgoose being now alone, then, partly to prevent too quick a circulation of the glass, and partly to give Wildgoose an idea of his consequence, and to convince a person of his *liberality*, who, he imagined, would never put it to the trial; Cullpepper filled up the intervals of each whiff of tobacco with the following ebullitions of vanity and self-importance.

Why, to be sure, there is not a man in the corporation (though I say it) that has a better interest in both the members than I have; though I make no other use of my power than to serve my friends. As for Sir Harry Plausible, he has a particular personal regard for me. (Sir Harry is certainly one of the *most agreeablest* men in the world.) It is not because I have a little interest in the corporation. No, no; it is not for that.—I dare say it is not, says Wildgoose.—No; I was acquainted with Sir Harry long before he had any thoughts of representing the city. The baronet is reckoned a proud man, indeed; but, I am sure, I never found him so. To be sure, the senator is a little reserved, when he does not like his company (and you know, sir, men that know the world are so;) but, when I and he are alone together, I can talk as freely to him as you can to your fellow-traveller here, Mr what-d'ye-call-him.—Ah! says

Wildgoose, nothing is more vain than the petty, distinctions which the children of this world are so fond of. Though we are not all members of parliament; yet all true Christians are *members* of Christ, and one of another.—Why, that is true, to be sure, sir, as you observe, says the alderman.

But did I never tell you how I got a living for our curate the other day?—I cannot say you did, replies Wildgoose.—I will tell you how cleverly I managed it. It was at the last treat Sir Harry gave the corporation. I sat next to the member. The glass went pretty briskly about.—Ah! says Wildgoose, I do not doubt it. Corporation treats are the devil's festivals.— Well, continued Cullpepper, without vouchsafing Wildgoose the least degree of attention, as I was saying, the glass went briskly about, and we had drunk pretty freely, but in a moderate way. *Howsoever*, the senator, who is a sober man too, began to wax mellow. Now, as I have pretty good intelligence, I had heard, that very morning, that the living of Ganderhill was become vacant. So *says* I to the senator, Yonder is our poor curate, *says* I, at the bottom of the table. He is a very worthy man, *says* I. He has been curate here these eighteen years. I have a great regard for him. I wish it were in my power to get him some little addition to his income. Indeed, he married a relation of mine: it was a distant relation. But the man is a very worthy man. Sir, says the member, if it ever lies in my power to oblige you, you may command me upon any occasion.

I believe the senator said this as words of course. However, I clinched him immediately. Well, well, sir, *says* I, remember your promise. I have a thing in my eye, if it should happen to fall: it is in the Chancellor's gift; but a word from you would do the business at once.

In short, having broken the ice, I said no more at that time. But, the very next morning, away goes I to the member's house, told him how lucky it was; that the very thing I had in my eye, was become vacant; and by his interest got it for my friend.

As soon as the alderman had finished his narration, and received the incense of a complaisant speech from Wildgoose, he began another, about his lending money to set up a young tradesman: neither of which was very interesting to Mr Wildgoose; yet, as his liberality had quite exhausted his stock of cash, he thought this a fair opportunity of trying

the force of his host's generosity in regard to himself.—Well, sir, this
was very good in you, to be sure. I shall never want to ask any favour
of that kind. However, sir, your generosity encourages me (as I have
this opportunity) to beg your assistance in a trifling affair; in which, I
know, it will give you pleasure to oblige me.—Ay, ay, Mr Wildgoose, any
thing that is in my way to serve you, I shall be very glad to do it, if it
is not any thing very much out of the way.—Why, sir, says Wildgoose,
since I have been in Bristol, I have met with several objects of charity;
and, as I brought but little money with me from home, my stock is
almost exhausted. [Here Cullpepper took his pipe from his mouth.] I
do not know, continues Wildgoose, that I shall want any money on my
own account (for I trust to Providence for my own necessities;) but if
you could spare me nine or ten guineas, to assist any poor brother in
distress—Nine or ten guineas! says Cullpepper, laying down his pipe,
and how can you be sure of returning it again?—Sir, says Wildgoose, I
hope I shall have some opportunity or other of doing it; but, if I should
not, as you will lend it in the support of so good a cause, you will be
sure of being rewarded a hundred fold at the great day of retribution.

Mr Wildgoose, says Cullpepper, I have nothing to say against the
cause you are engaged in; but I assure you, sir, the merchants of Bristol
understand business better than to lend their money upon so precarious
a security. In short, sir, I must take the liberty to tell you, that, from
what I have heard, you are very indiscreet in the management of your
money, and squander it away amongst a pack of idle rascals, who, instead
of working at their trades, run about from one meeting to another, and
take no care of their wives and families at home.

Whilst the alderman was haranguing in this lofty strain, and giving
Wildgoose advice, instead of lending him money, Mrs Cullpepper came
into the room, and, finding the cause of her husband's displeasure, soon
pacified him with a smile, and assured Wildgoose, with a nod and a
wink, that any little distress, which his charitable disposition might have
occasioned, would be relieved by their society; that nobody was more
generous than Mr Cullpepper; but that he did not quite approve of
one or two acts of liberality, which, he had heard, Mr Wildgoose had
performed—and the like.

Wildgoose said, it was no great matter; he could make very good shift for the present. And it being now near ten o'clock, the alderman's bed-time, he took his leave for that night; but at the door met Captain Gordon, who was coming to take a final leave of the alderman and his wife, having received an order to sail the very next morning for the West Indies.

Alderman Cullpepper was so full of this unexpected attack upon his generosity, that he could not forbear mentioning it to Captain Gordon; and Mrs Cullpepper, taking Wildgoose's part more warmly than was prudent, irritated her husband, and raised the jealousy of Captain Gordon; which produced an event which she could not have expected.

XI

MR WILDGOOSE BECOMES
A GREAT CASUIST

Mr Wildgoose had promised Mr Whitfield to attend him to Kingswood the next morning, and to give a word of exhortation to the poor colliers there. For which purpose, he was got up before six o'clock, that he might give his advice, in imitation of Mr Whitfield, to any poor people that came to consult him. Tugwell also was ready at the door, and with his inseparable companions, his oaken staff in his hand, and his wallet on his shoulders, stuffed with two or three stale rolls and cold meat (which the alderman's servant had given him,) for fear of accidents. Jerry had also put on his grizzled wig (to look more solemn;) but had left his full-trimmed coat in his bed-chamber, that he might not be incumbered in his walk.

Just as Wildgoose was coming out of his chamber, a fat elderly woman, tolerably well dressed, came to the door, grunting most bitterly, and casting up her eyes with now and then a pious ejaculation, and inquired whether Mr Wildgoose was stirring. Upon Tugwell's answering her in the affirmative, and showing her into his room, she begged leave to sit down a little; and, after a few more groans and ejaculations, she opened her case. She said, her name was *Placket*; that she kept a little coffee-house, where gentlemen and ladies sometimes meet to drink a dish of tea together, in a harmless way, for what she knew to the contrary; but that she had censorious neighbours, who had given her house a bad name.—Why, says Wildgoose, the world is very censorious, without doubt: but we should take care, not to give room for any *just* reflection upon our conduct.—Ah! sir, says she, why that is my business with you. God forgive me! I am afraid there may have been some little frolics now and then carried on at my house. When young people get together, you know, sir, they will be kissing and toying; and one does not always know where those things may end.—Why, by your account, Mrs Placket, you do not keep so good a house as you should do.—Dear sir, says she, that is what pricks my conscience; for, I must confess, I have sometimes taken money to bring young gentlemen and ladies together; and, indeed, always keep some young women in my house, to assist a friend or so.—Oh! Mrs Placket, I find then you keep a downright bawdy-house.—Why, to be sure, sir, says she, that is what ill-natured people call it; and I would willingly know, sir, whether it is a lawful employment or not: for you must observe, sir, I keep as good orders in my house as any woman in England; and though (I thank God) I have always had good custom, and have had twenty couple at a time taking their recreation, in my house, yet (I bless God!) I never had any murder, or riot, or daggers-drawing, since I have been in business. Then I make my poor lambs read the Bible every Sunday, and go to church in their turn; and, in short, though their bodies may be polluted, I take great care of their souls; and I hope God will wink at my poor lambs that *sport themselves together*.—Why, says Wildgoose, without doubt, our outward actions are indifferent in themselves; and it is the heart that God chiefly regards. God *sees* no sin in the *elect*. If we have true faith, that will sanctify our works. Thus Rahab the harlot, you know, was accepted through faith. But, as yours is an uncommon case, I will consult Mr Whitfield upon it.—Ah! God help me! says Mrs Placket: I am afraid I am not long for this world; and what will become of my poor lambs, when I am gone to my dear Redeemer?

Whilst Wildgoose was engaged in this conference, in comes the poor girl that was pricked through and through, by the power of the word, at his last preachment, attended by her mother. The girl looked very pale, and, upon coming before Wildgoose, was taken with an hysteric fit. Wildgoose bade the mother not be frightened; for, as Mr Whitfield had assured him, these were common symptoms of the New Birth. Lack-a-day! sir, says the mother, I wish it may be nothing more than the New Birth. But I have been very much terrified; and am sadly afraid my poor girl is with child.—With child! says Wildgoose; why, she is a mere child herself. Ah! sir, says the mother, so she is indeed; for though she is a fine-grown girl, yet, if she lives to Lammas-day next, she will be but fourteen years old, as sure as eggs is eggs. But a wicked rogue of a sailor, who promised her marriage, I am afraid, has had *cardinal knowledge* of her, and has now left her; and I shall never be able to maintain her and her child: times are so hard, and money so scarce, I can hardly maintain myself.— The case was, the poor woman had heard of Wildgoose's generosity, and was in hopes of partaking of his bounty, and therefore brought her daughter under pretence of consulting him as a Casuist. But he, having at present neither silver nor gold, gave her only some spiritual comfort; and told her that this accident was probably a very providential thing for her daughter, as it was a maxim with Mr Whitfield, the greater the sinner, the greater the saint; that she had nothing to do but to lay *hold* on Christ, as Mary Magdalen did, by an active faith; and she would enter into the kingdom of heaven, before those self-righteous, good sort of women, who fancy they need no repentance.

These customers were hardly retired, when a dirty-looking fellow was introduced by Tugwell, who, peeping round the room and shutting the door, spoke in a low voice to Wildgoose, and said, his was a scruple of a particular kind, upon which a friend had desired him to consult Mr Wildgoose.—Well, what is it? says Wildgoose.—Why, sir, whether it is not fighting against God, for a man in gaol to use means for making his escape.*—Wildgoose, after a short pause, answered, that, doubtless, self-preservation was the first law of nature; and a man in prison, it

---

* Vid. *Journal*, p.99.

should seem, might use all lawful means to gain his liberty; but nature is one thing, and grace another. A good Christian must submit to every ordinance of man, as the dispensation of Providence; and if he is committed to prison by legal authority, I question whether any other authority can innocently set him free. But, as this is a dubious point, Mr Whitfield and I will determine it by lot.—Ah! says the fellow, it is too late to cast lots about the matter; for I made my escape from Salisbury gaol last spring, and am now going on ship-board, but should be glad to go with a quiet conscience.

Before this man had done, a tall lanthorn-jawed fellow, whose features seemed lengthened by a long weather-beaten wig, which hung below his cheekbones, desired to lay his case before Mr Wildgoose, when the other was dismissed. He said, he was bred a dissenter, and a button-maker by trade; and in his apprenticeship had married an elderly woman, with a little money; but she was so bad tempered a woman, continued he, that I could not possibly live with her; so I went and worked in London, where, upon hearing Mr Wesley, I became a new man; and, meeting with a very *sober* young woman of my own trade at the Tabernacle, to whom I honestly told my situation, we agreed to live together for some years, and have had several children: but she is lately dead; and now my conscience pricks me, and I cannot be easy day nor night: but still I hope, sir, *God will sanctify every dispensation.*★

What became of the old woman, then? says Mr Wildgoose.—Why, sir, says he, as I had got me another wife, I believe she got herself another husband, more agreeable to her own age:—And so, says Wildgoose, by putting away your wife without a sufficient cause, you have caused her to commit adultery.—Why, says the button-maker, I am afraid I have: but I hope *God will sanctify every dispensation.*—Friend, replies Wildgoose, God cannot sanctify adultery. You must confess yourself a vile sinner, and *lay hold* on Christ by faith; for you can have no hopes but in him, who came into the world to save sinners.

★ A real fact.

XII

SOME UNEXPECTED INCIDENTS

Wildgoose, though not displeased with observing the good he was likely to do by awakening so many wicked sinners, was almost tired of his company, when in came Mrs Cullpepper's maid, courtesying and simpering, with her lady's compliments: and before Wildgoose could ask how she did, produced a little packet carefully sealed up; which being opened, to his great surprise he found it contained five guineas, with the following billet:

> My dear Brother,
>   Give me leave to contribute my mite towards the great work which is going to be wrought upon the earth; but do not come any more to our house, till you hear further from your sister in the Lord.
>   Rachael Cullpepper.

Wildgoose could not recollect any precedent in Mr Wesley's or Mr Whitfield's *Journals* of their having received money for their private occasions; as he was conscious, however, that his intentions were charitable, he did not refuse so seasonable a supply. He therefore returned his compliments to Mrs Cullpepper, with thanks for the contents of her packet; but was less pleased with the present which he had received, than shocked with the hint that accompanied it, not to repeat his visits to Mrs Cullpepper.

Wildgoose was now come out into the passage, and was observing to Tugwell, that the spirit testified he should do great things in Bristol; and that he had a call to tarry in that city many days. To which Tugwell seemed to have no manner of objection.

But, while they were yet speaking, another ill-looking Irish sailor, with one eye, and several scars on his cheek, came to consult Wildgoose. He said, he had been the vilest of sinners (to which confession his appearance bore sufficient testimony); that he had been guilty of every kind of uncleanness; nay, that, when on ship-board, he had an intrigue with a cat.—Ay, says Tugwell, and she has left some tokens of her kindness upon thy cheeks.—But, says the sailor, notwithstanding my sins are so numerous, I am so far from any sorrow, or contrition, that my greatest affliction is the being violently addicted to *laughing*, which, I am afraid, is a token of reprobation. Now, I should be glad to know, whether laughing be any sin or not; for I have heard that Adam never *laughed* before the fall.

Wildgoose stared with astonishment at this strange penitent; but Tugwell, who was impatient to get to breakfast, used this gentleman with less politeness. Come, come, friend, says he, this is no time for *laughing*; we have more serious matters upon our hands; you had better be going about your business. He then thrust him towards the door. Upon which the sailor gave the signal with a boatswain's whistle, and in rushed four or five stout fellows, amongst whom was the man that had escaped from Salisbury gaol. He immediately thrust a handkerchief into Tugwell's mouth; pulled his long wig over his eyes; twisted the wallet which hung over his shoulder, round his neck; and muffled him up in such a manner, that he could not make any sort of resistance. Some of the rest secured Wildgoose, who never offered to interrupt them; and led them both to a covered boat, which lay ready on the quay, and rowed away immediately for Kingroad; where when they arrived, they put the two pilgrims aboard a large ship, which was riding at anchor, and which set sail the moment they were on board.

XIII

Event of their voyage

Wildgoose was so well prepared to submit to the various dispensations of Providence, that he appeared quite calm upon the occasion, and let the sailors dispose of him as they pleased. But Tugwell, being less passive, struggled, and hung an a-se, and laid about him as well as he could; for which refractory behaviour, he got three or four hearty knocks on the pate; but as soon as he was restored to the use of his tongue, he expressed the transports of his grief and rage in a most vociferous manner. Sometimes he lamented the forlorn condition of his poor wife Dorothy: then fell foul upon Mr Wildgoose, for seducing him from home; then cursed himself, for leaving his cobbler's stall, and his own chimney-corner, to go rambling about the country: in short, though Jerry had read books of travels with so much pleasure, and often wished to accompany the adventurer in his voyages as he pursued them in his own stall; yet he found, in fact, the company of sailors, upon this occasion, not so agreeable as he expected.

Wildgoose endeavoured to comfort his fellow-sufferer, and desired him to trust to Providence, who would bring them, he said, to the haven where they *should* be: and notwithstanding Wildgoose so lately felt a call to remain in Bristol; yet he was now convinced, that he was chosen for some more important service, and was to 'preach the Gospel in other *cities also*.'★

Whilst they were thus engaged in lamentations on one side, and consolations on the other, the ship was falling gently down the channel; when who should come into the cabin, where the two pilgrims were stowed, but their old acquaintance Captain Gordon? The Captain started back; and affecting some little surprise, Ha! cries he, what, Mr Wildgoose! what, was it for this, then, that our friend Cullpepper sent my rascals a guinea to drink this morning? I was surprised at his generosity. Well, sir, he has played you a comical trick; for I am going a pretty long voyage.—Wildgoose, after expressing his surprise answered, that he did not know how he had offended the alderman but, however, continues he, I am convinced, that Providence has some important end to serve by this dispensation, to whatever part of the world I shall be transported. Why, sir, says the Captain, I am bound for North America, and am to join the fleet in the Gulf of St Lawrence. But, as I am to touch at Cork or Kinsale, to lay in more provisions, if you choose it, I can set you on shore in that part of Ireland. Wildgoose thanked the captain for his civility, not suspecting that this had been a scheme

★ *Journals.*

concerted between him and the alderman; the captain being jealous of him, as a rival in Mrs Cullpepper's good graces; and the alderman being suspicious, that his wife might supply him with *that* money which *he* had refused him.

When Tugwell heard of being set on shore in Ireland, he renewed his lamentations, and made sure of having his throat cut by *Papishes* and wild Irish: and, if they should be carried into America, he did not doubt, he said, but they should be left upon some desolate island, as Robinson Crusoe was, amongst the wild Indians; and, perhaps, be roasted alive, and have their bones picked by *hannibals* and *scavangers* (so Jerry called the cannibals and savages), as he feared his poor son Joseph was. The captain bid him not be afraid, for that they should not be used ill in any respect. He advised them, therefore, to come out of their cabin, and take a walk upon deck; where, the weather being fine, the water calm, and the vessel now in the midst of the channel, between the two opposite coasts, they had no unpleasant voyage for some hours.

Towards the evening, being got near the mouth of the Channel, the afternoon having been excessively hot, some black clouds began to rise towards the south-east, and a most violent thunder-storm soon after ensued, which lasted for several hours. Those who delight in descriptions of this kind may have recourse to any of the epic poets, ancient or modern. I shall only observe, that after being driven from their course, and tossed about a good part of the night, they found themselves, at break of day, near the Glamorganshire coast; and found it convenient, as their tackling had suffered a little, to come to an anchor in the Bay of Cardiff, where the captain, having carried the jest far enough, gave Wildgoose and his friend leave to be set on shore; which favour, when he heard they were on the coast of Wales, Wildgoose gladly accepted of. After giving them the word of exhortation, therefore, Wildgoose took his leave of Captain Gordon, thanked him for bringing them to the haven where he wished to be; and he and his fellow-traveller were safely set on shore.

BOOK VIII

I

THE TWO PILGRIMS ARRIVE AT CARDIFF

M R WILDGOOSE NOW THOUGHT HIMSELF a second St Paul; and that, in the late storm, God had given the lives of all those that sailed with him to the force of his prayers, though every common sailor knew there had been no real danger.

As for Tugwell, he was so sick at the coming on of the storm, that he had not been very attentive to what had passed, and was so rejoiced at reaching land again, that he dropped all resentment against the authors of this calamity. He had thrown off his great wig; but, grasping his oaken staff, and securing his wallet, he sprang eagerly upon the shore, without looking behind him: and desirous as he had formerly been of travelling, made a solemn vow, never to forsake the *terra firma* again as long as he lived.

The place where they landed was about three miles from Cardiff; and, it being early in the morning, and no living creature to be seen, Tugwell began again to wish himself at home, in his own chimney-corner, with a mess of onion-pottage, or a dish of Madam Wildgoose's pot-liquor, for his breakfast; for, having eaten nothing the whole preceding day but a sea-biscuit, he began to complain of hunger and fatigue. By good luck, however, upon searching his wallet, he found a couple of rolls and a piece of mutton-pie, which he had laid in at Bristol: he prevailed upon his master, therefore, without much difficulty, to sit down at the foot of a rock, and partake with him of what he had so providently laid in.

But, during their short repast, Wildgoose began to blame himself for having lived too luxuriously at Bristol, observing, that regular dinners and hot suppers were by no means expedient for those that were called to preach the Gospel.—Odzooks! cries Tugwell; why I did not see but Mr Whitfield, and other good Christians, ate and drank as well as we; and much good may it do them! I would have every one have a belly-full. To be sure, Madam Cullpepper keeps a good house, and gave me many a good meal, and money besides for that matter.

Wildgoose, upon hearing that Mrs Cullpepper's generosity had extended to his companion also, condemned himself for discovering his necessity to the alderman, and began to suspect that some jealousy of this kind (for he had no idea of any other) might be the cause of his getting them kidnapped, and sent on ship-board. He comforted himself, however, with the uprightness of his intentions, and with the conviction that the money would be spent in a good cause; and that he should make a better use of the unrighteous mammon than those to whom it properly belonged.

Though the sun was risen above the horizon, it was not yet four o'clock; and the two pilgrims having had little rest in the night, Wildgoose leaned against the rock, and took a short nap; and Tugwell, being now at ease, laid himself down on his wallet, and, according to custom, snored most profoundly.

Wildgoose, however, having paid a slight compliment to nature, and having in his sleep dreamed of nothing but spiritual conquests, starts up, and rouses his fellow traveller. Come, Jerry, cries he, this is no time for sleep; up, and be doing: the whole land of Canaan lies before us; we must subdue the idolatrous nations, the Hivites, the Perizzites, and the Jebusites. God has called us into Wales; and I make no doubt that he will send his angel before us (as he did before Mr Whitfield*); and we shall go on from city to city, like Joshua; and the Devil's strong holds will fall down at our preaching, as the walls of Jericho did at the sound of the rams' horns.†

Notwithstanding this spiritual rant, Tugwell grumbled at being waked so soon, and said, he did not find that conquering cities was so easy a matter. You know, master, says he, you talked of conquering the city of Bristol; but I think they have *conquered* us, and have transported us into this heathenish country, without our own consent, where there it nothing to be got, as I can see, for love or money.

The truth was, Jerry liked travelling well enough in a country where they could meet with refreshment at every ale-house; but, having been very sick in his voyage, and being a little chagrined at the desolate appearance of the sea-coast, compared with the pleasures of Alderman

---

* *Journals*, p. 20.

† *Ibid*.

Cullpepper's kitchen, he could not forbear venting his spleen against Wildgoose, for seducing him so far from home.

But the same cause which damped Tugwell's spirits roused Wildgoose's zeal. He languished for a little persecution (as Mr Whitfield had often done); and thought things were not right, whilst they went on so smoothly at Bristol. He said, the primitive saints were made perfect by sufferings; and I dare say, Jerry, you yourself will be the better for this slight persecution for the Gospel's sake.—Yes, to be sure, says Tugwell; I suppose, master, you would be glad to see me ducked in a horse-pond, or tossed in a blanket, for the Gospel's sake; but I do not see what occasion I have to run my head against a wall, when I can get my living very well by mending shoes; and I wish I were at home again in my own stall, or in my chimney-corner with our Dorothy.

Wildgoose said he would not prevent his returning home, if he desired it; and would pay him for the time which he had lost in attending him: and then, continues he, as you have been at no expense, you can have no reason to complain. Besides, you own that Mrs Cullpepper gave you some money; and, perhaps, other good Christians may have been as liberal; and much good may it do you! Mr Wildgoose, however, said, he did not want to call him to an account, but only to make him submit with patience to the accidents which might befall them in the pilgrimage in which he had voluntarily engaged to accompany him. But come, Jerry, says he, I believe we are not far from Cardiff, where we shall meet with better accommodations, and, what is of more consequence, with a society of true Christians, which I believe Mr Whitfield established there, when he visited the principality of Wales.

Accordingly, in less than half an hour more, they came within sight of that handsome town; which revived Tugwell's spirits, who wished for nothing so much as a cup of good ale, and a slice of toasted cheese, which, now he was in Wales, he hoped to have in perfection.

II

ADVENTURES AT THE INN IN CARDIFF

The first public-house which the two pilgrims came to, was one of those old, unsightly mansions which, having been a well-accustomed inn time out of mind, had had different conveniences added to it by different possessors; so that it made, upon the whole, a comfortable, though very irregular appearance. The house was at present very full; yet Tugwell contrived to get a nook in the kitchen chimney, to smoke his pipe, and drink his ale (which was his principal concern); and Mr Wildgoose had a little parlour, near the stable, for his breakfast and his meditations.

As the Cambro-Britons are a nation of gentlemen, jealous of their honour, and impatient of affronts, they are engaged in frequent litigations: and there happened at this time to be some lawyers upon a commission at that inn. Among the rest there was an eminent attorney from Bristol, who came post the day before, and whose clerk came into the kitchen, whilst Tugwell was eating a rasher of bacon, instead of toasted cheese, for his breakfast. As Jerry, by his master's order, had been slily inquiring, whether there were any Methodists at Cardiff? the lawyer's clerk interposing, said, they had too many of them in Bristol; but, thank God! says he, two of them were shipped off for North America yesterday morning, just as my master and I set out.—For what? says one of the company.—Why, one of the rascals, says the young lawyer, had been tampering with one of our aldermen's wives; and, by his cursed canting tricks, choused the poor alderman out of a hundred pounds, or pretty near it, to my certain knowledge.—What was the alderman's name, then? says Tugwell, interrupting him, with an eager look.—Why, Alderman Cullpepper, says the young clerk.—The devil is a liar, and so are you, says Tugwell; for I know Alderman Cullpepper better than you do; and I came from Bristol but yesterday morning, as well as you.—You know Alderman Cullpepper! returns the lawyer.—What, thou hast been carried before him for a petty-larceny I suppose.—I do not care a t—d for your *pretty lasses*, says Tugwell; but I know that what you say is a cursed lie.—Is it? says the lawyer; I had it from his own servant: and I will pull thee by the nose, if thou givest me the lie again, says he. One of them pretended to be a man of fortune, forsooth; but wanted to borrow money of the alderman; and the other was a broken cobbler.—How do you know I was a broken cobbler? quoth Tugwell. If I was a cobbler, thank God, I never was broke.—I will be hanged, cries the lawyer, staring in his face, if thou art not one of them; I have seen thy face in Bristol: and the alderman's servant told me one of them was a damned guttling fellow; that he caught him in an intrigue with a pigeon-pie, behind the pantry door, one morning before dinner; and that he had ravished above a dozen bottles of strong beer in less than a week's time.—I *trigue* with a pigeon-pie! says Jerry; it was nothing but a piece of pie-crust that the cook gave me, and a little best drink to stay my stomach, gentlefolks dine so plaguy late. What, must not a man, that preaches the Gospels eat and drink as well as other folks?—Thou preach the Gospel! says the clerk; thou art more fit to sweep chimneys, or black shoes, than to preach the Gospel.—As Jerry was going to retort with some vehemence, this dispute might probably have proceeded to an assault and battery, if the young lawyer had not been called away by his master: and Mr Wildgoose, having now dispatched his short breakfast, summoned Tugwell into his little parlour, to know what intelligence he had got about any religious society at Cardiff. Jerry related to him, with some indignation, the report which the young lawyer had brought from Bristol; but Wildgoose was less surprised at the exaggerations of vulgar fame, than shocked at the scandal which he and his friend Tugwell had given, by accepting of Mrs Cullpepper's favours: and again expressing his suspicion, that Tugwell might have tasted more largely of her bounty than he cared to own, Tugwell wished the devil might fetch him, if he had had above half a guinea or *sich* a matter, of any body's money, since he came from home. Wildgoose reproved him for his passionate exclamation; but his manner of expressing himself, and his being so touchy upon the occasion, only confirmed Wildgoose in his suspicions.

III

Wildgoose holds forth to a Welsh audience

Whilst the two pilgrims were debating what course to take, as people at an inn want to get rid of guests when nothing is going forwards for the good of the house, the drawer, or rather the tapster, came into the room to know whether *the gentleman called*. Wildgoose desired to pay for what they had had; and, whilst he was doing that, inquired of the waiter, whether there were any Methodists, as they called them, in the town. Yes, I believe there are, says he, more than are welcome: and we have got the famous preacher Howel Harris in town at this time.—Pray, who is he? says Wildgoose.—Why, he is a young fellow, replies the waiter, that goes all over the country to revels and fairs, and preaches two or three times a day. He does a great deal of mischief amongst the country people; but I hope somebody or other will beat his brains out one of these days.

What, I suppose, he spoils your trade, and would not have people get drunk, nor spend their time and money in wicked and idle diversions?—I do not know, says the tapster; I have nothing to say against the young fellow; I never saw any harm by him, not I: if you have a mind to hear him, I believe he preaches again to-night; and he lodges at a widow woman's, not far from our house.

As Wildgoose had heard Mr Whitfield make honourable mention of brother Howel Harris, he desired the tapster to give them directions, and went immediately and found him out. As soon as they met, like true free-masons, they discovered each other's occupations, almost by instinct; and, in the apostolical phrase, Wildgoose gave Howel the *right hand* of fellowship.

When Howel Harris discovered Wildgoose's inclination to harangue publicly, and that he had already been employed by Mr Whitfield, he engaged to procure the town-hall for him that very afternoon; where, by trumpeting the fame of this new preacher, he assembled above four hundred people. Wildgoose held forth from the judgment-seat; where he took occasion, without judge or jury, to *arraign* and *condemn* the whole race of mankind. Many were very attentive; but some mocked: and some jolly fellows, who had been drinking at the inn, one of whom kept a pack of hounds in the neighbourhood, having had intelligence of Wildgoose's intention by the drawer, got a dead fox, and trailed him round the town-hall, and laid on his dogs to the scent. The music of the hounds, and the noise of the sportsmen, was so loud and vociferous, that it almost drowned the voice of the orator: and the cheerfulness of the sound had such a mechanical effect upon the minds of many of the Cambrians, that they ran out to join them: nay, Tugwell himself, in the midst of the preachment, could hardly refrain from giving them a *tallio*! but the recollection of the jeopardy he had been in, when he mistook the jack-ass for a stag, checked his spirit, and prevented him from deserting his station near his master, and joining the cry.

The fox-hunters, however, were tired before the preacher, who harangued for above an hour, to a very attentive audience; and, what is remarkable, that part of the congregation seemed most affected, and bestowed the most hearty benedictions on the preacher, who did not understand a word of English. This, however, we ought not to attribute merely to affectation, but to the vehemence and apparent sincerity of the orator, and the mechanical and infectious operation of an enthusiastic energy.

It was towards evening before they dismissed the assembly, and Wildgoose, having been disturbed by the storm the preceding night, invited Howel Harris to sit an hour with him at his inn, where they settled their plan for the next morning; and the two pilgrims retired early to their repose, highly satisfied with the adventures of the day; which Wildgoose said (in the style of the Journals), was a day of *fat things*; to which Tugwell (applying in a literal sense to his rashers of bacon and Welsh ale) heartily assented.

IV

AN UNLUCKY MISTAKE

The house being very full, as was observed, our adventurers, being only foot-passengers, met with but scurvy lodgings. There was a room up five or six stairs, near the stable, with two miserable beds in it; in one of which the hostler usually lay; and the other was reserved for the drawer or tapster, or any of the other servants who might happen to be turned out of their own beds upon any extraordinary conflux of company, which was so much the present case, that the hostler himself was turned out by Mr Wildgoose, and forced to lie in the hayloft; and Tugwell took up the other bed contiguous to his master.

The two travellers were but just got into their first sleep, when Nan the cook, who happened to have a nocturnal intrigue with the hostler, slipped up to Wildgoose's bed-side, and calling the hostler two or three times in a low voice, disturbed Wildgoose, who began to mutter some rapturous ejaculation in his sleep, which Nan mistaking for the amorous expostulation of an impatient lover, began to disrobe herself with great expedition; when, as ill-luck would have it, one of the waiters, being driven from his bed to make room for a lawyer's clerk, came into the room with a candle, and discovered poor cooky half undressed. She was a handsome, plump girl, of about twenty-five; but, from the constant heat and unctuous steams of the kitchen, her complexion had more of the ruddy bronze of an Italian peasant, than the pale delicacy of a northern beauty.

However, she was agreeable enough to the gross appetite of an hostler, and, as the waiter imagined, to that of a modern saint; for Wildgoose, being now awaked (notwithstanding the surprise which he expressed at seeing such company at his bed-side, and the angry rebukes which he made use of for this intrusion), the waiter formed conjectures by no means favourable to his virtue. Poor Nan, pretending some mistake, collected her loose robes, and hurried down stairs as fast as she could, and the waiter with her. At the bottom of the stairs they met the hostler, who, having heard somebody go up into his usual apartment, suspected the mistake. The waiter told him, that he had caught Nan in bed with the Methodist Preacher which, though he did not entirely believe, yet it so far roused his jealousy, that he heartily joined with the waiter in publishing the story the next morning.

V

AN APPARITION

Tugwell, being thoroughly fatigued, and pretty well steeped in Welsh ale, never waked during the above transaction; but, about one o'clock, when the whole house was quiet, and he had a little satisfied the importunate demands of nature, he was disturbed by something at the feet of his bed; when, opening his eyes, he discovered by the twilight a most diabolical figure standing upright before him. It was about five feet high, of a grim aspect, with eyes that glared like fire, a long beard, and a monstrous pair of horns. In the name of the Father, the Son, and the Holy Ghost, cries Tugwell, what art thou?—The spectre made no other answer, but in a hollow tone cried, whare, whare. Jerry, who made no doubt but it was the Devil, and charitably supposing that his business was with the gentlemen of the law, replied, that if he wanted the lawyers, they lay in the best bed-chambers.—The apparition, as if he wanted no other intelligence, took his cloven feet immediately off the bed, and, like the Devil upon Two Sticks, went stumping down stairs again, and disappeared.—Tugwell, however, awaked his companion in a great fright. Master Wildgoose! Master Wildgoose! says he; for God's sake awake: Lord have mercy upon us! says he; the house is haunted; the Devil has just appeared to me, and is this moment gone down stairs.—Wildgoose, though in his discourses he frequently talked of the Devil, and the power of Satan, yet did not really believe his visible appearance to mankind. He took this opportunity, however, of reminding Jerry, how free he had made with the Devil's name about so trifling an affair as his receiving money upon the road! Lord have mercy upon us! says Tugwell; to be sure, that is the reason of his appearance. Talk of the Devil, and he will appear. I wished the Devil might fetch me if I had taken above half a guinea since we came from home; and to be sure, I have received three times as much from different people. But God forgive me, and defend me from the power of Satan, who is the father of lies.

Though Wildgoose did not trouble himself about Jerry's perquisites, he was sorry to find, that after so much good instruction, he had made no greater progress towards perfection. He desired him, however, to take another nap, for that the apparition was only a dream, or a phantom of his imagination.—The *fancy* of a *magic-lanthorn*! says Jerry; no, no; I have seen a magic-lanthorn at E'sham fair. It was no magic-lanthorn, says Tugwell; for I felt him as well as saw him. He patted my legs with his cloven feet; and he grew taller and taller, as I looked at him, till his head reached the ceiling; and I heard him walk down stairs: and I am sure the house is haunted by evil spirits; and I am for leaving this place as soon as it is daylight.

Mr Wildgoose, who had been haunted by the flesh (in the shape of a fat cook), as Tugwell had by the spirit (in the shape of a devil as he thought), and not knowing what use the drawer might make of such an incident; being also impatient to get back to Gloucester, for reasons which the reader may probably guess at, took Jerry's hint, and promised to set out by five o'clock, but desired Tugwell to compose himself till that time, which Jerry promised to do; and Mr Wildgoose, being still much fatigued, took another nap.

Tugwell, however, could not sleep soundly; but, being waked again by the clock's striking four, and still haunted by the terrors of his fancy, he calls out again to his fellow-traveller, Master Wildgoose! Master Wildgoose! says he.—What is the matter now? says Wildgoose.—O, nothing, says Jerry; I had only a mind to let you know, that you have but an hour longer to sleep.—Pugh! says Wildgoose; but you need not have waked me to tell me so.

The sun, however, began now to dart his first rays through the lattice, and discovered the ballads on the walls of their bed-chamber. People also began to move about the inn. Wildgoose, therefore, and his friend

Tugwell, thought it best to quit their beds, and decamp before the family were all stirring. Jerry, seeing his master kneel down to his devotions, just cast up a short ejaculation; but thought it more to his purpose to examine the state of his wallet, which being pretty well exhausted, he resolved to replenish it with what he could get before they set out.

As they came down into the stable-yard, a great shaggy he-goat, drawn by the smell of Jerry's wallet, came running towards them, which Mr Wildgoose espying, immediately observed to his friend, that was the ghost which had appeared to him in the night.—Tugwell said, the apparition had horns and a beard, like the goat; but that he was as tall as the house, and walked upright upon two legs; and he was sure it could be nothing but the Devil himself. Wildgoose did not stay to convince him; but, meeting with the tapster, who had waited on them the preceding night, paid him for what they had had; yet not before Tugwell had drunk a pot of ale, and furnished his wallet with some provision for their journey.

VI

RECEPTION BY THE PARSON OF NEWPORT

Though Wildgoose was not very solicitous about the ludicrous turn which the servants at the inn might give to his adventure with the fat cook; yet, as he had promised Howel Harris to hold forth again that day at Cardiff, and was unwilling to leave room for any suspicion in the mind of his friend, he thought it proper to call upon him at his lodgings and, though it was not yet five o'clock, he found him already up, and at his meditations.

As people who are good themselves are not apt to suspect ill of others, Mr Wildgoose found difficulty in convincing his brother Howel of his innocence. He would have persuaded Wildgoose, however, not to quit Cardiff so abruptly; but when he found him determined, he immediately took his staff, and set out with the two pilgrims towards

Newport, a considerable town on the great road; where he promised to introduce Mr Wildgoose to the parson of the parish, who, he said, was a friend to their cause, and had lent Mr Whitfield his pulpit, when he lately visited the principality of Wales.

They arrived at Newport before ten o'clock, and accordingly waited upon the doctor, who received them in a polite manner, and told them, as he was persuaded of Mr Whitfield's good intentions, and knew also how fond people are of a new preacher, and what an impression that very circumstance often made upon careless Christians, he had indulged his parishioners, for once, in hearing so famous a man; but that, in general, he did not at all approve of such irregular proceedings.

I have already, continued the doctor, found the ill effects of my complaisance to Mr Whitfield. My own people, who are very well disposed, and who were before entirely satisfied with my plain doctrine, now, forsooth, give out, that do not preach the Gospel, because I do not always harp upon the same string, of the new birth, faith without works, and the like. They also expect me to have private meetings two or three nights in the week, and compliment them with private expositions of Scripture, extempore prayer, psalm-singing, and what not; though I really believe, if I were to give them the very same sermons in a private room, lighted up with candles like a play-house, the very novelty of the thing would content them for a while, as well as the best of your itinerant preachers.

Though the doctor was not disposed to enter into the views of our spiritual adventurers; yet, as he kept a hospitable house, he entertained them with a good breakfast of coffee and hot rolls; after which Mr Wildgoose and Howel Harris parting with each other, the latter returned to Cardiff, and Wildgoose, with his fellow-traveller, pursued their journey to Gloucester.

VII

AN AGREEABLE SOLITUDE.
A HOLY FAMILY, IN THE FLEMISH STYLE

Though Mr Wildgoose's principal view was to make the best of his way into the North, agreeably to Mr Whitfield's destination; yet his more immediate object was to reach Gloucester as soon as possible, both to confirm the distressed brethren there, and perhaps, in a subordinate degree, in hopes of another interview with Miss Townsend before she left that place, as she daily expected to do. However, as both Mr Whitfield in his *Journals*, and also Howel Harris, had represented the inhabitants of Wales as sweetly prepared to receive the Gospel (going frequently twenty miles to hear a sermon); and as Howel had also informed him, that there was a considerable society established at Monmouth, and had given him a letter to a substantial tradesman, who was the chief ruler of the synagogue there; for these reasons Mr Wildgoose determined to take his route by the way of Monmouth.

Though Monmouthshire is now in some respects an English county, and is not so mountainous as many parts of Wales; yet, to those whose travels have never extended farther than Hammersmith or Brentford, or a few miles round the metropolis, the roads in this county would not appear quite so level as a Kidderminster carpet.

Accordingly the two pilgrims, after two hours travelling, had now just surmounted a Monmouthshire mole-hill, and were come down into a romantic valley, on the banks of the Uske, the coolness of which, as the sun was near its meridian, was extremely refreshing. After winding along the river's side for about half a mile, they came in sight of a pleasant village, at the foot of another hill, covered with hanging woods, which formed a beautiful amphitheatre, in the centre of which the parish church, with its little spire, rose amongst some old pine-trees; and the ruins of a monastery, near which the river formed a natural cascade, showed that the place had formerly been dedicated to devotion and solitude. Wildgoose could not but admire the sequestered situation, and observed, that if a true primitive spirit reigned amongst those people, they must be the happiest of mortals.

The first cottage they came to was a tolerably neat one, and appeared the constant residence of peace and tranquillity. A little wicket, painted white, led through a small court to the house, which was covered with honeysuckles and sweetbriar: the windows were glazed; and the chimney rose with a truly ancient British magnificence, two feet above the thatch.

As the road divided at the end of the village, Tugwell marched boldly up to the door, to inquire the way. On so near an approach, however, they found that peace does not always reside in a cottage; for their ears were saluted with the confused noise and squalling of children; and a female voice, with a Welsh accent (which is always expressive of anger), answered Jerry, and bade him go about his business; that there was nothing for him; and that they had beggars enough in their own parish.—Jerry replied, that they did not come to beg, but to inquire the road to Monmouth.

A little curled-headed boy, with shoes and stockings on, now opened the door, when they heard the foresaid female exclaiming, Why do not you make haste and scrape the bacon? I wish those books were all in the fire. Then seeing Jerry's wallet on his shoulder, she cries out, that they never bought any thing of pedlars; that her own father, who was a gentleman born, kept a creditable shop at Newport; and she would not encourage people who travelled about to the prejudice of the fair trader.

During this angry exclamation, Tugwell and Wildgoose had a full view into the kitchen; where, besides the boy that opened the door, they saw four or five more, and the poor woman far advanced in her pregnancy. The master of the house, who was no other than the vicar of the parish, was sitting down in his band and night-gown; but so far from being idle, that his eyes, his hands, and his feet, every limb of his body, and every faculty of his soul, were fully employed; for he was reading a folio that lay on the table to the right; was hearing his little boy read, who stood by him on the left; he was rocking the cradle with his foot, and was paring turnips.

As soon as he could disengage his attention from this variety of employments, he rose up, and with a stern air, asked the travellers what they wanted. Wildgoose repeated Tugwell's question, and desired to know which was the road to Monmouth. The vicar told them they were come near a mile out of their way; but that, with proper directions, they might easily recover the right road.

Observing Wildgoose, however, upon a nearer view, not to have the appearance of a common tramper, he asked them if they would sit down *at the door*, and refresh themselves a little in the heat of the day? I cannot desire you to walk into the house, says the vicar; for, amongst the other comforts of matrimony, I have that of sitting my whole life in a wet room. My wife, as you may perceive, is a very good housewife; but, unfortunately for me, she has taken it into her head, that a wet house and a *clean* house are the same thing: so that having only one room to sit in, and that being washed every morning, it is consequently as you now see it all the year round.

Mr Wildgoose said he was sorry to have given him the trouble of this apology, as he could not accept of his invitation. Tugwell, however, who seldom slighted an offer of this kind, said he would be obliged to the gentleman for a draught of small-beer. The vicar, therefore, himself took a cup, stepped to the barrel, which stood in a little shed, or *enclitical* pent-house, and brought Jerry, in a literal sense, some *small*-beer, the refreshing liquor which he asked for.

VIII

ECCLESIASTICAL PRIDE
IN THE DIOCESE OF LANDAFF

Whilst Tugwell was regaling himself with the foresaid potation, Wildgoose reposed himself upon the bench at the door; and, pointing to the ruins of the monastery, observed to the vicar by way of chit-chat, that there had been a religious house in his parish. Yes, says the vicar, there *has been a religious* house in the parish, I believe; but I am sorry to say it, it was long before my time; for I am afraid, at present, we have not one truly religious house in the parish. God forbid! says Wildgoose; for I dare say, sir, you do your duty amongst them. Why, says the vicar, I hope I do my duty as well as the generality of my brethren; but am afraid, from particular circumstances, it is not in my power to do much good in my parish.—How so, sir? replies Wildgoose.—You know, sir, replies the vicar, that at the reformation, in Harry the Eighth's time, when the revenues of these religious houses, by the act of dissolution, were granted to the crown, how slender a reserve was made in general for serving the parish churches. Now, you must observe, sir, that after spending seven years in the university, and taking a master of art's degree, I am possessed of a little rectory of about thirty pounds a year, and of this vicarage, which, if I could make the most of it, might bring me in near twenty more: now each of these preferments these poor people consider as a *noble benefit*; and, though you see, sir, in what way I live, yet because I am possessed of half a dozen spoons and a silver tankard, they envy me, as living in princely state, and lording it over God's heritage; and, what is worse, as my whole income in this parish arises from the small tithes, because I cannot afford to let them cheat me out of half my dues, they represent me as carnal and worldly-minded, and as one who regards nothing but the good things of this life, and who is always making disturbances in the parish: and this prejudice against me prevents my doing that good amongst them which I sincerely wish to do. One man has left his church, and walks three miles to a Methodist meeting, because I took one pig out of seven, as the law directs; another has complained to the bishop of my extortion, because I would not take three shillings and sixpence in lieu of tithes, for a large orchard, as my predecessor had done. In short, sir, here are two or three dissenters in the parish, who give out that all tithes are remnants of popery, and would have the clergy consider meat and drink as types and shadows, which ought to have been abolished with the Levitical law.

Well, sir, says Wildgoose, I cannot but think the situation of a poor vicar particularly disagreeable, and that of the clergy in general very much so, in a temporal view: and since 'all malice (as a polite writer observes) arises from an opposition of interests,' I think it is pity, even upon that account, that things could not be put upon some different footing between the pastors and their flocks. Why, says the vicar, if it could be done without too great a confusion of property, I am sure I should have no objection to it: and I have often thought, as things now are, to prevent that odium which every incumbent must bring upon himself, who is under a necessity of disputing with his parish the rights of the church, a method might be contrived to throw the burden upon the church itself, instead of any particular incumbent.—As how? says Wildgoose.—Why, says the vicar, that the bishop should be empowered, by a fund levied in some manner on the clergy of the diocese (in proportion to their income), to defend the rights of any particular parish; which, by reference to some neighbouring gentlemen, or other lenient methods, I should think might generally be done without much expense, and without involving a poor, miserable incumbent in continual squabbles with his parish, and preventing him from doing that good which probably he might otherwise do. But, continued the vicar, there is no perfection to be hoped for in any human institutions; and, perhaps, an attempt to remedy the present might be attended with still greater inconveniences.

I think, says Wildgoose, there can be no greater misfortune than a misunderstanding between a minister and his congregation, as it prevents all probability of the people's receiving any spiritual improvement, if the clergy were to take ten times the pains which they generally do.

But pray, sir, continues Wildgoose, where is that Methodist meeting which you mentioned? Is it in our road to Monmouth? This inquiry confirmed the vicar in what he had before suspected from Wildgoose's conversation, that he was a favourer at least of the Methodists. He told him, therefore, that if he wanted information of that kind, any of his parishioners would give him ample satisfaction, and would, upon occasion, leave the most necessary business, and walk twenty miles, to hear the extempore effusions of an illiterate mechanic.

IX

COLLECTS AN AUDIENCE

Tugwell had by this time dispatched his small-beer, with a piece of bread and cheese, and a pint of ale into the bargain; for the vicar's wife having, through her mistake, treated him at first with undeserved asperity, was willing to atone for her rudeness by a superfluous civility, especially as, during her husband's conference with Mr Wildgoose, Jerry had supplied his place, in rocking the cradle, paring turnips, and blowing the fire.

He was now, however, forced to leave the smell of the pot, being summoned to attend his master, and proceed on their journey. In return for the vicar's civility, Mr Wildgoose took the liberty to exhort him, to endeavour the regaining his people's good will, by some little popular acts of beneficence, by relieving the distressed, giving physic to the sick, or where he was obliged to exact his Easter groats from any very poor families, to give them a sixpenny loaf in the place of it; and the like innocent stratagems: but above all, sir, adds Wildgoose, if the poor people had the true Gospel earnestly and affectionately inculcated into them, I am convinced all these worldly considerations would entirely vanish, and you would dwell together in unity and love. The vicar thanked Wildgoose for his good advice, but said, he had already used his utmost endeavours to regain the good will of his parishioners, but was afraid nothing would succeed with people, who to save a groat would resign their eternal salvation. The vicar and the travellers then parted, with mutual good wishes.

When the two pilgrims came towards the end of the village, they observed an old tailor sitting on his board, with spectacles on his nose, and with more devotion than harmony quavering one of Mr Wesley's hymns. This was hint sufficient for Wildgoose to make further inquiry about the society of Methodists, which the vicar had mentioned. The tailor told them there was a weekly meeting at a village about three miles farther; but that this was not the night on which the preacher came. Tugwell soon let him know, that his master could supply that defect; and that, if it lay in their road to Monmouth, he would give them a word of exhortation that evening. Upon this the old tailor leaped nimbly off his board, and leaving a suit of clothes which he had promised to finish that evening, said he would accompany them if it were as far again, and immediately ran and communicated this intelligence to a blacksmith, his next neighbour, who leaves the farmer's horses half shoed, and with like speed acquaints the farmer's wife, who was a zealous disciple of theirs. She, slipping on her shoes and stockings, leaves her cows unmilked, and her child dangerously ill in the cradle; and, with half a dozen more, who, upon spreading the alarm, had left their several employments, joined the devout cavalcade.*

After many questions, who the gentleman was, and whence he came, they set forwards, and now marched cheerfully along the valley; Wildgoose making inquiry into the state of their souls, and Tugwell entertaining them with some account of their adventures, and what he called persecutions, which they had undergone since they entered upon their ministry.

The village whither they were bound, and where they soon arrived, was a considerable thoroughfare to Monmouth, and a populous place. The arrival of a new preacher was soon spread about the neighbourhood; and there assembled, in half an hour's time, above two hundred people. When Wildgoose (being always desirous of attacking the Devil in his strong holds), having first refreshed himself with what the house afforded, held forth at the door of a little inn, being mounted on a horse-block, under a shady elm, which had long been sacred to rustic jollity and tippling, and was thoroughly perfumed with the incense of ale and tobacco.

---

* Such was the active zeal of the last century:
  The oyster-woman lock'd her fish up,
  And trudg'd away to cry, No bishop!

X

Miracles and slight persecutions

As soon as Mr Wildgoose began to harangue from the horse-block, some servants belonging to the 'squire of the village, who was a very orthodox man, and no friend to these superfluous acts of piety, began to make some disturbance, and to beat a drum, that formerly belonged to the militia; which at first a little embarrassed the orator: but he appearing much in earnest, and a majority of the company being more inclined to be attentive, they soon silenced these scoffers, and Wildgoose proceeded in his harangue.

A considerable part of the congregation were seated on an orchard wall, which faced the public-house, and, whilst Wildgoose was declaiming with great vehemence to an attentive audience, in praise of humility and self-denial, and had just assured them, that he who humbled himself should be exalted, the whole wall on which they sat, being built of loose stones, fell flat to the ground, not one of them crying out, or altering his posture; nor was there the least interruption, either in the vehemence of the orator, or in the attention of the audience.★

But their tranquillity was soon after disturbed by a phenomenon of another kind. A poor fellow of a neighbouring hamlet, who used to be always quarrelling with his neighbours, but who had been greatly affected by hearing Mr Wesley preach two or three times, came galloping through the street upon a little poney, about the size of a jack-ass, hallooing and shouting, and driving men, women, pigs, and children, before him. He was without a hat, with his long red hair hanging about his ears; and, staring wildly, he rides up to Wildgoose, crying out, *Got* bless you! Master Wesley; hur is convinced of sin; and Got has given hur revelations, and visions, and prophecies; and has foretold that hur shall be a king, and tread all hur enemies under hur feet.†

★ Mr Wesley's *Journal*, 1740.
† *Ibid.*

As the preaching was interrupted by this poor man, some of the company told Wildgoose, that he had been almost mad ever since he had heard Mr Wesley preach. Mad! quoth Wildgoose, I wish all that hear me this day were not only *almost*, but altogether as mad as this poor countryman. No, says he, these are the true symptoms of the new birth and he only wants the obstetric hand of some spiritual physician, to relieve him from his pangs, from these struggles between the flesh and the spirit. He then desired those who were strong in faith to *wrestle* in prayer for the poor enthusiast; but he left them to wrestle by themselves: and, without waiting for the event of their application, galloped off again upon his Welsh tit, hallooing and whooping, and as frantic as before.

The preachment being ended, Tugwell, who had been vastly taken with the singing of hymns, which he had heard at Bristol, thought he might venture, in a country place, to exhibit a specimen of his own talent at psalmody, and give out the psalm; though Jerry's voice was as unharmonious as the falling of a fire-shovel upon a marble slab. Both his music and appearance, therefore, were so far from any thing of devotion, or solemnity, that the 'squire's servants, who had been awed to silence by the vehemence of Wildgoose's eloquence, could now hold out no longer: but one of them began again to beat on the drum, and another discharged two or three addled eggs, which he had brought for the purpose, at Tugwell's head, one of which flying directly into the aperture of Jerry's extended jaws, the unsavoury odour of the rotten eggs, and Jerry's resentment of the indignity offered to a man of his fancied importance, threw the whole congregation into confusion, and soon after dispersed the assembly.

Wildgoose now began to reflect upon the escape his audience had had from the tumbling wall, and to bless God for what he fancied so miraculous an attestation to the truth of his mission. But the farmer who owned the orchard, considered the affair in a different light; and, being no friend to the cause, insisted upon an indemnification; and made poor Wildgoose pay five shillings and sixpence for dilapidations.

As the evening now came on, and the two pilgrims were much fatigued with their early rising and long walk, they thought it best to set up their staff at the public-house where they had preached. Tugwell, indeed, complained likewise of his having been pelted with addled eggs.

But his master exhorted him, to count it all joy that he met with these divers temptations. Yes! great joy, indeed, quoth Jerry, in a pettish mood, to have rotten eggs in one's mouth, besides spoiling one's clothes, which I shall not get sweet again this half year. Tugwell, however, having got a rasher of bacon with his eggs, and smoked his pipe, was tolerably well pacified; whilst Wildgoose went about giving spiritual advice to different parts of the family; and then the two friends retired to their repose.

XI

RECEPTION AT MONMOUTH

The sun had been risen about an hour, when Wildgoose sprang from his bed, and it being likely to prove a very hot day, soon roused his fellow-traveller, and set out for Monmouth. Tugwell, however, could not leave a house of entertainment without laying in some provision for the journey of the day.

In all his travels, indeed, Jerry never wanted a substantial reason for making a good meal, and filling his belly. In the morning it was a maxim with him to make sure of a good breakfast, for fear they should not meet with a dinner. When dinner-time came, he pretended to be more hungry than ordinary that day, because they had breakfasted before their time; and at night he would observe, that his journey had got him an appetite, and he never was *so hungry* in his life before; though if Wildgoose had attended to his impertinence, he had probably made the like apologies every day since they came from home.

As their road lay through shady lanes or green meadows, they made pretty good speed; and without any thing worth recording, arrived at Monmouth early in the afternoon.

When Mr Wildgoose had found out the tradesman, who was one of the fraternity, to whom Howel Harris had given him letters of recommendation, he delivered his credentials. The man, casting his eye over the letter, and finding Wildgoose's business, received him at first with some little coolness; and said, they had of late had so many *strange* preachers, that the credit of their society had suffered greatly by their indiscretions. But, perusing the letter more carefully, and finding that Mr Wildgoose was no common itinerant, but a man of some fortune, and particularly delegated by Mr Whitfield, he altered his style, and, by way of apology for the suspicions he had expressed, related the following incident, which, he said, had lately happened in that neighbourhood.

A genteel young man, says he, came down from London, who pretended to have been a preacher at one of Mr Wesley's societies. He preached frequently at Monmouth, and was well received in a gentleman's family in the neighbourhood, who were religiously disposed. The gentleman had a daughter, whom he was upon the point of marrying, to great advantage, to a person of superior fortune; and the alliance would have made two families extremely happy.

This itinerant, however, finding the young lady rather indifferent in her affections for this gentleman, who was, indeed, fourteen or fifteen years older than herself, persuaded her, that she could not in conscience give her hand without her heart; and that it was a kind of legal prostitution, to dispose of her person merely for the sake of a genteel settlement in the world, and the like; especially to a man, whom he represented as *no Christian*, because he did not frequent their religious society.

In short, to prevent her yielding to the importunity of her friends, and even to the commands of her father, he persuaded the young lady to march off with him into Ireland, which was his native country, and where he had been a journeyman barber, and came to London in that capacity. But, by frequenting Mr Wesley's Tabernacle for a few months, he had learned a few Scripture phrases, which, by virtue of a modest assurance, he retailed to us in the country with great applause; though, it is to be feared, he had no true faith, nor, indeed, any religion at all in his heart. And this affair has brought a great scandal upon our society, and given too just occasion for our adversaries to blaspheme.

However, sir, continues the tradesman, I hope a gentleman so well recommended, will contribute to retrieve our credit; and I will acquaint the brethren with your arrival, and I hope you will this evening give a word of exhortation at my house.

Wildgoose said, he would do his best, as God should give him utterance: but would go to the inn for an hour or two, to rest and refresh himself, and about seven o'clock would meet the society.

XII

A STRANGER INTRODUCED TO OUR HERO

Our two pilgrims went to a second rate inn; where, whilst Wildgoose was eating some dinner in the parlour, Tugwell had published the good qualities and present occupation of his master (over a pipe) in the kitchen. This my landlord had communicated to a young officer, who was quartered there, and was lounging in the bar, and whom mine host, for the good of the house, contrived, as often as he could, to introduce to his company, to make one at a bottle of wine, or a bowl of punch.

This young man, however, had reasons of a more serious nature, for wishing to converse with a man of Mr Wildgoose's character and pretensions; and willingly consented to the landlord's proposal, of being introduced to this devout itinerant. As soon, therefore, as Wildgoose had finished his slight repast, the landlord told him, that a young officer, who was quartered there, would be glad to drink a glass of wine with him. Wildgoose replied, if the gentleman desired it, he should be very glad of his company; though he could not promise to drink much wine with him.

Accordingly there was introduced a tall, genteel young man, in his regimentals, who, throwing himself into a chair, and laying down his hat, with a smart cockade, upon the table, unbuckled his sword-belt, and hurled his sword, with some indignation across the room, crying out, Thus let the weapons of war perish!

Wildgoose was a little dismayed at this frantic behaviour, and stared at him with silent astonishment; when the man of war, looking wildly in his face, exclaimed again, with an air of distraction, Zounds, sir, can you give any relief to a soul that is haunted by furies?—Come, sir, says Wildgoose, do not despair of God's mercy, whatever your case may be: *Nil desperandum, Christo duce*. Never be cast down whilst you have Christ for your guide. I hope these are favourable symptoms of the new birth:—New birth, sir! God forbid! What! be born again? It is my misfortune that I ever was born at all.

> 'Why was I born with such a sense of virtue,
> So great abhorrence of the smallest guilt,
> And yet a slave to such impetuous passion?'★

As he was thus ranting in heroics, Wildgoose endeavoured to comfort him. Come, sir, says he, the first step to conversion is, to be convinced of sin, as I hope you are; but, that I may be able to administer a proper remedy, let me know the nature of your disease.

Well, sir, if you have patience to listen to a long series of irregularity and guilty pleasures, I will give the best account of myself that I can; as it is always some relief to the miserable, to lay open their griefs, where they can do it with safety, as I am convinced I may to a man of your character, though you are a stranger to me, and I have been guilty of murder; nay, parricide, I believe; adultery, and what not.—Well, well, so much the better, says Wildgoose; the more wicked and abandoned you have been, the more likely you are to be convinced of sin. But please to favour me with the particulars of your transgression. The stranger then began the following narration.

XIII

THE ADVENTURES OF CAPTAIN JOHNSON

My father, says the captain, was a merchant in London, where, for some years, he carried on a considerable trade; but his health declining, and having only one hopeful son (the wretch whom you here behold), he early in life retired from business. I was bred up at Westminster; and

---

★ Phædra and Hypolitus.

passed through the school, I believe, with some degree of credit; and was sent to the university with the character of an excellent classic.

My father, hearing that my parts and sprightly genius had introduced me to the *best,* that is, the most *expensive* company in the place, gave me very liberal appointments; of which I made a very ungenerous use; for, instead of improving myself in learning, or any valuable accomplishment, the only science, in which I made any progress, was that of a refined luxury and extravagance: and, in short, I was guilty of so many irregularities, that although the governors of the university were unwilling to expel me, yet they privately admonished my father to remove me from a situation, of which I was so far from making any proper use, that it must soon prove equally destructive to my health and to my fortune.

My father, who was too fond of me, thought it prudent to appear ignorant of my bad conduct, and wrote me word, that as I had probably by this time made a tolerable proficiency in polite learning and philosophy, he was willing to finish my education by letting me make the tour of Europe.

Accordingly, with no other governor than an honest Swiss, who served me in the double capacity of a tutor and a valet, I set out upon my travels; to make my observations upon the laws and customs, that is, to learn the vices and follies of all the nations in Europe.

During my stay at Paris I became intimate with an English gentleman of some distinction, who was settled with his family at R——, in Normandy, whither, in consequence of a pressing invitation, I accompanied him to spend part of the summer. As both he and his lady were fond of company, I was soon introduced to people of the best fashion, of both sexes, in that province.

There was a young lady of great beauty, the wife of one of the members of the parliament of R——, who was the most frequently of our party. She had a gaiety in her temper, and a coquetry in her behaviour; but not more than is common in the married women of that nation.—Ah! cries Wildgoose, I am afraid what you call by the soft names of gaiety and coquetry, are the lusts of the flesh, under a specious disguise; and that the French are an adulterous and sinful generation.—I am afraid they are, says the captain; and yet I question whether the inhabitants of this island are in that respect much inferior to their neighbours on the continent. But to proceed in my story.

XIV

THE ADVENTURES OF CAPTAIN JOHNSON CONTINUED

Lady Ruelle (which was this lady's name) had been something particular, as I fancied, in her behaviour to me. One evening, as we were walking in the gardens of my friend's house, with a large party of polite people, we found ourselves insensibly got into a private walk, detached from the rest of the company. Monsieur Anglois, says Lady Ruelle, I long to see Londres, and wish I could meet with an opportunity of going over into England.—As I thought this nothing more than unmeaning chit-chat, I imagined the most proper answer I could make her ladyship was, that I should be very happy in showing her our metropolis; and wished I might, some time or other, have that honour. She replied, with a sigh and languishing air, Ah! I wish, monsieur, you were sincere in those professions.—The manner in which she spoke this surprised me a little; yet, as a man of gallantry, I could not but repeat my acknowledgements of the honour she did me, and offered to conduct so fair a lady through the world, if she would permit me. She then declared, that she was serious in her intentions; but (as some company now walked towards us) said, she would explain herself more at large when she had an opportunity.

Lady Ruelle spoke no more to me that night; but the next time we met, she took occasion to let me know, that her husband used her extremely ill; that she had taken a fancy to me the first time she saw me; and would put herself, and ten thousand pounds sterling, in money and jewels, into my hands, if I would accept of the offer.

Though I was startled at such a proposal, it flattered my vanity so agreeably, that, without reflecting on the consequences, I affected to receive with rapture and gratitude so charming an overture.

Not to be too minute in this detail, she had laid her plan; and was determined, I found, to make her escape from a masquerade-ball, to which we were invited, near the suburbs of R——, the next night but one; when she knew also, that her husband would be engaged the whole evening from home. I had time enough to deliberate upon the wickedness and the danger of this expedition; the injury I was going to do the gentleman her husband; and the dishonour I should bring upon my English friend, who had introduced me to them; but, fired with the glory and gallantry of the action (as things then appeared to me,) I was blind to every other consideration.

The next morning, therefore, I sent my trusty Swiss to Dieppe, with orders to get a vessel ready to sail at a minute's notice.

On the night appointed for the masquerade, about ten o'clock, Lady Ruelle appeared, dressed like a young gentleman, in a sort of hunting suit of green and gold, and adorned with not less than five thousand pounds worth of diamonds, which she had contrived to borrow of her husband's relations, under the pretence of this masquerade-ball.

My servant had got the post-chaise ready, under a mount at the corner of the garden wall; and, after supper, when the company were separated into parties, Lady Ruelle and I easily contrived to give them the slip. I let myself down, and the lady, with great courage and alacrity, threw herself into my arms. I put her immediately into the carriage, and we drove off, attended only by the postilion, and by my Swiss, armed with a carbine, with great expedition, for Dieppe.

XV

THE ADVENTURES OF
CAPTAIN JOHNSON CONTINUED

As the distance, I believe, is not above ten leagues, or about thirty miles, we should probably have reached Dieppe without any interruption; but, upon our coming into a forest, where the road divided, our postilion drove us some miles out of the way, before he pretended to have discovered his mistake. We had just recovered our route, when we were overtaken by three men, well armed, who charged us to stop, in the king's name. I had time to cock both my pistols; and my servant, who was a bold fellow, bade them produce their credentials; which he received upon the end of his carbine, but shot the poor fellow dead upon the spot; the other two, like cowards as they were, fled with great precipitation; and we proceeded, without any further molestation, to Dieppe. I there dismissed the postilion, after presenting him with the post-chaise which I had bought, for his faithful service; though it appeared afterwards that he had betrayed us.

When we came to the harbour of Dieppe, we found the ship which my servant had bespoken, riding at her cable's length ready to sail. When we came on board, the master of the vessel demanded our passports. I produced one for myself and for my servant; but, when he found I had none for the young gentleman in green and gold, he shook his head, and refused to sail. I immediately cocked my pistol, and threatened to shoot him through the head, if he persisted in his refusal. He said, I might do as I pleased; but if he carried off that young gentleman, whom he suspected to be a person of consequence, he should be hanged the moment he returned to France. I was not yet so abandoned as to take away the life of an honest man upon so slight a provocation. After trying him again, therefore, with a round sum of money, to no purpose, we were forced to hire another chaise, and resume our journey by land; and proceeded to Boulogne.

Being come the next day within a few miles of that city, we were again overtaken by a man, whom, from his particular dress, I knew to be an emissary of the police. He made a pause, surveyed us all with an eager attention, and then made on, post-haste, towards Boulogne. As I guessed his intention was to apply to the magistrates of that place, and to take us into custody, I, therefore, ordered the chaise to halt a little, and with Lady Ruelle's permission, got out, mounted my servant's horse, changed part of my dress with him, and rode on full speed, to reconnoitre how matters were likely to go in the city.

When I came thither, I found the guards drawn out, and, with drums beating, patrolling the streets. I inquired for one of the principal inns, at the door of which I met by accident a young Englishman, whom I knew to have been a school-fellow at Westminster, though he did not recollect me. He immediately told me, by way of news, that the town was in an uproar, in expectation of seizing an English gentleman, who had carried off a lady of the first quality from R——; and that he would be secured the moment the chaise came within the gates of the city.

Upon this intelligence I immediately rode back as fast as I came; and, holding a council with my Swiss and the postilion, we resolved to turn back out of the great road, and go to a small fishing town, where the postilion told us, we had a better chance for hiring a vessel than at any of the more considerable sea-ports.

When we came thither I soon met with a petty commander of a fishing boat, who, for a small sum of money, readily agreed to convey us the next day to Brighthelmstone. But I, foolishly enough, pulling out a purse of fifty louis-d'ors, which I offered him if he would sail immediately; at the sight of so extraordinary a sum the fellow began to be alarmed, and then demanded our passports, which he had never thought of before. I again produced those for myself and my servant; and showed him a written paper, as a passport for the lady. As the man could not read, he said he would go with us to the curé, or minister of the parish, to have the passports examined.

The curé had a gentleman-like appearance. I took him aside, and told him I would express my gratitude to him, in any manner he should name, if he would assure the master of the vessel that the passport was good, and prevail upon him to sail immediately. The curé replied, with a very serious air, that he would not, for the whole world, abuse the confidence which his parishioners placed in him, by deceiving them in a matter of such importance; but very politely offered us an asylum in his house for that evening. As we had no alternative, we gladly accepted the curé's offer, that we might have time to consider what step was to be next taken.

XVI

THE ADVENTURES OF
CAPTAIN JOHNSON CONCLUDED

It was now the third night since Lady Ruelle had been in bed; and though she had slept a little in the post-chaise, she could not but be very much fatigued; with much difficulty, therefore, I prevailed on her ladyship to go to bed. And having myself sat up till about twelve o'clock with the honest curé, I lay down, and had just composed myself, on a settee in the parlour, when I was awaked by an alarm, that the house was beset by the officers of the police.

As we had reason to apprehend this, we had taken care to barricade the approach, and were determined to stand a siege. There was no way that they could attack us, but from a little garden near the parlour-window. I had armed my servant with his carbine, and myself with a pistol in each hand; and ordered him to keep his fire as long as possible; but he, having a fair mark at one of them by the light of the moon, let fly, and killed him upon the spot. But four more immediately marched up to the window, armed with blunderbusses. I fired one pistol without effect. Upon which, they rushing in upon us immediately, and threatening to fire if we did not surrender, it would have been madness to make any further resistance.

Lady Ruelle and I were seized, and put under a guard till near the morning; when we were placed back to back, and our hands bound behind us, in a sort of covered waggon; and in this manner conveyed to R——.

Lady Ruelle, however, had the generosity, at my request, to slip her watch and a pearl necklace of considerable value into my Swiss's hands; with which, by my orders, he contrived to make his escape into his own country; and this circumstance was of great weight upon my trial.

I could not but remark one particular in Lady Ruelle, quite in the French style. In the midst of her distress, her eyes swimming in tears, and when she could not but dread the consequence of this adventure, she runs up to the glass, adjusts her head-dress, and put some *rouge*, or red paint, upon her cheeks.

Ah! says Wildgoose, those are the works of the Devil, the father of lies, and of every kind of deceit.

Well, continues Captain Johnson, upon our arrival at R——, I was sent a close prisoner to the castle. From thence I was soon brought to my trial before the Parliament of R——; and, as one of their members was the injured party, should have been severely dealt with, if they could have proved either the murders, or the robbery, directly upon me; but as my servant was principal in the former, and also the only witness of the latter, and he had made his escape; and as the lady appeared rather more culpable than myself, having really seduced me; the chief party concerned seemed willing to drop the further prosecution of the affair, especially as my good friend at R—— had made a very powerful application, by means of our ambassador at the court of Versailles. So, after some little confinement, I was dismissed, with orders to quit the kingdom in three days' time; with which I cheerfully complied: and the poor lady was immediately dispatched to a convent.

Upon further inquiry into the cause of this lady's violent resolution, I found she had a suspicion of the most horrid kind, that her husband, who was much older than herself, had an intrigue with her own mother.

Wildgoose stared with tokens of horror. But after some pause,—Nay, says he, I wonder at nothing of this kind; for we are all by nature in the same state with the Gentiles of old, given up to vile affections, unnatural lusts, and a reprobate mind, and to work all uncleanness with greediness.

Well, says the captain, I am not yet come to the most material part of my story, especially so far as my own temporal interest is concerned; for, on my arrival in England, I found my wicked course of life had contributed to shorten my father's days, and my extravagance greatly diminished his fortune; for he was dead: and, instead of the affluence which I had always depended upon, he left but about two thousand pounds, to support me and a mother, who is now but a middle-aged woman, though, from grief and vexation, become very sickly and infirm.

Not to be tedious, I found myself in immediate possession of no more than five hundred pounds with which I purchased a lieutenancy, and am now doing penance in country quarters, strutting about in my red coat and cockade, but really a prey to melancholy, and tortured with reflecting upon those vices which have brought me so early in life to this wretched situation.

XVII

A TEMPORARY CONVERSION

Captain Johnson having finished his narration, Mr Wildgoose bade him not despond; that Providence often brought about our conversion by severe trials; and that it was a maxim with them, The blacker the sinner, the brighter the saint. But, says he, I am going to meet a society of true Christians; where, I make no doubt, you will find those, who have been as wicked as yourself, now full of peace and joy; and I assure you, sir, I have heard Mr Whitfield often say, that he had rather preach to a congregation of publicans and harlots, or what the world may call whores and rogues, than to a set of mere nominal Christians, or good sort of people, as they are called, who flatter themselves that they need no repentance.

The captain said, that, although he should be called a Methodist, and was really invited to dance at a sort of Welsh assembly, he would accompany Mr Wildgoose, by his leave, to their society.

Accordingly, having sat together till near seven o'clock, Mr Wildgoose took Captain Johnson with him, attended by his friend Tugwell, to the tradesman's house; where he found a pretty large congregation assembled in an upper room, over his warehouse in the garden.

Wildgoose harangued upon the usual topics with great pathos; and, as several people round him sighed and groaned, and even wept, the captain found himself variously affected, sometimes inclined to laugh, at other times to cry: but what he found most contagious were the tears of a very pretty girl, a grocer's daughter, who sat near him, with whom the captain would have been glad to have compared his feelings and experiences; for though he was probably sincere in the compunctions which he discovered in conversing with Mr Wildgoose, yet, when the passions have got strength by long indulgence they are not immediately to be subdued, but are apt again to take fire upon approaching a tempting object: nay, as twenty or thirty of the most zealous of them were desirous (according to a common practice) of spending the night in the society-room, the captain stayed among them for some time, and was thought to have been made a complete convert by this young female disciple.

As Mr Wildgoose, however, had been up early in the morning, and was fatigued with the toils of the day; he himself, about eleven o'clock, lay down upon a bed that was offered him by the pious tradesman; and Tugwell's devotion was so far from being enthusiastic this evening, that before Wildgoose had done preaching, he was fallen asleep in the corner of the room.

But, about two in the morning, Mr Wildgoose was waked* by a confused noise, as if a number of men were putting to the sword. He went up into the society-room, where the people had worked themselves up to such a pitch of religious phrenzy, that some were fallen prostrate upon the floor, screaming, and roaring, and beating their breasts, in agonies of remorse for their former wicked lives; others were singing hymns, leaping and exulting in ecstasies of joy, that their sins were forgiven them. Amongst the rest, there was a little boy,† of three years old, who had caught the infection, and acted the sinner with as much appearance of contrition as the best of them. The uproar increased when Wildgoose came into the room, and began to pray with them; but nature, having now been strained to its height for some hours, subsided into a calm. Wildgoose, therefore, dismissed them with a short exhortation, and lay down again till the morning, leaving Tugwell to finish his night's rest, where he had begun, upon some hop-sacks in the corner of the assembly-room.

The captain (he found upon inquiry) about eleven o'clock had conducted home the grocer's daughter, whose father and mother had

* Mr Wesley's *Journal,* 1739.
† *Ibid.* 1738.

sent for her; for, although they indulged her in going (with some other young people) to the Meeting, they did not approve of those late nocturnal vigils, which were frequently solemnized by the warmer devotees.

Amongst others in this devout assembly, there was a substantial miller's wife, who lived about a mile out of town, that was more zealous than any of them. She entreated Mr Wildgoose, if possible, to come home to her, and give her some private consolation, as Mr Whitfield, Mr Wesley, and other gentlemen, she said, had sometimes done. When Wildgoose found she lived partly in the road towards Gloucester (whither he intended to direct his course in the morning,) he promised the good woman to call and take breakfast with her about seven o'clock.

XVIII

A WARM BREAKFAST, CONCLUDED WITH COLD SAUCE

Jerry Tugwell, having been disturbed by the uproar in the night, no sooner met his master in the morning, than he began to vent his indignation with some warmth against the good people of Monmouth. Gad-zookers! says he, these Welsh people are all mad I think; I never heard such rantipole doings since I was born: a body cannot sleep o' nights for 'em.

Ah, Jerry, replies Wildgoose, this is a glorious time! these are the triumphs of faith! these are the true symptoms of the new birth! People are never nearer to the Kingdom of Heaven than when they are *mad*, as you call it; and have never better reason to hope for salvation, than when they are ready to hang and drown themselves.

But come, Jerry, says he, a poor sister is labouring under the pangs of the new birth, and wants our assistance. We must walk a mile or two before breakfast.—Walk a mile or two before breakfast! says Tugwell; why, I had no supper last night, and my stomach is so empty, that I can hardly walk at all without my breakfast. If the young woman is in *labour*, she has more need of a midwife than our assistance.

As Wildgoose, therefore, was taking leave of the tradesman, Tugwell got a piece of bread and cheese, and a cup of ale; and then they went to the inn, to call upon the captain: but, hearing that, notwithstanding his fancied conversion, he had gone from the religious meeting to the profane dancing assembly, and had not been come to bed above two hours, the two pilgrims set out upon their expedition.

When they came to the mill, which was not above a mile out of town, they found a good breakfast prepared for them by their kind hostess, the miller's wife; for the miller, having set out early in the morning, the good woman, who thought she could not do too much for such good people, had got some cakes baked and buttered, and all other requisites for a comfortable *dejeuné.* And in this manner, with the addition of some godly conversation, the poor woman frequently regaled herself; and always found herself more happy, than in the surly society of her morose husband; which happiness she ascribed to the power of religion, rather than to its more probable cause; the variety it introduced, and to the comfortable soothing doctrine of being saved by faith without works.

And, indeed, the miller, though fond of his wife (who was much younger than himself, and a tolerably handsome woman,) and unwilling absolutely to forbid her frequenting these pious meetings; yet, as he was often, by this means, deprived of his conjugal claims, and the company of his spouse, who, according to the old Liturgy, ought to have been *buxom both at bed and board*, he was generally out of humour upon these occasions, and could not forbear expressing his disapprobation of the many itinerants which came to the house, amongst his workmen and servants. These fellows, therefore, who were more in their master's interest than in that of their mistress, laid a plot, which they knew would not displease their master; but which, if he had been at home, he probably, out of regard to his wife, would not have suffered them to execute.

The nearest way for the two pilgrims to return into the great road, was through a meadow, into which they must pass over the mill-stream, by a narrow plank, which was laid across it. This plank the fellows contrived to saw almost in two, on the under side. When, therefore, the travellers had taken their leave of the miller's wife, Wildgoose leading the way, marched foremost nimbly over the bridge, which, though it cracked, did not entirely break down till he was landed, and Tugwell came upon the middle of it, who, being a heavy-a——d Christian, and moreover encumbered with his loaded wallet, fell plump into the stream, bawling out for help, to the no small diversion of the spectators. The men, ran, however, to Jerry's assistance with a feigned concern, and dragged him out of the water; but took care that he should first be dipped into it considerably above the waist.

The fright and the surprise at first took away Jerry's voice, that he could not vent his indignation. One of the fellows handing him up his wallet, 'Sblood! Honesty, says the man, thou hast but just *saved thy bacon.*—What the devil do you mean by saving my bacon? says Tugwell. It is nothing but my master's Bible and some good books in my wallet. The fellow, indeed, by that proverbial expression, only alluded to the narrow escape Jerry had had; but spoke the literal truth by chance: for the miller's wife it seems, out of her great regard to the godly, had offered Tugwell a piece of bacon, of about five or six pounds, which, for fear of accidents, Jerry (unknown to his master) had accepted of, and stowed in his wallet; and the consciousness of his greediness now made a discovery, which the miller's men, perhaps, would not otherwise have suspected.

One of the fellows asked Tugwell, with a sneer, if he would go back and dry himself, and have another dish of tea: but Tugwell, muttering some threats, trudged after his master as fast as he could, equally ashamed to be thus out-witted, and vexed to be wetted to the skin. And, upon Wildgoose's exhorting him to suffer tribulation with patience, Jerry replied, in great wrath, that he did not care who suffered tribulation, so that he was got safe home again in his chimney-corner.

XIX

A SEASONABLE RELIEF

They had now proceeded about three miles on their journey from Monmouth, when they came to a considerable brook, which ran at the foot of a steep hill, covered with extensive woods. There was a foot-bridge to pass over; but the rivulet being swelled by a violent thunder-storm which had fallen in the night, they could not possibly approach the bridge. Being obliged, therefore, to halt, they sat down upon the bank, and were deliberating what course to pursue, when Tugwell began to complain of being very chill, and of the head-ache, and said he was certainly going to have a fit of the ague, and should not be able to go any further. He then heavily bemoaned himself, and said, if he were at home, Dorothy would carry his water to the *cunning man*, who would cast a spell, or send him a bottle of *stuff*, which would cure him after the third fit; or else Madam Wildgoose would send him some *higry-pigry*,★ which would stop it at once.

Whilst they were thus engaged, Tugwell complaining, and Wildgoose endeavouring to encourage him, by the examples of martyrs, saints, and confessors, they observed a horse grazing at some distance by the wood-side, with a sort of pack-saddle upon his back, and the bridle hanging loosely between his legs. Having now waited near a quarter of an hour, and nobody appearing to whom the horse might probably belong, Mr Wildgoose observed to his friend, that Providence† had certainly delivered this horse into their hands, to promote the great work in which they were embarked. Tugwell, however, for more reasons than one, objected to taking a horse which certainly did not belong to them. Wildgoose owned, it was not lawful to steal, or even to covet our neighbour's ox, or his ass, or any thing that does not belong to us. But, says he again, we are commanded to use all diligence in our power, which must signify the using all the means to compass any end

---

★ *Hiera picra*, or sacred bitter.
† *Journal, passim.*

which falls in our way. Now we shall certainly make more speed on horseback than on foot; and, therefore, we may lawfully, I think, make use of this horse, which is thus providentially ready bridled and saddled for our use.

To this Tugwell made two objections; first, that perhaps the water was too high for them to ride through, and secondly, that he could not ride, having never been on horseback since he was ten years old.

Wildgoose replied, that as Jerry was afraid, he himself would first ride through, and, if it were safe, would return and take Jerry behind him, and convey him to the next inn; and, by putting him into a warm bed, he did not doubt but he would soon be as well as ever.

But, continues Wildgoose, to make sure of the lawfulness of what we are about, we will have recourse to our Bible, as Mr Wesley and Mr Whitfield have often done. Upon opening it, therefore, they dipped upon that passage where the disciples were ordered to bring the ass's colt, for their master's triumphant entry into Jerusalem. This Wildgoose considered as a case in point, and decisive in their favour. He went, therefore, to catch the horse, when he spied also an old blue great coat thrown into the ditch, which it puzzled him yet more to account for. But, as he intended to leave the horse at the first inn they came to, he thought it best to take the coat also, and wrap up his companion, who was still shivering with cold.

Upon searching the pocket of the great coat, they found in it an old crape hat-band, a pocket-knife, and an iron tobacco-box.

Wildgoose now leaped upon Rosinante; and, riding boldly into the brook, found it barely fordable (as the flood was abating,) which it probably had not been in the morning, when it was at the highest. He, therefore, returned, and with some difficulty dragged Jerry up behind him, wrapped in the great coat; and thus crossing the brook, they marched slowly up the hill, through a deep and rough hollow way. They descended the hill again; and, after riding about a mile further, came to a little village, where, meeting with a public-house, they stopped, hung the horse at the door, with the great coat upon the pad, and put Jerry into a warm bed, who desired a little treacle posset, which threw him into a perspiration, by which he soon recovered his usual vivacity.

Whilst Wildgoose was waiting in a sort of little parlour for his fellow-traveller's recovery, my landlord had prevailed upon him, as his beard was near a week's growth, to submit to the operation of a barber, who had just shaved my landlord. The operator had just finished one side of Wildgoose's face, when five or six men rushed into the house, armed with clubs, pitchforks, and an old gun; which was part of the hue-and-cry raised by a farmer, who had been robbed that morning, in his way to the fair above-mentioned, by a man upon the very horse which Wildgoose and his friend had made use of.

They inquired where the person was to whom the horse at the door and the blue great coat belonged. My landlord pointed to Wildgoose, as he was shaving in the next room, with his back towards them. The fellows surveying him pretty narrowly, one of them cried out, Aye, that is he, I can answer to him: he was a tall thinnish man, just his size. They then began disputing who should go first into the room, and seize the villain. The farmer that had been robbed said, it was the constable's duty to apprehend the criminal. The constable said, he would take him before the magistrate, but would not venture his life upon other people's business. A butcher, who was amongst them, made signs to the barber, to cut his throat without any more ceremony. But the honest barber, either not understanding their hints, or having more sense than to comply with them, the farmer's son, who had been robbed, a young man of about seventeen, snatched the gun out of the hands of one of them, and immediately seized Wildgoose, in the king's name, for *villoneously* robbing an honest farmer that morning upon the king's highway. And, without suffering Wildgoose to make any defence, or the barber to finish the other side of his face, they were hurrying him immediately before a justice of the peace, when my landlord informed them, that there was another of them, who came with the horse, and who wore the blue great coat which was left upon the pack-saddle.

At that instant, Tugwell finding himself pretty well recovered, and his returning appetite putting him in mind that he had acted the sick man long enough, he was just come down into the kitchen and the landlord tipping the wink, the constable seized him also by the collar, in the king's name. What the pox is the matter now? says Tugwell; what do you collar me for, and be hanged?—Only for stealing a horse, and robbing upon the highway, says the constable. The man who had been robbed seeing Jerry seized, and hearing his voice, cried out again; Aye, that is the very rogue that robbed me; I can swear to his voice. And he now said it was a short thick-set fellow; though he had before given just the contrary description of him.

The gentlemen of the hue-and-cry were going to tie the culprits' hands behind them, and their legs under the horse's belly, in order to carry them before the justice; but mine host observing, that there were enough to guard them without that precaution, they set them both upon the horse as they had been before; and thus they marched with them near four miles, to one Mr Aldworth's, on the borders of Herefordshire; Tugwell, according to custom, bewailing his misfortune, and Wildgoose administering his usual topics of consolation.

XXI

A JUSTICE, AND A JUSTICE OF THE PEACE

Mr Aldworth was an opulent country gentleman, and a very worthy magistrate. His way of living gave one the truest idea of that hospitality for which the English nation was formerly distinguished. I mean not in the days of Queen Elizabeth, when even the ladies breakfasted upon toast and metheglin, or cold beef (which days I consider, in that respect, as somewhat barbarous and semi-gothic;) but of that hospitality which subsisted amongst our gentry till the Revolution, and continued in some measure to the days of Queen Anne and George the First; when, instead of being tantalized with a dozen of French dishes (which no Frenchman, however, would ever taste,) and stared at by as many French servants, dressed better than yourself, or their own master; instead of being dragged out the moment you have dined, to take a walk in the shrubbery, and wonder at his lordship's *bad* taste, and then frightened away with the appearance of cards and wax candles; instead of this refined luxury, I say, you were sure to find at Mr Aldworth's, a ham and fowls, a piece of roast beef, or a pigeon-pie, and a bottle of port wine, every day in the week; and, if you chose to spend the night at his house, a warm bed, and a hearty welcome.

This hospitable temper and friendly reception generally filled Mr Aldworth's table; and none of his old acquaintance, who came within ten miles of him, ever thought of lying at an inn, when he was in the country; which, indeed, unless any extraordinary business called him to London, was usually the whole year.

The reader will pardon this tribute to such primitive merit, which, indeed, serves also to render more probable an incident in the sequel.

Mr Aldworth was at dinner, with some company, when the culprits and their cavalcade arrived at the door; they were, therefore, ordered into a little summer-house, at the corner of the garden: where the 'squire used both to take a sober glass with a particular friend, or to distribute justice amongst his neighbours with equal wisdom and impartiality;

'And sometimes counsel take, and sometimes wine.'

Amongst other company now at Mr Aldworth's, there was one Mr Newland, a young man of fortune, who, instead of going to the University, to Paris, or even to the Temple, to study the laws of England, had been educated under an eminent attorney in the country, and consequently was a rigid observer of the letter of the law; and, having but lately been put into the commission, he was impatient to act the magistrate, and flourish his name at the side of a mittimus.

Mr Newland, therefore, having paid a proper compliment to the second course, by swallowing a leg and wing of a duckling, and a plate of green peas; and, having drank hob-or-nob with a young lady, in whose eyes he wished to appear a man of consequence, he hurried out into the summer-house, where he made the clerk immediately swear the evidence, and take the depositions; over which, as soon as young Newland had cast his eye, and had surveyed Wildgoose's face, half shaved (which he took for a disguise;) Well, you rascal, says he to Wildgoose, what have you to say for yourself, guilty or not guilty!—Ah! says Wildgoose, shaking his head, I am but too *guilty*, God forgive me! and am laden with iniquities.—There, says the young magistrate to the clerk, you hear he confesses it. He then bid the clerk fill up the mittimus, and he would sign it, without giving Mr Aldworth the trouble of leaving the company.

XXII

A FRIEND IN NEED IS A FRIEND INDEED

While this was transacting, however, the good old gentleman, being aware of his young colleague's precipitate temper, came out, with the napkin tucked in his button-hole, and began to inquire a little into the circumstances of the affair. It appeared from the deposition, that the farmer had been robbed of seven guineas that morning about five o'clock, by a man upon that very horse, and in that blue great coat, with a black crape over his face, and armed with that very long pocket-knife; all which were found in Tugwell's and his master's possession.

Mr Aldworth, however, notwithstanding these particulars, and the suspicious circumstance of Wildgoose's double face (which, indeed, the landlord soon cleared up,) saw an appearance of honesty in Wildgoose, and even in his friend Tugwell, which inclined him to think more favourably of them than Mr Newland had done. He, therefore, asked Wildgoose, what account they could give of themselves, whence they came, and whither they were going?—Wildgoose replied, that they had come from Gloucester, and had been at Bristol upon a business of consequence; but, for some particular reasons, had been obliged to return through Wales and Monmouthshire.

This account appearing somewhat incoherent, Mr Aldworth asked, how they came by that horse and the great coat; which Wildgoose explained to him; and added, that probably the person who committed the robbery, finding the brook not fordable in the morning, on account of the flood, had made his escape into the woods on foot. But, however that might be, though he owned himself guilty of many other crimes in the sight of God, yet he was never guilty of robbery; and that he himself and his fellow traveller were at breakfast at a miller's, near Monmouth, at seven o'clock that morning; and that he could bring a hundred people to witness, that he had preached at a religious society at Monmouth the preceding night.

O, ho! says Justice Newland, are you at that sport? Your preaching at Monmouth last night does not prove that you did not rob upon the highway this morning. Many of these itinerant preachers have done the same.

Well, well, says Mr Aldworth, let us suspend our judgment till we have inquired more into this affair. Where is your proper place of residence? says he to Wildgoose; and what trade or profession are you of?—Upon Wildgoose's answering that he lived in the north part of Gloucestershire,—Mr Aldworth said, they should then probably get some light into his character, and give him an opportunity of clearing himself, by a gentleman who was then in the house. Here! says he to a servant, desire Mr Powel to step hither a moment.

Wildgoose, finding himself oddly affected at the name of Powel, though he did not immediately know why, changed colour; which Justice Newland observing, winked upon Mr Aldworth, with a sagacious nod. But, says he, this old rascal is the principal; and I suspect he is returned from transportation; for I remember his face at Monmouth assizes seven years ago, when I was first clerk to Mr Traverse.

Tugwell was going to clear himself of that aspersion, when Mr Powel appeared, who was no other than the parson of the parish where Mr Wildgoose lived, and whom we mentioned as the accidental cause of Wildgoose's disgust with the world. Mr Powel was returning from a visit to his friends in Wales, and had made Mr Aldworth's house a convenient stage by the way.

The mutual astonishment of Mr Powel and the two pilgrims, at meeting each other in this place, and on such an occasion, was proportionable to the improbability of such a rencounter.

Mr Powel expressed his concern at seeing his old neighbours in such a situation; but could hardly forbear laughing, to see one side of Wildgoose's face close shaven, and the other with a beard half an inch long.

Mr Wildgoose was in some confusion at this unexpected meeting with Mr Powel, as he did not like to be obliged by a man, against whom he had conceived so violent a prejudice; and also was afraid of being disappointed in what he really wished for, the being persecuted for the Gospel's sake, as he esteemed it, and (like honest John Bunyan) the singing of psalms in a gaol.

Upon Mr Powel's telling him, however, that his mother had been greatly affected with his absence, and had had a dangerous fit of sickness, he found some symptoms of humanity revive in his breast; an involuntary tear rose into the orbit of his eye; and he even expressed some hope that she was quite recovered.

But, as for Tugwell, his joy was excessive, and quite sincere, at meeting the vicar of his parish, for whom he had always a thorough reverence and esteem.—God in Heaven bless you, Master Powel! cries Jerry; how does our Dorothy do, and my poor dog Snap, and Madam Powel? Ah! master, we have been all the world over, by sea and by land, over mountains, deserts, and quicksands, since we went from home; and, after preaching the Gospel all over England and Wales, for pure love, here they have taken us up for horse-stealing, only for riding a horse, that we found grazing by a woodside, about a mile or two, when I was ready to perish with the ague.

Why, my friend Jerry, says Mr Powel, I think you might as well have been in your own stall, repairing old shoes, as rambling about the country to reform the world; but I will answer for it, Jerry, neither you, nor Mr Wildgoose, had any hand in stealing this horse.—I find, then, says Mr Aldworth, Mr Powel does really know these men. Appearances are by no means in their favour; but what can you say for them, Mr Powel?—Why, replies Mr Powel, I will be answerable for their honesty; and that neither of them is concerned in the fact of which they are accused.

I do not dispute Mr Powel's knowledge of the criminals, says young Newland; but the circumstances are so strong against them, that I think we have nothing to do but to make their mittimus.

Sir, replies Mr Aldworth, many an innocent man has been condemned and executed upon circumstantial evidence; we cannot, therefore, be too cautious in this affair.

I am not going to condemn, or to try them, rejoins Newland, with some quickness; that is the judge's business. I shall only commit them to a gaol till the assizes, when I hope their innocence will appear to the gentlemen of the jury. Mr Powel observed, however, that it would be a great hardship for innocent men to lie in gaol for three months upon so slight a suspicion. To which Newland answered, that the law did not consult the ease of individuals, but the good of the whole. Mr Aldworth was going to reply, when a great bustle at the summer-house door interrupted him.

XXIII

THE REAL HIGHWAYMAN PRODUCED. TUGWELL ESCAPES A GAOL, AND GETS A DINNER

The noise at the summer-house door was occasioned by another party of the hue-and-cry, who had gone a different way, that morning, in pursuit of the robber, and had actually taken the real culprit, who, having left his horse by the river's side, where Wildgoose and his friend found him, had escaped through the wood into a different road, where these people had seized him, from his guilty appearance; and had actually found upon him not only the exact sum of money, with two Portugal pieces, to which the farmer immediately swore, but also an old pocket-book, containing a regular account between the farmer and his landlord; which, with other circumstances, appeared so evident, that the justices had nothing more to do, but to commit him without further examination.

Mr Aldworth, having now turned over the rest of this ragamuffin assembly to the care of his butler (who never suffered any one that came about business, to leave the house without some refreshment,) desired Mr

Powel to conduct his two countrymen into a little breakfast-room, as he thought it in vain to ask Wildgoose, in his present trim, to go into the parlour where his company had dined. But Mr Aldworth himself, after making an apology to his other friends, returned, attended by a servant with a napkin and tray, and some remains of a plentiful treat, which was no unsavoury prospect to people in Wildgoose's and Tugwell's situation.

When the two pilgrims had now refreshed themselves, and Mr Powel had recounted most of the occurrences in the neighbourhood during their absence, he began to persuade them, with all the rhetoric in his power, to return to their respective homes. Tugwell listened with great complacency to this exhortation; but Wildgoose, with a religious obstinacy, persisted in his first resolution; said he was not at his own disposal, but should fulfil the engagements he was under to his friends; though he did not think fit to explain to Mr Powel the particulars.

Mr Aldworth, when he found that Wildgoose's elopement was contrary to his mother's approbation, shook his head, with a melancholy air, and said he heartily sympathized with every parent in that situation; and that he could not but join with Mr Powel in advising Mr Wildgoose to return to his mother. As I have suffered myself by the imprudence of an only son, I would endeavour to rescue any parent from the like distress; and I flatter myself, that on my late journey to town, I was instrumental in restoring a young lady to her friends, who from some unaccountable whim had eloped, entirely alone, in the stage-coach to London, and by my earnest persuasions prevailed on her to return the very next day, in the same stage, to her father: and I cannot but entreat you, sir, though a stranger, to restore your distressed mother to her tranquillity, by accompanying Mr Powel to your native place.

As the imprudence which Mr Aldworth lamented in his son was the pursuing his own inclinations, and marrying a young woman with less fortune than Mr Aldworth had destined him for; so the reader will probably guess, that the young lady whom he had rescued from destruction, was no other than Miss Townsend; in whose story Mr Wildgoose was so much interested.

Wildgoose's colour came immediately into his cheeks, and he could hardly forbear discovering the acquaintance he had with that young

lady, and also informing Mr Aldworth of the accident that had frustrated
his benevolent intentions; which, if Miss Townsend had been indifferent
to him, he would most certainly have done; but, as the delicacy of his
passion made him reserved in speaking of her, so his surprise passed off
without being remarked by the company.

As the afternoon was now far advanced, Mr Aldworth invited
Wildgoose (with his fellow-traveller), to take a bed there; and told
Wildgoose, that his butler should finish what the barber had been
prevented from doing by the insolence of the hue-and-cry. Wildgoose
thanked the old 'squire for his civility; but, not feeling himself quite
happy in Mr Powel's company, and finding a stronger attachment
towards Gloucester the nearer he approached to it, he chose to proceed
on his journey.

Wildgoose, however, sent his dutiful respects to his mother; and
Tugwell took an opportunity of whispering to Mr Powel, that he did
not half like this vagabond way of life; and wished the Spirit would give
Mr Wildgoose leave to return home again. But, master, says he, tell our
Dorothy we shall be no losers by it: and here, master, please to give her
this crooked sixpence, for a token. Mr Powel smiled at Jerry's instance
of generosity; but advised him to carry it himself.

The young magistrate, Mr Newland, on his return to the company,
had acquainted them with all the particulars of Wildgoose's story, which
raised the curiosity of the ladies; and, when they were informed of their
marching off, they all ran to the window which looked towards the
lawn, where the two pilgrims passed in review before them.

Tugwell's spirits being quite elevated by his good cheer, he took the
lead, in his short jerkin, his jelly-bag cap, which he had kept on since
the morning, and his wallet on his shoulder; which, by a kind of instinct,
he secured amidst all adventures; and which, like

> His oaken staff, which he could ne'er forsake,
> Hung half before, and half behind his back.

Mr Wildgoose, however, exhibiting only that side of his face which
had undergone the barber's operation, made no despicable appearance;

but raised a concern in the ladies, that so handsome a young man should have taken so odd a turn, and travel about the country like a Scotch pedlar.

XXIV

MAN OF ROSS

When the two friends were got clear of Mr Aldworth's premises, and were now alone in the road to Gloucester; whilst Mr Wildgoose was wrapped in meditation, Tugwell interrupted him, by commenting upon the adventures of the day, and observed what a narrow escape they had had from being sent to gaol. He said he would take care how he got on horse-back again, especially upon other folk's horses. What a fine story our parson will have to carry home! that I and your worship were taken up for horse-stealing!—Ah! Jerry, replies Wildgoose; how often must I remind thee of the blessing promised to those who are unjustly persecuted? Happy are ye, when men shall say all manner of evil of you, falsely, for my name's sake.—Yes, yes, that is true, says Jerry; but a man does not like to be counted a thief for all that, when a body does not deserve it. One's good name is one's livelihood; and I never was counted a night-walker, or a sheep-stealer, before I kept company with your worship (as I may say); and I had rather have been ducked in a horse-pond, or pelted with cow-turd, than have had the disgrace of such a scandalous thing.

But come, hang it! we did get a good dinner at the 'squire's, *howsomever*, and I believe he is a very honest gentleman.

Thus Tugwell went on, grumbling and consoling himself alternately, without much conversation from his master, till they came, towards the evening, to a tolerable public-house, where they thought it best to repose themselves, after the fatigues and distresses of the past day.

The first thing Wildgoose did was, by Tugwell's admonition, to finish what the barber had begun; after which, according to his usual custom, he went to impart some spiritual exhortation to the family that received him. There was in the kitchen an old gentleman-farmer, with locks as white as wool, and a face as red as a red-streak: he was smoking his pipe, and drinking cider with my landlord. Wildgoose, perceiving by his discourse that he came from the neighbourhood of Ross, in Herefordshire, took that opportunity of making some inquiries after the famous Man of Ross, so justly celebrated by Mr Pope, for his public spirit and unbounded generosity. What! old Kyrle! says the farmer; yes, I knew him well: he was an honest old cock, and loved his pipe and a tankard of cider as well as the best of us.—Well, says Mr Wildgoose, if he used them with moderation, there was no great harm in either of them; and though a man may endow hospitals without charity, and build churches without religion; and though I am afraid the Man of Ross relied too much upon his good works; yet he was certainly a very useful man, and a great benefactor to your country.

Yes, says the old farmer; he certainly made good roads, and raised causeways, and brought conduits of water to the town; but it was not *all* at his own expense; he made the country pay for it, by pretty handsome levies, and a tax upon the public.

Wildgoose was not a little shocked at the malignity of the vulgar part of mankind, in detracting from the merit of the most heroic characters, and bringing every one down, as near as possible, to their own level; which seemed to be the principle on which this jolly old fellow proceeded in his character of the benevolent and worthy Man of Ross.

XXV

FOREST OF DEAN. EQUALITY OF MANKIND

As Wildgoose was impatient to proceed on his journey to Gloucester, he had gone early to bed, and awoke early in the morning: but Tugwell having been thoroughly harassed and fatigued the preceding day, it was not in his master's power to rouse him from his bed till near eight o'clock; when, as soon as Jerry had taken a short breakfast (which he made a conscience of not omitting), they set forwards on their journey.

Their road lay through the romantic Forest of Dean; and the very name of a forest filled Tugwell's imagination with ideas of wild beasts, robbers, and out-laws; and though Jerry had no great matter to lose, all the stories which he had ever heard in the chimney-corner, or read in his penny-farthing histories, now occurred to his memory. But, upon Wildgoose's assuring him there was no danger to be apprehended now-a-days, either from wild beasts, giants, or out-laws, they jogged on pretty peaceably all the fore-part of the day; and about dinner-time, coming to a fine tuft of oaks, upon a bank by the side of a crystal brook, the coolness of the scene invited them to rest a little in the heat of the day, and to regale themselves with the contents of Jerry's wallet, which Mr Aldworth's butler had liberally furnished with provisions the preceding day.

While they were thus employed, Jerry began to make comparisons between the different situation of some poor fellows whom they had just passed by, (who, in the dog-days, were sweating at the forge belonging to a great iron-work in the forest), and the company which they had seen the day before at Mr Aldworth's. Jerry observed, how hard it was that some people should be forced to toil like slaves, whilst others lived in ease and plenty, and the fat of the land!—Ah! Jerry, says Wildgoose; true happiness does not consist in meat and drink, but in peace and joy in the Holy Ghost; and I am convinced, there is not that difference in the real enjoyment of men, which you imagine. You only see the outside of the wealthier part of mankind; and know nothing of the care and anxiety they suffer, which is frequently more insupportable than any bodily labour which poor people undergo.

Odsbobs! says Tugwell, if I had but as good a dinner every day as I had yesterday at the justice's, I would not value of a straw all the care and *hangciety* in the world.

Well, replies Wildgoose; but these distinctions amongst mankind are absolutely necessary; and whilst men have the liberty of doing as they please, it cannot be otherwise.

I suppose, continues Wildgoose, you would have every body provided for alike; so that no one should be either very rich or very poor.—Why, says Jerry, methinks it is very hard that one man should have five or six hundred pounds a-year, when another, mayhap, has not fifty.

Well, then, replies Wildgoose, we will suppose that you and I, Jerry, and all the people of our parish, and in the next parish, and in the next market-town, and so on, had each a hundred pounds a-year, and no more.—Aye, that I should like now well enough.—Well, then, but where should I get my shoes made? says Mr Wildgoose.—Troth, master, you must even make them yourself; for I should work for nobody but for myself and our Dorothy. Well, says Wildgoose, and where would you buy your leather?—Why, of Mr Jones, the currier, at Evesham.— Where would you get awls, hammers, and cutting-knives?—Why, from Birmingham.—Very well; and where would you get your clothes made?—O, Isaac, our tailor, should work for me; he is a very honest fellow.

Ah, Jerry, says Mr Wildgoose, thou dost not consider, that all these people would be fully employed in working for themselves; so that, for all thy hundred a-year, thou must not only make thy own clothes, but raise thy own corn, build thy own house, make thy own chairs and tables, thy own linen, stockings, shoes, and buckles; and, in short, either every man must work ten times harder than the poorest man now does, or if he were idle or extravagant, those that were more frugal and industrious would again grow rich, and the others poor; which shows the unavoidable necessity of that inequality amongst mankind, with which your complaint began.

Odzookers, master! why, I do not know but it may be true enough, as you say; and, perhaps, I may be as happy as 'Squire Pelican himself, though we brew nothing but small-beer: for though the 'squire can afford to get drunk every day in the week, yet he is laid up with the gout half the year; and, thank God! I have seldom any thing the matter with me, except the cramp now and then; and that I can cure by a cramp ring, made of hinge of old coffins.

XXVI

PERILS AMONGST FALSE BRETHREN

The two pilgrims having reposed themselves for a considerable time in the heat of the day, it grew almost dark before they approached the city of Gloucester. Tugwell again began to renew the subject of thieves and robbers; but as his master had before rallied him for his cowardly apprehensions, Jerry affected to talk of highwaymen in a jocular strain. He said the cleverest book he ever met with was, *The Exploits of Captain James Hind*, who lived in Oliver's days; and though, to Jerry's surprise, his master had never heard of him, he was born, he said, at Chipping Norton. Did you never hear how he served the parson? continues Jerry. Not I, indeed, says Wildgoose.—It is a comical fancy enough, says Tugwell. Captain Hind had just robbed a gentleman of two hundred pounds; but more company being just behind, he thought they would pursue him; and so, meeting a poor parson, who was a little pot-valiant, the captain pretended he himself was pursued by some highwaymen, and desired the parson to take one of his pistols, and fire it in the face of the first man he met, whilst Hind rode down to the next village to get more help: and so, in short, the parson did, and was taken by the gentleman, and had like to be hanged for it.

Another time the captain was enchanted for three years by an old hag. But the cleverest trick is what he served the old miser.—Well, well, says Wildgoose, I shall listen no longer to thy stories: I do not wonder that such foolish tales delighted thee in thy unregenerate state; but I am afraid, this sort of nonsensical books have brought many a poor wretch to the gallows, as they always interest one in favour of their heroes, and represent vice in too agreeable a light.

The road now lay through a dark lane, shaded with elms; and Wildgoose, being equally happy in the thoughts of seeing Miss Townsend, and in beholding the flourishing state of his little church, which he had planted under the care of the barber and Mrs Sarsenet, they moved along with profound silence, when out leaps a man from the edge, and, with a thundering oath, snapped a pistol full in the face of

Tugwell, who happened to be foremost; which, however, only flashed in the pan. Tugwell, though not deficient in courage, as we have observed, yet was extremely terrified at the sight of fire-arms, to which he had not been accustomed. He, therefore, bawled out, Murder! murder! and running back, knocked Wildgoose down, and himself tumbled, a-se-over-head, souse upon him. The footpad, holding the pistol to Tugwell's head, bade him and his master deliver their money, or they were dead men.—Wildgoose, who had more presence of mind, begged him to take away the pistol, and he would give him money enough to relieve his present *necessity*; as nothing, he observed, but the *utmost necessity* could possibly drive a man to such desperate acts of violence.

As Wildgoose was proceeding in his unseasonable exhortation, the robber, who knew his voice, cries out, God forgive me! Master Wildgoose! Is it possible that I should be so unfortunate as to make my very first attack upon you! Do not you know me? proceeds he.—Who are you, then? says Wildgoose.—Ah, sir! I am Tom Keen the barber, where your worship lodged at Gloucester.—The two pilgrims now recovered from their fright, but not from their surprise; and inquiring what could possibly tempt him to hazard both his life and his soul, by robbing upon the highway?—Oh! sir, says the barber, nothing but the most urgent necessity, as you rightly observe. You, yourself, however (without intending it) have been the principal cause of bringing me to this distress. My neighbour Fillpot, at the public-house, out of spite, paid off a year and a half's rent, which I owed my landlord, seized upon my goods, turned me out of my house; and now my wife, who has just lain-in, is destitute of the necessaries for a woman in her condition; and my children are, at this instant, crying for bread.

Well, says Tugwell, I pity any one that wants a meal of victuals. But, 'sblood! that is no reason why you should take away my life, and fire a pistol in my face.—Ah! cries the barber, you were in no danger of your life from my pistol; for you may see, if it were light enough, that it is nothing but a pistol tinder-box, which I took out of Mr Pasty's, the fat prebend's, bed-room, who has made no use of it these ten years.

Wildgoose then said, he was sorry to find that any degree of necessity could suggest to him this method of relieving his distress; but, as his first attempt had been providentially made upon himself, Wildgoose observed, it would be attended with no ill consequences; and, as he had been the cause of his calamity, he hoped it would be in his power, some time or other, to make him some amends for his temporal sufferings: but he hoped no distress would ever prevail upon the barber to be guilty of such another desperate attempt to relieve it.

XXVII

GLOUCESTER

As this worthy triumvirate were now travelling amicably towards Gloucester, Wildgoose inquired how Mrs Sarsenet went on? The barber replied, he did not know that her business declined at all; and Mrs Sarsenet was a very good woman. But, says he, charity begins at home. She has got an old infirm mother, and a lame sister to support; and yet she has of late so many spiritual bargemen and pious colliers, that come up from Bristol, whom she entertains at breakfast, with tea and coffee, and buttered rolls, that I am afraid it is more than she can well afford.

And then the young woman that lodged with her is gone away; and I suppose she paid handsomely for her board (for I find her father is a rich 'squire), and she was a clever notable young body, and of great use to her in her business.

This piece of news was a great disappointment to Mr Wildgoose; which, with the shock he received from hearing the ill consequences of his preaching (to the temporal interests of his disciples), threw him into a fit of musing, and put a stop to their conversation till they arrived at Gloucester.

It was near ten o'clock when Wildgoose and his fellow-travellers reached the town. Having, however, supplied the poor barber with half a guinea for his immediate necessities, which was full as much as he could prudently spare out of his present stock, he and Tugwell went to Mrs Sarsenet's, whom they found at supper, with her mother and sister, upon a bunch of radishes and some dry bread.

Mrs Sarsenet was greatly rejoiced to see Mr Wildgoose, to whom she was a most sincere convert. She offered to get the travellers something for supper; and also told Wildgoose, that as he was deprived of his old lodging, he should be welcome to the bed in which Miss Townsend had lain. Wildgoose, though he probably thought, what David said of Goliath's sword, that there was none like it; yet Mrs Whitfield, after she became acquainted with his merit when last at Gloucester, having pressed him to leave his lodgings at the barber's, and come to the Bell, he now thought it would be very convenient, at least for that night, to accept of her kindness, and prove the favourable opinion which she seemed now to entertain of him.

Having made all proper inquiries, therefore, after Miss Townsend, and being informed of all the particulars—that Mr Townsend had sent a carriage, and conveyed her to a relation's in Warwickshire; and having read three or four times over a direction, written with her own hand, to Miss Julia Townsend, at Dr Greville's, at ———, near Warwick, he sighed, and took his leave of Mrs Sarsenet for that evening, and went to Mrs Whitfield's, at the Bell, to the no small joy of Tugwell, who infinitely preferred the smoke and savoury smell of a greasy kitchen, to the meagre neatness of Mrs Sarsenet's parlour, notwithstanding it was adorned with a glass door, to peep into the shop, and the Ten Commandments, worked at the boarding-school, in a gilt frame; with King William and Queen Mary, and several other mezzotintos, painted on glass, which had been in the family ever since the Revolution.

XXVIII

THE PILGRIMS KINDLY TREATED BY MRS WHITFIELD

Mrs Whitfield received Mr Wildgoose with great cordiality, notwithstanding he brought no letters of recommendation from her brother-in-law, as the reader may suppose, on account of his precipitate departure from Bristol. Mrs Whitfield's husband, being fatigued with *too close attention* to the *proper business* of his calling, was retired to rest; so that she was at supper alone, upon a brace of partridges, with a large China *bason* of warm punch, which was no disagreeable contrast to the mortified repast of poor Mrs Sarsenet: and, as the relation she stood in to Mr Whitfield sanctified whatever she did, in the eyes of Mr Wildgoose, he made no scruple in partaking with her of the good things which were set before him. Mrs Whitfield laid Wildgoose in one of her bettermost rooms, the only good bed he had met with since he came from home; and Tugwell also shared the same kindness, which made ample amends for the contumelious reception they had met with on their first arrival at Gloucester.

Though the little church which Wildgoose had planted, was partly dissolved by the poor barber's calamity; yet, the next morning he collected as many of the brethren together as could be suddenly assembled, and gave the word of exhortation to them in a field belonging to Mr Whitfield at the Bell.

Before he departed, he recommended to them the barber's distressed condition; and, by consulting also with Mrs Sarsenet and Mrs Whitfield, they put him in a method of recovering part of his old customers; and Mrs Whitfield promised to get him the occasional custom at the Bell, as the barber who used to attend was going to settle at Bath.

XXIX

SET OUT FOR THE NORTH

The two pilgrims being now within a day's journey, or a little more, of their native place, Tugwell was impatient to return home, partly to see his good wife Dorothy, and partly to recount his adventures, amongst his neighbours, and exhibit the fancied improvements he had made in his travels. Wildgoose, indeed, was principally bent on pursuing the great object which had taken possession of his imagination; yet the impression which Miss Townsend had made on his heart, a little distracted his thoughts, and made him deliberate whether he should go the nearest way into Stafford and Shropshire (which was through Worcester), or go round by Warwick, where he had some prospect of seeing Miss Townsend. As in the latter case, however, he could not well avoid passing through his own village, where he might meet with some obstruction to his project from Mrs Wildgoose, he determined upon the former. Accordingly, after taking leave of his friends at Gloucester, and writing a tender epistle to Miss Townsend, and exhorting Mrs Sarsenet to join a little of the prudence of the serpent with the innocence of the dove, Mr Wildgoose and his friend Tugwell set out for Worcester.

BOOK IX

I

GOOD EFFECTS
OF MR WILDGOOSE'S LABOURS

BOTH WILDGOOSE AND HIS FRIEND Jeremiah, having each of them been somewhat disappointed (the former in his expectation of meeting Miss Townsend at Gloucester, and the latter in his hopes of returning home to his Dame Dorothy), travelled on for some time with a kind of sullen taciturnity. Tugwell, at length, ventured first to break silence, by observing, that they might now have got home in one day's time, if so be *as how* his worship had been so disposed. Wildgoose replied, with some degree of peevishness, Why, Jerry, to be sure, you are not my hired servant; and I cannot oblige you to attend me against your will; but how can you think so meanly of me, as to imagine I will desert my post, and not execute the commission which Mr Whitfield has given me: especially as Heaven has inclined the hearts of such numbers to listen to my instructions, and I have so fair a prospect of *converting* so many poor souls from the error of their ways?

Convart them! says Tugwell. Odhang it! master, why, to be sure, your worship does preach main well, that is certain; but, as for *convarting*, methinks some of them are only *converted* from bad to worse. There is the barber now; he was poor enough, I believe, when we first went to his house; but he is now *converted* from a poor honest shaver, to a wicked robber, and from *scarifying* men's faces, to terrifying folks upon the highway. Wildgoose was not pleased with being reminded of this unlucky instance; but said, the barber's was a particular case; that he was persecuted by his neighbours, and driven by necessity to one wicked attempt; and that he made no doubt, the barber was still in a state of grace, though appearances were against him.

Then there is Madam Sarsenet, says Tugwell; to my thinking, she was a very good sort of woman before she was *converted*, and maintained her mother and her sister; and I saw them at dinner upon some good roast mutton and baked pudding; and now, since she has been *converted*, it seems to be but poor with them, or else, methinks, they would have had a bit of soft cheese or butter, with their bunch of radishes last night.

Wildgoose not thinking it worth while to make any answer to his friend's observation, silence again ensued for some time; and, in short, nothing material befel the two travellers before they reached Tewksbury, about twelve o'clock; where they halted for an hour or two, to refresh themselves in the heat of the day.

II

THE HOTEL AT TEWKSBURY

Mr Wildgoose, inquiring of my landlord where they stopped, what he could have to eat, was answered, Whatever you please, sir; but, continues mine host, you may dine with us, if you choose it. We have a fine leg of veal, an excellent gammon of bacon, and a couple of charming fowls roasted; and only two very civil gentlemen and a lady, that quarter in the house, dine with us. Though Wildgoose was not very hungry, yet the bill of fare, and my landlord's account of the company, inclined him to accept of his invitation.

When dinner came in, there appeared, beside my landlord and his wife, an old lady about fifty, one gentleman about the same age, and the other seemed to be about twenty-five.

The leg of veal, which my landlord had mentioned, was only the knuckle, cut pretty close; and the bacon, the most bony part of the fore-gammon; the veal was *red*; and the bacon *white*, the lean part I mean; for the fat, being thoroughly tinged with smoke, was of a different complexion.

As Wildgoose was not very fond of boiled veal, he would not rob the company of this part of their short commons, but reserved himself for the second course.

When the fowls appeared, they were full-grown, nicely roasted, and frothed up, and looked tempting enough; but, when they were to be

carved, my landlord laid hold on one leg and his wife of the other, and
with some difficulty dismembered them. As the rest of the company
were less complaisant than Wildgoose, the wings were soon disposed
of; so that he and my landlord took each of them a drum-stick, which
Wildgoose said, he always chose;—and my landlord said, it was the best
part of the fowl.

But now came the difficult part of the achievement. The muscles of the
leg were so hard, that no human jaw could possibly make any impression
upon them. The gentlemen, indeed, observed, that even the wings were
a little tough.—Yes, says my landlord, the flesh is *firm*; they were well fed;
Jemmy Cockspur is one of the best feeders in the country.

And now the secret was out. They had had a cock-fighting the day
before; and these fine plump fowls had died in the field of battle, after
having triumphed victoriously for five or six years successively. In short,
poor Wildgoose, after sucking the drumstick, and licking up his parsley
and butter, concluded his dinner with a good slice of Gloucestershire
cheese and a crust of bread.

Tugwell, however, who regarded more the quantity than the quality
of his food, fared better in the kitchen, where was a good pan-full of
cow-heel fried with onions; on which Jerry made a very comfortable
meal.

III

THE LIFE OF A STROLLER.
CRITICISMS ON SHAKESPEARE

As Wildgoose had leisure enough, during his repast, to make observations
upon the company, he was studying their several characters, in order to
suit his spiritual advice accordingly. He was at first a little puzzled to
guess at their several professions. There was a sort of shabby smartness
in their dress, that suited neither with the rank of a gentleman, nor
that of a tradesman. The young man had on a faded green cloth, which

discovered the marks of a gold lace, that had probably been ripped off, to answer some particular exigency. Wildgoose observed that his companion called him—your highness. The elderly man had a black crape about his neck, a ramillie wig, and a pair of half jack-boots, with the tops of some old thread stockings pinned on; which riding-dress seemed to be no otherwise necessary, than to supply the want of shoes and stockings. The old lady had a long black cardinal, and something like a cambric handkerchief pinned round her head.

The old man happened to assert some trifling matter upon his *honour:* to which the young man replied, in heroics,

> Honour's a sacred tie, the law of kings:
> It is not to be sported with.—
> Syphax! thou art a false old traitor.

This speech convinced Wildgoose (of what he had before suspected), that they were part of a company of strollers. The company were on their route from the West of England to Birmingham; and were to perform Cato that night in a barn, to defray their expenses upon the road.

The old man was to play Syphax; and was the very character he intended to act. He had a most villanous physiognomy, and seemed, by his conversation, to have been a street-robber. The old lady was to appear in the character of Marcia, though she had lost one eye; and instead of an even twofold *hedge* of teeth, as Homer expresses it, her broken snags were more like park-pales, or what school-boys in Latin verse call a dactyl, that is, a foot of three syllables, the first long, and the two last short; yet the old lady resembled Marcia in one respect;

> The virtuous Marcia tow'rs above her sex;

for she was near six feet high, and (I will answer for it) had lived a most *virtuous* life for many years.

Juba had a swelled face, yet was really a genteel young fellow, and had had a good education; but, as he confessed to Wildgoose, had been

ruined by his vanity, and a humour for spouting tragedy, which he had
learned at school; for he had spent near two thousands pounds, which
his father left him; and, though bred to a genteel profession, could never
settle to business.

Then, I was quite an idolater of Shakespeare, quoth the player; and
having seen Mr Garrick play Hamlet and Othello two or three times
(he acts with so much *ease* as well as propriety, that) I imagined it no
difficult matter to succeed in the same parts; which determined me to
go upon the stage.

Why, says Wildgoose, I have seen a few plays some years ago; and
must own, Mr Garrick is almost the only actor I have met with, who
keeps sight of nature in his action, and has brought her back upon
the stage, whence, by all account, indiscriminate rant and unmeaning
rhodomontade had banished all truth and propriety time out of mind.
But, sir, I profess myself an enemy to all theatrical entertainments; and
even to Shakespeare himself, in some respects.

Oh! sir, cries the young player, stretching out his hand, I must not
hear a word against our venerable patriarch, and great founder of the
English drama.

I will allow every objection that you can imagine against him. I
will forgive Ben Jonson his malignant wish, that instead of one line,
he had blotted out a thousand. I will not pull Voltaire by the nose
(though he deserves it), for calling his Tragedies *monstrous farces*. I will
grant the Frenchman, he has offended against the laws of Aristotle and
Boileau, and slighted the unities of action, time, and place; that, upon
some occasions, he abounds in mixed metaphors, and uses some harsh
expressions, which the age he lived in might *tolerate*, and which are
become venerable only by their antiquity. But read one act, or even
one scene, in *Hamlet*, *Othello*, or *Macbeth*, and all these trifling criticisms
disperse like mists before the orient sun.

Wildgoose began to explain himself, and to give the conversation
a spiritual turn. In order to which, he first observed to the players,
that their situation was very unfavourable to the practice of religion.
Religion, cries the Prince of Mauritania, I only wish we had any
morality, or even common honesty, amongst us. No, we are heroes,

kings, or sultanas, upon the stage; but beggars, sots, or prostitutes, in our private lodgings. There is the lovely Marcia, says he, whispering to Wildgoose, would drink you two quarts of ale now, if you would give it her; and, if she had six-pence in her pocket, Cato's daughter would get drunk with gin, before she came upon the stage. In short, continues the young player, I intend to take my leave of them very soon.

Old Syphax, hearing part of this declamation against the life of a stroller, said, there was one agreeable circumstance attending it, that they frequently fell into company with some gentleman of fortune, who would treat them with a bottle of wine, or a bowl of punch.—This the wily African said in consequence of the intelligence he had gained from Tugwell in the kitchen, that his master had four or five hundred pounds a-year. But Wildgoose not taking the hint, and my landlord perceiving there was no more liquor called for, began to grudge such company the use of his parlour. He, therefore, bade the waiter bring a bill; and Wildgoose soon after took his leave, and with his trusty 'squire set out for Worcester.

IV

STATE OF RELIGION AT WORCESTER

Mr Wildgoose, impatient to execute the commission which Mr Whitfield had given him, traversed with hasty strides the spacious streets of Tewksbury and, getting clear of the town, the two pilgrims now ascended a little hill; when Wildgoose looking round him, I wonder, says he, how many miles it is to Warwick.—Then without waiting for Jerry's reply, he trudged on again at a round rate.

Tugwell's inclinations still pointing homewards, he likewise made a soliloquy in his turn. Odzookers! one might almost see our steeple, now, from this hill, and the smoke of my cottage. I wonder what our Dorothy is doing at home: and our poor dog!

The travellers now proceeded without any interruption, and arrived at Worcester about eight o'clock in the evening.

Mr Wildgoose made immediate inquiry, whether there was any religious society in that city; and found that only a few of the lower sort of people met once a week at a private house, whose zeal was kept alive by now and then an occasional preacher that came amongst them; that a considerable part of the town had their attention taken up by their china-work, lately established there under the auspices of the ingenious and excellent Dr Wall; that the learned prebends were immersed in profound studies, or engaged in the care of their health; as their wives and daughters were at whist or quadrille. The two pilgrims, therefore, set out again early in the morning, and took the road towards Wednesbury, Dudley, and Walsal; which are the chief collieries and manufactories in that part of the country.

V

AN UNEXPECTED RENCOUNTER

Towards the middle of the day, our travellers came into the gravelly bottom of a deep valley, through which a silver stream ran winding along, shaded with alders, and invited them to repose a little in so cool a retreat. Wildgoose, according to custom, pulled out a little godly manual, and began to read; as Tugwell, by a kind of instinct, began to rummage his wallet for something to eat; whose example having stronger attractions for the former, than his amusement had for the latter, Tugwell soon brought over Wildgoose to his party; and they took a comfortable noonchine together.

Whilst they were thus employed, two more travellers came, the contrary road, to the same spot; and without much ceremony, sat down to partake of so agreeable a shade. One of them looked like some mechanical handicraft; but the other (though his long hair was somewhat in the style of Ralpho in Hudibras) had a gentleman-like appearance, both in his dress and his address.

Wildgoose making some overtures by a few general topics and introductory preludes, they soon entered into further conversation.

Two or three small birds coming to drink and bathe themselves, with great boldness and security, as the travellers were sitting in a calm repose; Wildgoose said, that he could never sufficiently admire the beauty, elegance, and harmless innocence of those little animals of the winged creation and that he had often thought the familiar, friendly, and almost conversible air, with which some birds and other animals approached mankind, till they were alarmed and frightened away by some violent motion or menacing altitude, seemed to give credit to the doctrine of transmigration, as if some of our own species were doing penance in those animals, and wanted to express their sufferings or complaints, or to renew their intimacy with some old friend, or former acquaintance. At least, continued Wildgoose, one is puzzled, without some supposition of this kind, to account for the *final* cause of their creation; many animals being frequently persecuted and tortured in such a manner, as to make their being rather a curse than a blessing.

The stranger replied, that, when we come to talk of final causes, or the ends proposed by Providence in any part of the creation, we soon get out of the depth of our shallow understandings; though I am convinced, says he, that God has formed all his creatures with a capacity of being happy, if they do not forfeit it by their own fault.

This discourse on pre-existence, brought on the subject of predestination, election, and reprobation; which his puritanical library, and his conversing with Mr Whitfield, had taught Wildgoose to maintain in its strictest sense.

The stranger opposed his opinions with great vehemence; and said, he would sooner renounce his Bible, than believe those doctrines, as Calvin of old, or Mr Whitfield had of late, taught them. Sir, says Wildgoose, I suppose then you are a follower of John Wesley's. No, replies the stranger; I am John Wesley himself.

Wildgoose started up with the utmost surprise, and accosted him with the most profound reverence and respect; and by way of apology, said, that although he had lately become personally acquainted with Mr Whitfield, and confessed himself a convert to most of his opinions, yet he had so great a regard for all those who embarked in the same general cause, that he was extremely happy in this opportunity of conversing with a man whose character he had so long admired. He then acquainted Mr Wesley who he himself was; when he found Mr Wesley was no stranger to his character or conversion. Mr Wesley returned the compliment with a pious wish, that he might be able to give him any spiritual assistance. After which, Wildgoose let him know his present situation, and his intentions of visiting the poor colliers at Wednesbury, Walsal, and so forth. But Mr Wesley began immediately to dissuade him from pursuing his scheme at present; for that he himself was, at this instant, escaped from a most violent persecution; that a large and enraged mob, stirred up by some interested people, were now in arms, and in search of every preacher of their denomination; and that it would be tempting Providence to run into the very jaws of that many-headed monster, a drunken multitude, who knew not what they did.

An enthusiast, like a man of courage, is so far from being dismayed by an appearance of danger, that he generally becomes more resolute. Wildgoose, therefore, was still more inclined to try the strength of his eloquence, and to proceed to Wednesbury, till Mr Wesley assured him it would be injuring the cause, to attempt to convince them, whilst their passions and prejudices were so strongly engaged on the other side.—Wildgoose, therefore, stood corrected: and a man now coming up with Mr Wesley's horses, which he had been obliged to leave behind, Wildgoose took his leave; and, instead of pursuing the intended road, turned off towards Birmingham, in order to make the best of his way to the Lead-mines in the Peak of Derbyshire.

VI

A JUST CHARACTER OF LADY L——N, FROM A DISCARDED SERVANT

Our two pilgrims being a little fatigued with travelling in so hot a day, they halted in the afternoon at a public-house in the neighbourhood of Hagley. Wildgoose seeing a number of people drinking under a tree at the door, observed to my landlord, that *his* seemed to be a well-accustomed house.—Yes, says mine host, with an air of piety (taking Wildgoose for a clergyman), blessed be God! I have my share of custom at this time of the year, please God to send fine weather, as every body comes to see Hagley Park here.—Wildgoose replied, that his house seemed to stand well for the refreshment of travellers; but that he did not understand how he could bless God for some of his idle customers, who spent the money, which ought to support their families, in getting drunk, and making brutes of themselves.—Mine host replied, that, to be sure, poor men that worked hard, and had no beer at home, would now and then have a little good drink; but then, says he, I never suffer them to have more at my house, than they have money to pay for.

Wildgoose then said, he supposed sir George L——n's house was worth seeing, as so many people came thither for that purpose.—Yes, says a young man in a livery frock, Hagley is a noble seat, and *abundance of quality resort* thither at this time of the year.—Ah! says my landlord, and Sir George has something at Hagley better worth seeing than his fine seat. He has for his wife the finest woman, and the best Christian, in England. But, says he, my son here knows all about it; he was under-butler at Sir George's; and, sir, as you seem to be a gentleman, please to step into this parlour, and I will tell you more (coming, sir; coming). My landlord then showed Wildgoose into a little nook, divided from the kitchen by a partition of deal boards, which prevented you from being seen, but not from being overheard by any one that was disposed to listen. Now, says my landlord, as I was telling you, sir, my son was under-butler at Hagley. But, sir, betwixt you and I, the house-keeper is the d—ndest b-tch in England.—Well, well, says Wildgoose, I do not want to be let into family secrets. But my lady, you say, is a very good woman. That she is, says mine host; and, if she had had her way, my son would never have lost his place. Though my landlord was very full of this subject, he and his son did great justice to Lady L——n's character that there was not a poor person, a sick person, or a wicked person, within five miles of the place, but she found them out, and gave them money, physic, or good advice; and, what is more, says he, there is not an *idle* person, but she contrives to employ them, and keep them out of harm's way; and they mind what my lady says more than all the parson preaches, or the doctor can say to them when they are sick. Then, continues he, my son says, my lady has wit at will, and will *hold discourse* with, any lord or bishop that comes to Sir George's table; and knows every thing that happened in former days,★ or in foreign parts,★ as well as the best of them.

Mr Wildgoose said, he did not in the least doubt the justness of my landlord's panegyric; for that he had known Lady L——n from a child (she being his country-woman); though he had not seen her for some years. He was then going to give mine host some spiritual instructions, when Tugwell came to the door, to remind his master that it was very dusty travelling, and that he seemed to have forgotten their intention of calling at a public-house. My landlord then asked what they would please to drink? But there being no great variety of liquors or provisions at this hotel, they refreshed themselves with some fresh ale, and some new cheese; and then proceeded in their journey towards Birmingham.

VII

A SKETCH OF THE LEASOWES, AND OF THE CHARACTER OF THE WORTHY POSSESSOR OF THAT PLACE

The sun was now far upon the decline towards the west, when the two pilgrims had passed a little market-town on the Birmingham road, called Hales-Owen. As they walked on they saw an object amidst the woods, on the edge of the hill, which, upon inquiry, they were told was called Shenstone's Folly. This is a name, which, with some sort of propriety, the common people give to any work of taste, the utility of which exceeds the level of their comprehension.

★ The vulgar definition of history and geography.

As they ascended the hill, through a shady lane, they observed a gentleman, in his own hair, giving directions to some labourers who were working beyond the usual hour, in order to finish a receptacle for a cataract of water, a glimpse of which appeared through the trees on the side of the road. As Wildgoose and his friend, partly out of curiosity, and partly to take breath, made a little pause, the gentleman turned his face towards them, when Wildgoose immediately discovered him to be no other than his old acquaintance, the now celebrated Mr Shenstone, whose place began to be frequented by people of distinction from all parts of England, on account of its natural beauties, which, by the mere force of genius and good taste, Mr Shenstone had improved and exhibited to so much advantage: and this had discovered to the world his own fine poetical talents and polite learning, which, from his modesty, would otherwise probably have been buried in solitude and obscurity.

Mr Shenstone soon recollected his old academical friend and associate; and, with that warmth of benevolence for which he is distinguished amongst those that know him, insisted upon his staying that night at least with him at the Leasowes; which invitation Mr Wildgoose was sufficiently inclined to accept of, though he had not been prompted to it by his fellow-traveller, who never was so cynical as to slight the least overture towards a hospitable reception.

As they passed towards the house, Mr Shenstone pointed out to his friend many of the beauties of his place. He showed him his cascades, which are so deservedly admired, and the reservoirs that supplied them; the prospects of the country from various points of view; his grove, dedicated to Virgil; his urns, statues, and his admirable inscriptions. He mentioned several people of the first quality, and, what Mr Shenstone valued more, of the first taste, who had done him the honour to visit his place: and particularly he informed him, that he expected Lord D—tm—h, and some other company the very next day, on which account he had been inspecting his reservoirs, got his walks cleaned out, and made the men work so late, in order to finish the cataract, where his friend had first seen him.

As Wildgoose knew the elegance of Mr Shenstone's taste, he could not but add his suffrage to those of the rest of the world, in admiring his place, and observed, that doubtless the pleasures we receive from gardens, woods, and lawns, and other rural embellishments, were the most innocent of any *amusements*; but then we should consider them as *amusements* only, and not let them engross too much of our attention; that we ought to spiritualize our ideas as much as possible; and that it was worth while to inquire, how far too violent a fondness for these merely inanimate beauties might interfere with our love of God, and attach us too strongly to the things of this world.

This gave Mr Shenstone an opportunity, in his turn, of combating his friend's enthusiastic notions; who, he found by his own account, had deserted the station in which his own choice and his mother's approbation had fixed him, to sally forth and preach the Gospel, without any other call to that office than what a warm imagination had suggested, and which a romantic view of converting sinners *at large* had prompted him to undertake.

The two friends, however, supped together very amicably; and, after drinking a cool tankard, and spending a pretty late evening in talking over the incidents of their youth, which they had spent together in the University, Mr Shenstone showed his friend into an elegant bed-chamber, fitted up in a Gothic taste; to which the bed itself, the rest of the furniture, and the painted glass in the window, all corresponded. Contiguous to this he lodged Tugwell, his trusty 'squire and fellow-traveller, and wished them a good night.

VIII

A PRACTICAL LECTURE AGAINST THE VANITIES OF THIS WORLD

As soon as Mr Shenstone rose in the morning (which was not always at a very early hour), he went up to his friend's apartment, to summon him to breakfast, when, to his surprise, he found both him and his companion departed, without taking leave of him? and upon Wildgoose's table was left the following letter:

My good friend,

I am called hence by the Spirit: in the visions of the night it was revealed unto me. I must own, that, like the good Publius, you have received and lodged us courteously, and my bowels yearn for your salvation. But, my dear friend, I am afraid you have set up idols in your heart. You seem to pay a greater regard to Pan and Sylvanus, than to Paul or Silas. You have forsaken the fountains of the living Lord, and hewn you out cisterns, broken cisterns, that will hold no water: but my conscience beareth testimony against this idolatry. Bel boweth down, Nebo stoopeth. I have delivered my own soul, and will pray for your conversion. I am

Your brother in the Lord,

GEOFFRY WILDGOOSE.

This extraordinary letter, and his friend's abrupt departure, greatly alarmed Mr Shenstone: but, going out to view his principle cascade, he soon discovered the mystery; that his friend, imagining he was too much affected with the applauses which were bestowed on his good taste in laying out his place, had forced open his sluices, and emptied his reservoirs; so that, in a literal sense, his *cisterns could hold no water*, nor his cascades make any great figure that day: and what was more distressful, he had thrown down a leaden statue of the Piping Fawn from its pedestal, which was a damage that could not easily be repaired before the arrival of his illustrious guests.

Mr Shenstone was a little provoked at the first discovery of this incident; but, upon reflection, could not forbear laughing at his old friend's frantic proceedings; and thought the singularity of the adventure would afford his guests as much entertainment, as a greater flash from his cascades, or as viewing his place in more exact order.

IX

A DISCOURSE ON IDOLATRY

When the travellers were got into the Birmingham road again, Tugwell, who did not rightly comprehend nor approve of his master's conduct on this occasion, nor understand what he meant by saying, that Mr Shenstone quite idolized or worshipped those lifeless objects; Jerry, I say, began now to express his apprehensions of the consequences of what they had done. Odzooks! says he, it is well if the gentleman does not get a warrant for us, and *trouble* us, for robbing his fish-ponds (as he may think we have), or for damaging his images.—He observed, moreover, that as he seemed to be a sensible gentleman, he could not think he would be so foolish as to *worship* images, as the *Papishes* do. Why, continues Jerry, there is our 'squire has got a naked *thing-em-bob* stands up in the middle of the grove (it is either the Virgin Mary, or fair Rosamond, or Dinah,★ that was ravished by the Jacobites), and yet I never heard that the 'squire, or any of the family, ever said their prayers to it, or worshipped it.

Why, Jerry, says Wildgoose, a person may be guilty of idolatry by setting his affections too much upon any thing, upon riches or pleasures, a fine house or a fine child, and in those cases it is an act of friendship in any one to take some method (as I have done with Mr Shenstone) to wean them from those objects: and Providence, out of mere kindness, often deprives us of those things which we have so entirely fixed our hearts upon.

Why, to be sure, says Tugwell, God Almighty may do what he pleases for that matter; but then, if one *man* was at liberty to take away from another whatever he had *set his heart* upon, they might take away one's wife, or one's cow, or one's dog, or one's cat; and then there would be no living at peace in the world. Now there is my dog Snap; I *loves* him almost as well as I do my wife, and if the best man in Gloucestershire were to steal my dog, I would *take law on him*, if there was any law to be had in the kingdom.

★ It was most probably Diana, that Jerry meant by this confused account.

Wildgoose did not think it material to continue the dispute; but it occurred to him in the course of this conversation, how much his affections were attached to Miss Townsend. This, however, he considered as a spiritual attachment, he intending only the good of Miss Townsend's soul by a union, which, from the little encouragement she seemed to have given him, he had some slight hopes of effecting. This project engaged his thoughts in an agreeable reverie, which prevented any further conversation till they arrived, about eight o'clock in the morning, at Birmingham.

X

SLIGHT PERSECUTIONS

As Mr Wildgoose intended, if nothing very extraordinary prevented it, to visit the colliers at Wednesbury on his return; he made no longer stay in Birmingham than whilst he himself took some slight refreshment, and Tugwell a hearty breakfast, at the first inn they came to, and then proceeded towards Litchfield, in their way to the Peak of Derbyshire.

As they walked through Birmingham-streets, they heard two or three fellows in a workshop, up two pair of stairs, quarrelling, swearing, and cursing, in a most tremendous manner. Wildgoose, thinking it incumbent upon him to reprove their profaneness, made a halt, and beckoning with his hand, called out to the vociferous garreteers, to hold their blasphemous tongues. The litigants observing a man of a tolerable appearance addressing himself to them, were silent for a moment; but when they heard Wildgoose, with an air of authority, charging them, in the name of the King of kings, not to take the name of God in vain, with a mixture of mirth, indignation, and contempt, they redoubled their oaths and imprecations upon the preacher; and one of them emptied the stale contents of an unscoured piss-pot full upon the heads of him and his companion. As Mr Wildgoose was got almost into the middle of the street, in order to direct his voice to them more commodiously, he received only a slight sprinkling of their intended kindness; but as Tugwell stood just under the window, with his mouth open, waiting the event of his master's exhortation, he received a more liberal portion, part of which came full into his mouth, and penetrated pretty deeply into the cavity of his throat.

Wildgoose, observing the inefficacy of his rebuke, cried out in the apostolical style, Well, my brethren, I have delivered my own soul, look you to it; your *blood* be upon your own heads.

Tugwell, being less patient (at this ill return of their intended favour), spitting and rubbing his face, and shaking his clothes, exclaimed with some indignation against his master for this unseasonable interposition; Pock-i-cat take it! for me; the *blood* and guts, and the devil and all, I think, is upon our heads; and it was no otherwise likely: what the *dickins* had we to do with folks that were quarrelling up in a garret, and never troubled their heads about us?

Well, quoth Wildgoose, as the Roman emperor said, when he laid a tax upon urine, the smell of money is sweet, whencesoever it comes, so I can say, persecution is sweet and wholesome in any shape whatsoever.— Yes, says Tugwell, even in the shape of a piss-pot, I suppose. The smell of money may be sweet; but I am sure neither the smell nor the taste of what was thrown upon our heads was either sweet or wholesome; at least I had rather your worship should have it than I, if you think it so very sweet and so wholesome.

The hapless pilgrims now passed on through Birmingham, Wildgoose leading the way, and Tugwell at some little distance behind him. Wildgoose, reflecting upon what had just happened, said he began to wonder what they had done that the world was so civil to them.

Odsbobs! cries Jerry, looking up to the window of a little shop, there is a fine plumb-pudding!

The friendship of the world is enmity with God, continues Wildgoose.

It is smoking hot, just out of the oven, says Tugwell.

My zeal began to cool, and I grew quite remiss in my duty, proceeds the master.

I have a great mind to have a pennyworth of it, says the man.

But, come, let us make the best of our way, to rescue the poor miners from the power of Satan, says Wildgoose.

I must and will go back, and have a slice of that pudding, says Tugwell.

Thus the master and man proceeded in a kind of soliloquy, entirely inattentive to each other: but, when Wildgoose discovered his fellow-traveller's gluttonous intention, and saw him return with a good slice of pudding in his hand. Ah! Jerry, Jerry, cries he, swallow thy spittle, and subdue thy appetite. I thought thou hadst just satisfied the demands of nature with a hearty breakfast; and now thou art at it again: if thou hadst but a grain of true faith, thy mind would not be thus continually hankering after these carnal indulgences.

Odsbodikins! cries Tugwell, as soon as he could empty his mouth, cannot a man have true faith that loves plumb-pudding? Why, master, I was very hungry to-day; and then I wanted to get the taste of the *persecution* out of my mouth, which, your worship says, was so sweet and wholesome. Wildgoose smiled to himself, but made no reply, and trudged on.

XI

A GLIMPSE OF MISS TOWNSEND

Being now got clear of the town, the two travellers came to a direction-post, where the road divided. On one of the hands was written, the road to Litchfield; on the other, to Warwick.—As Wildgoose had as strong a hankering after the place of Miss Townsend's residence, as Tugwell had after his own fire-side, they kept their eyes for some time fixed on the hand which pointed towards the object of their respective inclinations; and, as a string of Coventry pack-horses had raised a cloud of dust, they did not perceive a chariot and pair, bowling along on a brisk trot, till it had almost passed by them.

There seemed to be in it an elderly gentleman and his wife; and a young lady sat side-ways on the stool, with a very white arm resting upon the window of the chariot. The young lady, with a female curiosity, thrusting herself out to have a view of the travellers, dropped a cambric handkerchief (probably without perceiving it), which Wildgoose immediately picked up; and was going to return it, when casting his eyes upon the mark, he instantly knew it to be Miss Townsend's cipher. This occasioned such a surprise, as fixed him motionless for a moment, and would have prevented him from overtaking the chariot, if, upon recollection, he had thought it either prudent or advisable to endeavour it. Though Wildgoose had hardly a glance of Miss Townsend's face, yet, as imagination magnifies every object beyond its real dimensions, this incident, and the initial letters of Julia Townsend, contributed more perhaps to keep alive Mr Wildgoose's passion, than the most tender epistle, or a complete view of her might have done.

Wildgoose was deliberating with himself, whether he should not return to Birmingham, and find out Miss Townsend, especially when he had so good a pretence as that of returning her handkerchief, when Tugwell came up to him, with his jaws yet in motion from masticating his baked pudding, and cries out, Well, master, as God sends good luck, let us be thankful, and spend it at the next public-house. This white handkerchief will buy us a quart of best drink, I will warrant you, though, mayhap, it is only cut out of the tail of an old smock.

Wildgoose was so provoked at Jerry's gross ideas, that he could hardly forbear striking him.—Best drink! cries Wildgoose, pressing the handkerchief, which breathed the fragrance of lavender and *eau-de-luce*, with rapture to his breast, I would not part with it for the richest wines of Canary or Cyprus, nor for all the wealth of the Indies.

Odsbobs! master, says Tugwell, you seem to be as fond of the young woman's handkerchief, as I am of plum-pudding. One would think it was a love-toy, and that it was given you by your sweet-heart and, for that matter, it seemed to be a good plump young woman that dropped it out of the coach, and drest like a queen. I suppose, she was daughter to some 'squire, or some topping button-maker here in Birmingham, at least.

Ah! Jerry, replies Wildgoose, I value this handkerchief, because it belongs to a very good girl. That young lady in the chariot was no other than the Miss Townsend, whom we saw at Mrs Sarsenet's at Gloucester.

What! the young woman that came after us to Bristol, says Jerry, and was taken with *compulsion* fits at the Tabernacle? I thought I had seen her face before, continues he; but then she is got fatter than she was. I suppose she has her belly-full now; which, belike, she had not at poor Madam Sarsenet's, at Gloucester.

Wildgoose did not like to have the object of his affection treated with so much familiarity; and was also afraid of discovering to Jerry the situation of his heart. Neither was he yet determined, whether he should return to Birmingham or not, and endeavour to get an interview with Miss Townsend. But, recollecting that the races at Warwick would be within a fortnight, which being the nearest meeting to his own native place, and fancying he had a particular call to bear his testimony against the lawfulness of those diversions, he was determined in himself (as soon as he had opened his commission in the Peak) to attend them. He, therefore, dropped the subject at present, and trudged on at a good rate towards Litchfield.

XII

MEET WITH A SEASONABLE INVITATION

The two pilgrims having pursued their journey above three hours, and the turnpike road being very hot and dusty, Tugwell proposed, where they could commodiously do it, to walk through the fields within the hedge. This insensibly led them too far from the great road, and brought them where two foot-paths led different ways; and they were puzzled which to pursue. Tugwell, therefore, went to make inquiries of a fellow that was at plough, in the adjacent field. At the end of the furrow, they saw an odd figure of a man, standing upright, with his eyes shut, and his mouth open, his neck stretched out, and his hands hanging straight down, in the attitude of the Pierro in the pantomime. Though the sun was burning hot, he had a green surtout coat on, with the cape over his head, and buttoned round the neck.

Wildgoose, as his ideas ran constantly upon religious objects, thought immediately it was some poor soul under the agonies of the new-birth, and waiting for the influx of the Spirit. He accosts him, therefore, in his own way, God comfort your soul my good friend, says Wildgoose.—The gentleman, starting from his Swiss meditation or reverie, in which he had been unexpectedly surprised, and throwing himself into a tolerably genteel attitude; sir, says he, I do not know you; but am obliged to you for your good wishes, though my body has more need of comfort than my soul, at present.—What is the matter then, says Wildgoose, if I may make so free? What is your complaint, sir?—Ah! Says the gentleman, if I could tell you that, I should tell you more than all the physicians in England have been able to tell me.—Where does your chief disorder lie, then? says Wildgoose.—Why, sir, I have a complication of disorders, replies the gentleman. I have the gout, the rheumatism, the scurvy, a dropsy, and an asthma, and what not; I have a *cachexy*, or bad habit of body, which has brought on a nervous *atrophy*; so that nothing I eat or drink will *nourish* me: and what plagues me more than all these is, a disorder which, perhaps, you never heard of.—Pray what is that? says Wildgoose.—Why, a sort of convulsion, or hiccup in the ear. In short, sir, I believe mine is a total decay of nature; and I do not expect to live a month to an end.

Ha! says Wildgoose, that is very surprising. Why, sir, you look extremely well in the face.—Ah, sir, says the stranger, shaking his head, that is the very thing that alarms me. I eat, drink, and sleep well: and so did a friend of mine look; and ate, drank, and slept well, to the very last, and yet died suddenly this last winter.

I have, as you see, sir, rather a ruddy complexion: but then, if you observe, there is an odd sort of bluish cast mixed with it, which is a sure sign of an apoplectic habit.

Come, sir, says Wildgoose; I fancy you are a little hippish, and I hope you fright yourself without any reason. But, pray, sir, what crop are you ploughing for at this time of the year?—Why, says the gentleman, I have had no other crop, than what you see, from this field these five years, and yet these three acres pay me better than any land I have.—In what respect? replies Wildgoose.—In saving my doctor's fees, and apothecary's bills, answered the gentleman. You know, I suppose, continues he, that nothing is so wholesome as the smell of new-ploughed earth. I keep this little field, therefore, in my hands for no other purpose; and make my servant, every day before dinner, turn up two or three furrows, and follow the plough, as I have been now doing; which gives me an appetite to my dinner, and I am convinced, has kept me alive these five years.

Wildgoose thought this gentleman somewhat whimsical; but having listened with a more serious attention to the detail of his maladies than many people would have done, the gentleman was prepossessed in his favour; and when Tugwell came up with his intelligence, that it was still three miles to Litchfield, the gentleman said, as Wildgoose, he supposed, had not dined, he should be very welcome to take pot-luck with him; that his house was but at the end of that avenue of firs; and he was just going to dinner. Why, yes, says Tugwell, before his master could speak, as Providence has directed us to so good a house, you had best accept of the gentleman's good-will.—As Wildgoose always flattered himself with the hopes of doing good, or, what he esteemed the same thing, of making converts to his opinions, he was easily prevailed upon to accompany the gentleman to his house, to which he was so hospitably invited.

XIII

SOME ACCOUNT OF THIS STRANGER

As they went along, Mr Slicer (which was the gentleman's name) made some efforts towards gratifying his own curiosity, and discovering Wildgoose's profession, and what expedition he was bent upon. This Wildgoose evaded, by inquiring of Mr Slicer what first brought him into this low-spirited way, or, as he called it, this indifferent state of health? to which Mr Slicer answered, that he had formerly been in considerable practice as a solicitor in London, where he underwent great fatigue, yet never knew what it was to be sick; but a relation leaving him an estate in that country, and having no family, he retired from business, in hopes of finding in retirement a more complete felicity than what he enjoyed in the hurry of business, and in the noise and smoke of the town. However, I was soon convinced, continued Mr Slicer, that happiness is not the product of any particular place or way of life; much less is it to be found in a state of absolute inactivity; that some employment was necessary, to divert the mind from preying upon itself; and whereas I enjoyed good health, ate with an appetite, and slept soundly when fatigued with business; I now found every thing reversed; my sleep went from me, my appetite was palled, even venison lost its relish, and though, by constant attention, and the use of several excellent medicines, I have a little recovered my strength and spirits, yet I am convinced it is all forced and unnatural; for, though I am not sensible of any particular complaint, yet, as I said before, I am daily apprehensive of a sudden dissolution.

Wildgoose was going to observe, that he had not yet found the true road to happiness; that there was no real cordial for the miseries of life, but an assurance that our sins are pardoned, and the witness of the Spirit in our souls, that we are the children of adoption; but they were now arrived at the door of the gentleman's house, which prevented any further conversation for the present.

XIV

THE LIFE OF A DYING MAN

The moment they had entered the hall, Mr Slicer's old housekeeper, Mrs Quick, met him with consternation in her looks. Good lack-a-day, sir, says she, we have had a most terrible accident. You would not let the chimney be swept; I told you how it would be.—What! is the chimney

on fire, then, says Mr Slicer.—Oh, no! says she; but a whole heap of
soot has fallen down into the fish-kettle, and entirely spoiled the carps.
I very providentially caught up the loin of veal upon the spit, or else
that would have been covered with dust and ashes.—Well, well, says
Mr Slicer, accidents will happen; it is well it is no worse; we must dine
without the carp then.—But, lack-a-day, sir, continues Mrs Quick, why
did you stay so long? the fowls are boiled to a rag; and the veal is roasted
to powder; and there is not a drop of gravy left; and the parson and Mr
Selkirk have been here waiting for their dinner this half hour.—Well,
well, says Slicer, if that be all, there is no great harm done.—But—

Let me see; I took my Bostock's Cordial this morning. Come, bring
my Stomachic Tincture: I will just take a few drops of that, to strengthen
my stomach; and a little Balsam of Life, and one or two of my *Pilulæ
Salutariæ*; and then you may send up dinner as soon as you will.

But, says Mrs Quick, if I had known you would have brought any
strangers, I would have made a custard pudding. However, I can just beat
up two or three eggs, and a spoonful of cream, and a little orange flower
water, and make a little pudding, in the catching up of a saucepan.

Mr Slicer said she might do as she would. Then bidding her show
Tugwell into the kitchen, he took Mr Wildgoose into a handsome
parlour, where they found Mr Slicer's niece, who was come on a visit,
with her little boy and girl; Mr Selkirk, abovementioned, who was a
schoolmaster in the village; and a little sleek divine, whose spruce wig,
short cassock, japanned shoes, and silver buckles, (worn smooth with
the daily strokes of the brush,) gave him rather the appearance of an
archdeacon, than what he was, the parson of the parish.

After an apology for making his company wait, Mr Slicer introduced
Wildgoose to them, and then took his Stomachic Tincture, his Balsam of
Life, and his *Pilulæ Salutariæ*, one after another; strongly recommending
a dose of the Stomachic Tincture to Mr Wildgoose, as an excellent
medicine to fortify the stomach, and create an appetite. Wildgoose
waved the offer, and said, he thanked God he had a very good appetite,
without any assistance of that kind.

Slicer then bade the servant bring him Mrs Stephens's Medicine for
the Stone and Gravel, which he never omitted, he said, since it was

first discovered,—What! are you afflicted with the stone and gravel, then? says Mr Selkirk.—*Afflicted*! says Slicer; no, sir, God forbid! nor ever was *afflicted* with it; but I suppose I should have been *afflicted* with it before this time, if I had not taken this admirable medicine: and, as every one is subject more or less, to gravel and sabulous concretions, it is madness to neglect so easy a precaution as this noble lithonthriptic, which Providence has permitted to be discovered, and for which the parliament has granted so handsome a reward.

The servant having brought the preparation, with a large liaison of veal broth, Slicer swallowed the nauseous prescription with great alacrity; though the virtues, or even the safety of that medicine have justly been questioned, notwithstanding the decision of our wise legislators in its favour.

Wildgoose could not but express his astonishment at Mr Slicer's credulity in this respect; and said, he was afraid he might injure his health, by mixing together too many of those *excellent* medicines, with which the world now abounded.

Sir, says Slicer, I despise the common quack medicines as much as you can do, and never take any but what perform their operations in a rational manner, and whose effects I can in some measure account for (for I know something of physic myself, by experience at least;) such I mean, as either *brace* up the *relaxed fibres* of the stomach, and assist the concoction, or such as *cut*, *divide*, and *attenuate* the *tough* and viscid *humours*, and prepare them to be thrown off by insensible *perspiration*, or such as strengthen the *nerves*, *comfort* the *brain*, and revive the spirits; or, as an ingenious writer expresses it, 'such as, *ambitious* of *immortal fame*, fly *immediately* to the *part* affected, and enter into contest with the *peccant* humours, and either expel or subdue them.'*

Wildgoose and the rest of the company could with difficulty suppress their mirth, to hear poor Slicer thus retail the studied panegyrics of interested empirics in favour of their own nostrums. But the little fat rector of the parish, who was a good-natured and polite man, turned the conversation to some general topics; and dinner soon made its appearance.

---

* All expressions taken from advertisements.

XV

A REMEDY FOR WANT OF APPETITE

When dinner came in, Wildgoose found that the old housekeeper's apology was only words of course, for there were three fine full-grown pullets, an excellent Yorkshire ham, a loin of veal, and the custard-pudding, which Mrs Quick had tossed up, adorned with currant-jelly, a gooseberry tart, with other ornamental expletives of the same kind.

Wildgoose observed, that although Mr Slicer was careful enough about the *quality* of his food, yet he was less scrupulous about the *quantity* of what he ate. He would not touch a morsel of skin or fat, nor eat any butter with his veal or his boiled fowl, because it *eluded* the *concoctive powers*, as he said; but he made shift to pick the very bones of a pretty large pullet, with two good large *vertebræ*, and half the kidney of the loin of veal; not to mention a good quantity of supplemental pudding, gooseberry-tart, and apple-custard; so that it appeared probable, Mr Slicer palled his appetite by over-loading his stomach; that he destroyed his health by too great a quantity of *wholesome* food, and made work for the doctor, by an unnecessary use of quack medicines; by infallible nostrums, restoratives, cordials, balsams of life, tinctures, elixirs, and the like; for he could never read an advertisement of that kind, but he longed to make the experiment; taking it for granted that every medicine had all the virtues it pretended to, and really performed all that its vender engaged for in his feeling recommendation of it to the public.

XVI

HISTORY OF A LONG-LIVER, AND OTHER CHIT-CHAT

After dinner Mr Slicer put round the bottle of port, but had the servant bring *him* his *Scorzonera*-water. Mr Selkirk asked him, what the virtues of that Scorzonera-water were, which he observed he drank every day after dinner.—I do not know what the particular virtues are, says Slicer; I only know, that it has contributed to prolong life to above a hundred years.

Did you never meet with the history of Francis Hongo, surnamed Hyppazoli, who died at an hundred and fourteen (the beginning of this century) at Smyrna, where he was consul for the Venetians?

Hongo never was sick; his sight, hearing, and intellectual faculties continued entire to the last. He would walk seven or eight miles every day. At a hundred his white hairs are said to have turned black again; and, what is equally surprising, having lost all his teeth, at a hundred and ten he cut two large ones in his upper jaw.

This gentleman drank no other liquor than a water distilled from scorzonera, or viper-grass; no wine, strong liquors, coffee, or tea; nor used tobacco. Towards the last he lived chiefly upon broths and ripe fruits, which he always ate with bread.

He was a man of great merit, wit, and honour; his only failing was too great an attachment to the fair sex. He had, by his wife and two or three concubines, nine and forty children.

As soon as Mr Slicer had finished his little history, all on a sudden he bent down his body, and leaned his elbows upon his knees, distorting his face into a variety of wrinkles. Bless me, uncle, says the lady, what is the matter? I am afraid you are ill.—Oh! nothing at all, says Slicer, smiling; only a little touch of the cholic, which my pills have given me. I love to have the cholic sometimes; it is the best symptom in the world; it is a sign the peccant humours, instead of entering the mass of blood, are spending their force on the *primæ viæ* or intestines, where they will soon find themselves a passage; and then the pleasure of being at ease again is greater than the pain one suffers from the complaint.

Slicer now fell into a musing posture for near a minute, with his eyes fixed upon the lady. Niece, says he, your husband's father lived to above ninety, merely by walking; and I *will walk*. He had no sooner formed his resolution, than forgetting for a moment that there was any company in the room, he started up, and put it in execution. After a turn round the garden, recollecting that some of the company were strangers, he returned to them again, with an apology, that he found, by experience, his dinner never began to digest till he had taken a little turn or two in the garden.

The little divine told him, with a smile, it was well he was not born at Sparta.—At Sparta! Why so? says Slicer,—Why the Spartans, you know, were a military establishment, and spent most of their time in athletic exercises; they thought it an idle thing, therefore, to *walk* merely for walking's sake; and, being informed that the inhabitants of a certain city under their jurisdiction, used to take *evening walks* merely for recreation, instead of making a decree, with a long preamble like a modern act of parliament, the magistrates sent them this laconic message, *Μὴ ὦεριπατεῖτε, Do not walk!*★ which immediately put a stop to that unnecessary consumption of time, as they esteemed it.

Well, says Slicer, I should be sorry, on account of my brethren of the quill, to have that *laconic* style introduced into our law proceedings. But you put me in mind of another instance of Spartan severity, not foreign to our purpose, on the subject of health.

Lysander going upon public business into Ionia, amongst other presents sent him upon his landing, there was some ox-beef and a large cheese-cake. He surveyed the latter with some curiosity; and, in the modern phrase, inquired, what the devil it was? Those that brought it told him it was a composition of honey, cheese, and other ingredients.

Oh, very well, says he, give that to my servants; for I am sure it is not fit for a gentleman to eat. He then ordered the beef to be dressed in the Spartan way and on that made an excellent meal.†

Why, to be sure the only way to preserve health, is to eat plain food, says the Scotchman; and the only way to destroy it, is to cram in such mixtures as you do in England, since French cooks have been in vogue.

★ Ælian. Var. Hist.
† *Ibid.*

XVII

RULES FOR HEALTH

The little rector observed, they had had a long dissertation upon the subject; and, doubtless a good state of health was an inestimable blessing, as it was the foundation of all other enjoyments. But, continues he, too great a solicitude on that account is not only unworthy a man of sense and a good Christian, but is really destructive of what we are so anxious to preserve. I know, with regard to myself, says he, that, having gone through a course of anatomy in the university, and observed how fearfully and wonderfully we are made, and having dabbled a little in books of physic, I brought myself, by my whims and apprehensions, and by tampering with my own constitution, into a very bad state of health. I have read a treatise upon sleep, that has kept me awake all night; and I studied Dr Cheyne upon *Health* and *Long Life*, till I brought myself to the brink of *death*.

Why, says Wildgoose, I have heard of a young man at Oxford, who going through a course of anatomy, and hearing the doctor expatiate upon the beautiful contrivance of nature in guarding the *ductus thoracicus*, or the tube that conveys the whole chyle of the body into the arteries, by the ribs on one side, and the back-bone on the other, and being told that the least touch almost on that part would be immediate death, the young fellow was met the next day, leaning forwards, with one hand held up to guard his breast, or thorax, and the other stretched out, and desiring every one he saw to stand off; for, says he, if you do but touch my *ductus thoracicus* I am a dead man.

Yes, says Slicer, and I have heard an addition to that story, which I suppose you do not care to mention.—Sir John Shadwell, physician to George the First, was telling this very story at court to Lady D——, who laughed heartily at it; and meeting the doctor the next day, she put herself in the same attitude, and desired him to stand off; for, says she, if you do but touch my—*what do you call it*?—I am a dead woman.

Well, says the little rector, it is certainly better to be really ill sometimes, than to be so hippish, and perpetually anxious about one's

health. A friend of mine, a jolly fellow, finding me in my room with
Cheyne's book upon Health and Long Life before me, threw it into the
fire, partly to cure me of my whims, and partly, I believe, for the sake of
a distich, which he pretended to repeat extempore:

> I'd scorn the health such rigid rules must give;
> Nor sacrifice the ends of life to live.

As this observation seemed obliquely to glance at Mr Slicer,
Selkirk said, by way of countenancing his friend, Why, to be sure,
my countryman might carry the matter too far, yet I think no man
can be too careful of his health, nor be blamed for studying the rules
which have been laid down by physicians for that purpose.—Why, says
Wildgoose, as most diseases incident to the human body are generally
allowed to proceed from indolence and repletion, I should think there
can no rules be wanting to preserve or even to restore it, but exercise
and temperance; and, in many cases, even *fasting*, or an entire abstinence
from all kinds of food; this at least if made use of at the beginning of
a disease, I have always found sufficient to check its progress, or put a
stop to most complaints.

As you all seem to be proposing compendious rules, or laconic
precepts for health, says the little rector, I think there can be none better,
or more comprehensive, than those which Dr Scarborough, physician
to Charles II gave to the Duchess of Portsmouth; Madam, says he, you
must either eat less, or use more exercise, or take physic, or—be sick.

XVIII

A NEW SYSTEM OF EDUCATION

Mr Slicer now, by way of shifting the conversation, asked Selkirk how
his pupil went on? which was Slicer's little cousin Johnny, and who was
in the room, with his black string and blue silk waistcoat.

Mr Selkirk (as we have already observed) was the schoolmaster of the village. He had formerly been a travelling Scotchman; but marrying a farmer's daughter with four or five hundred pounds, had opened a shop, and set up a little school, and professed to teach not only reading, writing, and accompts, but Latin and Greek, algebra, logarithms, and trigonometry, and all the most abstruse parts of the mathematics. He had really had the rudiments of a learned education, and was intended for the university, and some learned profession; but, being of a rambling disposition, like many of his ingenious countrymen, chose to travel southwards, and carry a pack for his amusement, as he would sometimes humourously confess.

Mr Slicer then informed the company of Selkirk's excellent plan of education; that, instead of the rigid severity of the usual method in our public schools, he taught his boys all the rudiments of the Latin tongue, amidst their childish sports, by way of diversion.—What, in Locke's method, I suppose? says Wildgoose.—What, *Johnny Loke*? No, says Selkirk, I hope I have improved upon *Johnny Loke,* and Milton too.—In what manner, sir, says Wildgoose.—Here, *Jockey*, replies Selkirk, let the gentlemen see you decline the pronoun article, *hic, haec, hoc.*—Master Jacky immediately began hopping round the room, repeating *hic, hæc, hoc*; gen. *hujus*; dat. *huic*; acc. *hunc, hanc, hoc*; voc. caret; abl. *hoc, hac, hoc,* &c.

There now, says Selkirk, in this manner I teach them the whole grammar, I make eight boys represent the eight parts of speech. The noun substantive stands by himself; the adjective has another boy to support him; the nominative case carries a little wand before the verb; the accusative case walks after, and supports his train: I let the four conjugations make a party at whist, and the three concords dance the hay together, and so on.

The company laughed at Selkirk's project; but the little fat doctor, who had been bred at a public school, observed, that it was very pretty in theory, and so was Milton's and Locke's method, and might please fond mothers; but, he imagined the great men in Queen Elizabeth's time had studied this affair more deeply than has been ever done since; yet they thought some *coercive* power in the teacher was very necessary;

and, if boys were suffered to lay by the pursuit of dead languages as soon as it ceased to be *agreeable* to them, he was of opinion they would make but a very slender progress in Greek and Latin.

Instead of continuing the dispute, Mr Slicer observed, that Mr Selkirk, though a Scotchman, taught the true pronunciation of the English language much better than the generality of schoolmasters; and, as a proof of his assertion, took up a common prayer-book that lay in the parlour-window, and made little Johnny give a specimen of his abilities in that respect.—Mamma, says Jacky, I am to have a new hat next Sunday.—Yes, my Jacky, mind your book and you shall.

Jacky then, by Selkirk's direction, began to read with an audible voice the exhortation in the Morning service, where the words *humble* and *acknowledge* come two or three times over. He pronounced the *h* in *humble* very strong, and *ac-knowledge* as it is written. There doctor, says Mr Slicer, you gentlemen of the clergy never read that right. You leave out the asper in *humble*, and pronounce knowledge as if it were written *knolledge*, which is absurd.

Why, says the doctor, as languages were not originally formed by a committee of philosophers, but arrived gradually at perfection, and were established by *custom*, I think *custom*★ ought to regulate the pronunciation; and I cannot but think it a good rule in this case, as well as the rest of our conversation, to think with the wise, but to talk and pronounce with the vulgar. The rules of grammar cannot, in any language, be reduced to a strict analogy; but all general rules have some exceptions. True, sir, says Selkirk; but we ought to come as near to perfection in every thing as possible.—According to that rule, says the doctor, why do not you pronounce the *h* in *honest* and *honour*? why do not you pronounce the word people *pe-ople*, as it is written? and why does not every body say *bu-rial*, as my clerk, and the grave-diggers in *Hamlet* do? In short, says the doctor, there is something so disagreeable to me in pronouncing the word humble with an aspirate, that I could as soon chew tobacco (which I mortally hate) as bring myself to pronounce it so.

★ *Quem penes arbitrium est, et jus et norma loquendi.* Hor.

XIX

FURTHER ACCOUNT OF
THE LITTLE FAT RECTOR

The company smiled at the little rector's delicacy on that point, and Mr Slicer said, that to be sure there was some truth in what Mr *Griskin* observed.—Upon hearing the little doctor called Griskin, for the first time, Wildgoose looked at him with some attention; and inquired whether he had not a near relation, one Mr Rivers, near Bath, in Somersetshire? After a few questions, Wildgoose was soon convinced, that this was no other than Mr Gregory Griskin, whom he had so often heard of, kinsman to the Mr Rivers, whose adventures were related in the former part of this history.

Mr Griskin lamented the disappointment he had met with in Rivers's imprudent match; that he had flattered himself with the hopes of his nephew's making some figure in life, and even distinguishing himself in the learned world; and had intended to have done something handsome for him at his death, and the like.

Wildgoose began to make some excuse for his friend's imprudent conduct, by encomiums on Mrs Rivers's personal accomplishments and behaviour; to which Griskin (looking down with a reserved air) made no reply.

When Mr Griskin found, however, by several circumstances, that Wildgoose had been intimate with his nephew in the university; and also that he had only come accidentally to Mr Slicer's house for refreshment on his journey, he said he should be glad to have more conversation with him upon the subject; and invited him to go and drink coffee at his house, and even to take a bed there, if consistent with his engagements.

As Wildgoose was in hopes of doing his old friend Rivers some service, and also knew the little doctor to be piously disposed, he accepted of his invitation, having first provided for the reception also of his fellow-traveller; and, taking leave of his benevolent host, Mr Slicer and his company, went to the rectory with Mr Griskin.

The parsonage house was a modern building, and neatly furnished; and the gardens, instead of being laid out, in the present taste, with sun burnt lawns, and barren shrubs, were comfortably enclosed with fruit-walls, filberd hedges, and codlin trees; with a good pidgeon-house, poultry-yard, and fish-ponds; and, in short, with every thing that could contribute to the comfort and convenience of this life.

Griskin was a man of the old-fashioned piety, that showed his faith by his good works. He gave much in charity, prayed often, and fasted now and then. Having the tithes in his own hands, it enabled him to keep a plentiful table, to which every sober honest man was welcome. He every Sunday invited by turns some of his parishioners to dine with him; one or two of the most substantial in the parlour, and as many of the oldest and poorest in the kitchen. This made them pay their tithes and dues cheerfully, which Griskin exacted of them punctually, but not with rigour. If a farmer had any loss, or remarkably bad year, he made him some little allowance; and if a cottager paid him a groat at Easter, which he could ill spare, perhaps he would give his family a sixpenny loaf the Sunday following. By this means he kept up his dignity, and secured his right and the love of his parish at the same time.

XX

FURTHER ACCOUNT OF THE LITTLE FAT RECTOR

When Mr Griskin was alone with Wildgoose, he told him, that he should not have been so much displeased with his nephew Rivers, for pleasing himself in marrying, if he had staid till he had finished his studies, and had married a prudent woman; but that he found his wife was a proud minx, who regarded nothing but dressing, visiting, and going to the public rooms and balls at Bath; and that by what he had heard of her extravagance, his nephew would soon be in a gaol.

Wildgoose was very much surprised at this complaint of Mr Griskin, and said, he would venture to assure him he had been misinformed with regard to Mrs Rivers's character and turn of mind; for, from what he himself had seen of her, he was certain the very contrary was the truth of the case, and that she had not the least taste for that sort of gaieties; and from the unreserved friendship which had subsisted between himself and Mr Rivers, he could depend upon the account he had given him of Mrs Rivers's conduct, and their retired way of life, especially as he had given him that account as a matter of course, to satisfy his friend's curiosity, when there was not the least probability that he could ever have the present opportunity of doing that justice to their character which he now was favoured with.

Mr Griskin replied that he had very good authority for what he had asserted; which Wildgoose found was that of a splenetic old dowager, who went sometimes to Bath, and who had seen Mrs Rivers at the only ball she had appeared at, when they first went into the country; and that she had picked up two or three malicious gossiping stories, with which Bath as much abounds as any country town in the three kingdoms.

Wildgoose then proceeded to describe the amiable qualities of Mrs Rivers, and the manner in which she seemed to pass her time, in the care of her children and family, which, though it did not immediately convince, yet it gave great satisfaction to Mr Griskin, and he seemed to wish it might be true.

The conversation then took a different turn, and Mr Griskin (as his nephew had informed Wildgoose) being very piously disposed, Wildgoose made no scruple of letting him into the secret of his present undertaking; and they soon fell upon the subject of religion. Their sentiments did not correspond, indeed, with regard to some speculative points; but Griskin was much pleased with Wildgoose's zeal for the conversion of sinners. He lamented the great decay of Christian piety; and informed Wildgoose of the methods he himself had taken to revive it in his own parish, by reading prayers publicly every Wednesday and Friday, and privately every morning and evening in his own family.

He told him likewise, that having a public-house belonging to him in Litchfield, in order to sanctify in some measure the unrighteous mammon, he had endowed a little charity school with the annual rents of it.

Though Wildgoose had rather a contempt of these formal devotions and good works, he was too polite to shock his kind host with any reflection of that kind; and, in short, by his simplicity and sincerity, he gained so much upon the good opinion of Mr Griskin, that he insisted upon keeping him and his fellow-traveller all night; and the next morning, before they parted, he gave Wildgoose a commission to write to his old friend Rivers, that a visit from him and Mrs Rivers would be no ways disagreeable to their relation, Mr Griskin. This commission Wildgoose executed immediately; and it was attended with the desired effects on both sides.

Wildgoose now took his leave of Mr Griskin, being rejoined by his friend Tugwell, who had spent the evening as much to his satisfaction in the kitchen, as his master had done in the parlour.

XXI

Set out for Ashbourn, near the Peak

When the two friends were now alone in the Litchfield road again, Tugwell began to express his approbation of the hospitable way of life which Mrs Griskin lived in; and that he thought him a true Christian; and that if any body went to heaven, Mr Griskin certainly would.

Wildgoose, without mentioning Mr Griskin's name, endeavoured to regulate Jerry's opinions by his own standard; and said, a man might fast and pray, and give all his goods to feed the poor, and yet not have true Christian *charity*, or what Saint Paul calls faith working by love.—Tugwell clinched his observation by echoing back some of his own expressions; yet still remained a convert in his heart to Griskin's more comfortable system of Christianity.

Having made a hearty breakfast at Mr Griskin's, our travellers staid no longer in Litchfield, than whilst Wildgoose found out the post-office, and put in his letter to his friend Rivers, and then trudged on with great alacrity, without halting, till they came to Uttoxeter, in their way to Ashbourn, the first town of any note in Derbyshire.

There was a nearer way through the Forest of Nedwood, but more difficult to find; and Tugwell could not yet separate the ideas of robbers, outlaws, and wild beasts, from that of a forest, notwithstanding his master assured him there were no wild beasts to be found, except herds of deer, in any of our royal forests; nor so many robbers as there were upon the great roads, or in the streets of London.

They kept the great road, however, and, without any damage to their persons or property, and without any adventure worth recording, arrived at Ashbourn-in-the-Peak, as it is usually called, about six o'clock in the evening.

BOOK X

I

A PHENOMENON

THE TOWN OF ASHBOURN BEING a great thoroughfare to Buxton Wells, to the High-peak, and many parts of the North; and being inhabited by many substantial people concerned in the mines; and having also three or four of the greatest horse fairs in that part of England, every year, is a very populous town.

There had appeared at Ashbourn, for some market-days past, a very extraordinary person, in a character, and with an equipage somewhat singular and paradoxical: This was one Dr Stubbs, a *physician* of the itinerant kind. The doctor came to town on horse-back, yet dressed in a plaid night-gown and red velvet cap. He had a small reading-desk fixed upon the pummel of his saddle, that supported a large folio, in which, by the help of a monstrous pair of spectacles, the doctor seemed to read, as the horse moved slowly on, with a profound attention. A portmanteau behind him contained his cargo of sovereign medicines, which, as brick-dust was probably the principal ingredient, must be no small burden to his lean steed.

The 'squire, or assistant, led the doctor's horse slowly along, in a dress less solemn, but not less remarkable, than that of his master.

The doctor, from his Rosinante, attended by his merry-andrew (mounted on a horse-block before the principal inn), had just begun to harangue the multitude, when Mr Wildgoose and his fellow-traveller arrived; and the speech with which he introduced himself each market-day was to this effect—

II

A MODEST PLEA

My friends and countrymen! you have frequently been imposed upon, no doubt, by quacks and ignorant pretenders to the noble art of physic; who, in order to gain your attention, have boasted of their many years' travels into foreign parts, and even the most remote regions of the habitable globe. One has been physician to the sophi of Persia, to the great mogul, or the empress of Russia; and displayed his skill at Moscow, Constantinople, Delhi, or Ispahan. Another, perhaps, has been tooth-drawer to the king of Morocco, or corn-cutter to the sultan of Egypt, or to the grand Turk; or has administered a clyster to the queen of Trebisond, or to Prester John, or the Lord knows who—as if the wandering about from place to place (supposing it to be true) could make a man a jot the wiser. No, gentlemen, don't be imposed upon by pompous words and magnificent pretensions. He that goes abroad a fool will come home a coxcomb.

Gentlemen! I am no high-German or unborn doctor—But here I am—your own countryman—your fellow subject—your neighbour as I may say. Why, gentlemen, eminent as I am now become, I was born but at Coventry, where my mother now lives—Mary Stubbs by name.

One thing, indeed, I *must* boast of, without which I would not presume to practise the sublime art and mystery of physic. I am the *seventh son* of a *seventh son*. *Seven* days was I before I sucked the breast. *Seven* months before I was seen to laugh or cry. *Seven* years before I was heard to utter seven words; and twice *seven* years have I studied night and day for the benefit of you, my friends and countrymen: and now here I am—ready to assist the afflicted, and to cure all manner of diseases, past, present, and to come; and that out of *pure love* to my country and fellow-creatures, without fee or reward—except a trifling gratuity, the prime cost of my medicines; or what you may choose voluntarily to contribute hereafter, out of gratitude for the great benefit, which, I am convinced, you will receive from the use of them.

But come, gentlemen, here is my famous* Anti-febri-fuge Tincture; that cures all internal disorders whatsoever; the whole bottle for one poor shilling.

---

* A celebrated quack made this blunder; that is, in plain English, a tincture that will *bring on* a fever.

Here's my *Cataplasma Diabolicum*, or my Diabolical Cataplasm: that will cure all external disorders, cuts, bruises, contusions, excoriations, and dislocations; and all for sixpence.

But here, gentlemen, here's my famous *Balsamum Stubbianum*, or Dr Stubb's Sovereign Balsam; renowned over the whole Christian world, as a universal remedy, which no family ought to be without: it will keep seven years, and—be as good as it is now. Here's this large bottle, gentlemen, for the trifling sum of eighteen-pence.

I am aware, that your physical gentlemen here have called me quack, and ignorant pretender, and the like. But here I am.—Let Dr Pestle or Dr Clyster come forth. I challenge the whole faculty of the town of Ashbourn, to appear before this good company, and dispute with me in *seven* languages, ancient or modern: in Latin, Greek, or Hebrew—in High-Dutch, French, Italian, or Portuguese—Let them ask me any question in Hebrew or Arabic, and then it will appear who are men of solid learning, and who are quacks and ignorant pretenders.

You see, gentlemen, I challenge them to a fair trial of skill; but not one of them dares show his face: they confess their ignorance by their silence.

But come, gentlemen: who buys my *Elixir Cephalicum, Asthmaticum, Arthriticum, Diureticum, Emeticum, Diaphoriticum, Nephriticum, Catharticum.*—Come, gentlemen, seize the golden opportunity, whilst health is so cheaply to be purchased!

III

THE GENEROSITY OF A QUACK

After having disposed of a few packets, the doctor told the company, that as this was the last time of his appearing at Ashbourn (other parts of the kingdom claiming a part in his patriotic labours), he was determined to make a present, to all those who had been his patient, of a shilling a-piece. He therefore called upon all those who could produce any one of Dr Stubb's bottles, pill-boxes, plaisters, or even his hand-bills, to make their appearance, and partake of his generosity.

This produced no small degree of expectation amongst those that had been the doctor's customers, who gathered round him, with their hands stretched out, and with wishful looks. Here, gentlemen! says the doctor, Stand forth! hold up your hands, I promised to give you a shilling a-piece. I will immediately perform my promise. Here's my *Balsamum Stubbianum*; which I have hitherto sold at *eighteen-pence* the bottle. You shall now have it for *six-pence*.

Come! *gemmen*, says the merry-andrew, where are you? Be quick! Don't stand in your own light. You'll never have such another opportunity—as long as you live.

The people looked upon each other with an air of disappointment. Some shook their heads, some grinned at the conceit, and others uttered their execrations—some few, however, who had been unwilling to throw away *eighteen-pence* upon the experiment, ventured to give a single *six-pence*; and the doctor picked up eight or nine shillings more by this stratagem, which was more than the intrinsic value of his horse-load of medicines. He then took his leave; and was retiring to his inn, to enjoy the fruits of his public-spirited labours; when Wildgoose, seeing an audience ready to his hands, immediately mounted the horse-block, which the merry-andrew had quitted; and in order to draw their attention, bade Tugwell give out the hundredth Psalm. Many of the people were greatly surprised, but two or three itinerant preachers having of late passed through the town, some of the company understood the signal, and even joined the two pilgrims in their oddly-timed melody.

IV

ECCE AUTEM ALTERUM!

After singing a couple of stanzas, Wildgoose began his address to the mob, by observing how anxious they were about the health of their bodies,

when they could listen with patience to every itinerant pretender to
the art of physic; who, without any previous instruction or experience,
boasted of that complete knowledge of diseases, which physicians of a
regular education, after many years' study, find it so difficult to obtain;
and without any regard to different cases or constitutions, often sell the
same remedies for contradictory complaints.

Wildgoose then (by an easy transition) proceeded to direct them to
the true Physician of their *souls*: and recommended *faith alone*, as the
infallible catholicon for all their maladies.

Yes, yes, cries Tugwell; here is the true spiritual mountebank,
gentlemen: here is the quack-doctor of your souls.

Yes, says the merry-andrew, and thou art the true spiritual tom fool.

Doctor Stubbs himself (also having stopped on his horse at the gate-
way of the inn, to hear and see the event of Wildgoose's mounting the
rostrum), observing the obvious parallel between Wildgoose's irregular
practices in the theological way, and that of a mountebank in the
medical, could not forbear appealing to the mob, whether an itinerant
preacher, (such as these methodists) were not more of the quack than
he was, who pretended to have discovered a more compendious way to
heaven; and to prescribe *faith* alone, as the universal cure for all diseases.
Let the parson keep to his church; the farmer to his plough; and the
cobbler to his stall,—says the doctor.

Tugwell, thinking the doctor had discovered something of their
profession, now took up the cudgel: and said, he was no cobbler; but
made shoes, as well as *mended* them: that his master was no *farmer*; but as
good a gentleman as the doctor for all his red-cap! and kept as good a
horse, if he had a mind to make use of him.

The merry-andrew, hearing his master treated with such familiarity
by a fellow of Tugwell's mean appearance, laid hold on his wallet, which
hung over his shoulder, and almost pulled him backwards; telling him,
at the same time, that he supposed it was filled with old shoes. Tugwell,
who was afraid of nothing but ghosts and fire-arms, began to retort
upon Pil-garlic with the arm of flesh; but he having more wit and agility
than courage, gave Jerry a swinging blow on the face with his sword
of lath; then made his escape amongst the crowd. This raised Tugwell's

choler, together with a loud laugh and a hubbub; and, the mob being by this time pretty well tired, the assembly was soon dissolved: each party, the doctor with his merry-andrew, and Mr Wildgoose with Tugwell, retiring to their respective apartments, in the same hotel.

V

AN AFFECTING SCENE.
TUGWELL IN JEOPARDY

Mr Wildgoose, before he went to rest, having made proper inquiries which was the most unfrequented part of the Peak, yet abounded with the greatest number of mines, arose pretty early; and having, at Tugwell's request, taken a slight breakfast, he was preparing to sally forth; when a woman, who (as she returned from the doctor) had heard Wildgoose hold forth the preceding night, came and entreated him to go and pray with her husband; who, she said, had been in a languishing condition for some time, and was now, she feared, near his end.

Wildgoose was pleased with the opportunity of doing a charitable action, as well as with the compliment paid to his eloquence and his piety. He, therefore, immediately complied with the woman's request.

When he came, he saw a very affecting, though, at the same time, a somewhat ridiculous scene. The poor man had one son, who was a great *schollard;* that is, he could read without spelling: and, by way of comforting his father, the young man had got an old folio Common Prayer-book; and was reading the *act of uniformity* to the sick man, with a very *audible* voice: to which the poor man listened with great attention; and said, it was very comfortable doctrine. Wildgoose asked him, as he seemed so well disposed, why he had not sent for the minister of his parish? The sick man said, he had done so, when he was first taken ill; but that the minister had given him no comfort; for, the poor man confessed, he had lived a very wicked life, and had gained a livelihood by very dishonest means; and had it not in his power, if he

were inclined to do it, to make restitution, as the minister would have
him do. Wildgoose bade him not despair; for that he and all mankind
were equally sinners! and that he had nothing to do but to lay *hold* upon
Christ by faith; and all would be well. The poor man *said,* he did so,
and trusted only to *his* mercy. Wildgoose then assured him, his sins were
forgiven; and they parted entirely satisfied with each other.

When Wildgoose returned to the inn, he found, to his great surprise,
his friend Tugwell taken into custody by a constable, who was hurrying
him away before a justice of the quorum that lived very near the town;
for Jerry, though far advanced in life, had had but little experience of
the ways of men. Being, therefore, in his political principles, as we have
already observed, rather attached to the Stuart family; and the town
of Ashbourn, since the late march of the rebels through that place,
being divided into two parties (who persecuted each other with great
violence); Tugwell, it seems, had somewhat imprudently taken the
part of an honest barber; who, as he was drinking his morning cup
in the kitchen, had fallen into a dispute about the rebellion, with a
dissenting baker, who was very zealous for the government, and, upon
Jerry's interfering, had charged the constable with him as a disaffected
subject.

Upon Mr Wildgoose's interposing in his friend's behalf, Doctor
Stubbs, who had joined the crowd assembled in the gate-way of the inn,
whispered the constable, that, to his knowledge, Wildgoose was a Jesuit
in disguise; that he had seen him in York gaol during the rebellion; that
he had let his hair grow to conceal the clerical tonsure; and that several
Jesuits had of late appeared, in the character of Methodist preachers, in
several parts of the kingdom. The constable, therefore, charged some of
the company, in the king's name, to assist him in carrying them both
before a magistrate; and the doctor pretended to follow them, and make
good his allegations.

VI

A JUDICIOUS MAGISTRATE

When they came before the justice, all that could be proved against Tugwell was, that he *seemed* to *favour* the rebels; that he said, he loved to read about battles and massacres, and that he should have been very *glad* to have seen the young Pretender. The justice, who was a sensible man, and endeavoured, as much as possible, to restore and preserve the peace amongst his neighbours, observed, if that were all, he could find nothing treasonable in what the prisoner had said; especially as he spoke of the *Pretender* as such, and not as having the least shadow of right to the crown of England. In short, it appeared to him, that all he had said, seemed to proceed from *curiosity*, rather than from *disloyalty* to King George.

The justice then asked, what they had to say against the other prisoner, Mr Geoffry Wildgoose by name? The constable said, there was a gentleman present, who knew him to be a Jesuit, and had seen him in York gaol during the rebellion; and would take his oath of it. Doctor Stubbs was then called upon, to make good his charge. But the doctor, who only owed Wildgoose a grudge for speaking disrespectfully of his profession, and was conscious all he had said was an impudent lie, had given them the slip; and had taken this opportunity of marching out of town, without being pelted by the mob, as he richly deserved.

An old man, however, whose wife was a favourer of the Methodists, said, such fellows as Wildgoose and his companion ought to be punished, for making a disturbance, and hindering people from their work; that they had *converted* his wife in particular, who used to mind her knitting, and bustle about, and scold at him all the day long: but, since these Methodists had come about and *converted* her, she minded nothing but reading and praying, and singing psalms, from morning to night. The good justice said, if the *converting* his wife was all the mischief they had done, he wished they would *convart* all the *scolds* in the parish. And so, after asking Wildgoose a few questions, he ordered the constables to release them, and dismissed the company from his presence.

The Jacobite barber, whose cause, as we observed, Tugwell had espoused, as soon as his worship was out of sight, clapped Jerry on the shoulder, by way of triumph, and said, as he himself was acquainted with the butler, and Tugwell, he found, was a curious man, he would show him a curiosity.—The *Prince* is in this house now, says he, whispering in Tugwell's ear. Jerry starting with surprise, the barber got his friend the butler to take him up the back stairs, into a long gallery, which led to the principal bed-chambers; on the doors of which had been written by the quarter-master with chalk (and afterwards traced over with white lead by way of curiosity) the names of *the Prince*, Lord Ogilvy, Pitsligo, and other rebel chiefs, who, in their way to Derby, having halted one night in Ashbourn, had been quartered in this gentleman's house.

Tugwell expressed great surprise at seeing the very place where so renowned a personage had lately lodged; whose name he had often heard read in the *Gloucester Journal*; which Mrs Wildgoose had lent the vicar, the vicar had smuggled to his clerk, who had frequently retailed it to the whole parish, under the great elm at Tugwell's cottage gate.

Wildgoose returning to the inn before his fellow-traveller, and finding a number of people, who had been assembled on the report of Tugwell's being taken into custody, still loitering about, took the opportunity of mounting the *suggestum*, or horse-block, once more, though without much effect; people's passions being rather calm in a morning, and not so well disposed to catch the fire of enthusiasm in open day-light, as amidst the dazzling lustre of sconces and chandeliers at the evening tabernacle. Some of those who had taken a cup in the morning were a little riotous; some few, however, seemed affected, and consulted with Wildgoose what further was to be done towards their conversion; and also informed him which were the most uncultivated parts of the Peak, and stood most in need of the labours of his mission.

VII

THEY SET FORTH TOWARDS
THE HIGH PEAK

Our Spiritual Quixote was now impatient to sally forth, in quest of more spiritual adventures: but Tugwell, hearing so romantic an account of the mountainous country they were going to traverse, entreated his master not to do any thing rashly, nor set out upon an empty stomach; and, it being now past the middle of the day, they made a pretty hearty meal upon some cold mutton-pie; a good segment of which, for fear of accidents, Jerry stowed in his wallet; and about three o'clock they set out on the Buxton road for the High Peak.

After travelling about an hour and a half, our two pilgrims imagined they had climbed to the summit of the mountains; but they still found 'Alps on Alps arise.' At length, however, they came upon an extensive plain, to the extremity of which their sight could not reach. Jerry, after reading so many books of travels, and having been near two months on foot, now lifting up his hands with astonishment, cried out, he did not think the world had been half so wide.

As the sun had now journeyed far towards the west, and they could see neither village, hut, nor even a single tree to shelter them from the dews of the night, Jerry's heart began to fail him; and he could not forbear again to wish himself at home with Dorothy, in his own chimney-corner, or at least at the inn at Ashbourn, which they had quitted so late in the day.

As the road led them by degrees towards the extremity of the moor, they heard, at a distance on the left-hand, the sound of a French-horn, which a little revived Tugwell's spirits, though it revived at the same time the jeopardy he had been in amongst the stag-hunters, as related in the beginning of this history.

Jerry, however, entreated his master (as the evening was coming on) to turn aside, and try whether they could find any place to lodge at, especially as there was nothing to preach to, but a few sheep and some black cattle, which were feeding amongst the rocks.

Though Wildgoose was unwilling to listen to any overtures of indulgence, he thought it prudent enough to comply with his friend's proposal. Proceeding, therefore, towards the edge of the plain, they came to a precipice of an astonishing height, from which was a stupendous view into a deep valley; the hill rising on the opposite side, covered with woods, near half a mile perpendicularly. The river Dove ran winding at the bottom, amidst pyramidical rocks, that rise detached from the hill, with shrubs growing from their tops, and the roots hanging down in a grotesque manner. In some places they almost meet, and intercept the view; in others they open, and discover rocks beyond rocks, in long perspective up the valley, in a most beautiful profusion.

VIII

FALL IN WITH A MUSICAL PARTY

The French-horns which were blown by two servants, placed in the opposite woods, now ceased; and upon their approaching, out of curiosity, to the edge of the precipice, the two pilgrims were surprised to hear (seemingly about half way down the hill) an angelic voice, accompanied by two German flutes, singing a song from the masque of Comus.

> On ev'ry hill, in ev'ry grove,
>   Along the margin of each stream;
> Dear, conscious scenes of former love!
>   I moan and Damon is my theme.
> The hills, the groves, the rocks remain;
> But Damon there I seek in vain.

Wildgoose was filled with rapture at the sound and, when the song was finished, could not forbear repeating to himself (yet loud enough for his fellow-traveller to hear) these beautiful lines from Shakespeare, with whom, as we observed, he had formerly been conversant:

I thought that all things had been savage here;
——————But, whate'er you are,
That, in this desert inaccessible,
Lose and neglect the creeping hours of time:
If ever you have lived in better days;
If ever been where bells have knolled to church—

Ah! says Tugwell, I wish I could hear our *bells knoll to church* this very moment; I would soon be at home again in my own stall. I am quite tired with this *vaggibond* life. But come, master, let us go and inquire our way to the next town, and not wander about this wilderness country all night.

Jerry then looked about and found a sheep-track, that led winding down the hill; but they were forced to descend above a quarter of a mile, before they could discover the place from whence the music proceeded; when they beheld a lofty arch, or natural cavity in the side of the rocks, to which there was an artificial ascent by near a hundred steps, guarded by a slight rail: at the mouth of this grotto there was a broad space like a balcony; from which there appeared a genteel party of nine or ten people well dressed; some with musical instruments, others with books in their hands, and one or two with bottles and glasses before them, amusing themselves as was most suitable to their several tastes and inclinations.

Upon Tugwell's appearing in sight, a servant came to him, and in a surly tone, demanded what he wanted there?—Jerry answered, that they did not come to beg or to steal; that, he thanked God, his wallet was well stored, and his master had money in his purse: but that they had lost their way upon the moors, and desired him to direct them to the nearest town, or place of entertainment for travellers.

The servant asked him, who, and what the devil he and his master were?—Why, says he, my master is a gentleman of four or five hundred pounds a-year (but no matter for that); he is a good Christian, and travels about the country to *convart* people from their wicked ways, and *sich* like.

Well, says the servant, I can tell thee, for thy comfort, there is no town, nor hardly a house within these five miles, except the village which we live at; but if thou wilt stay till we go home, which will not be long, I will direct thee to a public-house, where there is good quarters and good liquor; and what wouldst have more?

When the servant had given Jerry his answer, and was returning, a young lady (whose curiosity was very impetuous) ran down a few steps, to inquire what those men wanted? and, having satisfied herself, ran and told the company, that there were two droll *creachers*, who had lost their way; and one of them pretended to be a gentleman of fortune; but, she supposed, by the servant's account, was a Methodist preacher.

This company consisted of Sir William and Lady Forester, who lived in the neighbourhood, and some friends that were with them in the house, who came to enjoy a fine evening in this romantic scene, which Sir William had a little decorated, as above described.

IX

CHARACTERS OF SIR WILLIAM AND LADY FORESTER

Sir William Forester was a gentleman of fine sense and (what is not always a consequence) of fine taste, not only in the polite arts, music, painting, architecture, and the like; but in life and manners. He had the art of making every company happy; and the greater art of making himself happy in every company. Some of his wise neighbours, indeed, were a little scandalized at his admitting people of inferior rank so frequently to his table; but Sir William, like Swift's virtuoso, who could extract sun-beams from cucumbers, had the skill of extracting entertainment from the most insipid companions; of discovering humour in the most phlegmatic divine, or solid sense in (the most trifling of all characters) a country dancing-master.

Lady Forester was a woman of uncommon merit, considering the peculiar circumstances attending her education. She was the daughter of Lord ——, who was a professed infidel, and absolutely forbade those who were about his children to instil any religious prejudices (as he called them) into their tender minds, by teaching them their catechism, or by suffering them to read any books on religious subjects. Nay, he severely punished his favourite child, of ten years old, for presuming to look into a Bible.

He was of Lord Shaftesbury's opinion, that there is no necessary connection between religion and virtue; and even that people may be good moral men and good members of society, without the belief of a God. And he considered himself as an instance of his assertions, as he lived a tolerably sober life, and performed several generous and charitable actions, without the pretence of any religious motive, though it is well known, that, for want of a uniform principle, he was frequently guilty of the most flagrant instances of vice and immorality.

Lady Forester's mother, however, who was a very pious and a very sensible woman, had taken care to instil some short principles of religion into her daughter; but, dying whilst Lady Forester was very young, she underwent a trial of a different kind from the capricious indulgence of her father, who settled her, when she was just sixteen, in a house in town, with an equipage, and suitable domestics and attendants, entirely at her own command. Her ladyship's good sense, however, supported her without the least censure, in this critical situation; and the utmost indiscretion which the severest critic could ever charge her with, was of a romantic kind, the rambling once or twice into Hyde-Park, at a distance from her equipage and attendants, and reading under a tree, accompanied only with a female friend, with all the security of rural innocence.

Lady Forester was now, however, the mother of several children, whom she bred up in the strictest principles of religion and virtue, which will probably make them ornaments to the rising generation, though her ladyship herself was a little inclined to the mystic, or rather the seraphic theology, being a great admirer of Fenelon's, Norris's, and other works of the same kind.—But to return to our story.

X

CHARACTER OF COLONEL RAPPEE

Miss Kitty Forester (who, though much younger, was sister to Sir William, and the lady whose voice they had heard), having made her report, that the travellers had lost their way, the company voted, by way of fun, to send for them up to *Reynard's-hall*, which was the name given to this natural grotto, or cavity in the rock, where the company was sitting.

As Wildgoose, though in his travelling dishabille, had a gentleman-like appearance, he was desired to sit down amidst this *belle assemblée*, and Tugwell, with his wallet, was turned over to the care of the servants. After some little conversation with Wildgoose upon his journey, and the like, the company sat down to (what in romance would be called) a cold collation, which in plain English was a good quantity of cold ham and fowls, cold tongue, orange cheese-cakes, and other portable provisions of the best kinds.

Wildgoose, having made a hearty meal at Ashbourn, ate little; but drank two or three glasses of Rhenish wine. The evening was now extremely fine, the heat of the day being succeeded by an agreeable *fraicheur*; the parting sun gilded the summit of the mountains, and the river Dove ran murmuring at their base. The French-horns, at proper intervals, enlivened the scene; and, in short, by the politeness of Sir William and Lady Forester, Wildgoose found himself much at ease, and very happy, notwithstanding the sneers and stifled titterings of some of the company.

Among the rest there was a Colonel Rappee, an officer in the guards, who was upon a visit at Sir William Forester's. The colonel had made a very shining figure in the army, during a thirty years' peace, and had behaved with the greatest courage and magnanimity in above twenty engagements and reviews—on Hounslow-heath, or Hyde-park.—But, at the battle of Preston-pans, in the year forty-five, he was one of those gentlemen who retreated with so much precipitation, as to outride the express, and bring to London the first news of their own defeat.

The colonel, however, appeared by no means deficient in personal valour, for though he had never fought any duel in form, he had frequently given the look of defiance, and kicked two or three impertinent fellows, who were dismayed at the ferocity of his countenance, and his military dress.

The colonel's person, indeed, gave him the advantage over any common antagonist, and also recommended him to the notice of people of rank, for he was near six feet high: and, though

> Lambent dullness played about his head,

he had an air of sagacity and importance which commanded respect from the less discerning part of mankind; nay, and having 'a little kind of an odd sort of a small wit,' as Congreve says, and uttering now and then a tolerable thing with a decisive air, he even passed for a man of sense; and by a discreet management, was received upon a decent footing in many families of distinction.

From being much in company also, the colonel had picked up a few common-place maxims and topics of ridicule, upon matrimony, religion, Scotchmen, parsons, and old maids, which he applied indiscriminately upon all occasions; but frequently with so little propriety, as could not but shock the delicacy of Sir William and Lady Forester, who accordingly rather endured than enjoyed his company; and considered his *visits*, or rather his *visitations*, as afflictions from heaven, to which they were in duty obliged patiently to submit.

XI

A CONVERSATION ON RELIGION AND OTHER SUBJECTS

The colonel then looked a little sour upon Mr Wildgoose, and having too much pride, or rather too little penetration to discover what was really valuable in his character, considered him as a common stroller, and was quite affronted at Sir William's presuming to introduce such company to a man of his consequence. He began, therefore, to say rude things upon impostors and hypocrites, and to give hints how much Sir William was the dupe of parsons and buffoons.

Lady Forester, however, contrived to change the discourse, and to introduce some religious topic; upon which she gave Wildgoose an opportunity of displaying his knowledge of the subject in such a manner, that Rappee was afraid to interpose, for fear of discovering his own ignorance.

By way of venting his spleen, however, the colonel began throwing out common-place invectives against religion in general, and Christianity in particular, from the constant feuds and animosities it had accidentally occasioned amongst the different sects, and the like; and said, if people would but live according to nature and reason, it would be better if there were no such thing as religion in the world.

Sir William said he was glad that was only Rappee's private opinion, unsupported by any reasons; but begged the colonel, if he had discovered any new arguments against religion, which he thought of any force, he would keep them a secret from his wife, his children, and his servants, as he was convinced it was for the good of mankind, that they should not be undeceived in that particular, supposing religion to be all a cheat, or a political invention.

But, colonel, continues he, you are frequently uttering complaints of this kind; notwithstanding the king, your master, is the defender of the faith, and Christianity is at present the religion of your country, by law established. If you find yourself aggrieved by it, why do not you, or some of your wise associates, draw up the heads of a bill, and join in a petition to the parliament? and I will undertake to present it to the house, for the redress of those grievances which this oppressive institution has brought upon mankind.

The colonel saw the absurdity of his usual complaints against religion, when set in so strong a light, and was struck silent for a few minutes: but soon rallying his spirits, he shifted the discourse in his turn; and, with a more placid air, contrived to bring another subject upon the carpet, and at the same time to display his own importance, by mentioning a magnificent entertainment to which he had lately been invited by a noble lord.

Bob Tench, a sporting companion of Sir William's, and a near relation of the famous Will Wimble, who was waiting till the first sickle was put into the corn, in order to go a partridge-shooting.—Bob said, he never desired to be entertained better than he was this morning at Sir Harry Hotspur's, where was a cold venison-pasty, and some excellent strong beer, which he was sorry to see banished, to make way for tea and chocolate, and other hot liquors, unknown to our sporting ancestors.

The conversation now turned upon genteel, or on magnificent entertainments in general, which any of the company had either been present at, or had read of in history.

Miss Forester said she could never sufficiently admire Cleopatra's gallantry in her entertainment of Mark Antony; and was particularly pleased with her dissolving a pearl of immense value, and presenting it in a golden cup of rich wine. Colonel Rappee ridiculed this, by mentioning some modern wh-re, who had been suffered by her fond keeper to swallow a hundred pound bank note between two slices of bread and butter, at breakfast. Somebody mentioned the Roman emperor, I think, who presented each of his guests with the gold cup which they drank out of.

But Sir William Forester said, he never read of a more polite reception, than what Vokeèr, the rich Augsburgh merchant gave the Emperor Charles V. He had lent the emperor a very considerable sum of money, for which his majesty had given him a promissory note, or order upon his exchequer, or some written security of that kind. Soon after the emperor, on his march (by way of doing honour to his friend), lay at his house in Augsburgh. The merchant gave him a most magnificent supper, and when the emperor retired to his chamber, there was a fire laid of cinnamon-wood, which Vokeèr himself set alight, with the emperor's note of hand, or order for the money; and then wished his majesty a good night.

Well, Sir William, says a young Templar,★ who was of the party, you have told us how a subject entertained an emperor of Germany. I will tell you of an entertainment, or rather a family dinner, that was given

★ Now at the top of his profession.

by the emperor of Morocco to an English subject, Dr Shaw, who has lately published his travels into Africa and Egypt.

At the top there was a dish of fish, consisting of a young whale boiled, and a few sturgeons and porpuses fried round it. At the bottom was the hind quarter of an elephant. On one side a brace of lions, fricasseed; on the other the neck of a camel, made *kabab* (as the doctor calls it), or, in plain English, *cabob'd*.

The second course, a brace of ostriches roasted, at the upper end, with the ropes on a toast: at the lower end, a griffin: on one side a dish of cranes and storks; on the other, a potted crocodile.

There was no butcher's meat but a roasted buffalo at the side-table.

The doctor says, he only picked the short ribs of a lion, which, to use his own expression, was *a delicious morsel*.

His majesty asked the doctor, whether he should help him to the leg or to the wing of the griffin? which being half bird and half beast, his majesty thought facetious.

You must observe, griffins are looked upon as great rarities, even in Africa.

I suppose, says Sir William, this is some piece of humour upon the *marvellous* in the doctor's *Travels,* though I have heard them spoken of as very learned, as well as entertaining; and that the doctor has rectified several errors in the geography of the countries which he passed through.

I have heard, says the young Templar, when the doctor was introduced to the king, on his return from his travels, that he told his majesty, amongst other things, he had really eat the short ribs of a lion, and that it was a *delicious morsel*.

Well, says Wildgoose, smiling, and looking round upon the prospect, and pointing to the French-horns, which were placed in the woods at some distance from them, I have no idea of a more agreeable entertainment than that to which Sir William has done me the honour to admit me.

The company having finished their collation, Miss Forester was desired to favour them with another song; which Sir William and the young gentleman from the Temple again accompanied with their German flutes. After which, the sun being now setting, the ladies were taken up in a carriage, which came to the edge of the hill; and the gentlemen walked to Sir William Forester's, which was not above a mile across the plain; only the noble colonel thought it beneath his dignity to march with the infantry; he had, therefore, ordered his servant to bring his horses, and mounting his iron-grey, with his *demi-pique* and furniture, flanked the coach upon the *grand pas*; and Wildgoose, with his fellow-traveller, at Sir William's request, joined the cavalcade.

XII

A SCENE IN THE NURSERY

Sir William had by this time fully discovered Mr Wildgoose's intention of preaching to the subterraneous race of lead-miners in the High Peak; and, as he was sensible, from their situation and constant employment, they could have but slender means of instruction, either in the principles of religion or morality, he by no means discouraged Wildgoose from pursuing so disinterested a project. He desired him, however, to halt a day or two at his house, and he would make some proper inquiries where his instructions might be applied to the best advantage. He told Wildgoose, moreover, that Lady Forester was herself very religiously disposed, and would be pleased to have him talk to her children and her domestics upon that subject.

When they came to Sir William's house, which was a venerable pile of Gothic building, fitted up in an elegant modern taste, Lady Forester, who paid great attention to Wildgoose, told him she always went into the nursery as soon as she came home, especially in an evening, to visit her little folks, and hear them their prayers. She likewise invited Wildgoose to attend her thither. At the nursery door, Mrs Molly, her ladyship's maid, met her, with a little boy of about a year old in her arms, as the most agreeable service she could perform to her lady; for he, being the least, and the most helpless, possessed of course the largest share in Lady Forester's affection. She clasped him in her arms, kissed him, and gave him her blessing; and then, went round to three or four more, heard them their prayers, and made them ask a blessing; and then, wishing them a good night, returned to the company.

Wildgoose was struck with Lady Forester's affectionate care of her amiable progeny, which she observing; You see, sir, said she, where my treasure is, there will my heart be also. I am afraid, indeed, continues her ladyship, you will think these dear children engross too much of my affection but I assure you, sir, they are the most infallible pledges of my devotion to heaven. Their health is so dear to me, and I have so constant a sense of their depending for every pulse of life upon the good-will of Providence, that my whole life almost is one continued prayer for their preservation.

Wildgoose answered, nothing could be more amiable than the tenderness her ladyship expressed for the welfare of her offspring. He only wished, in his way, that she did not love that little child in the nurse's arms more than the *holy child* Jesus, through whose mediation alone, says he, we are entitled to the favour and protection of Providence.

XIII

FAMILY PRAYERS, FOLLOWED BY REPARTEES

They now came into the great hall, and Wildgoose was not a little surprised to find the whole company, except the colonel, assembled; and Sir William waiting for Lady Forester, with a large quarto Common Prayer Book on the table, in order to read prayers to the family.

This would have appeared more extraordinary, if he had known, that Sir William, before his marriage, had lived a remarkably gay life, and had even been tainted with many of the fashionable opinions of the age; but his regard for Lady Forester, and a sense of the importance of religious principles to every individual of society, had made Sir William so much a domestic man, as, even when in town, to read prayers every evening, unless any thing very extraordinary prevented it; and a sermon every Sunday night, to his family.

As soon as prayers were ended Colonel Rappee again made his appearance; but was rallied by Miss Sainthill, (a very sensible maiden lady, a friend and companion of Lady Forester's), on his fondness for private meditation, and the care he took to avoid all appearance of hypocrisy.—Rappee said, he knew no reason why a man could not say his prayers as well in private as in public, in a walk upon the terrace as well as in a closet; that religion was a mere personal affair, and the like. He hinted, however, that he might have as much true devotion as those who were always canting about religion, and pretended to set up for reformers.

Miss Sainthill replied, that, to be sure, people might say their prayers in any place, or in any posture, and even in a warm bed; but she could not but think there was a natural decency of behaviour due to the Supreme Being, as well as to our fellow creatures; and she was afraid, she said, those who deferred their prayers till they lay down upon their pillows (as she fancied the colonel did), very frequently fell asleep without saying them at all.

Well, says the colonel, there is one part of my devotions which I never forget, and that is thanksgiving; I have always thanked God for three things.—Pray let me hear those curious particulars, says Miss Sainthill. I suppose the first is that you are not an old maid.—No, says Rappee; the first is, that I was not born in Russia.—What, because you are afraid of the cold, I suppose, says Miss Sainthill.—No, says the colonel, because I am afraid of the knout, and do not like arbitrary governments. —Well, and what is the second particular?—Why, that I was not bred a cheesemonger.—What, because you do not love the smell of cheese? says Miss Sainthill; but, for a like reason, you should not have been bred a soldier, continued she.—Why go? says the colonel.—Why? because you do not love the smell of gun-powder.

Rappee bowed, and smiled; but said, he was most thankful for the third particular.—And pray what may that be? says Miss Sainthill.—Why, that I have not a very *long nose*, cries the colonel.—Miss Sainthill curtsied, and took a long pinch of snuff, being conscious how liberal nature had been to *her* in that respect; and being willing to give Rappee a short triumph, by inviting a laugh in his favour, at her own expense, of which he was not a little conceited. Miss Sainthill, however, retorted, and said, a long nose would certainly be very inconvenient to the colonel in the day of battle, especially if he should ever *face* the Highlanders again; as it would be more exposed to the stroke of a broad-sword. Well fought, Miss Sainthill, says Sir William. Colonel leave off, whilst you are well. *Cedant arma togæ*: 'Let heroes to the gown give place.'

There was now a side-board laid, with some anchovies, olives, and a few trifling things for those that chose to eat again, after their collation amongst the rocks in Dove-dale.

The company now appearing disposed to retire to their several apartments, candles were brought in by the butler, attended by Mrs Molly with a wax-light for her lady. Molly was a very pretty girl, and had a pair of eyes most perniciously piercing, which she played off upon Mr Wildgoose, as thinking him a guest not much above her own level. As the eyes are known to have a fascinating power, Wildgoose could hardly avoid returning Mrs Molly's amorous glances, which was perceived by the jealous eyes of Mr George, the butler, who was her admirer.

Mr George was ordered to wait on Mr Wildgoose to his apartment; which office he performed with tolerable civility. But Mrs Molly officiously inquiring, whether there was a bottle and bason carried into the gentleman's room, Mr George, with a surly air, bade her mind her own business. He then proceeded with his charge up the grand staircase, and wished him a good night.

XIV

A MORNING CONVERSATION
ON THE BACK STAIRS

It was now eight o'clock in the morning, when Betty the house-maid was sweeping the back stairs; but suspended the motion of her brush, and leaned against the rails, to make way for Mrs Molly, who now made her first appearance, with a ruffle half hemmed in one hand, and a volume of *Pamela* in the other.

So, Mrs Molly, you were up late again last night, I suppose.—Yes, pretty late, says Mrs Molly.—Ah, Mrs Molly, cries Betty, I *wou'dn't not* do it; no, not for the best mistress that ever trod upon shoe-leather.—Why, Betty, replies she, to be sure my lady is a very good lady; and we are so fond of each other's company, that we never know when to part. We were talking till after twelve o'clock about this strange gentleman. To be sure the gentleman is very much of a gentleman, for that matter, if he did not travel about on foot like a Scotch pedlar.—Why what trade is the gentleman, then?—What trade, you fool! Why, he is a gentleman, I tell you; and has got a good estate of his own; but he is going to preach to the poor miners in the High Peak.—Why, I thought nobody could preach but parsons, quoth Betty.—No more they could in former times, says Mrs Molly; but people are more *cute* and *cleverer* now-a-days, than they were formerly. Why, there is our George, the butler, can read a play or a sermon better than our curate.—Oh, says Betty, I thought you and George would have *fit* last night about this gentleman.—George, indeed! says Molly, a jealous-headed *cretur*! if *any body* does but speak to *a body*, *a body* must be called to an account by him, forsooth! What is the gentleman to me? The gentleman never spoke a word to me, nor I to him; only wished me a good-night.—Well, says Betty, Mr George swears he will be a match for him and the cobbler, his fellow-traveller, if my mistress keeps them here another night.

Here the lady's bell rang, and put a stop to the dialogue; and Mrs Molly and Betty hastened to their several departments.

XV

ON THE NECESSITY OF A REGULAR ORDINATION

Though Mr Wildgoose had of late been very negligent of his person, yet, being now in a genteel family, by the time the bell rung for breakfast, he had got himself shaved, his hair rubbed up with pomatum, and had supplied himself with clean linen from Tugwell's wallet; so that when he joined the company in the bow-window, he made no despicable appearance.

After the usual compliments of the morning, Lady Forester again introduced the subject of Wildgoose's preaching to the miners, and said, his intention was certainly very laudable; but wondered, as she found he had had a university education, that he did not get into regular orders, before he engaged in an undertaking of that kind.—Yes, says the colonel; Don Quixote himself, mad as he was, would not enter the lists, nor undertake any achievement of consequence, before he was dubbed a knight; and, though I hate all preaching, I am for a proper subordination, and would have people keep to their *ranks* in life. A commissary, or a quarter-master might as well pretend to rule an army, or to give the word of command in an engagement as a layman to interpose in the parson's trade, and mount the rostrum.—Why, says Wildgoose, if the commanding officers neglected their duty, it were better, sure, that a quarter-master, or any body else, should give the word of command, than that a whole army should be cut to pieces.

I should think, says Sir William, interposing, the cases are by no means similar; for, though the life of a Christian be justly compared to that of a soldier, yet, to make the cases parallel in the present view, you must suppose that the officers neglect their duty, not merely in a single engagement, but during a whole campaign; in which case, there would be room for complaint to be made to the superior powers, and get them punished, or removed from their commands. So, if a clergyman is negligent of his duty, not in one or two single instances, but in the general conduct of his life, the officers of a parish are bound, by oath, to present and make complaint of him to the bishop of the diocese; but the churchwarden, for that reason, has no *right*, supposing he had *abilities*, to exercise the sacerdotal function, mount the pulpit, and harangue the people. Such a conduct would necessarily be productive of disorder and confusion.

Wildgoose replied, that in a political view, those regulations might be of some consequence; and that, in general, he did not think it right to break through the restraints of society; but that, upon extraordinary occasions, those formalities were to be dispensed with: and I cannot but think, continues he, that Providence approves of the proceedings of Mr Wesley and Mr Whitfield, by the extraordinary success he has given to their labours.

That is a very fallacious way of arguing, cries the young Templar, because Providence often brings about good ends by very bad means.

Well, says Sir William, if such irregular proceedings can be proper upon any occasion, they are so in the present instance, which Mr Wildgoose has determined upon, that of preaching to our poor miners in the Peak, who are properly as sheep without a shepherd. Sir William then said they intended, the next day, to go upon a scheme of pleasure to Matlock, and to show some young people the wonders of the Peak, as they are called; and that, if he chose it, Mr Wildgoose might accompany them in their expedition. Wildgoose promised to attend them; but it proved otherwise in the event.

XVI

A LECTURE IN THE SERVANTS' HALL

After breakfast the company began to separate, and amuse themselves as suited their inclinations. As Bob Tench and his party proposed to angle upon the river Dove, they asked Wildgoose to accompany them. But Lady Forester said, she would be glad of his company to attend her and Miss Sainthill in their walk into the park, after she had visited her young people in the nursery, and dispatched some domestic affairs which required her attendance.

Whilst his master was thus entertained in the parlour, Tugwell was entertaining the second-rate gentry in the servants' hall. The butler had given Jerry a horn of strong beer with his breakfast, which opened his heart and loosened his tongue. Jerry therefore, diverted the company with the adventure they had met with in their travels: how well they had fared at Alderman Cullpepper's, Justice Aldworth's, and Parson Griskin's; and also what perils they had gone through by land and by sea. He gave them likewise a sketch of his master's private life; the credit he had lived in at home, and the converts he had made in his travels; but gave hints, at the same time, that he thought him a little crack-brained sometimes; and that he himself was fool enough to leave his wife and a good trade, and ramble about the country upon such a *wildgoose* chase.

Whilst Tugwell was yet speaking, Mr Wildgoose was come, at Lady Forester's request, to the servants' hall, to examine and instruct her domestics in the principles of religion; and, hearing Tugwell prating full-speed about himself and his adventures, he shook his head: Ah, Jerry, says he, I was in hopes you were edifying these good people with some religious discourse, instead of entertaining them with your carnal buffooneries. I find thou hast not yet put off *the old man*, with his affections and lusts.—Well, well, master, says Jerry, being a little pot-valiant, if I am an *old man*, that is my misfortune, rather than my fault; we shall all be old men, or old women, if it please God we live long enough.

Mr Wildgoose then addressed himself to the servants, who had not quite finished their breakfast, and said, he was sure they had a very good master and mistress.—That we have, cried all of them with one voice, the best in England.—The butler, however, said he had one complaint against Sir William; that if he should dismiss him from his service, he had spoiled him for any other place, as he could never submit to the arbitrary and capricious treatment which servants met with from too many masters. Mrs Molly, who stood at the door, with her work in her hand, said she had a complaint of the same kind against her lady. Wildgoose replied, if that was all their complaint, he hoped they would not, like too many servants, make it their whole business, when they got together in their hall, to abuse their master and mistress, to waste their victuals, damage the furniture, notch the tables, and do all the little mischief in their power.

But, continued Wildgoose, we have all one great Master, of whose favour we ought to be more ambitious, and with a view to whose approbation and we ought to serve our earthly masters with fidelity and care.

Wildgoose then proceeded to ask each of the questions about the principles of religion; and found Lady Forester had taken great pains in instructing them; but as he thought them yet ignorant of the true faith, and the doctrine of the new birth (as he and Mr Whitfield understood it), he began to talk to them a little mysteriously on that subject when some of his expressions being necessarily capable of a *double* meaning, Mrs Molly cast down her eyes, but gave Mr George a side look, with a wanton archness; who, being apprehensive that the same tender glances might be directed where he would not wish them to be, told her, with a jealous surliness, that she had better go to her lady's dressing-room, or to the nursery, which was her proper sphere.

Lady Forester, indeed, now rang the bell; on which the servants all dispersed to their several stations; and, after her ladyship had given the housekeeper her necessary orders, she summoned Mr Wildgoose to attend her and Miss Sainthilll in their morning walk.

XVII
LADY FORESTER'S MORNING ENGAGEMENT

Lady Forester always made it a rule to answer every demand of *duty*, before she indulged herself in any kind of amusement; and accordingly went her circuit almost every morning amongst the poor people in the village, however she might be engaged the remaining part of the day. Having made up some linen for a poor woman that was near her time, her ladyship's first visit was made to *her*, to whom she delivered the bundle. As the woman had generally a child every year, Lady Forester had got the linen made of a strong new cloth, that it might serve for more than one child. The poor woman turned it about, and surveyed it with some attention; and, upon Lady Forester's asking her how she liked it? she said it was pretty coarse, but she believed it *might* do.

Miss Sainthill asked the woman, if she did not thank her ladyship for her trouble? The woman replied, Ah! my lady has so many maidens to work for her, it is no great trouble to she.

Wildgoose shook his head, and Lady Forester smiled, and proceeded to another cottage, where lived a poor woman, with seven or eight small children, almost naked, and who appeared to be half-starved.

Lady Forester inquired, why she had not sent for some broth for her children, as she used to do? The woman replied, Why, to tell you the truth, my lady, the broth is not so good as it used to be, since this new cook came.—I am sorry for that, says my lady; but what is the matter with it now?—Ah! cries the woman, Mrs Filch, the old cook, used to give a poor body a bit of meat now and then with one's broth. Mrs Filch had some charity, and was very good to the poor.

I am afraid not, says my lady; she was good to some of them when she was in the humour for it, and bad to others: she would give what was very improper to those that were her favourites, and send others away with reproaches and empty pitchers, just as the whim seized her; and that was a principal reason for my parting with her.

In the next house which they came to lived a poor man that had had an ague for some time; to whom Lady Forester had sent a cordial infusion of the bark. She inquired, how it agreed with him, and whether he had yet got rid of his ague?—The man replied, the stuff had done him no good at all.—Perhaps you did not take it regularly? says my lady.—Ah, no, replies the man; it was so *bitter*, I could not bear the taste of it. Lady Forester told him, all the virtue of it consisted in its bitterness; and, if he would not take that, there was no other remedy for an ague. The man said, then it must be as it pleased God; for he could not take *doctor's stuff*, if he died for it. And so they left him.

They now met a poor miserable-looking old fellow, who seemed to be just slipped out of an ale-house, which stood by the road side, near the end of the village. Well, John, cried Lady Forester, I am glad to see you abroad again; I thought your lameness had still confined you. How do you like the book which I sent you to read in your confinement?—I don't know, my lady; to be sure it is a very good book; but I have been so busy, I have not had time to read a word of it.

Wildgoose could not but observe, that her ladyship had been rather unsuccessful in her endeavours to do good amongst her poor neighbours; but added, that she would not lose her reward.

Lady Forester replied, she was sufficiently rewarded, in the consciousness of having discharged her duty. Wildgoose added, if her ladyship could but bring them to have a true faith, she would see the effects of it in bringing forth the fruits of the Spirit, meekness, humility, sobriety, and every Christian virtue.

Well, replied Lady Forester, that you may not think all my efforts entirely fruitless, I will take you to one of my more promising institutions.

XVIII

A SCENE MORE AGREEABLE THAN THE LAST

Lady Forester now took Wildgoose to a more neat, or rather an elegant habitation, on a little eminence near the park wall. There was a small court before it, planted with sweet herbs, shrubs, and flowers. On their approach the door immediately opened to them, and discovered near twenty little girls and boys, working or reading; and a genteel elderly woman in the midst of them instructing them in their needle-work or in their books.

The moment Lady Forester entered one of the little girls threw herself upon her knees before her and begged her ladyship not to send her home, and she would never be guilty of stubbornness any more. This, it seems, was a piece of discipline observed by the matron of the school, that when any of the children were refractory, and a slight punishment proved ineffectual, she turned them over to her ladyship's visitatorial authority, which kept them more in awe, than the severest corporeal chastisement would probably have done.

The children were all clean and neat; and their dress was reduced to a kind of uniform, by a sort of band, or handkerchief, with which they were presented when they came to the school: and, as the children were employed part of the day in weeding the garden, or other necessary business about the house, several useful servants had been sent out from this seminary, within the nine or ten years that Lady Forester had been in the neighbourhood.

Wildgoose asked the school-mistress, what religious books she taught the children; and whether she had met with any of Mr Wesley's excellent tracts for that purpose?—She replied, that she had taught them the Church Catechism, and a short Exposition of it; and endeavoured, from thence, to inculcate into them their duty to God, their neighbour, and themselves; but did not think children of that age capable of any speculative notions, or any of the mysterious doctrines of Christianity.

Wildgoose replied, that there had been of late many instances of children at five or six, nay, even at three years old, who had had great *experiences*, and had *assurance* of their sins being pardoned; and had also been favoured with visions and revelations of an extraordinary nature;[*] and that we had no reason to doubt, that even now, as well as in times of old, God could make even babes and sucklings instruments of his glory.

The school-mistress expressed some surprise at this discourse, as being ignorant of Wildgoose's peculiar character; but Lady Forester said, they were going to take a walk in the park; and so put a stop to the dialogue.

XIX

A SLIGHT ALARM

They were now come to one of the park gates, to which Lady Forester had a key. The park had a fine sylvan appearance, and they were beginning to admire the prospect, when they heard at some distance a most dismal outcry, of Help! help! Murder! murder! I shall be murdered. Wildgoose desired Lady Forester and Miss Sainthill to retreat back again to the park gate, and ran full speed to the assistance of the person in distress. Passing round a thicket of oaks, he saw, with astonishment, his friend Tugwell lying upon the ground, rolled up as round as a wood-louse, with his head between his knees, and guarding himself with his elbows; but could discover no visible cause of this terrible vociferation.

---

[*] Mr Wesley's *Journals, passim.*

At the same instant Mr Bob Tench, who, not getting any body to angle with him, had been poaching about the park with his gun, was running also to Jerry's assistance. Upon their calling to him once or twice, Jerry ventured to look up, and began to give an account of what had befallen him.

The case was, Tugwell being so little versed in the natural history of animals, as not to distinguish a stag from a jack-ass (which sufficiently appeared at his first setting out on his travels) he had rambled into the park, to see the deer; where, meeting with a large herd, one of them, which had been bred up as a tame fawn, advanced before the rest, and offered his forehead to be scratched; with which instance of familiarity Tugwell was at first highly delighted: but the young deer, who was now above a year old, waxing wanton, began by degrees to be more familiar than Jerry approved of; who, therefore, poking him off with his staff, the deer began to be in earnest, and drawing himself up, attacked Tugwell in front with great vehemence, and soon overset him; and when down, battered him with his young horns so furiously, that Jerry had good reason to cry our for assistance. The young pricket, however, at sight of Bob Tench, had made off, and joined the herd; so that Wildgoose thought his friend had again been alarmed, as he was at Cardiff, by the vain terrors of imagination.

Wildgoose now returned to find out the ladies, and acquaint them with the cause of the outcry they had heard; but they were so terrified, that they had run home, and alarmed the whole family, many of whom were by this time come to the park gate; and, being informed of the truth of the affair, were greatly diverted with the bastinado Jerry had received from the tame deer; and only lamented, that they had not come soon enough to be witness to the ludicrous operation.

But though Tugwell was not much damaged in his person by this accident, Sir William, for fear of the stag's becoming more mischievous, as his horns became more capable of doing mischief, ordered the poor animal to be shot at the first opportunity.

XX

THE LAWFULNESS OF EATING
A GOOD DINNER

It being now dinner-time, most of the company were assembled in the dining parlour, where (as Sir William kept a constant table) the cloth was laid, and the side-board set out with some degree of splendour. Wildgoose could not forbear making a comparison between the elegance with which Sir William lived, and the scenes of misery which they had just been viewing amongst the poor people in the village; and, addressing himself to Lady Forester, said, he ought not to indulge himself in *faring sumptuously*, whilst the poor miners were perishing for want of that spiritual food with which he had undertaken to supply them. Well, says Lady Forester, but there is a time for all things we will not detain you when you have fixed upon a plan of operation.—Why, I think, says the young Templar, it would he a proper act of mortification for the gentleman to set out upon his mission immediately, now dinner is coming upon the table; as I have heard Mr Wesley and his friends (when they first set up this scheme of reformation in the university) used frequently to bespeak a handsome dinner, and as soon as it was brought in, send it immediately to the prisoners in the Castle; and dined themselves upon dry bread and green tea.—Yes, says the colonel, but they know better, I believe, by this time; and are not often guilty of those popish austerities. They love feasting, as far as I can see, as well as other people.

Why, says Sir William, I do not apprehend it at all unlawful for the best Christian to frequent occasionally, the festival entertainments of their friends and acquaintance. If that were the case, our Saviour, instead of giving us prudential rules for our behaviour on those occasions (when thou art bidden to a wedding, go and sit down in the lowest room,) would probably have said, when thou art bidden to a wedding, do not go.

Pray, says Lady Forester, now you are talking divinity, what is become of our chaplain to-day, the parson of the parish?—Oh! says Mr Tench, I can tell your ladyship; he is gone to the Bowling-green club. I promised to attend the doctor thither; but forgot it till it was too late.—Ah, Mr Wildgoose, says Lady Forester, those are things that I disapprove of as well as you.—Madam, replies Wildgoose, I disapprove of those things, because I really have no relish for them; and if it would be as great a penance to me, if I were obliged play a whole afternoon at bowls, cards, or back-gammon, as it was to the primitive saint,★ to stand all night upon a pillar forty feet high; and I suppose your chaplain has no more taste for books or spiritual joys, than I have for those carnal amusements.

Sir, says Bob Tench, the doctor is a very learned man, and *publishes* something almost every month.—In the magazine, I presume? says Wildgoose.—No, in the church, replies Mr Tench; he *publishes* the banns of marriage between the lads and lasses who want to be joined together in holy matrimony.

As dinner was now upon table, all conversation began to grow insipid. Wildgoose, indeed, still kept harping upon the same string for some time, and said, that no one who had tasted the pleasures of a divine life, could any longer relish such trash as the amusements of this world generally were.—Mr Wildgoose, says Lady Forester, let me help you to some of this hashed calve's head. The savoury smell of this dish soon put to flight Mr Wildgoose's spiritual ideas. He accepted the calve's head; and began to fancy himself in the land of promise; and, with a true patriarchal appetite, he feasted most devoutly.

XXI

PROTESTANT NUNNERIES.
THE DISCONSOLATE WIDOW

Dinner being ended, Lady Forester's favourite topic, religion, was again brought upon the carpet; upon which subject, she and Miss Sainthill

---

★ Simon Stylites.

talked with pleasure. The colonel, however, could not bear with patience the compliment which he thought was paid to a mere vagabond in this respect; and at last said with some wrath, that he was of the same opinion, in regard to the Methodists, which Charles the Second was in regard to the Presbyterians—that there never was a *gentleman* of that religion, since the first propagation of it.

Sir William Forester replied, that he had always considered that observation of King Charles, if he really made it, as a compliment to the dissenters of that reign, when the *gentleman* meant a fellow of a genteel address, perhaps, and polite accomplishments; but who would drink, whore, or debauch the wife of his friend or companion; and, when called to an account for it, run him through the body without any more ceremony.

Miss Sainthill, out of opposition to the colonel, took the part of the Methodists with some spirit—to all which the man of war only replied in the words of Hamlet—

Get thee to a nunnery, Ophelia; get thee to a nunnery.

So I would, says Miss Sainthill, if there were in England any such thing as a Protestant nunnery; and I could spend my life, in such a situation, with great satisfaction.

Why, says Rappee, I should think it a very proper way of disposing of some part of your sex—of the old and the ugly; of old maids, and of young women who were too homely to get themselves husbands.— And, I assure you, says Miss Sainthill, I should think it a very happy refuge from the impertinence of fools and coxcombs, with which the world abounds.

Why, says Lady Forester, jesting apart, Miss Sainthill and I have often been laying a plan for an asylum of this kind; and I cannot think, if there were such an institution, in every country, under proper regulations, it would be attended with any bad effects. I do not mean to draw in young thoughtless creatures upon every disappointment in love; or young women, who might be useful in the world, as servants, milliners, or mantua-makers, and other necessary employments; but as a refuge for young ladies of good families and small fortune, who are now forced to live in a dependent state, or, perhaps, to take up with matches of mere convenience, which make them miserable their whole lives.

There should be a proper succession of working, reading, and amusement. They should enter voluntarily into them, and not before a certain age, as thirty or forty, suppose; yet to guard against the caprice and inconstancy of human nature, they should be under some little restraint, and not be released from their engagement, without some considerable forfeit for the good of society. The number should be limited; and, to make it an honourable situation, the queen, perhaps, for the time being, or some of the royal family, would vouchsafe to patronise these institutions; who should also have a power of visiting them, and be the judges of the qualifications of persons to be admitted, and of the causes for which they might plead to be released.

Well, says the young Templar; but, by a statute of the 27th year of Harry the Eighth, all monasteries, nunneries, and religious houses, are for ever dissolved; and I do not imagine any thing of this kind could be established without an act of Parliament.

Ah! says the colonel, in his common-place way, and besides,

Vows of virginity should well be weigh'd;
Too oft they're broke, tho' in a convent made.

There was a widow in ——shire, the other day, who was so disconsolate upon the loss of her good man, that she made a *vow*, not only to live single, but absolutely to renounce the world, and never to behold the face of a man again.

To sooth her melancholy she sat constantly in her dressing-room, with her curtains half-drawn; and, with folded hands, kept contemplating a miniature picture of her husband, fixed in the pedestal of a little pyramid, or mausoleum, formed of her jewels; which she had gotten worked up into that form, and placed upon her toilette, from morning to night.

After carrying on this farce for near three months, some affairs respecting her jointure, which was very large, made it absolutely necessary for her to go to London. When she took coach for that purpose, her men servants were ordered to be out of sight; and she was handed in, veiled, by her own maid.

A friend of mine, in the guards, who though not personally known to her, was (by means of a servant who had lived in the family) acquainted with every circumstance of her fortune and the present state of her mind (by a few half-crowns properly applied,) got intelligence of her intended journey, and of all her motions. My friend, therefore, contrived to meet her equipage at the first stage: and taking his station in the bar, as soon as the dowager's maid stepped out of the coach, he flies to the step; thrusts the Abigail aside; and, with a gallant yet submissive air, seized the lady's hand, and offered to conduct her to the parlour.

At the sight of a man, even through her veil, she gave a faint scream, and affected to be extremely angry with her maid for deserting her in such a manner. She felt something contagious, however, in the touch of a handsome young fellow in his regimentals; and, though she charged her servant to be more careful for the future, her curiosity prompted her to inquire, whether she knew who the gentleman was? then repeated her charge, to make sure that the coast was clear, at the next inn they came to, before she got out of the friend staid and dined at the inn as the lady also did; and suffered the carriage to set out before him; but ordered his servant (by means of a bowl of punch with which he treated the lady's coachman) to get strict information, where and at what inn they were to lie that evening.

Nay, as her servants had no idea of the lady's delicate distress on the loss of her spouse, they considered her behaviour as mere affectation; and as that sort of gentry are always pleased with such cheerful events as promote feasting and jollity, were much inclined to facilitate a good understanding between their lady and so generous a lover.—They contrived, therefore, a stratagem to overcome the dowager's reserve, and to lay her under a necessity of another interview with the captain, by loosening some of the traces of the carriage, and, when my friend overtook them, by alarming the poor lady with an outcry of danger; which forced her to get out of the coach, whilst they pretended to set matters to rights. At this instant the captain made his appearance, leaped off his horse, and again handed the lady out of her carriage. She could not avoid admitting him to converse with her, whilst they stood waiting for her equipage in the public road. The captain made the best use of his time; ogled, sighed, and played all the artillery of love so effectually, that the lady condescended at length to thank him for his civilities; and added, if he *happened* to go to the same inn, she would be glad of his company to sup with her.

In short, there was so close an intimacy commenced from that evening, that when the poor dowager came to town, she found her affairs so perplexed, and herself (a poor helpless woman) so little able to conduct them, that she began to consult with her maid, whom she had best call in to her assistance. Mrs Abigail had seen too much of the rapid progress of her lady's passion, to hesitate on the choice, and immediately determined that the captain was the only man in the world for her purpose.

In short, the exigence of her affairs was such, and her *distress* so urgent, that she thought any longer delay would be quite imprudent. So that, in less than six months, she laid aside her weeds, had her *jewels new set*, married the captain, and was as fond of her second spouse as she had been of her first.

XXIII

FRAILTY NOT CONFINED TO FEMALES

Well, says Lady Forester, and what do you infer from this gossiping tale? That women are poor frail creatures, and do not thoroughly know their own hearts; but frequently act contrary to their best-formed resolutions?

Yes, says Wildgoose, and we are all equally frail and impotent, without the assistance of the Divine Spirit. This lady, indeed, seemed sensible of her own weakness, by her first resolution to avoid the very sight of a man for the future: for there is no security, but by guarding every avenue of the soul against the approach of our spiritual adversary.

I am afraid, however, says Sir William, there are as many instances of frailty to be met with in ours, as in that which is called the *softer* sex. The lady whom the colonel has mentioned, was guilty of a very common, and, I suppose, a very innocent frailty. She buried one husband, and married another. But there has lately happened a very shocking instance of frailty, or rather of an irregular indulgence of the passions, in one of our sex; the particulars of which (as I believe it was in his neighbourhood) Mr Wildgoose, perhaps, may be able to inform us of; I mean, the dreadful story of Sir W. Keyte, who in a fit of jealousy (as I have heard) burnt himself and a magnificent house, which he had built to please the fancy of an imperious mistress, whom he kept; though he had really been as fond of his own lady, as the dowager (Colonel Rappee talks of) was of her husband.

Wildgoose replied, that the particulars of that affair were known to all the neighbourhood in which *he* lived: but the catastrophe was too tragical to entertain so cheerful a company. Yet, says he, if Sir William desires it, I will take some opportunity of relating the whole progress of that affair.

The ladies, according to a laudable custom, now leaving the gentlemen at liberty to enjoy a more liscentious conversation, and to drink bumpers; and neither Sir William nor his company being disposed to make use of that indulgence; they also soon after dispersed; and Sir William invited Mr Wildgoose to accompany them to a very romantic place (which he was going to show to the young Templar,) being the seat* of a gentleman in the neighbourhood, where the river Manifold, after running three or four miles under ground, bursts forth from a hollow rock in the garden, which is laid out with grottoes and cascades, suitable to so grotesque a scene.

Wildgoose would have declined this gratification of his curiosity, but for the sake of a small lead-mine, which Sir William told him they should pass near in their walk thither; where he thought he might reconnoitre the ground, in order to begin his operations at the first opportunity.

---

* Ilam, the seat of Mr Porter, now well known to people of taste in most parts of the kingdom.

The colonel, conscious of the advantageous figure he made on horse-back, chose to ride, attended only by his servant. But Bob Tench accompanied them, for the sake of throwing his fly by the way, and angling for trout in the river Dove: and one or two of the servants took Tugwell as far as the lead-work, notwithstanding his bruises from the tame deer in the morning, in hopes of having some sport with him when they came thither.

XXIII

Wonders of the Peak

One of the servants that attended Tugwell in his walk was the old gardener, who was a man of some humour; and had read many books of travels and of natural history, as well as those which more immediately related to his own profession. He entertained Jerry, as they went along, with some account of the wonders of the Peak; which, he said, they would see, if he and his master went with the company to-morrow, as he found his lady intended they should.

The gardener told him, there was a hill called Mam-torre (as big as any of the Welsh mountains which he had been talking of) that was continually mouldering and shivering down earth and parts of the rock; and yet neither was the hill visibly diminished, nor the valley beneath raised up, in the memory of man.

There is also a perpendicular chasm, or opening into the very bowels of the earth, called Elden-hole, above fifty feet wide; and which has been fathomed above eight hundred yards, and no bottom discovered.

Then there is Chatsworth, the finest house in England, belonging to the Duke of Devonshire. The frames of the windows are all gilded with gold; and the gardens are the most beautiful that can be conceived.

Well! but where is the Devil's A-se o'Peak, which they talk so much of! says Tugwell. Why that is the greatest curiosity of all, says the gardener. It is a monstrous cavern, as high as the inside of a cathedral church, at the bottom of a prodigious mountain. In the mouth of the cavern are several cottages, where the poor people make pack-thread, &c. and across it run three different streams, which are lost under ground. Two of them you may pass over in a flat-bottomed boat: but the rock closes almost entirely over the third; so that it is generally thought to be impassable. This, however, a man of great curiosity once ventured to pass over, laying himself flat on his face in the boat, and being shoved over by his companions; but he was near a whole day before he returned.

And what, *the dickens*! did he see, says Tugwell, when he got thither?

Why, says the gardener, as soon as he landed, he came into a fine green meadow, not covered with grass, but paved with green emeralds; at the extremity of which was a large city, inhabited by people about a span long. Upon inquiring the name of the country, he found they understood his language, and did not seem much surprised at his appearance; having often seen and conversed with the inhabitants of this outward surface of the globe, in the remoter parts of their dominions: for, you must know, the place where he landed was the mineral kingdom, and the town which he saw, the capital city of the King of Diamonds. They are a race of fairies, that preside over the different productions of the mines: not only gold, silver, copper, lead, and all the useful metallic ores; but also the precious stones which mortals are so fond of, diamonds, rubies, emeralds, sapphires, and the like: which they crystallize, ripen, purify, and refine, by incessant chemical operations in the bowels of the earth. Their city was surrounded with walls of common agate or cornelian; the gates were either brass or iron; their houses were built of different-coloured precious stones; regard being chiefly had to their several ranks or professions. The royal palace was of rubies and garnets, the doors of gold and silver. The bishops' houses were of purple amethysts, those of the inferior clergy of blue or sapphires, and so on: though most of them were lined with cornelian, or some stone that was not transparent, to keep out the scorching rays of the sun, and to prevent the inspection of their impertinent neighbours. They set no great value upon diamonds, on account of their want of colour; but prepared them chiefly for traffic. They had plenty of the finest liquors;

their conduits ran with a liquor called nectar, honey-water, and eau-de-luce; and their springs with the most spirited mineral waters, such as Spa or Pyrmont produce. But, it being very hot weather, our poor adventurer would rather have had one quart of small beer, than all the gold and precious stones in the universe.

Well, says Tugwell, but how the deuce did he get back again?

You shall hear, says the gardener. He was going to pocket a few loose diamonds, with which the highways were mended, and to pluck up an old silver gate-post, when he found himself pinched all over his body, and received a great blow upon his back, with a stone; and the boat was driven down the stream to a good landing-place, where he returned to his companions; being uncertain whether he had not fallen asleep in his passage, and whether what he saw was a dream or a reality.

This strange description put Jerry in mind of the Utopia of school-boys; he said, he had rather have gone into the country which he had heard of, where the houses are built with plumb-cake, or gingerbread, and thatched with pan-cakes; the streets paved with apple-dumplings; and where the roasted pigs ran about with knives and forks stuck in their buttocks, crying, Come, eat me! Come, eat me! Though I should like to see the *mineral kingdom* too, says Jerry, if I could see it without crossing the water.

XXIV

VIEW OF A LEAD MINE

They were now come to the lead-mine, at the bottom of a high hill; where they saw only three miners, who were winding up a basket of ore; but the gardener told Jerry, there were probably twenty more under ground; and that he had better go down and preach to them, or at least prepare them a little for what his master had to say to them when he came; and then you will see something of the mineral kingdom into the bargain.

As Jerry had heard Wildgoose harangue so often on the same subject, he
was a little conceited in his own proficiency, and really fancied he could
almost equal his master; and seemed at first well enough pleased with
the compliment that was paid him. But when he approached the shaft or
mouth of the mines, he was greatly terrified at the appearance; and said,
for his part, he did not pretend to preach; that God had not bestowed
upon him the gift of utterance, and of understanding hard words; but that
he only went with Mr Wildgoose for company's sake, who, he did not
doubt, would some time or other pay him for his trouble.

Well, says the old gardener, but as your master may not come in time,
you would not suffer so many poor souls to perish, for want, perhaps,
of what little instruction you can give them.—Tugwell replied, he was
nothing but a poor cobbler, and it was not his business to *save souls*.—
That's true, says the gardener, as you are a cobbler; but, as you pretend to
be a Methodist, you ought to preach 'in season and out of season,' above
ground or under ground, wherever you have an opportunity.

'Sblood! cries Jerry, with a licentious air, I am no Methodist, I tell
you; and would not go down into such a hole as this, to save all the
souls in purgatory.

The servants, however, as soon as the miners had emptied their load,
winked upon them, and made signs to put Tugwell in the basket, which
two of them very dexterously performed, notwithstanding Jerry laid
about him, and made great resistance; and the third got into the basket
with him, and held him fast, whilst the other two, by means of the
windlass, let them several fathoms down the shaft; Tugwell roaring out,
like a mad bull, as he descended into the horrid chasm.

Just at that instant Mr Wildgoose, attended by Bob Tench (having left
the company as soon as they had taken a slight view of the romantic
gardens at Ilam) came to the lead-mine, and hearing the outcry,
inquired with some eagerness what was the matter? The gardener told
them, that they had persuaded Mr Tugwell to go down and preach to
the miners; but that now he was got into the shaft, he seemed a little
frightened at the manner of going down.

Wildgoose, being no stranger to Jerry's want of courage in adventures
of that unusual kind, was apprehensive of some bad consequences; he,

therefore, desired them to wind him up again; which, upon Bob Tench's likewise insisting upon it, they immediately performed: so that Jerry saw but little of the mineral kingdom.

As soon as Tugwell was safely landed again, he began rubbing his fists and spitting in his hands, and challenged to fight any two of the miners who had treated him in that treacherous manner; when, perceiving his master (who attempted to moderate his resentment,) Jerry fell foul upon him with bitter complaints; and said, if Mr Wildgoose had a mind to preach to the miners, he should go by himself; for he would not be buried alive upon other people's business; and, I am sure, adds Jerry, if I had gone much lower, the cold damps would have taken away my breath.—Well, says Wildgoose, I don't desire you to run any risque; but I myself will immediately go down amongst these poor people, and open my commission; and they shall not remain one night longer under the dominion of Satan.

Wildgoose then desired the miners to let him down the shaft, as he understood there were several more of their fellow-labourers under ground. But the miners then told him, that there were no more than themselves there, and that the mine had been under water for this week past; and that they had been employed to bring away some ore, that was left in a cavity about half way down the shaft; and that they only took the other honest man, (meaning Tugwell,) to frighten him a little, by way of diversion. Wildgoose, therefore, having asked them some few questions more, he, Mr Tench, and the rest of the company, returned towards Sir William Forester's.

Tugwell, by not submitting to his fate with Christian patience, had got a broken head in the scuffle; which, though he did not perceive it at first, bled pretty freely. But, as Bob Tench was never at a loss for expedients, and had always a little phial of Friar's Balsam in his pocket, some gold-beater's skin and court-plaister, as well as his cork-screw and mohock, he soon set Jerry's skull to rights; and stopped the bleeding.

Upon Wildgoose's lamenting his disappointment in not finding any number of people at the lead-mine, the old gardener told him how precarious those operations were; that a great copper-mine in that neighbourhood, which had brought in six thousand pounds a year, was now under water, and would probably be the ruin of a very worthy family: that one gentleman had spent eight or nine hundred pounds in quest of a vein of ore, and was then obliged, for want of money, to desist: another gentleman pursues the same work, and within two feet of the spot where the former adventurer had left off, discovers a rich vein, and makes a fortune of ten thousand pounds.—Ah, says Wildgoose, I wish people would seek after righteousness, as they do after silver; and search after true religion as they do after hidden treasures.—Troth, says Tugwell, I had rather work for eight-pence a-day above ground, than venture down into a mine for all the hidden treasure in the world.

As they went along, Bob Tench left them for an hour, to angle upon the Dove for trout; and it being a fine calm evening, he soon caught a brace and a half, which he brought home in triumph; and said, that was the finest prospect he had seen today.

XXV

BEAUTIES OF NATURE

Sir William and the young Templar, and the other parties, all came to the rendezvous pretty near the same time. When they were come into the parlour and sat down, Mr Wildgoose appearing rather more serious than usual, Lady Forester said, he seemed tired with his walk, and asked him how he liked Ilam? Wildgoose answered, it was certainly a most romantic place, and he enjoyed prospects of that kind as much as any one formerly. But—But what? says Miss Sainthill, with some quickness. Why, to be sure, replies Wildgoose, the natural man cannot but be delighted with these terrestrial beauties; yet, considered in a religious light, these stupendous rocks and mountains appear to me as the ruins of a noble palace, designed for man in a state of innocence; and I own it makes me serious, when I reflect on the fallen state of mankind; and that the whole creation suffers for our guilt, and groaneth for redemption.

Well, says Lady Forester, all this may be true; but you don't think it any sin to be charmed with the beauties of nature? You say, the *natural man* is delighted with them; that is, every thing great, beautiful, or uncommon, is *naturally* agreeable to the imagination; and I can never think it unlawful to enjoy, under proper restrictions, what Providence has formed us for enjoying.

No, says Miss Sainthill, if it were, David must have been a very wicked man, who always speaks with rapture of the beauty of nature, of the magnificence of the heavenly bodies, the moon and stars, which thou hast created, the variety of seasons thou hast made, summer and winter; the sweet approach of even and morn! Thou that makest the out-goings of the morning and evening to praise thee. 'O Lord, how manifold are thy works!' says he, 'in wisdom hast thou made them all.'

Well prayed, Miss Sainthill, cries the colonel. Why, Lady Forester has no occasion for a chaplain; you quote chapter and verse as well as the best divine in Christendom.

Supper now appeared, and the *natural man* again resuming his place in Mr Wildgoose, he ate as heartily as the best of them. After supper, when they had taken a glass or two round, Sir William put Mr Wildgoose in mind of the promise he had made, to give them the particulars of Sir William Keyte's unhappy affair.

Wildgoose replied, that he could not, without some reluctance, recollect so tragical a story, which concerned a family for whom he had a great regard. But, says he, as the thing is public, and shows in a striking light the dreadful consequences of irregular indulgences, and also how corrupt the *natural man* is when destitute of divine grace, I will relate the particulars with as much brevity as I can.

XXVI

NARRATIVE OF A LICENTIOUS AMOUR

Sir William Keyte was a baronet of very considerable fortune, and of an ancient family; and on his return from his travels, had so amiable a character, and was reckoned what the world calls so fine a gentleman, that he was thought a very desirable match for a worthy nobleman's daughter in the neighbourhood, of great beauty, merit, and a suitable fortune.

Sir W. and his lady lived very happily together for some years, and had four or five fine children; when he was unfortunately nominated, at a contested election, to represent the borough of W—r—k; in which county the bulk of his estate lay, and where he at that time resided. After the election, as some sort of recompense to a zealous partisan of Sir W.'s, Lady Keyte took an inn-keeper's daughter for her own maid. She was a tall, genteel girl, with a fine complexion, and an appearance of great modesty and innocence.

Molly I——n (which was her name) had waited on Lady Keyte for some time, before Sir W. appeared to take the least notice of her; though Lady Keyte (perhaps from some sparks of jealousy, and to try how Sir W. stood affected) would frequently observe, what a fine girl Molly I——n was grown: to which Sir W.'s usual reply was, that he saw nothing extraordinary in the girl; and even affected to speak slightingly of her person, and to censure her awkwardness and her vanity; for which, as there was not the least foundation, Sir W. probably intended it to conceal his real sentiments.

After some time, however, the servants in the family began to entertain some suspicions, that Molly I——n was too highly in her master's favour. The housekeeper in particular (who in the course of forty years had been actually engaged in at least forty intrigues) soon perceived there was too much foundation for these suspicions. Knowing, therefore, that the butler had himself made overtures to Molly, she set him to work, whose jealousy made him so vigilant, that he soon discovered the whole of the affair; and that it had proceeded much further than was at first apprehended. The housekeeper (as that sort of gentry are apt to triumph in the indiscretions of young people) made use of the butler's name, as well as his intelligence, to her lady; and this threw every thing into confusion.

Lady Keyte's passion soon got the better of her discretion. For if, instead of reproaching Sir W. with his infidelity, she had dissembled her resentment, till his first fondness for their new object had abated (which, for her own sake, as well as that of her children, she ought to have done) she might probably have reclaimed her husband; who, notwithstanding this temporary defection, was known to have a sincere regard and esteem for his lady.

The butler's officious sedulity, however, had like to have been fatal to the poor fellow. For his name being mentioned as having made the discovery, and Molly I——n having told Sir W. that he was only piqued at her rejecting his addresses, Sir W. went up into the servants' apartment the very next night, and ran his sword several times through the bed where the butler used to lie; who had, for some reason or other, changed his lodging, and happily escaped his destruction. And this rash proceeding of Sir W. shows how true it is, that whoever offends against the laws of God in one point, is often, in a literal sense, guilty of violating the whole law.

XVII

The narrative continued

The affair being now publicly known in the family, and all restraints of shame, or fear of discovery, being quite removed, things were soon carried to extremity between Sir W. and his lady, and a separation became unavoidable. Sir W. left Lady Keyte, with the two younger children, in possession of the mansion-house in W——shire, and retired himself, with his mistress, and his two eldest sons, to a large farmhouse on the side of the Cotswold-hills. The situation was fine, with plenty of wood and water, and commanded an extensive view of the vale of Evesham. This tempted him to build a handsome box there, with very extensive gardens, planted and laid out in the expensive taste of the age: and, not content with this, before the body of the house was quite finished, Sir W. added two large side-fronts (if I may so express it) for no better a reason, as I could hear, but that his mistress happened to say, 'What is a kite without wings?'

I mention these particulars, because I believe the expense of finishing this place (which was at least ten thousand pounds) was the first cause of Sir W.'s encumbering his estate; and the difficulties in which he was involved making him uneasy, he, as is too natural, had recourse to the bottle for relief. Sir W. kept, what is called, a hospitable house, and too many people being fond of the freedom and jollity which is usually found at a table where no lady presides,★ he was seldom without company, which brought on a constant course of dissipation and want of economy; by which means Sir W.'s affairs, in a few years, became almost desperate though, it must be confessed, Mrs I——n, in her situation, behaved with great care and frugality.

Well; Sir W. was now turned of fifty, and his eldest son (the present Sir J——s) being grown up and returned from the university, Sir W. instead of sending him abroad, or giving him the advantages which a young man of his rank might have expected, kept him at home, and made him a witness, and, in some measure, a partaker of his debaucheries; and, what is most to be lamented, in a temporal view, drew him in, by some plausible pretence, or wrong indulgence, to part with his reversionary right to his mother's jointure, which was very considerable, and almost the only part of the estate which had not been already mortgaged for its full value.

XXVIII

ITS FATAL EVENT

But to hasten to the catastrophe of my tale. There was taken into the family about this time, a fresh-coloured country girl, in the capacity of a dairymaid, with no other beauty than what arises from the bloom of youth; and, as people who once give way to their passions, and are

---

★ It was a point of decency at this time, not to bring a mistress amongst strangers. I believe the custom is now altered.

unrestrained by grace, know no bounds, Sir W. in the decline of life, conceived an amourous regard for this girl, who was scarce twenty. This event produced still further confusion in the family. Mrs I———n soon observed this growing passion; and, either from resentment, or from the apprehension, or, perhaps, the real experience of ill usage, thought proper to retire to a little market-town in the neighbourhood; where she was reduced to keep a little sewing-school for bread.—Aye, and good enough too for such hussies, cried some of the ladies.

Well, continued Wildgoose, young Mr Keyte, whether shocked at this unparalleled infatuation of his father, or, as was commonly said, finding himself considered as a rival in the affections of this poor creature, sought an asylum, and spent most of his time with Lord L———, a friend of his, in W———shire.

Sir W. though he had now a prospect of being successful in this humble amour, and of indulging it without molestation; yet began at length to see the delusive nature of all vicious pursuits; and, though he endeavoured to keep up his spirits, or rather to drown all thought by constant intoxication, yet in his sober intervals he became a victim to gloomy reflections. He had injured a valuable wife, which he could not even now reflect upon without some remorse: he had wronged his innocent children, whom he could not think upon without the tenderest sentiments of compassion. His son, who had been a sort of companion to him for some years, had now left him, through his ill usage. And, as she had been for some time useful to him, he was shocked at being deserted even by the woman for whose sake he had brought this distress upon his family; and he found himself almost alone in that magnificent but fatal mansion, the erecting and adorning of which had been the principal cause of ruining his fortune.

Tormented by these contending passions, he had, for a week past, raised himself, by constant inebriation, to a degree of phrenzy; and had behaved in so frantic a manner, that even his new favourite, the poor Blowselinda, could bear it no longer, and had eloped from him.

On the morning of the day on which he executed his fatal resolution, Sir W. sent for his son and for his new mistress; with what intention can only be conjectured; but luckily, neither of them obeyed the summons.

Early in the evening (it being in the month of October, I think) the butler had lighted two candles (as usual), and set them upon the marble table in the hall. Sir W. came down and took them up himself, as he frequently did. After some time, however, one of the house-maids ran down stairs in a great fright, and said, the lobby was all in a cloud of smoke. The servants, and a tradesman that was in the house upon business, ran immediately up, and, forcing open the door, whence the smoke seemed to proceed, they found Sir W. had set fire to a large heap of fine linen, piled up in the middle of the room, which had been given by some old lady, a relation, as a legacy to his eldest son. Whilst the attention of the servants was entirely taken up with extinguishing the flames in this room, Sir W. had made his escape into an adjoining chamber, where was a cotton bed, and which was wainscoted with deal, as most finished rooms then were. When they had broken open this door, the flames burst out upon them with such fury, that they were all glad to make their escape out of the house; the principal part of which sumptuous pile was, in a few hours, burnt to the ground; and no other remains of Sir W. were found the next morning, than the hip-bone, and the *vertebræ*, or bones of the back; with two or three keys, and a gold watch, which he had in his pocket.

This was the dreadful consequence of a licentious passion, not checked in its infancy; or rather, thus may every unregenerate man expect to be drawn on from one degree of wickedness to another, when deserted by the Spirit, and given up to his own imaginations.

XXIX

A REMEDY AGAINST SUICIDE

Well, says Colonel Rappee, we are obliged to the gentleman for his story—and for a sermon into the bargain.—Why, it is a very serious affair, says Sir William, for a man to destroy himself, and rush into the presence of his offended Judge, with all his sins and follies unrepented of about him.—The colonel replied, if life was given as a blessing, when it ceased to be such, he thought a man might resign it again, without offence to any one.—Yes, yes, says Sir William, if he were under no obligations to any law, either of nature, or reason, or society: not to mention the revealed will of God, by which all murder is forbidden. But I would desire no other argument against self-murder, continues Sir William, than its being contrary to the very first law of nature, self-preservation, and its shocking the natural feelings and common apprehensions of all mankind.

The young Templar said, that as suicide was the most horrid of all murders, a friend of his proposed to have it punished as other heinous murders are.—How is that? says the colonel.—Why, by being hanged in chains, says the Templar.—O, says Sir William, but that would be rather a punishment to his surviving family, than to the deceased offender.—Yes, says the Templar, and that is the very thing proposed; as the thoughts of bringing such a reproach upon his innocent wife and children would probably restrain many a man from so rash an action, who was deaf to every other consideration.—Well, says Miss Sainthill, but this penalty would be no restraint upon you and me, colonel—upon old maids and old bachelors.

The colonel was going to make some reply, when the attention of the company was attracted by a burst of loud laughter from the servants' hall; and a sort of riotous mirth not usual in Sir William's family. Miss Forester, attended by Mr Bob Tench, took upon her to go and inquire into the cause of this boisterous merriment. When they came to the door of the servants' apartment, they found it was Tugwell who had 'set the table in a roar,' by getting upon the end of it, and holding forth in imitation of his master and Mr Whitfield.

The truth was, Jerry being pretty thirsty after his long walk, and the numerous perils he had undergone that day, the butler plied him with strong beer, till he began to wax mellow; in which state of things, Jerry thought proper to mount the table, and harangue in praise of *temperance*; and, in short, proceeded so long in recommending *sobriety*, and in tossing off horns of ale, that he became as drunk as a piper. This inconsistency of conduct exposed our orator (as it has done more respectable characters) to the ridicule of his audience; so that the cook had made so free with the preacher, as to pin a dish-clout to his rump; and the other servants, in their different ways, had offered Jerry many indignities. Nay, they proceeded so far at last, as to give him the strappado, or ancient discipline of the boot, with no feeble arm upon his posteriors; and then conveyed him hand and foot, like a dead pig, decently to bed.

When Miss Forester returned into the parlour, she laughed to herself, and whispered Lady Forester in the ear. Sir William asked Bob Tench what was the cause of all that noise below stairs? Bob cast a sneering look at Wildgoose, as if he were answerable for the absurdities of his comrade, and said, Mr Wildgoose's friend was entertaining the company with a dissertation upon *sobriety*; but his long walk, and a horn or two of ale, were a little too much for him.

Wildgoose could not forbear blushing at the indiscretion of his fellow-traveller; being sensible that he must rather injure the cause than promote it, as his zeal was probably much greater than his knowledge or his abilities.

XXX

LOVE TRIUMPHANT OVER SENSUALITY

It being now bed-time, Mrs Molly brought candles for the ladies; and in allusion to what had passed in the servants' hall, simpered upon Wildgoose. But there was something so lascivious in her smiles, that he considered it as almost an act of sensuality to return them, which yet it was almost impossible to avoid.

The gentlemen sat talking near half an hour after the ladies were gone, and then retired to their several apartments. When Wildgoose was got to his chamber, had shut the door, and was going to his devotions by the bed-side, he was surprised with the sight of a pink petticoat, a cotton gown, a pair of white stockings, and some green stuff shoes, thrown carelessly upon the floor; and, upon looking within the curtains, saw a girl, as he thought, in a laced night-cap, her face turned from him, and, as he supposed, fast asleep. Wildgoose was struck silent with astonishment at first; but imagining that Mrs Molly, who had ogled him so frequently since he came, had laid this snare for his virtue, he broke out into this kind of soliloquy:—Ah! wretch that I am; I have brought this poor creature to the very brink of destruction, by my own carnal concupiscence. I have encouraged her amorous wishes, by returning her wanton glances, instead of nipping her hopes in the bud, by a severity of countenance, as I ought to have done. But how shall I resist such a temptation! The spirit is willing; but the flesh is weak. I can renounce the world, and defy the devil. But the flesh—O, the flesh is weak, Heaven protect me! Whilst he was uttering this rhapsody, he, by an almost involuntary motion, pulled Miss Townsend's cambric handkerchief out of his pocket; the ambrosial scent of which immediately revived her agreeable idea, and the tender sentiments which Mr Wildgoose entertained for that lady, and gave a new turn to his thoughts.—But O! wretch that I am, continues he, how can I forget the kind looks and modest blushes of the incomparable Miss Townsend, and be guilty of any act of infidelity to so amiable a lady? Avaunt, Beelzebub! Get thee behind me, Satan, says he, with a vehement emphasis; which threw the counterfeit Mrs Molly into a fit of laughter: and out leaped Tom the stable-boy, whom the butler had got to act this farce, and, running to the chamber-door, joined Mr George, and some others of the servants who were in the secret, and who were waiting in the lobby for the event of their stratagem.

Mr Wildgoose stared with surprise, and was at first a little angry at the joke which was put upon him. But immediately recollecting that he had invited this insult by his own indiscretion, he thought it best to take no further notice of it. He, therefore, went to bed; but was kept awake an hour or two, by his vexation at this incident, and other meditations of various kinds.

XXXI

MORE NOCTURNAL PERILS

Mr Wildgoose was just composing himself to sleep, however, when he heard his door open again, and was afraid of some real attack upon his chastity, when, to his astonishment, he heard the lamentable voice of his friend Tugwell.—Master Wildgoose, Master Wildgoose! says he, for God's sake awake: I will not stay a moment longer in the house. Why, what is the matter? says Wildgoose.—Why, quoth Jerry, the house is haunted, and the bedclothes are bewitched; and I would not go to bed again for a hundred pounds.—I am afraid, replies Wildgoose, thou art not sober yet, Jerry; for I hear thou gottest fuddled to-night in a most ungodly manner.—Ah, master, cries Jerry, I am as sober now as ever I was in my life, and have had two or three hours good sleep. But, I am sure, the bed is bewitched; for there was not a soul in the room besides myself, and a witch, or a spirit, kept pulling the bed-clothes off me, twenty times, as fast as I could pull them on me again: and I am certain it could be nothing but witchcraft.

The case was, the cook and the house-maid, by a common contrivance amongst girls who love to be playing tricks with young fellows, had tacked the bed-clothes together, and, by a long packthread fixed under the quilt, and brought under the door, as they went up to bed, had played off this piece of fun, to the terror and annoyance of poor Tugwell.

Mr Wildgoose desired Jerry to go to bed again till the morning, when he himself, he said, intended to depart; as he found the servants, instead of minding the things which belonged to their salvation, were all in a conspiracy to put tricks upon them, and to defeat their pious intentions.

Yes, says Jerry, and so are the miners too, as far as I can see; and I am for getting out of this heathenish country as fast as we can.

Why, says Wildgoose, Sir William and Lady Forester are very good people; but we have done wrong to entangle ourselves in the pleasures of this world; and, though I have promised to accompany them into the

Peak to-morrow, yet the servants, perhaps, may prejudice the miners against us. In short, says he, I am afraid, the hour is not yet come for their conversion. Therefore, Jerry, go you and lie down for an hour or two longer, and at dawn of day we will leave this place.

Tugwell, however, could not be prevailed upon to return to his own bed, which he considered as haunted by some invisible being, or evil spirit; but, putting on his clothes, and laying his wallet under his head, slept upon the carpet in his master's room.

As for Wildgoose, he composed himself for a few hours; but awaking between three and four o'clock, he roused his fellow-traveller, and they set out before any of the family was stirring.

Wildgoose left a note upon the table, expressing his obligations to Sir William and Lady Forester, and making an apology for his abrupt departure; but said, God had called him elsewhere; and the end for which he had come into the Peak being, as he thought, frustrated by some unexpected incidents, he would defer his visitation of the miners to some more favourable opportunity; when he hoped again to pay his respects to his worthy friends, Sir William and Lady Forester.

BOOK XI

I

THE TWO PILGRIMS DECAMP
WITHOUT BEAT OF DRUM

THE TWO PILGRIMS SET OUT from Sir William Forester's as was related, about four o'clock in the morning; and, as Tugwell did not know what his master's intentions were, he was much pleased to see him turn his face towards the south. He was surprised, however, to find him so easily give up his project of preaching to the miners in the Peak, with which view they had travelled so many tedious miles.

But the truth was, that besides his apprehensions lest the servants might make a ludicrous use of the adventure of the stable-boy whom the butler had put into his bed, Mr Wildgoose had a more powerful motive for hastening his departure towards the south. Mr Bob Tench, in their walk from Ilam, had told him, by way of conversation, that he had promised to attend Sir Harry Hotspur to Warwick races, which, he said, were within two or three days at farthest. Mr Wildgoose, therefore, having determined, as a *coup d'eclat*, to bear his testimony against those ungodly meetings, thought no opportunity could be more proper than the present, when he should have a good chance for an interview with Miss Townsend, for which he so eagerly longed.

Mr Wildgoose now travelled on for two or three hours in profound silence, reflecting on the disgrace he should probably bring upon himself, and the cause in which he was embarked, if the servants should maliciously misrepresent the ridiculous adventure above-mentioned.

At length, however, Jerry ventured to ask his master, what o'clock it was? Wildgoose looking at him with a serious air, answered,—Ah, Jerry, do not be so anxious to know the times and the seasons: for my part, continues he, I am resolved for the future, *to know nothing but Christ crucified*; nor, as far as I can answer for myself, ever to laugh again as long as I live, that I may not, by any levity of behaviour, inspire any weak Christian with wanton thoughts, nor give occasion for any suspicions to the prejudice of my own character.

I will tell you what, then, master; if you are resolved never to *laugh again*, you must never do two things more—you must never read Scoggran's *Jests*, nor ever hear the merry-andrew at Evesham fair; for they will make you burst your belly with laughter, in spite of your resolution. Wildgoose had almost broken his vow at first setting out; and could not but *smile*, at least, at Jerry's idea of wit and humour.

About eight o'clock our travellers came to a public-house, at a small distance from a nobleman's seat; where they thought it proper to halt and refresh themselves. There were two smart servants, with guns and pointers, in the kitchen, who, as well as the neighbouring seat, they found belonged to Lord B——, Lady Forester's father. The servants were going a partridge-shooting; and as soon as they marched out of the house, my landlord shook his head, and said, it was a shame to turn their pointers into the corn before the farmers had begun harvest.—Yes, says my landlady, they are a sad pack of them; they have debauched the whole country; there is hardly a sober man, or an honest woman, within ten miles of my lord's house. I do not desire their company here; for I know they only want to ruin my daughter, if they could have their will of her. Wildgoose thought this a melancholy contrast to the character of Lady Forester, the force of whose good example had diffused a spirit of religion and virtue as widely round, as her father's vicious principles had extended their baleful influence.

Wildgoose answered mine hostess, that he imagined my Lord B—— was a good-moraled man, though he knew he was no great friend to religion.—Yes, says she, my lord does some generous things, to be sure; but then there is no depending upon him: he will be very charitable to a poor man one day, and, if he happens to affront him, send him to gaol the next.

He almost starved our whole market-town last winter, to be revenged upon them for an affront which they had put upon his lordship.—How was that? says Wildgoose.—Why, says my landlady, he went and bought up three or four thousand pounds worth of coals (for my lord is very rich, you know); so that there was not a bit of coal to be got at any of the pits for ten miles round the place. This account confirmed Wildgoose in his opinion of the precarious nature of mere human virtues, when unsupported by principles of religion, or, as he called it, when void of faith or divine grace.

II

A LEARNED INN-KEEPER.
WILDGOOSE MEETS AN OLD ACQUAINTANCE

Mr Wildgoose and his fellow-traveller having had but little rest the preceding night, they made a short stage that day, lodging at a small public-house on the edge of the forest of Nedwood; and the next morning reached Litchfield again about eleven o'clock. They observed upon a sign there a Greek motto,★ to this purpose, *Either drink, or depart about your business*; which they imagined to have been supplied by some learned prebend, who either frequented or patronised the house. They complied with the first part of the precept, and *were drinking* a pint of ale upon a bench in the yard, when my landlord, who was a genteel sort of man, vouchsafed to speak to them, and soon finding that Wildgoose had had a liberal education, sat down by them, and began to inform them, that he himself had been bred at Cambridge as a physician, and had actually practised at Litchfield; but, finding the fees but small, and that, such as they were, they came in but slowly, he had married a young widow, who kept the inn. And here, says he, I see a good deal of genteel company: I am *master* of a good house; have the most amiable woman in the world for my wife, and live as happy as a king. Whilst my landlord was thus displaying the felicity of his situation, the amiable Mrs Brewer, his wife, rang the bar-bell with some vivacity; and, with no very melodious voice, cried out,—Dr Brewer, where are you? What the devil are you about? Why *don't-chee* come and shell some peas? Here's a family coming in, and you sit prating to your foot-passengers, who are drinking three-halfpenny-worth of mild-ale—forsooth!

★ Ἤ πίθι, ἤ ἄπιθι.

The doctor moved like clock-work at the sound of the bell and Mrs Brewer's voice; and told the travellers, he would wait upon them again immediately.

The case was just at that instant, there rode in, at the back-gate, a young man in a silver laced hat and a blue great-coat, and called the hostler with great authority. Here, master; here am I, says the hostler; who's a coming?—Who's a coming? why, I am coming, you puppy, says the young man.—Yes, master, I see you be, returns Robin: but what family, what equipage have you got? and how many stands shall you want for your horses?

My landlady, hearing the hostler ask these questions, took it for granted some grand family was at hand. But the gentleman who caused all this uproar, turned his horse into the stable, bade the hostler bring in his *saddle-bags*, and ordered a mutton-chop for his dinner.

As he passed by our two pilgrims upon the bench, Mr Wildgoose thought it was a face which he had seen before, and, indeed it was a pretty remarkable one; yet, being engaged with his own thoughts, he did not on a sudden glance recollect him. But the young man having got rid of his great-coat, (which, though in the midst of the dog-days, he had chiefly worn to conceal his saddle-bags on the road), he again exhibited himself at the door, when Wildgoose immediately knew him to be Mr Rouvill, or Beau Rueful, whom he had remembered at college, and met with at Bath.

As there were now no *persons of distinction* in the case, Rouvill did not disdain to recognise his old acquaintance. Wildgoose being now an itinerant by profession, Rouvill expressed no surprise at meeting him there: but Wildgoose asked Rouvill what had brought *him* to Litchfield?—Why, business of consequence, replies Rouvill; and, if you will dine with me here, I will explain the affair to you; and, indeed, should be glad to consult with you upon the subject.

Though Wildgoose was rather impatient to get into Warwickshire; yet, as the races did not begin till the day following, he had time enough upon his hands. He, therefore, accepted of Mr Rouvill's invitation.

III

THE LAST EFFORTS OF EXPIRING VANITY

When Mr Wildgoose and Rouvill were alone together, Rouvill acquainted him with his present situation; that having been jilted by a woman of fortune, whom he thought himself upon the brink of marrying, he had, in a fit of disappointment, married an agreeable woman with a few hundreds, who was really the widow who kept the house where he had lodged at Bath; that he was now determined to live a more retired and regular life; and, in order to that, had accepted of a presentation to a living, given him by one of the members for Coventry; and that he was now going to the bishop for orders.

To the bishop for orders! cries Wildgoose; what, in a laced hat?—O, says Rouvill, that is only to gain a little respect upon the road, as I could not conveniently bring my servant with me; but I shall immediately get that piece of finery ripped off, before I wait upon the bishop. I must confess, however, continues he, I have been so long accustomed to the gaiety of the world, and to dress like a gentleman, that I do not at all relish the peculiarity of the clerical habit. Indeed, I can see no reason why a clergyman should be distinguished from the rest of the world by such a funereal appearance, nor what connection there is between religion and a black coat, as if Christianity were such a gloomy affair, and so fatal an enemy to all kind of enjoyment.

Why, says Wildgoose, I do not imagine there is any virtue in a black coat; but it seems proper, by some external mark, to put the clergy in mind of the gravity and importance of their function; as also, to prevent their following the vain fashions of the world, and changing their dress according to the caprice of mankind, it seems advisable to confine them to some one particular habit, which, I have heard, was the common dress about the time of the reformation.

Well, says Rouvill, I can assure you I think it a great act of mortification for a young fellow of eight and twenty to give up so material an article as that of dress; and could not forbear expressing my sense of this hardship t'other day, in a ludicrous advertisement which I will show you. Rouvill then pulled out a smart morocco-leather pocket book, and read the following advertisement:

'Whereas, on Sunday last, (being Trinity-Sunday) between the hours of ten and twelve, two or three ill-looking fellows, disguised in *crape* (expressly contrary to the *black* act), did lay violent hands on a poor young gentleman, near the bishop's palace at B—d—n; putting him. in *bodily fear*, by bidding him *stand* and *answer* them several odd out-of-the-way questions; and did insist upon his taking several horrible oaths, and extort from him several unreasonable concessions, particularly that they, and all the gentlemen of their profession, were very honest, civil gentlemen (contrary to his real sentiments and their known practices), and had a right to treat in that manner, and impose their opinions upon, all that fell under their clutches; and moreover, did rob him of twelve and sixpence in money; and did strip him of all his wearing apparel, namely, a smart coat with a red silk lining, a laced waistcoat, and a pair of red breeches, with about half a dozen ruffled shirts, and as many pair of white stockings; and did even rip the silver button and loop off his hat.—Now, this is to give notice, that whoever will bring any of the said offenders to the two-faced pump in Oxford, or to any of the pumps, or horse-ponds, in Oxford or Cambridge, so that they may be brought to condign punishment, shall receive a handsome reward.

'*N. B.* The head of this gang is an old offender, and has followed these practices for many years; and has brought up several of his sons in the same idle way, who desired to follow some genteel trade, and to get their bread in some honest gentleman-like way of life.'

Well sir, says Wildgoose, there is no great harm in this piece of humour; I only think it a sort of jesting, which, as St Paul says, is not quite so convenient or decent, especially in a man that is going to the bishop for holy orders. Many a man has paid dearly for his jest. A candidate for the consulship at Rome, you know, lost his election, by jesting upon a poor mechanic for the roughness of his hand. However, I should think the change of character, which is expected in a clergyman a more weighty consideration than the mere change of dress; and that it is a greater sacrifice in a young man to give up the gay amusements of life, than to lay aside his laced waistcoat or white stockings.

Why, says Rouvill, I should imagine it would be no disadvantage to religion, or to the clergy in particular, if they were to remit a little of that solemnity of character, which has exposed them to the imputation of hypocrisy, and the ridicule of the world; and to mix a little more of the gentleman, both in their dress and in their deportment, which frequently prejudices people against very worthy and ingenious men. And, now my pocket-book is out, I will show you another ludicrous composition, which a friend of mine gave me when I first talked of taking the gown. Wildgoose said he did not approve of that sort of buffoonery; but as he would hear all the objections Rouvill had to the profession he was now engaging in, Rouvill read the following parody on Shakespeare's celebrated description of the seven ages of human life.

IV

A PARODY ON THE SPEECH OF JAQUES IN SHAKESPEARE'S AS YOU LIKE IT

As this parody is put into the mouth of a fop, says Rouvill, it is rather a compliment to the clergy, than any reflection upon them.

—————————————Sir Plume,
——————————————religion's all a farce;
And parsons are but men, like you or me
They have their foibles and their fopperies:
And one sees amongst them sundry characters.
To mention only seven.————And first, the curate,
Humming and *hawing* to his drowsy herd.—
And then the pedagogue with formal wig,
His night-gown, and his cane; ruling, like Turk,
All in his dusty school.—Then the smart priest,
Writing, extempore, forsooth! a sonnet
Quaint, to his mistress' shoe-string.—Then the vicar,

Full of fees custom'ry, with his burying gloves;
Jealous of his rights, and apt to quarrel:
Claiming his paltry penny-farthing tithes,
E'en at the lawyer's price.—Then the rector,
In sleek surcingle with good tithe-pig stuff'd;
With eyes up-swoln, and shining double-chin;
Full of wise nods and orthodox distinctions:
And so he gains respect.—Proceed we next
Unto the old incumbent at his gate,
With silken scull-cap tied beneath his chin;
His banyan with silver clasp wrapt round
His shrinking paunch, and his fam'd thund'ring voice,
Now whistling like the wind, his audience sleeps
And snores to th' lulling sound.—Best scene of all,
With which I close this rev'rend description,
Is your Welsh parson, with his *noble living*,
Sans shoes, *sans* hose, *sans* breeches, *sans* every thing.

Why, says Wildgoose, this parody might be characteristic of the clergy of the last age; but, I am apt to think the descriptions are now obsolete, and the clergy of these times are rather too polite than too awkward, and have more of the gentleman than either of the Christian or the pedant in their characters. They read more plays and pamphlets, than sermons or commentaries on the bible; they are rather witty in conversation, than wise unto salvation;

Polite apostates from God's grace to wit.

But I am most sincerely of opinion, continues Wildgoose, that the only way for the clergy to escape the ridicule of the gay world, and to keep up their credit, is not to join in its fopperies, but to revive the primitive manners, and to preach up the genuine doctrines of the reformation. And I cannot but hope, Mr Rouvill, that whatever levities you may have hitherto indulged yourself in, you will lay them aside, with your ruffles and your laced hat.

Rouvill replied, that he had seriously resolved to do every thing in his power to redeem his lost time; and that, although he might not be able to do much good by his learning or eloquence, he was determined not to do any mischief by an immoral or indecent behaviour.

This serious conversation was now interrupted by the appearance of a leg of lamb and cauliflowers, and a custard pudding, which Rouvill had ordered for dinner; and, though they differed something in their theological opinions, the two travellers were unanimous in their approbation of Mrs Brewer's cookery, and ate very heartily.

After dinner Rouvill called for a bottle of port, and said he would take a decent leave of the laity; but, as Wildgoose did not choose to drink his share, they proposed inviting Dr Brewer, in the character of mine host, to partake with them; who graciously condescended to honour them with his company, and assist them in the arduous task of dispatching a bottle of his own manufacture; as pleasant a revenge as making a physician swallow his own prescription.

Wildgoose having resumed the subject of Rouvill's taking orders, and having earnestly exhorted him to consider the importance of the office which he was going to take upon him; the afternoon was far advanced before they parted; Rouvill setting off for the bishop's palace at Eccleshall, and Wildgoosee, attended by his trusty friend, pursuing his journey towards the borders of Warwickshire.

V

TRIFLING DIFFICULTIES

Our spiritual adventurers, having sufficiently refreshed themselves, travelled at a good rate; Wildgoose being desirous to reach Sutton-Colfield, in his way to Warwick, that night; so that little conversation passed between them. Tugwell, however, could not but express his surprise, that the gentleman—whom he had seen to-day in a laced hat (and whom he had taken for a gentleman's servant) was to be a parson to-morrow.

As it was now some time past the summer solstice, night overtook them sooner than they expected; and when they came into the forest, or chase, near Sutton, it was quite dark, and they had wandered considerably out of the great road. At length, however, they came to what they took for a direction-post, when Wildgoose told Jerry, if he could but climb up the post, and trace out with his finger the first letter upon either of the hands, he could tell which way to turn; as, he took it for granted, one road led to Birmingham, and the other to Warwick. That I can do, then, master, says Jerry; for, when I was a young fellow, there was not a boy in the parish could climb a crow's nest so well as myself. Tugwell, therefore, desiring his master to take care of his staff and his wallet, ran up the post like a cat; but when he was got about seven or eight feet high, he made a sudden pause, and squelch he came down again, bawling out, with great consternation, Lord have mercy upon us! as sure as I am alive there is a dead man hanged up. Which indeed was partly true; for a highway-man, who had committed a murder, was hanged in chains there two or three years before; but, the body being decayed, only part of the skeleton remained, for a terror to these honest men, rather than to those hardened wretches for whose edification it was intended.

They now travelled on, therefore, under the direction of Providence, and in half an hour more saw some lights at a distance, which proved to be Sutton-Colfield, whither they were bound.

The two pilgrims, coming in late, soon retired to rest, without meeting with any incident worth recording; only finding a drunken blacksmith in the house, whom mine host pretended he wanted to get rid of, Wildgoose began preaching to him about the new birth, which soon put him to flight, and sent him home to his wife and family.

VI

TUGWELL COMPELLED TO DRINK STRONG BEER INSTEAD OF SMALL

Wildgoose having been assured by my landlord, that the races did not begin at Warwick till the next day, notwithstanding the strong attraction which he felt in his heart towards the residence of Miss Townsend, they did not set out till near nine o'clock. After travelling three or four hours in the heat of the day, about one o'clock they passed near some corn-fields, where they saw a company of reapers, who had just begun harvest, sitting at dinner under a shady oak, and laughing and singing with great glee and alacrity.

As making converts was the game which Wildgoose had constantly in view, he fancied he had a call to give a word of exhortation to these honest people, whom he considered as indulging a culpable festivity.

When they came up to them, therefore, Jerry introduced himself by asking whether they could give a poor man a draught of small beer this hot weather?—Aye, and of strong beer too, says one of them, as much as thou canst drink: it costs us nothing; and we give it as freely as we receive it.

This hospitable invitation encouraged Tugwell to sit down by them without any more ceremony, and he began to rummage out a crust of bread and a piece of cheese, which he had stowed in his wallet. But a young farmer told him he should not eat bread and cheese there; and, taking up a basket, he cut him off a good slice of some boiled beef, and a piece of plumb-pudding; of which, at Tugwell's request, Mr Wildgoose vouchsafed to partake. After eating pretty heartily, and drinking a draught or two of strong beer out of a leathern bottle, one of the company desired the young farmer (who appeared in a genteeler style than any of the rest) to entertain them with a song, as he was going to do when he was interrupted by the arrival of Tugwell and his master.—Mr John, said one of them, can sing in the playhouse fashion; for he has lived two or three years with my Lord in London.—But what must I sing? says he.—Why, the harvest-home song, that your brother made last year, replied the other.—Well, says he, I have got a sad cold;

but I will sing it as well as I can, though we have many a weary day
to come yet before our harvest-home.—He then sang, with a tolerable
grace, the following ballad:

The
TRIUMPH of CERES, or the HARVEST-HOME.
To the Tune of
What beauteous scenes enchant my sight!

What cheerful sounds salute our ears,
   And echo o'er the lawn!
Behold! the loaded car appears,
   In joyful triumph drawn.
The nymphs, and swains, a jovial band,
   Still shouting as they come,
With rustic instruments in hand,
   Proclaim the harvest home.

The golden sheaves pil'd up on high,
   Within the barn are stor'd;
The careful hind, with secret joy,
   Exulting, views his hoard.
His labours past, he counts his gains;
   And, freed from anxious care,
His casks are broach'd; the sun-burnt swains
   His rural plenty share.

In dance and song the night is spent;
   All ply the spicy bowl;
And jests and harmless merriment
   Expand the artless soul.
Young Colin, whispers Rosalind,
   Who still reap'd by his side;
And plights his troth, if she prove kind,
   To take her for his bride.

> For joys like these, through circling years
>   Their toilsome task they tend:
> The hind successive labours bears,
>   In prospect of the end.
> In spring, or winter, sows his seed,
>   Manures or tills the soil;
> In summer various cares succeed;
>   But harvest crowns his toil.

When the young farmer had finished his song, Wildgoose said, it was rather better than the common ballads, and inquired whether his brother really made it, as the reapers hinted? The farmer assured him he did; for that his brother had been bred at Cambridge; and though his father would have been glad to have had him assist them in the field when he came home in the long vacation, yet, instead of binding up the sheaves, or making hay, he would sit half the day under a tree, and make verses.

Mr Wildgoose was now going to exhort them to sanctify their labours, by singing hymns and spiritual songs, instead of those ungodly ballads; when Tugwell, observing a company of women who were gleaning in the field, wished his old wife Dorothy were amongst them, for that she would make a better hand at leasing than any of them.

She would hardly make a better hand of it, says the young farmer, than a young woman did here last harvest, and to whom we are obliged for our good cheer to-day.—How much might she earn in a day then by her leasing? says Jerry.—Why, more than this field and the next to it will produce these ten years, says the farmer. Tugwell expressing some surprise, the young farmer said, the story was remarkable, and if they would give him leave he would tell it them. Accordingly he began the following narration.

VII

THE FORTUNATE ISABELLA

This manor, the greatest part of which my father rents, was purchased by our 'squire's father, a great counsellor in London, who died before he had taken possession of it. The young 'squire, being fond of the country, came and settled here about two years ago. He took a small part of the estate into his own hands, for his amusement, and having a few acres in tillage, used to ride out most days in the harvest-time, to view his reapers at their work.

Amongst the poor people who came to glean in the field, there was a young woman, whose mother came a stranger into the parish, and had lived there for nine or ten years, with no other family than this one daughter, who was now about sixteen, and so handsome, that several young farmers in the neighbourhood admired her; and if she had had a little money, would probably have been glad to marry her. She dressed like our other parish girls, in a coarse stuff gown, straw hat, and the like; but some how or other she put on her clothes so cleverly that every thing became her. Her caps and her handkerchiefs, which were of her own making, were in a better taste than those of our other country girls; and, when her gown was pinned back, an under-petticoat appeared, with a border of flowers of her own work.

The young 'squire could not but take notice of her genteel shape, and elegant motions; but she was so bashful, that he could hardly get a sight of her countenance. He inquired who she was; and as nobody could give much account of her, because neither she nor her mother went out amongst their neighbours, he one evening, as she returned home, followed her at a distance, up a winding valley, to the cottage where she and her mother lived. It stands by a wood side, at a distance from our village, near a lonely farm-house, which is the only neighbour they have.

The 'squire hung his horse to the gate, and went in, where he found the old gentlewoman (for so we all thought her) knitting some fine stockings, and surveying with pleasure the produce of her daughter's labour. The house was very plainly furnished; but the 'squire was surprised to see a handsome harpsichord, which took up half the room, and some music-books lying about, with other books proper for young ladies to read.

Isabella, which was the name the young woman went by, blushed up to the ears when she saw the 'squire come in; and, making a courtesy, retired into another room.

He made a short apology to the mother for his intrusion; but said, he was so struck with her daughter's appearance, that his curiosity would not suffer him to rest till he had made some inquiries about her, as there was something in her manner that convinced him she must have had a different education from what usually falls to the lot of young women in that humble sphere of life.

The mother told him they had lived better formerly, but had been reduced by misfortunes; that, however, by her daughter's industry and her own work, they contrived to live very comfortably in their present situation.

As she did not seem inclined to be more communicative, the 'squire took his leave, but not without offering her a handsome present of money, which, to his surprise, she absolutely refused.

VIII

FURTHER ACCOUNT OF ISABELLA

The next day Isabella appeared again in the field, and was as intent upon her leasing as usual. The 'squire could not keep his eyes off her; and, having now a pretence for inquiring after her mother, entered into some further discourse with her; and found she expressed herself so properly, and discovered so much good sense and delicacy, that her personal charms appeared to much greater advantage, by the beauty of her mind; and, in short, the 'squire became quite enamoured of this rural damsel.

After two or three days he went again to her mother, and begged with the most earnest importunity, to be further informed of her story, and by what accident she had been brought to submit to her present obscure way of life; for that he was greatly interested in her's and her daughter's welfare, and hoped it might be in his power, if she would give him leave, to make their situation somewhat more agreeable to them, than it could possibly be whilst both she and her daughter were forced to work so hard for a subsistence.

There appeared so much sincerity and modesty in our young gentleman's manner, that the mother could not avoid gratifying his curiosity. She then told him, that her husband had enjoyed a genteel place under the government, and by his care and frugality had saved a considerable fortune; but that, not being in the secret, he had lost the whole in the iniquitous project of the South Sea, the shock of which had proved fatal to his health; and he died a few years after, leaving her and this one daughter, who was then about six years old, without any support, but what she could raise by the sale of a few jewels, which did not amount to three hundred pounds.—To avoid the slights of my former acquaintance, continued she, I retired into this part of the country, where I was pretty sure I should not be known; and have taken the name of Fairfax; for my real name is ——.

The young 'squire heard this short account with an eager attention; but upon hearing the name of ——, good heavens! cries he, is it possible you should be the widow of that worthy man Mr ——, to whom our family is under the greatest obligations? as I have often heard my father declare; who always lamented that he never could hear what was become of you and your daughter; and I am certain, would have been extremely happy in an opportunity of showing his gratitude to the family of his worthy friend. I hope, however, that happiness is reserved for me. But, continued the 'squire, did not you know that my father had purchased this manor, and that he was the friend of your late valuable husband?—Why, replies Mrs Fairfax, my time is so constantly taken up with the instruction of my daughter, and with the business necessary for our support, that I converse but little with our neighbours, and though I may have heard that a Mr —— had purchased the manor, and know that my dear Mr Fairfax (so I call him) had a friend of that name, yet I never thought that your father was under any further obligations to assist his friend's distressed family than many others were, from whom I never received the least act of friendship, though I knew they had it in their power to alleviate our distress.

The 'squire then told Mrs Fairfax, that he hoped there were various ways by which he could render their situation more happy than it seemed to be at present; but that there was only one way by which he could do it with complete satisfaction to himself, which was, with her permission, by laying himself and his fortune at her daughter's feet, which he should do with the greatest pleasure.

Mrs Fairfax was astonished at so generous an offer; but desired the young gentleman not to engage in an affair of so much importance, and to consider thoroughly how he could support the raillery of his acquaintance, and, perhaps, the resentment of his friends, which he might reasonably expect from so imprudent an alliance. The young 'squire replied, that he was his own master; that he was sufficiently acquainted with Isabella's personal charms, and would rely upon Mrs Fairfax's care of her education for every other accomplishment; and should think himself completely happy, if the proposal proved agreeable to the young lady's inclinations.

In short, the fair Isabella was immediately sent for; and the 'squire left the mother to propose it to her daughter, who, after a decent parley, with gratitude surrendered her charms to so generous a lover. They were married in a fortnight's time; and are now as happy as the day is long.

The old lady will not be prevailed upon to forsake her little cottage by the wood-side; but has enough allowed her to keep a maid-servant; and the coach is sent almost every day to carry her to the great house.

As a compliment to his lady, the young 'squire every year gives us a dinner out in the field on the day we begin harvest; and another at the hall, by way of harvest-home; on which occasion last year my brother made the song which I have now sung.

Well, says Tugwell, when the young farmer had finished his story, this is right now to take care of the old gentlewoman; and I dare say she now makes three meals a-day, and a supper at night. Why this is just, for all the world, like a story in a history-book.—Yes, says Mr Wildgoose, it is like a story in the Book of books, the story of Boaz and Ruth.—Well, says Tugwell, the squire is a man after my own heart; and I will drink his health in another draught of strong beer, if you will give me leave.

The leathern bottle then went round, and Jerry began to talk apace; when Mr Wildgoose endeavoured to give the conversation a religious turn; and, amongst other things observed, in allusion to their present employment, that the harvest, indeed, was great, but the labourers (meaning the true ministers of the Gospel) were few. The reapers, not understanding his allegory, said, they were enough of them to cut down that field, and as much more, in a week's time. But considering Wildgoose's speech as a hint that it was time for them to resume their labour, they leaped up, and fell to work with great cheerfulness and alacrity, leaving the two travellers to pursue their journey at their leisure.

IX

A CURIOUS INSCRIPTION

About eight in the evening Mr Wildgoose and his humble friend came to a public-house near Menden, on the Chester road; whose sign being suspended in a shady elm, it has obtained the name of the George in the Tree. Wildgoose during this peregrination, had adopted a laudable custom, though attended with some little expense as well as trouble, which was, when he came to an inn, to read whatever he found written either on the walls, or in the windows; and, wherever there was any thing obscene or immoral, either to write under it something by way of antitode; or, if it were very shocking, he would entirely erase it, if written upon a wall, or if in a window, break out the pane, and pay the damage.

As he was examining the parlour windows in this little hotel (which, affording entertainment for horse as well as man, *might* be called an inn) he observed the following remarkable inscription:

J. S. D. S. P. D. hospes ignotus,
Patriæ (ut nunc est) plusquam vellet notus,
Tempestate pulsus,
Hic pernoctavit,
A. D. 17—.

Jonathan Swift, Dean of St Patrick's in Dublin, here a stranger
unknown, but in his own country (such as it now is) better
known than he would wish to be, being driven by a storm, lodged
here all night, in the year of our Lord, 17—.

Mr Wildgoose, having at present little curiosity of that kind, did not
take out the pane, as he probably might have done for three halfpence,
and as was done soon after by some more curious traveller.

He then went into the kitchen, according to custom, to give some
little spiritual instructions to the family, or to any one he might
accidentally meet with, where he saw two travelling women, who
seemed much fatigued, as they had sufficient cause, having travelled
on foot that day above twenty miles. One of them seemed a pretty
genteel woman, but had a melancholy dejected look, which attracted
Wildgoose's particular attention; and he addressed himself to her as a
person under affliction, applying the common topics of consolation for
the evils of life. But the poor woman making little reply, Wildgoose
soon left her, without satisfying his curiosity for the present, and went
early to rest.

X

MAKE A NEW ACQUAINTANCE

As they had but a short stage to Warwick, and the races were not to
begin till the afternoon, the two pilgrims did not set out very early;
but, travelling a good pace, they soon overtook the two women whom

they had seen the preceding night, though they had set out some time before them. As they were to travel half a mile farther the same road, Tugwell asked them, by way of conversation, whether they were going to London or not? One of them answered, no; but into ———shire. The lady then asked Mr Wildgoose, if he knew any thing of one 'Squire Townsend in that county?—'Squire Townsend! replies he with some surprise; yes, I know something of the family. She then inquired, if he knew whether either of the daughters were married lately, or likely to be married? Wildgoose answered, that he did not know that they were, and that he could venture to assure her to the contrary; though I have heard, continued he, that a half-pay Irish officer had made pretensions to one of them; but her father, I am pretty sure, will never listen to the proposals of such an empty coxcomb, and one who has no visible fortune to support his daughter.

The poor woman turned pale as Wildgoose was speaking, and all on a sudden burst into a flood of tears. Wildgoose expressing great astonishment, the other woman, who was the lady's maid, said, that Irish officer was the vilest of men; that he was this poor lady's husband, with whom he had had a good fortune, and by whom he had three fine children; but he had gone to England, under a pretence of soliciting better preferment in the army, and left her destitute of any other support than what she could meet with from her own friends; and, what was more base (if their intelligence was true), he was going to draw in another young lady of family and fortune, by a marriage which must necessarily be invalid.

This intelligence greatly alarmed Mr Wildgoose, as he did not know what impression this Irish hero might have made upon the object of *his* affection. But when the lady, finding him so well acquainted with the family, produced the letter which she had received upon that subject, he was struck dumb with astonishment; for the person who gave the intelligence, and who had been a servant to the late Captain Townsend, mentioned Miss Julia Townsend, as the lady to whom Captain Mahoney was going to be married. So that Wildgoose began to suspect, either that Miss Townsend had not been sincere in the contempt which she expressed of Captain Mahoney, or that, since he had seen her, some

scheme of that kind might have been brought about by the widow
Townsend's influence over her father.

Mr Wildgoose, however, carefully concealed how much he was
interested in the affair; and, knowing how whimsical Mr Townsend was
in giving Roman names to his children, he told Mrs Mahoney, that
the person who wrote the account must certainly have mistaken Miss
Julia Townsend for Miss Lucia; as, to his knowledge, the former had
been some months from her father, and was now with a relation near
Warwick; and that he himself was in hopes of seeing her there, either
that very night, or the next morning at furthest, after he had dispatched
some business which he had upon his hands that afternoon. He added,
moreover, that the nearest way she could go to Mr Townsend's was,
to leave the great London road, and go through Warwick, whither he
himself would conduct her.

Mrs Mahoney and her companion thought themselves very fortunate
in meeting with a man who seemed capable of assisting them in the
affair which had brought them to England, and gladly joined them.
This droll party, therefore, united by an odd concurrence of interests,
trudged on very amicably together, and about dinner-time arrived at
the borough of Warwick.

Mr Wildgoose was at first inclined to go immediately to Dr Greville's,
and inform Miss Townsend of the discovery he had made; but, thinking
it sinful to prefer the temporal felicity of one family to the immortal
happiness of thousands, which he flattered himself depended upon his
preaching, he rejected with horror that design.

XI

AT WARWICK

Mr Wildgoose took his company to the first inn that presented itself.
They found every one in motion, and preparing to set out for the
course, which was some little distance from the town. They got some

dinner, however, and all sat down together; during which Tugwell observed, how comical it was they should happen to meet with the lady so cleverly, and said, if he could but meet with his son Joseph again, he should think his time well bestowed. It was but last night, added Jerry, that I dreamed about him. I thought *as how* they were going to let me down in the lead-mines again; and *as how* our Joe came and drew his sword, and beat the miners off, and *drawed* me up again. But I shall never see poor Joe any more; if he had been alive, we should certainly have heard from him in five years' time; but, perhaps, one reason why Joe has never wrote to us, is, because he can neither write nor read.

As the company had more important concerns of their own to engage their thoughts, they paid little attention to Jerry's disquisition. But, as soon as they had made a short meal, and Mr Wildgoose had safely deposited Mrs Mahoney and her companion, under a promise to wait at the inn till his return, he set out with his friend Tugwell, conducted by an intelligent lad belonging to the inn, who, as they walked together, promised, at Mr Wildgoose's request, to furnish him with a table, or joint-stool, from their booth; for the lad taking Wildgoose for a conjurer, the poor boy imagined he should, by that means, see his legerdemain performances, or slight of hand, for nothing.

XII

OLYMPIC HONOURS

The two pilgrims approached the scene of action just as the horses were going to start. Their ears were saluted with variety of sounds; the trumpet had just given the signal to prepare for the first heat; a recruiting party, with drums and fifes, were beating up for volunteers; and in every part of the field,

Steed answer'd steed in high and boastful neighings

as Shakespeare expresses it. The whole course was in motion; the coaches and chariots whirling towards the starting-post, or other convenient stands; the horsemen scampering different ways, according as they imagined they should get the best view of the sport; in another part, the knowing ones, with great composure, though with horrid oaths and imprecations, were settling the bets, and, with profound skill, deciding the fates of the different horses.

Wildgoose was moved with compassion, or, to use his own expression, his bowels yearned for his poor brethren, to see with what thoughtless eagerness, and vain curiosity they scowered across the plain, in pursuit of they knew not what; each miserable mechanic apparently as solicitous about the contest, as if their salvation depended upon the event. Amongst other objects, he could not but take notice of a young man of fortune, an old Oxford acquaintance, exalted in the stand, or balcony, of the starting-post, who looked down with the utmost contempt upon all below him, fancying himself superior to a Roman general in his triumphant car, or even to Mr Whitfield, when he preached from the starting-post at Northampton.

Wildgoose's zeal for the cause he was engaged in was raised almost beyond control. He thought it best, however, to defer his harangue till after the first heat; when the people would be more inclined to listen to his admonitions, than in the present tumultuous agitation of their spirits.

XIII

WILDGOOSE'S FAREWEL SERMON

Accordingly, the heat being now over, and people a little composed from their eager attention to the sport, Mr Wildgoose applied to his young friend at the booth that belonged to the inn where they had dined, who procured a table, which Tugwell placed upon a little eminence; by which means his master was sufficiently exalted above the crowd; who, with several chariots and horsemen, soon gathering round him, Mr Wildgoose, without more ceremony, began to harangue them with great vehemence, both of language and gesticulation.

Though Wildgoose insisted strenuously upon the unlawfulness and bad tendency of these paganish diversions, and the bad effect they had upon the mind of a Christian; yet his principal intention was, to make use of this opportunity to inculcate his peculiar tenets, and to make proselytes to true Christianity, or, what he always thought equivalent, the doctrines of Mr Wesley and Mr Whitfield.

But, whilst Wildgoose was enumerating the evil consequences of these ungodly assemblies, and amongst the rest, graphically describing the sad effects of drunkenness and intemperance; a young fellow on horseback, who was drinking with some more company, having a glass decanter in his hand, before it was quite empty, hurled it with great vehemence at the preacher's head, bidding him, drink, and be d-mn'd!

The decanter struck Wildgoose just above the left temple; and (being, in order to deceive the customers in the measure, fluted and crumpled into various angles) not only brought him senseless to the ground, but also cut a branch of the temporal artery, from which the blood issued forth in great abunadance, and alarmed all the company, who thought Wildgoose killed upon the spot.

Poor Tugwell, seeing his master struck down, and, for aught he knew, mortally wounded, broke out into doleful lamentations; being equally concerned, both for his friend and for himself. He said he should be hanged for enticing Mr Geoffry from home; or, at least, should lose Madam Wildgoose's custom, and be forbidden the house.

Jerry, however, thrust away and shoved off the crowd, in order to assist his master; and was so angry with every body about him, that he gave one a blow in the face, another a punch in the guts, and another a knock on the pate with his staff, which brought three or four surly fellows upon Jerry's back; and he would probably have suffered as much in the scuffle as his master had done, had not a young fellow in a military habit, with a knapsack on his back, and a cutlass by his side, pushed through the crowd very opportunely, and come to his assistance.

Jerry, in his hurry, could hardly forbear striking even his deliverer; but seeing a hanger by his side, he was kept a little in awe, and made a bow to the gentleman soldier, for his friendly aid. The soldier, catching hold of Tugwell with both his hands, cried out, Dear father! do not you know me? Give me your blessing. How does mother do?

Tugwell stood staring for some time, before he knew his son Joseph; who (as the reader may, or perhaps may not remember) has been mentioned more than once, as being sent for a soldier, and supposed to have died in America. Jerry threw his arms about his son's neck, expressing the utmost joy and surprise; and said, Now his dream was out! And began to ask twenty questions in a breath; which, Joseph said, he would answer at a proper time.

They now, therefore, assisted in carrying young Wildgoose, whom Tugwell had announced to his son, into the booth, that proper care might be taken of their friend in this unhappy situation.

XIV

WORK FOR THE DOCTOR

Amongst the horsemen whose curiosity had drawn them to hear Wildgoose, was a well-booted Grecian, in a fustian frock and jockey cap, who seemed greatly affected with this accident, and rode immediately with great trepidation in quest of a surgeon. This was no other than the benevolent Mr Bob Tench, who, the reader may recollect, became acquainted with Mr Wildgoose at Sir William Forester's in the Peak, and said he was to attend Sir Harry Hotspur to Warwick races. Bob was directed by some of the company to Dr Slash, an elderly surgeon, who was smoking his pipe over a tiff of punch, by himself, in the next booth. Bob summoned him, with great authority, to come immediately to the wounded itinerant, who, he said, would bleed to death.

The surgeon continued smoking on with great composure; and asked who was to pay him for his trouble? observing, that he could not work for nothing; that their education was very expensive; that, besides serving seven years apprenticeship, they were obliged to walk the hospitals, to attend anatomical and pharmaceutical lectures, and the like.

D-mn your *anno-domical, farta-shitical* lectures! cries Bob: why, the man is dying, and, if you don't come immediately, will bleed to death.— Come along, I myself will see you paid.

Dr Slash then beat out his pipe; took another glass of punch; and, with a very important air, rose up, and went to attend the wounded orator, who by this time was carried into the other booth, and was come a little to himself again. The doctor, however, shook his head; magnified the danger of the contusion; and took several ounces of blood from the patient, notwithstanding what he had lost from the wound. While the doctor was preparing his bandages and dressings, the company, according to custom, were very officiously giving their advice. Bob Tench was for applying only some Fryar's Balsam, and some goldbeaters' skin; which, as we observed, he always carried in his pocket. Jerry Tugwell wished, that his namesake, Dr Tugwell, the great bonesetter of Evesham was there; who, he said, would cure his worship in the twinkling of an eye. Young Tugwell said, *if so be* the surgeon of their regiment were there, he would cut off a leg, and tie up the arteries, and stop the blood, in the firing of a pistol. My landlord belonging to the booth, putting in his verdict, said, a little *permacetty* and a dram of brandy was the *sovereignst* thing in the world for an inward bruise.

Dr Slash, you may suppose, did not look very pleasant during these wise instructions. On the contrary, he gave himself no small airs; and said, if they made such a noise, and the patient could not be kept more quiet, the devil might dress the wound, for he would have no more to do with it.

XV

AN OLD GENTLEMAN IN BLACK ARRIVES

Just as Mr Slash had mentioned the devil, a tall elderly gentleman in black came into the booth; and, applying himself to Slash, inquired whether the patient might be removed without any danger, as he could not have proper care taken of him in such a place as that?—The surgeon bowing with great respect, answered, that, to be sure, there would be some danger in removing him; for, if the artery should bleed again, he did not know how it would be stopped; but, however, with great care, he added, that he *might* be removed.

Wildgoose himself said, he should be glad to be conveyed, if possible, to the inn at Warwick, as some company waited for him there, with whom he had business of great consequence. He then called Tugwell to him, and told him, he would have him go, that very night, with a note which he would write, to Miss Townsend, to acquaint her with the discovery which they had made in regard to Captain Mahoney. He then ladled out his pen and ink, and some paper out of his letter-case, and wrote a short note, which he sealed, and directed it, To Miss Townsend, at Dr Greville's, at ———, near Warwick. This direction he showed to Mr Slash; and asked him whither he could instruct his fellow-traveller how to find out the place?—Why, says Slash with surprise, this gentleman in black is Dr Greville himself. He then informed the doctor of Mr Wildgoose's request. Wildgoose, who was agreeably surprised at this unexpected interview, desiring to speak with Dr Greville in private; the doctor replied, that they would get into his chariot, and then they might converse without interruption. Wildgoose, therefore, taking leave of Bob Tench, and directing Tugwell, with his son Joseph, to meet him at the inn at Warwick, was lifted into the chariot; and he and Dr Greville, who gave the surgeon orders where to see his patient the next day, set off together.

XVI

CHARACTER OF DR GREVILLE

Doctor Greville was a clergyman, in whom the sacerdotal character appeared in its genuine dignity, not in an assumed solemnity of aspect, or formal grimace, and a pompous perriwig as big as Dr Sacheverell's; but in a serious, yet affable behaviour; the result of a sincere piety, sanctity of manners, and goodness of heart. He had a considerable independent fortune, which enabled him to obey the impulse of a generous and humane disposition: and it was a maxim with him, that, while a single person in his neighbourhoood wanted the necessaries of life, he had no right to indulge himself in its superfluities.

He undertook the care of a large and populous parish; but with no other motive than that of doing good, the stipend being hardly sufficient to maintain a resident curate.

Dr Greville really was what Mr Wesley and his associates ought to have been, and what, I sincerely believe, they at first intended to be. He revived the practice of primitive piety in his own person, and his own parish; and, by his example and admonitions, excited many of the neighbouring clergy to be more vigilant in the discharge of their duty. He had a *faith* which worked by *love*; or, in modern language, his belief of the truths of the Gospel made him consider as an indispensable duty those acts of beneficence which his humanity prompted him to perform.

If Dr Greville had seen the poor man who fell, amongst thieves, he would not, like the priest and the Levite, have passed by him on the other side; but like the good Samaritan, would have set him upon his own horse, would have bound up his wounds, and poured in *oil* and *wine* (if the modern practice had adopted so excellent a balsamic), which, upon so good authority, I should think, by the way, at least equal to Fryar's Balsam, or Opodeldoc.

Dr Greville, then, would have been the first to have run to the assistance of poor Wildgoose, had not his attention been engaged by an object nearer home; I mean a young lady in the chariot with him, who, upon the sight of Wildgoose's accident, had fainted away, and who the reader will easily guess, was no other than Miss Julia Townsend.

When Mr Wildgoose first began his harangue, Miss Townsend told Dr Greville, that she had seen him at Gloucester, and that he was a young man of a pretty good fortune; which partly induced the doctor to drive up, and make part of the audience; though he was glad of this opportunity of seeing young Wildgoose, on account of what had happened previously to this, and which it is proper to explain.

Wildgoose had written to Miss Townsend a letter from Gloucester (as was mentioned), which she received, and carefully preserved in her morocco-leather pocket-book; but which she had accidentally left upon her toilette, one morning, whilst she was gone with Dr Greville to take a walk in the fields. Mrs Greville going into Miss Townsend's room, female curiosity got the better of the point of honour, and she could not forbear examining the contents of this letter; which, indeed, was a liberty that Miss Townsend's situation, since her imprudent elopement, sufficiently warranted so good a friend to take. This letter was written in so ambiguous a style, that it was difficult to determine whether Mr Wildgoose were more solicitous for Miss Townsend's happiness, or his own: and there was such a mixture of the amorous and the devout, that it might be taken either in a spiritual or in a carnal sense; though, to any one that knew human nature so well as Dr Greville did, there could be no difficulty in what sense such a correspondence between two young persons of different sexes ought to be interpreted. Dr Greville was not displeased, therefore, at this opportunity of making some observations upon Miss Townsend's behaviour on such an occasion; and the violent effect which Wildgoose's accident had upon this young lady, left Dr Greville no room to doubt of the tender regard which she entertained for him.

Dr Greville was greatly alarmed at Miss Townsend's fainting away, and sent the footman, in a great hurry, to procure some water from the next booth; who, seeing the lady of their manor in her coach with her two daughters, acquainted them with the accident. She immediately sent one of her daughters to Miss Townsend's assistance; and by Dr Greville's permission, took Miss Townsend into her coach for the rest of the afternoon; which left him at liberty to make proper inquiries after the wounded pilgrim, and to take him into his chariot, as has been related.

XVII

DR GREVILLE, AND MR WILDGOOSE

As soon as they were alone together in the chariot, Wildgoose related to Dr Greville the circumstances of his getting acquainted with Miss Townsend at Gloucester; and then his accidental meeting with Mrs Mahoney, and the discovery he had made of Captain Mahoney's villanous design upon some one of Mr Townsend's daughters; which greatly alarmed Dr Greville, though he said that all Mr Townsend's friends had a very bad opinion of the widow Townsend, whom he had taken into his house.

It is very lucky, however, added Dr Greville, that Mr Townsend will be at our house this very evening, if he is not yet arrived; in expectation of which, Mrs Greville stayed at home to-day. And for that reason (and because, I believe, you will be better taken care of at my house than at an inn), I would have you by all means go home with me to my parsonage-house. Wildgoose found no great reluctance in complying with so kind a proposal, which would give him the opportunity he so long wished for, of seeing and conversing with Miss Julia Townsend. After a decent apology, therefore, for giving so much trouble to strangers, he told the doctor, he would gladly accept of his offer.

They now arrived at the inn at Warwick, where they found Mrs Mahoney waiting with patience for Wildgoose's return. She was not only surprised, however, to see him return in that manner; but his pale look, and the bandage about his head disguised him so much, that she could hardly be persuaded he was the same man. But, when that point was cleared up, and she was informed of Dr Greville's connection with Mr Townsend's family, she confirmed what she had said to Mr Wildgoose; and also produced the letter which she had received upon the subject.

When Dr Greville, however, found Miss Julia Townsend mentioned, he laid but little stress upon this intelligence. But, after talking the affair over, they concluded there would be no harm in showing Mr Townsend the letter, who would be able to judge what stress was to be laid upon it. And they advised Mrs Mahoney to rest contented at the inn till the next morning; and then Dr Greville, with Wildgoose, took their leave.

As they travelled gently along, Dr Greville took the liberty to expostulate a little with Wildgoose about his present romantic and irregular undertaking; and his eloping from his mother, without, and even contrary to her approbation; who he found, by Miss Townsend, was greatly affected by his extravagant and enthusiastic proceedings.

Wildgoose replied, he was sorry for that accidental consequence of his performing his duty; but, says he, whosoever loves father or mother more than Christ, is not worthy of him. And, in short, adds Wildgoose, a necessity is laid upon me; yea, woe unto me if I preach not the Gospel!

Dr Greville smiled at Wildgoose's application to himself of what was only applicable to St Paul and the primitive apostles, who certainly had a *divine call*; and wondered that a young man of so much good sense as he seemed to be in other particulars, should be so strangely imposed upon by a spirit of enthusiasm, that had possessed his imagination. Wildgoose was going to defend the *call* of the *spirit*, which he was convinced he had received in as ample a manner as any apostle of them all. But Dr Greville was afraid of bringing on too violent an agitation of spirits, and of renewing the hæmorrhage, or bleeding of the artery, and, therefore, changed the discourse for some other topic, which lasted till they arrived at the parsonage-house.

XVIII

AT DR GREVILLE'S

Mr Townsend being not yet arrived, they found Mrs Greville alone. She had been so much used to Dr Greville's acts of humanity, that she was less surprised at seeing a person in Wildgoose's situation, than at not seeing Miss Townsend in the chariot with them. But she was more surprised to find, that this was the very person who had written to

Miss Townsend from Gloucester, and a little wondered at Dr Greville's conduct in bringing him into the house to Miss Townsend, with whom she was by no means pleased, for admitting a private correspondence with a mere stranger, and (as she found by Miss Townsend's own account he was) an enthusiastical itinerant. She soon acquiesced, however, in Dr Greville's private reasons, who thought he might, at the same time, perform an act of humanity, in getting Wildgoose cured; and, perhaps, a greater act of charity, in reclaiming him from his erroneous opinions; and also make proper observations upon his general character, or, if he found it worth while, make a more particular scrutiny into the circumstances of his family and fortune.

Dr Greville would have persuaded Wildgoose immediately to lie down upon the bed; but, as he found himself very easy, and able to sit up till the evening, Mrs Greville ordered some tea, and said, the maid should get a proper room in readiness for him, whenever he should be disposed to retire to rest.

Before Mrs Greville had finished the ceremony of the tea-table, Mr Townsend's servant came to the gate; and brought word that his master was at the end of the village, and would be there very soon; that he had met with the old woodman as they came along, who told Mr Townsend that he had found some other curiosity as he was digging in the old camp on the brow of the hill; and that his master waited whilst the old man fetched it from his cottage.

Accordingly, in a few minutes more, Mr Townsend arrived, and was met by Dr Greville at the court gate; but not seeing Miss Townsend as he approached the hall door, which stood open, he cried out, Where is Julia? what, she has not eloped again, I hope. Ah! continues he, shaking his head, I every day hear fresh instances of her imprudence. Captain Mahoney was at Gloucester last week, where he was assured, that the little slut had like to have gone off from thence with a rascally Methodist preacher. Well, the Romans were a wise people; and, in the best ages of the republic, they gave fathers a power of life and death over their children, which kept them under a proper subjection.

Dr Greville said, Miss Julia was very well, but was not yet come from the course, where she was in Mrs Mowbray's coach. I am sorry, however, adds the doctor, to find you give so much credit to Captain Mahoney's intelligence, who, I believe, is no friend to any part of the family.

Mr Townsend was going to reply; but coming now into the hall, and seeing Wildgoose, he stopped short; and, paying his compliments to Mrs Greville, So, cousin, says he, you have got a patient to nurse, I see, according to custom. Pray, whom have you here?—Dr Greville answered, it was a young gentleman who had met with an accident at the race, and whom he had brought thither in his chariot, till he could be conveyed to his friends, who lived at some distance. He carefully concealed Wildgoose's name, however, and the nature of his present adventure.

Mrs Greville made some fresh tea for Mr Townsend; and, as it was not thought proper to discuss family affairs before a stranger, as Wildgoose appeared to be, the conversation became general for some little time. Well, cousin, says Dr Greville, you have been inquiring after antiquities according to custom, of our old woodman.—Yes, replies Mr Townsend; I thought, by his account, he had found a Roman stylus, which they used to write with; but I am afraid it is nothing more than an old iron skewer. Wildgoose then observed, that Mr Townsend had lost the principal day's *sport*, as it is generally *called*.—Why, that is the very salvo which I should have made, replied Mr Townsend; for what is *called sport*, I assure you, is not so to me; and though I have been used for some years to make my cousin Greville a visit at this season, my principal pleasure is in viewing the noble castle, and other antiquities in the neighbourhood of Warwick; which, I am convinced, was the *præsidium*, or chief station of the Romans in Britain, as being seated in the very centre of the island; and I value it more for having been the station of the Dalmatian *horse*, as Camden assures us, than for its paltry *horse-race* here once a-year.

If Wildgoose had not recollected Mr Townsend's person, his conversation would immediately have convinced him that he was the same virtuoso whom he had met in Lord Bathurst's woods. And Mr Townsend likewise, after a little time, said, he had seen Wildgoose somewhere before; and though I cannot recollect your name, says he, I know your face as well as I do that of Marcus Aurelius, or Caracalla. As Wildgoose did not care to discover too much, he only said, as he had

been rambling about pretty much of late, that probably Mr Townsend
might have seen him before, though he fancied he had never been
acquainted with his name.

XIX

MRS MAHONEY'S INTELLIGENCE
CANVASSED

When the servant had removed the tea-equipage, Dr Greville thought
it best not to defer the acquainting Mr Townsend with Mrs Mahoney's
intelligence, as he did not know how far the affair between Captain
Mahoney and Miss Townsend, if there was really any truth in it, might
have proceeded.

After a proper introduction, therefore, he showed Mr Townsend
the letter that Mrs Mahoney had received; which, when he had read,
and seen the name with which it was subscribed, and that Miss Julia
Townsend was mentioned as the object of Captain Mahoney's affection;
pshaw! says Mr Townsend, this is all a contrivance of a rascally fellow
who was a servant to Captain Mahoney when he was quartered at
Cork; and he having dismissed him, Captain Townsend hired him, and
brought him into our neighbourhood, where he is married and settled;
and, out of a pique has been endeavouring to do Captain Mahoney
some prejudice. Why, Captain Mahoney is *brother* to the widow
Townsend, and never was married in his life.—Sir, says Wildgoose,
the lady who calls herself Mrs Mahoney, assured me he never had any
sister; and that very circumstance looks very suspicious.—Well, I don't
know, says Mr Townsend, who this pretended Mrs Mahoney may be;
but I am pretty sure that Mrs Townsend would not connive at Captain
Mahoney's making overtures to my daughter without my approbation,
as she must know that her place depends upon her fidelity to me.

Well, says Dr Greville, I wish this intelligence may be without any
foundation; but the lady to whom this letter was written seems very

sincere in her apprehensions, and gives a very plausible account of herself; and so you will say, when you see her, which you may do to-morrow morning.

XX

WILDGOOSE RETIRES TO REST

It now began to grow dusk, and as Wildgoose looked very pale and fatigued, Dr Greville prevailed on him to go to rest, and himself very politely waited on him to his chamber, though he was extremely desirous of sitting up till Miss Townsend came home; for though we have not yet taken notice of it, we may be sure Mr Wildgoose could not take Miss Townsend's place in the chariot (as he found by Dr Greville he had done), nor be in the very house where she was expected every moment, without very sensible emotions of tenderness and expectation.

When Wildgoose was gone out of the room, Mr Townsend immediately asked, who he was? observing, that he seemed a very sober sensible young man. Mrs Greville replied, that he was a young gentleman of pretty good fortune in Gloucestershire, and, she believed, a humble admirer of her cousin Julia.—Is he? says Mr Townsend, with some quickness, then, for God's sake let him have her; for I know not who else will, after her imprudent elopement; and, I believe, the poor girl wants a husband. I am sure, at least, I don't know what to do with her, for my part.—Why, says Mrs Greville, these are partly my sentiments of the matter; and I fancy, between you and me, such a scheme would be no ways disagreeable to Miss Julia; and this was Dr Greville's chief motive, I believe, for bringing the young man to our house.

When Wildgoose, attended by Dr Greville and the servant with candles, came into his bed-chamber, he was making apologies for the trouble he gave; but the servant setting down one of the candles upon the toilette, Wildgoose immediately espied a miniature picture of Miss

Julia Townsend, hanging under the glass; which fixed his attention so entirely, that Dr Greville wished him a good night, smiling to himself at this further discovery which he had made of Wildgoose's attachment to his cousin Julia.

When Dr Greville returned to the parlour, he found Mr Townsend and Mrs Greville in close debate on the subject above-mentioned, and added his suffrage to the scheme proposed. But, while these good people were in the midst of their deliberations, Mrs Mowbray's carriage came to the door, to set down Miss Townsend, whom, Mrs Mowbray said, she had brought safe home; though she desired proper care might be taken of her, as she had been very languid and low-spirited the whole afternoon.

Dr Greville made an apology for leaving his cousin to Mrs Mowbray's care, as he was sensible she must have been rather a troublesome companion; but that he himself had been engaged in a charitable office, which required a more immediate attention.

Miss Townsend flew with a sincere transport into her father's arms; in whose breast, notwithstanding his slight resentment, nature resumed her place; and he received his favourite daughter with great tenderness and affection.

Book XII

I

THE INN AT WARWICK

Tugwell, with his son Joseph, went, as Mr Wildgoose had ordered him, to the inn at Warwick; where he found Mrs Mahoney and her companion; who informed Tugwell that Dr Greville had taken Wiidgoose to his own house.

As Mrs Mahoney desired to have Tugwell's company in a little parlour which she had got adjoining to the kitchen, Jerry desired to introduce his son also, with whose unexpected return he acquainted her.

When Joseph came into the room, he and Mrs Mahoney's maid expressed a mutuual surprise at sight of each other: for, though Mrs Mahoney was too attentive to her own distress, the maid immediately recollected, that he had come over with them from Dublin to Park-gate, in the same vessel.

When young Tugwell heard Mrs Mahoney's name, he said, he remembered a Captain Mahoney at Cork, when he was there two years ago, and that he was one of the gentlemen who had like to have married the woman that Captain Townsend married.

This account startled Mrs Mahoney, as she knew her husband had been quartered there about that time; and though she could not guess what Joseph meant, by his being likely to marry Mrs Townsend, yet she shook her head, suspecting, with too much reason, that it was some other instance of his infidelity.

Joseph, however, alluded to what he had told his father, in the circumstantial account which he had given him of his five years' adventures, as they returned together from the course. But, as a great part of them would be uninteresting to the reader, we shall only mention, that Joseph, upon enlisting for a soldier, to avoid marrying a common strumpet (as was mentioned in the beginning of this history,) was put on board the transports that accompanied the grand fleet upon the ever memorable expedition against Carthagena.

All the world knows the disastrous event of that expedition. After sacrificing the lives of so many brave fellows, in forcing the straits of

Bocca-Chica castle; and when the Spaniards were ready to abandon Carthagena upon the first attack, by the unaccountable delays and strange conduct both of the admiral and the commander in chief of the land forces, the affair was protracted till the rainy season set in; when our troops became a prey to sickness, and it was thought advisable, after a general council of war, to reimbark them aboard the transports; where, though there were several young surgeons aboard the fleet, who longed to assist their perishing countrymen; yet, the general disdaining to ask, and the admiral to offer any assistance, the poor people dropped off like rotten sheep.

Young Tugwell, however, by good luck, got leave to wait on Captain Townsend; who, being reduced by sickness to a declining state of health, as soon as the fleet returned to Jamaica, got leave to return to England; and, at his request, got young Tugwell's discharge.

They landed at Cork in Ireland; where Captain Townsend, being laid up with the gout, staid for some time; and, amongst other gentlemen, became very intimate with a celebrated bar-maid at a tavern there; and, thinking a nurse of some sort was necessary to a man in his situation, he robbed the public, and married that girl; who was the identical widow Townsend, who has been mentioned so often in this history.

Amongst her gallants, Captain Mahoney, being at that time a handsome young fellow, was distinguished as her favourite; which made Joseph think that he had like to have married her.

Young Tugwell, having taken the liberty to advise his master (Captain Townsend) against this match, was of course dismissed as soon as it took place. He met, however, with another English officer on the Irish establishment, who expected every day to return to England; but, being disappointed from time to time, Joseph at length left his service at Dublin, and happened to embark in the same ship with Mrs Mahoney; and was now on his way home, to visit his father and mother, and his native place.

II

KITCHEN STUFF

As Tugwell and his company were at supper in their little parlour, which was only separated from the kitchen by a deal partition, they heard a fellow holding forth over a pot of ale; and, with the air of a politician, abusing all the gentlemen shoemakers in the country. Jerry, thinking himself concerned in the affair, and fancying likewise that he was not entirely unacquainted with the voice, listened to the following harangue:—I have looked into their shops, master Crisp, and I don't approve of their knavish proceedings. I might have been foreman to Mr Cutwell of Coventry: but, sir, I assure you, they are the most *roguishest* set of people upon earth. Why, I remember when a pair of shoes was sold for two shillings; nay, for eighteen-pence, when I was 'prentice in London.—Why, were you 'prenticed in London? says Mr Crisp.—Yes, that I was; and served seven years in Whitechapel. And I have an uncle, that is a topping shoeblack near the Royal Exchange. Ah! London's the place; and yet London is not half the place it was formerly—for *old shoes.*

Well, cobbler, says master Crisp, I hope you are a better husband than you were.—Yes, thank God; I hope I am. Indeed, if God Almighty gives one health and money, one ought to take a cheerful glass now and then with a friend or so—But hang it, what signifies money in the country? If I had a hundred pounds, I would not spend a farthing of it in the country. In London you have something for your money. There's liquor! There you may take a glass in a genteel *discreet* manner. There is not a landlord in the country that knows common sense.—Come, come, says the landlord, a little offended at this freedom, come, pay as you go, cobbler; you have had two pots, and have paid for none.

The dialogue being now at an end, Tugwell went out into the kitchen, to see who this fluent orator might be; and found, to his surprise, it was his old friend, Andrew Tipple, who had worked for Jerry in his prosperity as a journeyman; but was now become quite an itinerant cobbler, and peripatetic politician. Andrew was as much surprised at the sight of his old master, and cried out, Ha! master Tugwell; why, we heard you were sent to gaol for horse-stealing. What have you done with young Mr Wildgoose? I was at your town but last week. Your wife Dorothy is very angry with you for leaving her; but says, she should not have minded it, if you had not gone in your best waistcoat. And madam Wildgoose threatens to disinherit Mr Geoffry; and has actually taken two of her grand-children to live with her, since the young 'squire took to these vagabond courses.

Jerry looked a little foolish at this account of the state of affairs at home; but, clapping his hand upon his pocket, with a gallant shake of the head, said, they should make matters up again when they got home.

Jerry then called for a pot of ale, with which he and his old friend drank an health to their friends in Gloucestershire; and so they parted, Tugwell returning to his company.

III

AT DR GREVILLE'S

When Mrs Mowbray's coach came to the door with Miss Townsend (as was related) Mr Wildgoose was just going to bed; but flew to the window, like a hawk at his quarry; where, by the light of the moon, he had a full view of Miss Townsend, as she ran up the court, drest, on the occasion, much more splendidly than he had ever seen her at Gloucester. This slight glance threw poor Wildgoose into such a palpitation and hurry of spirits, that it was a considerable time before he could compose himself to sleep; and Miss Townsend was the prevailing idea in his dreams for the whole night.

It was now eleven o'clock, and Dr Greville's family were all in bed, when they were awaked by a hasty rapping at the door; and were greatly alarmed, when the servant brought up word, that a man was come out of ——shire, with a letter for Mr Townsend. This messenger proved to be the old coachman, who was mentioned to have assisted Miss

Townsend in her elopement to London; and who, partly to atone for his imprudent conduct in that affair, and partly out of regard to the family, had taken his horse, and rode thirty miles after five o'clock that evening, to bring a letter, which his wife had intercepted, addressed to Miss Lucia Townsend, from Captain Mahoney. This letter being carried up to Mr Townsend, he opened it, and found the contents to be as follows:

To Miss Townsend

My dear Lucia,

Every moment is an age till my happiness is completed: and the deferring our departure another day is a contradiction to the impatience of a fond lover. But I am disappointed of the phaeton which I had bespoke; and was obliged to send to Oxford, whence I have ordered one of those post-chaises which are lately come into vogue, and which will convey us with more expedition either to London or Bristol; though I now think the latter is more advisable; as we can be conveyed from thence to Cork in eight-and-forty hours.

You and Mrs Townsend will be ready to-morrow evening, as soon as it grows dusk, with your baggage, behind the grove of firs: till which time, my dearest Lucia, I remain

Your impatient lover,

Patrick Mahoney.

P. S. Write me a line by the bearer.

Mr Townsend was greatly provoked at this discovery; but, upon reflection, became sensible that he had no one but himself to blame for the confusion which his imprudent connection with the widow Townsend had introduced into his family.

He at first thought of setting out again immediately; but as the time fixed by Mahoney for executing his wicked scheme was not till the following evening, he thought he might take a few hours' rest, and get out very early in the morning. He, therefore, sent for the old coachman up to his bed-side, and inquired how he came by that letter: in answer to which he gave him the following account:

Ben, the hostler at the George, says he, (where Captain Mahoney quarters,) is third cousin to my wife; and, having been sent by the captain with this letter to Miss Townsend, Ben thought it proper to let my wife know what he had heard from the hostler at the Black Bull, who told Ben, that Captain Mahoney, having been disappointed of *their* phaeton, had sent him to Oxford for a post-chaise; which was ordered to be at the captain's quarters the next day about ten o'clock, who was going a long journey; and as all the neighbourhood talk very freely about the captain's designs upon Miss Townsend, my wife was willing to forward this letter to your honour at a venture; and sent Ben back to the captain with an answer from Miss Townsend, by word of mouth, that it was very well.

Mr Townsend said, he was obliged to the coachman for the trouble he had taken; bade him feed his horse, and then go to bed; and that he himself would set out by four o'clock in the morning: which, as he found by the letter that the captain had put off his scheme till the next night, he hoped would be soon enough to prevent it.

Dr Greville had slipped on his night-gown, and was come into Mr Townsend's room, to inquire into the cause of this alarm; which being informed of, though he secretly triumphed over Mr Townsend's credulity, yet he begged him to lose no time in an affair of that consequence; and said, that he himself would take the liberty to awake Mr Townsend at three o'clock, by which time he would be a little refreshed after his day's journey; and that he would take care to convey Mrs Mahoney by a man and double horse, if it should be thought necessary; though he did not imagine, he said, that the captain would stay to dispute the matter with Mr Townsend.

IV

AT MR TOWNSEND'S

Notwithstanding Dr Greville's caution, and his eager desire to hasten Mr Townsend's departure, it was near five o'clock before he set out; and near eleven before he reached his own house in ———shire; when he found it deserted both by his daughter and the widow Townsend, which we may imagine shocked him to the utmost degree.

But, upon inquiry, he found the case not quite so bad as he at first expected; for the servants who were left at home informed him, that Mrs Townsend had sent a letter by the stable-boy, early in the morning, to Captain Mahoney; who came with a post-chaise, about half an hour before Mr Townsend came home, and had taken away Mrs Townsend, with all her luggage in two large trunks. But that they were both in great confusion, at not finding Miss Townsend, who had been missing all the morning; and of whom the servants could give no other intelligence.

Whilst Mr Townsend was deliberating what method to pursue, the coachman's wife came very opportunely, and relieved him from his distress, by giving the following account of Miss Townsend:

That she (the coachman's wife) being apprehensive that Captain Mahoney might suspect his plot was discovered, by his receiving no answer to his letter, and, therefore, might hasten the execution of it; she, therefore, consulted Mr Thompson, the 'squire's principal tenant, and whom, she knew, he greatly confided in upon all occasions; and he had contrived to get Miss Townsend to his house pretty early in the morning, under a pretence that somebody wanted to speak with her; and that Mrs Thompson had locked herself up with Miss Townsend in their parlour till the 'squire himself should come home, as they supposed he would do, in consequence of the letter which the coachman had conveyed to him.

Mr Townsend, therefore, went immediately to farmer Thompson's, where he found Miss Townsend confined, as the coachman's wife had informed them.

Mr Townsend gave his daughter a proper lecture upon the occasions; and explained to her with great tenderness the escape she had had; and the discovery which he had made of Captain Mahoney's being already married, by means of a young gentleman who was now at Dr Greville's, and had providentially met Mrs Mahoney upon her road from Ireland.

When they returned to the manor-house, Mr Townsend found that the widow Townsend had carried off not only her own property, but likewise some of his; particularly a gold repeating watch of his late wife's, a valuable ring or two, a great many fine laces, and a brocaded suit of clothes; in all, to the value of above two hundred pounds. But, as he had placed so unlimited a confidence in her, this was to be considered rather as a breach of trust than a robbery; and, having now sufficient proof of her infidelity and wicked designs, he was really glad to get rid of her upon any terms.

As for the two fugitives, it may be proper to have done with them here; and to inform the reader, that they made the best of their way to Bristol; where, embarking for some remote part of Ireland, they lived together for some time upon the fruits of the widow Townsend's plunder; till, satiated with each other's person, a mutual disgust ensued; and the captain, having shared the best part of the widow's fortune, his fickle temper soon dissolved a connection which was built upon so precarious a foundation.

V

AT DR GREVILLE'S

Let us now return to our wounded hero, Mr Geoffry Wildgoose.

For fear of any accident in the night Dr Greville had ordered the footman to lie in a closet adjoining to his room: who, coming down in the morning, told the maid, that the gentleman had slept very soundly all night; but that, ever since he had awaked, he had been lamenting and bemoaning himself like a child. I asked him, says the fellow, whether he was in pain; but he says he is quite well again! only I fancy he is troubled in mind. I suppose, says the footman, he has lost money by betting at the races; or, perhaps, he has left a sweetheart behind him somewhere or other.

Dr Greville, being informed of what the footman had said, went up to Wildgoose's bed-side, and asked him how he found himself. Wildgoose took the doctor by the hand, and thanked him for the great care he had taken of him; and said he had had a fine night, and found himself quite well: and thank God, says he, I find my head much clearer than it has been for some months. But, sir, I confess many things appear to me in a very different light from what they have lately done; and I am particularly shocked at having left my disconsolate other so long in a state of anxiety and concern on my account. For, O, sir, I am now convinced, that no doctrine, no religious opinion, can be true, that contradicts the tenderest feelings of human nature, the affection and duty which we owe to our parents.

Dr Greville replied, that he was glad the mist was dispelled from his mind, and that he seemed to see things in their proper light; though, perhaps, says the doctor, your last assertion ought to be admitted with some little restriction; as there may be some parents so unreasonably wicked, as to expect their children to prostitute their very consciences, as well as sacrifice their reason, to *their* absurd opinions, or dishonest practices; in which case children are evidently under a prior obligation to religion and virtue: though they should be very certain of the justice of their cause, before they venture to oppose so sacred an authority as that of parents over their children. But I am afraid, sir, indeed, that you left your unhappy mother, merely from the blind impulse of an over-heated imagination; to engage in an undertaking directly opposite to the laws of the land, without any pretence of a divine commission: and therefore I cannot but conclude you were under a wrong influence.

I am afraid I was, says Wildgoose; but yet, in times of general defection from the principles of the Gospel, and the doctrines of the Reformation, I cannot but think that every one has a divine call to stem the torrent, and endeavour to revive the practice of true Christianity.

I own they have, replied the doctor, by their example and their persuasion, within the sphere of their own neighbourhood. But then nothing, I think, is so evident, as that we are commanded, to submit to every ordinance of man, for *the Lord's* sake; to let every thing be done decently, and in order; and, therefore, no one has a right to break through the regulations of society, merely from the suggestions of his own fancy, and unless he can give some visible proof of a supernatural commission.

As to a 'general defection from the truths of the Gospel;' we are very apt to judge of the state of religion, as we are of the politeness, knowledge, or learning of the age, from what we feel in our own breasts. We fancy the world is more knowing, because we ourselves know more than we did in our infancy; and we think the world less religious, because we, perhaps, have thrown off the restraints of religion, and are more wicked or debauched than we were in our youth or childhood.

The most likely method of convincing any one, is to make our adversary some concessions. For a general opposition to his whole system, not only irritates his passion; but, finding you mistaken in some particulars, as you probably are, he concludes, at random, that you are wrong in all.

I grant you, continues Dr Greville, that there may be some cause of complaint against the negligence of the clergy; and that, if the people had plenty of wholesome food or sound doctrine, they would not be hankering after the crude trash of *some* of your itinerant preachers. But does this warrant every ignorant mechanic to take the staff out of the hands of the clergy, and set up for a reformer in religion.

There are corruptions, perhaps, or neglects at least, in every branch of the civil administration; as no human institution can be perfectly administered. But suppose an honest country justice to be a little negligent in his duty, or not very accurately versed in the subtleties of the law; would this warrant any neighbouring attorney, who spies out his error, to take upon him to administer justice in his room? No, an appeal is open to a superior court; and his errors must be rectified in a legal manner; otherwise strange confusion would ensue.

The parson of your parish, suppose, neglects his duty, or is immoral in his life and conversation. Let application be made to the bishop of the diocese; who, at his visitation, not only receives his synodals, but sends out articles of inquiry, relative to the conduct of every individual clergyman within his jurisdiction. 'Does your minister lead an exemplary, or at least, a sober and regular life? Does he do his duty decently, and in order? Does he catechise and instruct the children, and other ignorant persons, in the principles of religion, at several times of the year, as the canons direct?' If he does not, why is not he regularly presented by the officers of the parish, and complaint made to the bishop? who will not fail, first of all, to exhort him in private; and, if he does not alter his conduct, to censure him publicly at the next visitation; and, if he continues obstinate, to suspend him entirely from the exercise of his function.

Nothing, I think, can well be contrived better, or more wise, than our ecclesiastical polity is in itself, if properly put in execution.

As to the particular doctrines which the Methodists pretend to have revived, and on which they lay so great a stress, I do not imagine the advantage which they seem to have *gained* over the regular clergy arises from those cobweb distinctions, which I am convinced, not one in ten of their followers really comprehend; but from the seriousness of their lives, and the vehemence and earnestness of their harangues, which may have a temporary effect upon their audience whilst the impression on their fancy lasts; and have, I believe, really awakened many indolent and careless Christians to a sober and devout life.

As to the doctrines themselves, that of justification by faith, for instance; I know no clergyman that expects to be saved by the merit of his own works. We do not preach up the *merit* of *good* works, but the *necessity* of them; and unless a good man and a good Christian are inconsistent characters, I do not see how good works, which is only another name for virtue, can be dispensed with. In short, though the negligence of too many of the clergy may have given these reformers some little advantage over them; yet the extravagant proceedings, and monstrous tenets of many of their itinerant preachers, have given them an ample revenge. One man declaims against the lawfulness of some of the most necessary callings. Mr H——ll, who married a near relation of Mr Wesley's, having used the poor lady ill by an intrigue with another woman, defended the lawfulness of polygamy. One Roger Ball asserted, that the elect had a right to all women. These are not the necessary consequences, I own, of any of their principles; but they are the probable effects of an unlimited toleration of unlicensed, or rather such licentious teachers.

I would by no means undervalue the great talents, and the pious labours of Mr Wesley, and many of their leaders. They are, I am convinced, men of sound learning, and true devotion; and whilst they live to inspire and give vigour to their new establishment, some good may probably result from it. But when they come to be succeeded by men, who, instead of a zeal for religion, will be led by interest, to prefer the ease and advantage of a teacher to the drudgery of a mechanic trade; the same indifference and negligence will soon prevail amongst them, which they have complained of in the established clergy. And their classes will probably be as much neglected, as some of our parishes now are. So that after prejudicing the people against their proper pastors, they will leave them a prey to the ignorance, and, perhaps, much greater immorality of illiterate plebeians; and so will have made another schism in our church, to very little purpose.

Well, says Mr Wildgoose; but suppose Mr Wesley and his friends really convinced of the great decay of Christian piety, and that they were obliged in conscience to use their utmost endeavours to revive the practice of it, what course were they to take?

Why, says Dr Greville, I should think, if their little society, when it was first formed in the university (before they had made themselves obnoxious to the clergy by their irregular proceedings,) had quietly dispersed themselves, and settled upon curacies in different parts of England; and had there formed little associations amongst the neighbouring clergy; the influence of their example would gradually have spread itself, and produced more real, and more permanent effects, than it is now likely to do; without any bad effects, which I am afraid must proceed, as I have observed, from such licentious proceedings.

Dr Greville was going on to convince Mr Wildgoose of the mistake he himself had laboured under, in regard to his late conduct: and Wildgoose seemed to listen with great attention, and showed signs of confusion in his countenance, when the servant brought word, that Mr Slash, the surgeon, was come; whom Mrs Greville attended up to Wildgoose's room.

The surgeon first of all, with the air of a Radcliffe or a Freind, felt his pulse; which he pronounced to be in a healthy state. Then, taking off the bandage, he found, that although Mr Wildgoose had been stunned by the blow, and lost a great deal of blood, yet the wound in itself was very trifling; and, knowing that Mrs Greville was herself a skilful practitioner in surgery, he showed her the wound; who was surprised to see how slight it was. Slash, therefore, paid her the further compliment of leaving a few dressings, which he said, with truth enough, she could apply as well as he could; adding, that if the patient did not heat or fatigue himself, he might travel whenever he pleased. And Wildgoose intending, at farthest, to set out the next morning, took his leave of the surgeon, by slipping half a guinea into his hands, with which Mr Slash, having no great expectation from a knight-errant, was very well contented; and Wildgoose himself was obliged to limit his generosity, having but a few shillings left, to defray the expenses of his journey.

VI

AN INTERVIEW

Mr Wildgoose, being now left alone, that he might equip himself for breakfast, finding his mind much more easy since his conference with Dr Greville, and the thoughts of seeing Miss Townsend giving him fresh spirits, he adjusted his cravat, rubbed up his hair with some pomatum, and, in short, made his whole person as spruce as his present circumstances would permit; and his bandage being now reduced to a decent patch of black silk, Wildgoose made no despicable appearance.

When he came into the breakfast-room he was greatly smitten with the sight of Miss Townsend who was so much more elegantly dressed than in her state of humiliation at Gloucester. Dr Greville introduced them to each other, observing, with a good-natured smile, that they were two old acquaintances. This speech raised a blush in Miss Townsend's countenance, which still heightened her charms; and, what is not common, her real appearance surpassed, even the bright idea, which, for a month past, had glowed in the imagination of poor Wildgoose, her absent lover.

Well, continued Dr Greville, you have both been a sort of fugitives, and have given your friends some uneasiness; but, as the cause of Miss Julia's ill usage at home will, I hope, soon be removed, so I flatter myself, sir, your motive for rambling abroad will also cease. Not that I wish to see you less serious in the practice of religion, nor even less an enthusiast, in some sense; as I am convinced nothing great can be effected without some degree of enthusiasm; but I would not have your zeal transport you so far, as to hurry you into any irregularities, which only expose you to danger and ridicule, and can never answer any really useful purpose.

Miss Townsend, though herself in some little confusion, began to rally Mr Wildgoose upon the accident he had met with, and hoped it would cure him, for the future, of such romantic undertakings. Wildgoose replied, that he should not be deterred from doing what he thought his duty, from any danger which might accrue to his person; but that Dr Greville had almost convinced him, that such irregular proceedings were inexpedient, if not unwarrantable.

Wildgoose then asked Miss Townsend, whether she had heard from their friend, Mrs Sarsenet, at Gloucester lately; which gave Mrs Greville an opportunity of observing, that Mrs Sarsenet was a very worthy, *good creature*; and, she believed, had judged very rightly of the widow Townsend's character; but yet had been the accidental cause of poor Miss Julia's ill usage at home, and of her consequent elopement; though, she added, no usage which a child could be supposed to receive from a parent would justify such a violation of the duty which every child owes to its parent, or such a defiance of the authority which nature has given a parent over his offspring.

VII

MRS MAHONEY'S STORY FINISHED

Dr Greville, by way of changing the subject, which could not be very agreeable to the young people, said, he would take his horse, as soon as

they had breakfasted, and ride to Warwick, that he might acquaint Mrs
Mahoney of the further discovery which they had made of Captain
Mahoney's intrigue, and consult with her about her future proceedings.
But, whilst they were talking about it, Tugwell and his son Joseph arrived
from Warwick, in order to inquire how Mr Geoffry did; and to propose
their going home, and acquainting Madam Wildgoose of the accident.
But to this Wildgoose would by no means consent, as he said, it would
be too great a shock to his mother, and he himself was well enough to
set out with them that afternoon. Dr Greville, however, said, that would
be very wrong, and that he would run a great hazard of inflaming his
wound, and, perhaps, of renewing the hæmorrhage. But, says he, if you
are determined to travel so soon, I will to-morrow morning give you a
lift in my carriage, as far at least as the turnpike-road extends; which, I
imagine, is within a mile or two of your village.

And as for these honest men, they shall stay and dine here; and then,
if they choose it, they may go part of the way to-night, and halt for us
to-morrow morning at Stratford, if they can find their way thither.

O! says Jerry, I know Stratford-upon-Avon well enough: it's the place
where Shakespeare, the great jester,★ was born. Grandfather's father
lived a servant with the jester himself; and there is a mulberry-tree
growing there now, which he helped Mr William Shakespeare to plant,
when he was a boy.

Well, master Tugwell, says Dr Greville, you may go and visit the
mulberry-tree which your great grandfather helped to plant, and meet
us to-morrow morning about eleven o'clock, at the White Lion; and
then we will proceed together.

Mr Wildgoose then inquired after Mrs Mahoney, when Jerry cried
out, Odsbobs! I forgot to tell you, that the gentlewoman is very bad, and
has not been able to get out of bed to-day; and her maid says, she does
not know how she will be able to travel any further.

This account moved Mrs Greville's compassion, as her curiosity had
been raised before, and she immediately ordered her chariot, and went

---

★ All the idea which the country people have of that great genius, is, that
 he excelled in smart repartees, and *selling of* bargains, as they call it.

alone to Warwick, that, if it should be necessary, she might bring Mrs Mahoney with her to Dr Greville's.

When she came to Warwick, however, she found Mrs Mahoney just come down stairs. And upon Mrs Greville's inquiring after her health, she answered, that her complaint was nothing more than excessive fatigue: that she had been so intent upon the object of her journey, as not to perceive herself in the least wearied for three or four days; but that since she had lain still, her spirits began to flag, and she found herself unable to travel any further.

After informing Mrs Mahoney of the fresh discovery which had been made of Captain Mahoney's designs upon Miss Townsend, and of the means which Mr Townsend had used to prevent its taking effect, Mrs Greville added, that she had come alone in the chariot, with an intent to take Mrs Mahoney with her, if she approved of it. Mrs Mahoney, after recovering her spirits from the hurry into which this intelligence had thrown her, thanked Mrs Greville for her kind invitation; but said, she had a near relation in London, an elderly lady of good fortune, who had often importuned her, by letter, to make a visit; and, as she might be a friend to her children, she had made that a secondary object in taking this journey. She intended, therefore, to get a place in some stage-coach the next day, and go to London; as it seemed to no purpose, at present, to pursue her graceless husband any further.

And here the reader may like to be informed, that this relation, who was the widow of a rich merchant, died soon after Mrs Mahoney's return to Ireland; and was so well pleased with her visit, that she left her a handsome competence, vested in trustees' hands, independent of her husband; that, after Captain Mahoney was tired of the widow Townsend, and had contributed to the squandering away her ill-got wealth, Mrs Mahoney admitted him to share her little fortune with herself and children; and his dependence on her for a subsistence secured his respect and fidelity, and by degrees reconciled him to a life of domestic happiness and sobriety. So various are the methods of Providence to reward the virtuous, and, if possible, to reclaim the vicious from their wicked pursuits.

VIII

AT DR GREVILLE'S

While Mrs Greville was gone to Warwick, Dr Greville, according to custom, walked out to visit some of the poor and ignorant part of his parish; so that Mr Wildgoose was left alone for some time with Miss Townsend, which opportunity he did not throw away upon theological speculations; but employed it upon a practical subject, more to his present purpose.

He introduced a sort of amourous conversation, by producing the cambric handkerchief which Miss Townsend had dropped from the chariot-window, when Wildgoose had that transient view of her near Birmingham. Miss Townsend immediately knew the mark; but said, she had no idea that it had fallen into his hands: for though from the slight glance she had of him in a cloud of dust, she at first imagined the person whom they passed was Mr Wildgoose; yet, as she heard no more of him, she had taken it for granted that she was mistaken.

Wildgoose replied, it was merely out of respect that he had not gone to Birmingham to inquire after her; and he declared he never underwent a greater mortification. But, says he, putting the handkerchief to his breast, I have preserved this pledge with as much devotion, as the most zealous papist does his imaginary relics of saints and holy virgins.

Miss Townsend endeavoured to evade an application of this intended compliment, by her sprightly raillery; and said, she hoped Mr Wildgoose was now almost tired with rambling about in so strange a manner, and would settle at home with his disconsolate mother.

Wildgoose, still pursuing his point, said he should return to his mother, in compliance with Miss Townsend's advice; and should probably quit his present rambling way of life, in condescension to Dr Greville's opinion: but, says he, it will be impossible for me to *settle* at a distance from the object of that enthusiasm of another kind, which you have raised in my breast.

Though the meaning of this declaration was too obvious to be misapprehended, and though Miss Townsend was by no means insensible to Mr Wildgoose's tender expostulations, yet she affected to treat them in a ludicrous style; and when Wildgoose came still closer to the point, she answered with a very serious air, that notwithstanding she had been guilty of one imprudent and undutiful act, in eloping from her father, on account of what she thought severe treatment, yet she could not listen to a conversation of that kind, without his knowledge and approbation.

This little repulse cast a sudden damp upon Mr Wildgoose's spirits. But as Miss Townsend's declaration, that she would not listen to his overtures *without* her father's approbation, might be interpreted to imply the contrary if his approbation were obtained, he was not entirely destitute of some pleasing hopes. But their further conversation was soon interrupted by Mrs Greville's return from Warwick, and the doctor's from his morning walk.

IX

AN INVITATION TO MR TOWNSEND'S

After dinner, Tugwell and his son Joseph, as had been agreed, set out towards Stratford; but with a strict intention to wait at the White Lion till Mr Wildgoose should come thither, which Dr Greville promised he should the next morning.

Wildgoose spent the afternoon very agreeably with Miss Townsend and her two worthy relations: and, as he now talked very rationally upon religion, as well as upon common subjects, Dr Greville and his lady were highly entertained with his company.

About ten o'clock in the evening, when they were just retiring to rest, they were again surprised with the arrival of a servant from Mr Townsend; who brought them the agreeable intelligence of the widow Townsend's having withdrawn herself with Captain Mahoney; and also a letter from Mr Townsend, earnestly requesting Dr Greville and his lady to conduct Miss Julia Townsend home again, and to spend a week or a fortnight with Mr Townsend, to assist him in re-establishing the economy of his household; which invitation, for the sake of performing the friendly office annexed to it, they were very ready to comply with.

X

AT STRATFORD-UPON-AVON

Mr Wildgoose, having made a comfortable breakfast, and drunk some excellent tea from the fair hands of Miss Julia Townsend (which quite reconciled him to domestic and social life,) took his leave of Mrs Greville and Miss Townsend; not without a sigh and a languishing glance directed to the latter. Dr Greville and he then set out in the carriage for Stratford; where they arrived about twelve o'clock, and found Tugwell and his son waiting for them; whom they again dispatched to pursue their journey.

Whilst the coachman stopped to water his horses, my landlord, out of civility, came to pay his compliments to Dr Greville, who knew the man to have been a son of the learned Dr Welchman,★ well known for his *Illustration of the Thirty-nine Articles*: which piece of history, as he had not much literary merit of his own to boast of, mine host never failed to acquaint his customers with. Gentlemen, he would say, you have doubtless heard of my father: he *made* the Thirty-nine Articles.

While they were talking to my landlord, the church bells struck up, and rang with great cheerfulness: upon which, as the canonical hour was just expired, Dr Greville supposed they had had a wedding. No, says my landlord; but we are going to have a funeral; and the bells ring upon that occasion.

★ Mr Welchman probably soon quitted this station, as the White Lion has been kept for some years by Mr Peyton; who, by a secret peculiar to publicans, of making general favours appear particular ones, has brought the house into great vogue.

How so? says Dr Greville.—Why, have not you heard of old Mr Shatterbrain's whimsical will? He was born in this town, and kept a tavern in London; and got ten thousand pounds in the lottery, and has left it all to his nephew, who was a tradesman in this town. But I will fetch you the newspaper, and you may see all about it. He then brought the *Gloucester Journal* to Dr Greville, in which was this clause from Mr Shatterbrain's will:

Provided also, that my said nephew, on the day of my funeral, do distribute six pounds six shillings to six young women tolerably skilled in dancing; who, being dressed in white calico, with black ribbands, shall join with six young men, to be procured by the undertaker (or the undertaker himself to make one, if agreeable,) who, being dressed in mourning cloaks, with black crape hat-bands, shall, in a grave and solemn manner, dance to a good tabour and pipe, the ancient dance called the Black Joke, in the church-yard (if approved of by the minister;) if not, as near to the place of my burial as convenient may be; the church bells ringing from twelve o'clock at noon to six o'clock in the evening.

Provided also, that my said nephew do cause to be inscribed on my tomb the following moral distich:

Since *dust* we are all, let us moisten our clay;
Let us drink, let us dance, and dust it away.

Dr Greville observed, that Mr Shatterbrain seemed to be actuated more by the love of fame, than by the love of mankind, when he made that will; and that he seemed more ambitious of being celebrated in a newspaper, than of being blessed by the poor, after his death: that six guineas properly distributed, would make six poor families happy for a month, instead of making the testator ridiculous for ever. Indeed, added the doctor, I have observed several of these ridiculous bequests of late years; but, if I were lord chancellor, I should make no scruple, upon the slightest application, of setting aside such absurd clauses, and applying the donations more advantageously, either to the public, or to the distant relations of the testator.

XI

MORE LUMBER YET;
A WIFE AND TWO CHILDREN

The chariot was now going from the inn, when a two-wheel chaise drove into the yard, with a gentleman, a lady, and two children in it, attended by a servant on horseback. The gentleman leaped down, and began to lift out a little boy and girl, when Wildgoose was agreeably surprised at discovering his friend Rivers and his lady, whose long story, (if he did not fall asleep in the middle of it) the reader must recollect; and who, in consequence of Wildgoose's letter, was going to pay his respects to his kinsman, Mr Gregory Griskin, the little Staffordshire divine, from whom he had considerable expectations.

Mr Wildgoose begged leave to detain Dr Greville a few minutes, whilst he just paid his compliments to his old friends.

After explaining his present situation, Wildgoose began making a sort of apology for his travelling in so different a manner from what he had done when they met last. Come, come, says Rivers; this is only a sneer upon my ecclesiastical equipage of a one-horse chaise. What sport would our old Oxford acquaintance make at a man packed up in this leather convenience, with a wife and two children.

Why, yes, says Wildgoose, we laugh at these domestic concerns, in the university; but, when married and settled in the country, our elegant ideas give way to ease and convenience; and many a delicate man, I believe, has condescended to warm a clout, and many a learned one to rock the cradle.

Mr Rivers then thanked Wildgoose for the service he had done him with his kinsman, Mr Griskin, and said he had had a letter by the same post from Mr Griskin himself, expressing great satisfaction in the account Mr Wildgoose had given him of Mrs Rivers's character and conduct; and inviting him to bring her and her children into Staffordshire, as soon as he conveniently could.

Wildgoose then told Rivers, that from hints which Mr Griskin had dropped, he fancied his design was to get Rivers into orders, that he might assist him in the care of his parish; and he made no doubt but that Mrs Rivers's agreeable behaviour would soon restore Rivers to the same place which he formerly possessed in his cousin Gregory's esteem.

Wildgoose having now paid his compliments to Mrs Rivers, and wished them a good journey, was unwilling to detain Dr Greville any longer; so, after desiring Rivers to write him word of the success of his visit, they parted, and he and Dr Greville resumed their journey.

XII

A PLAN FOR REFORMATION

After travelling about a mile beyond Stratford, they met a young man, in a shabby sort of livery, who appeared very sickly, and applied to them for alms. The coachman, by way of favouring the suit of a brother servant in distress, stopped his horses, whistling to them, as if to give them an opportunity of staling. Dr Greville asked how so young a man came to beg upon the road? The man said he had been dismissed his service, on account of a long sickness; and was travelling into Shropshire, to try his native air; that he had lived with Lord —— in London; who was a very good master, kept a good house, and gave his servants good wages; but, in case of sickness, always dismissed them.

Dr Greville gave the man sixpence, observing to Wildgoose, that although he did not like to encourage common beggars, he generally gave them some little matter to relieve their present distress; but not without a sharp reproof to those who appeared to be habituated to that idle practice.

This incident again introduced the subject of a reformation: and Dr Greville observed, that neither the preaching of the clergy, nor even the many penal laws, which were daily multiplied, would avail any thing towards the end proposed, unless some alteration could be produced in the manners of the people by the influence of their superiors: the luxury and extravagance of the great, and people in high life, descends as a fashion amongst the crowd, and has infected every rank of people. If, says he, an association were formed amongst some of our principal and most popular nobility, to set an example of frugality and temperance, by reducing the number of their servants, and the number of dishes at their tables; and if the prince on the throne would condescend to enforce the example, by regulating the splendour of the dress and equipages of those who appeared at court, it would soon be established as a fashion; and that crowd of useless servants, who are now supported in idleness and luxury, and who, when dismissed from service, or married and settled in the world, propagate the prices and follies which they have learned of their masters, amongst the middling rank of people; these dissolute idle rascals, I say, would be left in the country, where they are wanted to till the land, or to supply our handicraft trades or manufactures with useful and industrious hands. And we might then hope to see virtue and frugality restored amongst us.

XIII

THE SAME SUBJECT CONTINUED

As to the clergy, continued Dr Greville, all I shall add upon that subject is, that I could wish they would, in general, be a little more cautious and reserved in their conduct.

I do not expect them to renounce the world, or to shut themselves up entirely in their closets or studies. Neither would I absolutely forbid them, in great towns, going to a coffee-house or tavern, upon necessary occasions: but I would not have them make those places their constant rendezvous. I do not think there is any indecency in their playing at cards, or joining in other cheerful transactions in private company: but am sorry to see them dancing or gaming at Bath or Tunbridge; and, as a Cambridge friend of mine expresses it, *shining* in every *public* place—except the pulpit.

As to their preaching, added the doctor, I could wish they would make their discourses more systematical, and connected one with another. I know, by experience, that a man may preach for seven years together in the common way, in unconnected sermons, and our people be never the wiser. But a set of plain regular discourses, upon the principles of natural and revealed religion; the being, attributes, and moral government of God; and the peculiar doctrines and duties of the Gospel; such a system, I say, repeated once or twice a-year, would teach the people their duty, and make them more willing to attend the church; and even pay their tithes more cheerfully, when they were sensible they had some equivalent for their money.

Well, sir, says Wildgoose, and I will venture to add, from my own experience, that I wish the clergy would be a little more earnest in their delivery, and enforce their precepts with some little vehemence of tone and action; as I am convinced what an effect it would have upon the most rational Christians.

I am sensible, indeed, from what I felt when I first heard Mr Whitfield, that too violent gesticulations are not agreeable to the modesty and reserve of an English audience; and there is certainly a difference between the action of the pulpit and of the stage. But when a preacher reads his sermon with as much coldness and indifference as he would read a newspaper, or an act of parliament, he must not be surprised, if his audience discover the same indifference, or even take a nap, especially if the service be after dinner.

Why, there is no doubt, replies Dr Greville, but an impassioned tone of voice, a suitable gesture, and a pathetic style, have more effect upon the middling and lower ranks of mankind, for whose use sermons are chiefly intended, than the most rational discourse, delivered in a dry uninteresting manner. And this certainly is one great advantage which the Methodists and other fanatical preachers have over the regular clergy, in rousing so many indolent drowsy Christians to a sense of religion.

There is a remarkable instance of the persuasive power of this enthusiastic eloquence in a Capuchin friar, one Philip de Narni,* a

---

* So Rapin and Balzac call him; but his true name was Jerom de Matini, of Narni.

popular preacher at Rome, near the middle of the last century; from whose sermons the people never departed without tears, many of them crying out for mercy in the streets. And what is more extraordinary, we are told, that, preaching before Pope Gregory the Fifteenth upon the subject of non-residence, he struck such a terror into his audience, by the vehemence of his oratory, that no less than thirty bishops set out post, for their dioceses the very next day. And yet it is added in the life of that friar, that when his sermons came to be printed, there was nothing very striking in them. We are told also, that the good man was so far disgusted with observing the great numbers who came to hear him out of mere curiosity, without reforming their lives, that he retired to his cell, and spent the rest of his days in writing the history of his order.

Why, to be sure, says Wildgoose, that will always be the case with too great a number of people, from the necessary imperfection of human nature.

But we should use the most probable means of doing all the good in our power, and leave the event to Providence.

XIV

Mr Wildgoose's reception at home

In this kind of discourse were Dr Greville and Mr Wildgoose engaged, when they came to the point where the road turned off towards the village to which Wildgoose was bound. Here Tugwell and his son Joseph had again made a halt; and, while they were waiting for Mr Geoffry under some shady trees, by a brook side, regaled themselves with a slice of cold roast-beef, which Dr Greville's servant had stowed in the wallet.

Mr Wildgoose was now at a loss how to act; as he could not press Dr Greville to convey him any farther, through a long and dirty lane, to his native place; nor yet dismiss him without an invitation to rest his horses, and to take a dinner, or at least some refreshment, at his mother's house.

But from this perplexity Dr Greville himself delivered Mr Wildgoose. As the long summer had made the road better than usual, and very passable for a carriage, the doctor insisted upon carrying Mr Wildgoose quite home.

Indeed one principal end in his taking this journey was, to make some inquiries into the circumstances of Mr Wildgoose's fortune; and, if he should find it agreeable to his expectations, to make some overtures to Mrs Wildgoose, for a match between her son and Miss Julia Townsend.

The carriage now proceeded, with Tugwell and his son in the rear; and, after many jolts and jumbles, in half an hour's time, brought them in sight of their village spire, which arose amidst a grove of pines, at the foot of the Cotswold hills; the sight of which, after near two months' absence, rejoiced the very cockles of Jerry's heart; though not without a mixture of solicitude, about the reception he might meet with from the offended Dorothy, whose indignation his friend Andrew Tipple had announced.

As for Mr Geoffry, he was impatient to restore his mother's peace of mind; whose maternal fondness for him he was too well acquainted with, to fear any thing from her resentment, when once he should have returned to his duty.

It being now the midst of a very sultry day, and most of the village people out in the fields, they arrived at Mr Wildgoose's gates without much speculation. Mrs Wildgoose's old hind, Stephen, was just gone into the yard with a load of wheat; and a little boy and girl, whom Mr Geoffry was surprised to see there, ran in, crying out, a coach! a coach!

These little folks were no other than Mrs Wildgoose's grand-children, by her daughter, whom we mentioned in the beginning of this narrative, to have married contrary to her parent's approbation; and of whose children, therefore, very little notice had been taken, till since Mr Geoffry Wildgoose's elopement.

Though Mrs Wildgoose never dressed fine, yet, as she was always neat and clean, she was consequently always sufficiently prepared, for a woman of her time of life, to see company. By the time, therefore, the chariot came to the door, she was come out to receive them. Having not, for some years, seen her son in his own hair, she did not immediately know him; especially as the black patch on his temples added to the paleness of his complexion, which his loss of blood had occasioned. But when he stepped out of the chariot, and, agreeably to a custom now obsolete, bent one knee to receive her blessing, Mrs Wildgoose's surprise was so great, that she almost sunk to the ground. Wildgoose supported her in his arms, till Dr Greville also coming out of the chariot, they attended her into the hall; by which time she had recovered her spirits; and Wildgoose began to introduce the doctor, and to inform his mother of the great obligations which he had to him.

Mrs Wildgoose made proper acknowledgements to the doctor; and then, looking on her son, Oh, Geoffry! says she, how could you desert me in such a manner without once acquainting me with your intention, or where I might make any inquiries after you? Your unkindness might have been fatal to me; and if I had died under the first sense of your undutiful behaviour, it would have been a great misfortune to you. I find you have taken a pique against poor Mr Powel; but, I assure you, it was entirely owing to his honesty and discretion that I did not pursue the dictates of my resentment, and make a will greatly to your prejudice.

Dr Greville made answer for Mr Geoffry, that he believed he had been for some time under the influence of a deluded imagination; but that the mists which clouded his reason, seemed now to be dispelled, and he saw things in a more proper light; and that he could venture to answer for him, that he would never be guilty of the like act of unkindness for the future.

Mrs Wildgoose's flutter of spirits being now a little composed, she began to reflect, that it was high time to order the cloth to be laid, and to consider in what manner she should entertain Dr Greville; which, however, as a plentiful dinner was provided for her harvest-people, gave a woman of Mrs Wildgoose's good sense but little trouble.

XV

TUGWELL'S RECEPTION AT HOME

Though I have lived to speculate near half a century on the humours of mankind, I hardly remember a more remarkable instance of self-partiality, than the desiring to *perpetuate*—or of deference to fortune, than the submitting to *unite*—the poor, pitiful, and almost obscene monosyllable of *Dunk*, with the noble high-sounding polysyllable of M-ntague, Earl of H-lif-x; yet I had a personal regard for the worthy Mr Dunk himself, and a great respect for the noble earl; and only make this remark, to show the fascinating, or rather the omnipotent power of accumulated riches—though not to my present purpose, which was, to describe the interview between Jerry Tugwell and his wife Dorothy.

Dame Tugwell was infinitely exasperated against poor Jerry, for presuming to elope from home, in downright defiance of her sovereign authority; and had meditated with herself, as she sat at her spinning-wheel, every variation of phrase, expressive of the most furious resentment, to attack the hapless culprit with, whenever he should make his appearance.

But, as Jerry knew Dorothy's blind side, and the only part where, on these occasions, she was vulnerable; instead of any supplicating apology, or endearing caresses after so long an absence, Jerry approached her with a free and joyous air, as she sat at her wheel, but extending his right hand, filled with silver, two or three half-guineas being interspersed amongst it; the sight of which precious metals immediately softened Dorothy's features, from the truculent fierceness of the fury Tisiphone, to the simpering smiles of a Galatea, a Hebe, or an Euphrosyne.

Some deep politician might here suggest, that Jerry's wisest and most certain way to make peace would have been, to send their long lost son Joseph into the house before him. I think otherwise; for, after the first transports of that happy meeting were over, Jerry's offence would still have remained in full force, the subject of a severe reprehension; but by convincing dame Dorothy at once, by so evident a proof, that he had not neglected the main chance, and that she would be no loser by his long absence, the way was smoothed for a thorough reconciliation; and nothing now remained, but to indulge their mutual congratulations on account of their son's happy return.

As for Dame Tugwell's surprise and joy on the sight of her son Joseph, I shall not pretend to describe it. Instead of any concern about Jerry's travels, she would have asked as many questions about Joseph's adventures as his father had done at their first unexpected meeting at Warwick races. But her affection was more active than her curiosity; and she immediately began puffing up the fire, and was going to set on her best scoured pot, and to cut an untouched flitch of her best bacon, to entertain her guests, when a boy from Mrs Wildgoose's came, to invite Jerry, his son Joseph, and even dame Dorothy, to eat some beef and pudding with her harvest-people in the kitchen; which invitation in the present gaiety of her heart, Dorothy was no more inclined to refuse than Jerry himself was.

XVI

THE GRAND POINT SETTLED

Young Wildgoose, after dinner, having gone out to pay his compliments to his fellow-travellers and Dame Tugwell, Dr Greville took the opportunity of opening his commission to Mrs Wildgoose. After acquainting her with the rise and progress of the intimacy between her son and Miss Julia Townsend, and informing her what fortune Mr Townsend would probably give his daughter at present, and her expectations in future, he desired to know if she approved of the match, what kind of settlement she could enable her son to make. Mrs Wildgoose seemed at first to hint, it would not be in her power to settle any thing in the least proportionable to Miss Townsend's fortune and expectations: but, when Dr Greville said, that as the young people seemed to have conceived an extraordinary affection for each other, very rigorous terms would not be insisted upon, she said, that she could give up three hundred pounds a-year, provided a proper provision were made for herself during her life: that the whole estate was about four hundred pounds a-year, and only charged with five hundred pounds for her daughter's fortune; but that, since her son's undutiful elopement, she had taken two of her grandchildren, and intended to add five hundred pounds more to her daughter's fortune.

In short, this affair was soon settled between Mrs Wildgoose and Dr Greville, who, after drinking a glass of wine, walked out with young Wildgoose to view the place, and then first opened his intention to him; which he received with equal rapture and surprise.

Dr Greville then told him, that he should go over to Mr Townsend's, with Miss Julia, in a day or two, and stay there a fortnight at least; in which time, if Mr Wildgoose would come over, Dr Greville would endeavour to gain Mr Townsend's consent to their scheme. But sir, added the doctor, as my principal reason for interesting myself in this affair is, that I had rather see my cousin Julia married to a sober, religious young man, with a moderate fortune, than to some of your gay men of the world, with ten times your income: so, if I thought you intended ever to resume your late irregular way of propagating your religious opinions, I would by no means promote such an alliance; for, as a true rational system of religion contributes to the happiness of society, and of every individual; so enthusiasm not only tends to the confusion of society, but to undermine the foundation of all religion, and to introduce, in the end, scepticism of opinion, and licentiousness of practice.

Wildgoose replied, that whatever his opinions on some particular points were (though they were yet so far from being entirely settled,) he was determined for the future, to keep them to himself, and only endeavour to enforce the practice of religion in his own family, and amongst his neighbours; and that he should want no other motive for settling at home, if he were blessed with so agreeable a companion as Miss Townsend.

Dr Greville repeated again, that he had a very good opinion of Mr Wesley and Mr Whitfield, and of their first endeavours to revive the practice of primitive piety and devotion; but I am afraid, says he, that there have already, and will hereafter, from their examples, start up mechanical teachers, who will preach themselves, instead of Christ;

aiming at applause and popularity, to fill their pockets, or to fill their bellies; to please the young ladies, or the old women; and bring religion into contempt with all virtuous and sensible people.

XVII

MODERN TASTE, AND THAT OF OUR ANCESTORS

After viewing the garden and orchards, which, according to the old taste, were surrounded with high walls and quickset hedges, Mr Wildgoose proposed, if he should be so happy as ever to bring Miss Townsend thither; to modernize his place, and lay it out agreeably to her fancy.

Dr Greville replied, that he would sacrifice a great deal to good taste; and, says he, as the hills rise very prettily round you, I would endeavour to catch an opening or two from the bottom of your garden to those grand objects.

But, for my part, I prefer the plentiful taste of our ancestors, in whose gardens Flora and Pomona amicably presided, to the barren taste of the present age. Why would you destroy this south wall, covered with peaches and plumbs; and root up these pinks and carnations, to make way for some half-starved exotics, or, perhaps, poisonous shrubs, which nothing but mere fashion can recommend?

I like to see a grand edifice in the middle of a lawn; and would gladly give up old moss-grown orchards, clipt hedges, and endless avenues, for extensive views elegantly diversified with groups of trees, hanging woods, and sloping hills. But to think of exposing your irregular mansion, by removing walls, and aiming at a lawn no bigger than a Persian carpet, is a prostitution of taste, and a burlesque upon magnificence.

But the old clock now striking five, Dr Greville recollected that he had four hours' driving to his own house. After settling the plan, therefore, with young Geoffry, and taking leave of Mrs Wildgoose, he ordered his carriage, and departed.

XVIII

OTHER MATTERS ADJUSTED

Soon after Dr Greville was gone, Mr Powel the vicar of the parish, and his wife, in consequence of a private message from Mrs Wildgoose, came to drink tea; whom Geoffry immediately received with his usual freedom and cordiality. Mr Powel took an opportunity of telling young Wildgoose, that he was sensible he had taken some pique against him, though he could not guess upon what account. But, to convince him how much he was his friend, Mr Powel showed him the instructions his mother had given him in regard to a will, greatly to his prejudice, and which he had prevailed upon her not to execute. Mr Wildgoose thanked him for the service he had done him; though, he said, he was glad to find his elopement had been the accidental cause of having his sister taken into favour; which was what he always desired. He then confessed, that he had taken some little prejudice against the vicar upon a very trifling occasion; but that it had pleased God lately to open his eyes; and that a weight of gloom had, he did not know how, been removed from his mind; and he hoped they should for the future live together in their usual friendship and good understanding.

The news of Tugwell's return being likewise soon spread about the parish, Jerry and his son were visited that very evening, by every man, woman, and child in the village; except by his rival in trade, the other shoemaker; and by Dorothy's nearest neighbour the blacksmith's wife. Their mutual emulation will account for the conduct of the former; and a jealousy of a particular kind in the blacksmith's wife for that of the latter.

Mrs Enville, it seems, valued herself upon her family; her grandfather, by her mother's side, having been a supervisor: yet, by her extravagance and want of economy, she was become much inferior in her circumstances to Dorothy Tugwell; and, whilst the latter was saluted by the respectable appellation of *Dame* Tugwell, the former was dwindled down from Mrs Enville, to plain Betty. When, therefore, she was told of Jerry's return, she received the news with a sullen contemptuous silence;

and, when it was added, that he had brought his pocket full of silver and gold, she only said, it was well if he came honestly by it.

When Jerry came to examine the state of his shop, he found an accumulation of business upon his hands—old shoes, which wanted variety of repair, and which Dorothy had taken in, under a daily expectation of Jerry's return. But he was so full of his late journey, and so much embarrassed in answering questions put to him from every quarter, that it was in vain to think of business for that night; and Dorothy was so deeply engaged with her son Joseph, and so well satisfied with the cash that Jerry had thrown into her lap (he having only reserved a *new* shilling to himself, for *antickity's* sake, which was Jerry's word for *curiosity;*) Dorothy, I say, was in such harmonious spirits, that she connived at Jerry's keeping holiday for that evening.

But the next morning, when Dorothy got up to her spinning, having locked up Jerry's best waistcoat, she sent him to his stall with a grave rebuke, that it was high time to settle to business again, and leave off preaching and rambling about the country. And though Jerry's shop was the general rendezvous every evening, for a week after his return, Dorothy watched him narrowly, and kept him close to his work. And Jerry himself, having satisfied his curiosity, and being handsomely rewarded by Mr Wildgoose for his trouble, seemed very well contented to spend the rest of his days in his own shop, and in his own chimney-corner.

CONCLUSION

Mr Geoffry Wildgoose, and his trusty friend having now finished their summer's ramble, and we having fulfilled our engagements to our readers, we might fairly enough dismiss them without any further ceremony, especially as the reader probably may not be very deeply interested in the affairs of a hero, who meets with no other adventures than what any man might expect to meet with, who travels through a country that is under a regular civil government, and in an age which appears to be under the direction of a general Providence.

But, as this history may probably be banished from the circles of the polite, to some remote province, for the winter evening's amusement of some artless nymph, Chloe or Rosalind, whose curiosity is not yet grown callous, by a constant intercourse with the marvellous vicissitudes which abound in modern romance; methinks I hear poor Rosalind exclaiming, Oh! I long to know, whether Miss Julia and young Wildgoose made a match of it at last.

Now, as I own myself to be nothing at a temptation, and could never withstand the charms of youth and innocence—in spite of the practice of Virgil, or the precepts of ancient critics, who are for leaving many things to be supplied by the reader's imagination—I am determined, I say, to gratify the ladies' curiosity with a peep behind the curtain, and inform them of a few subsequent particulars.

That Mr Wildgoose, having equipped himself, not in pea-green or pompadour, but in a plain drab coat, with a crimson-satin waistcoat, laced with gold, peeping modestly from under it, mounted his chesnut gelding, and attended by young Tugwell, whose military air, and the flavour of a brass button added to his brown coat, gave him a tolerably smart appearance, though Mrs Wildgoose would not yet consent to his having a livery—thus equipped, young Wildgoose waited on Miss Julia Townsend, at her father's house in ——shire; where, by the mediation of Dr Greville and his lady, a match was soon concluded upon, and, after another visit or two, solemnized at Mr Townsend's in the Christmas holidays.

That Mrs Wildgoose, having fitted up a sort of neat cottage for herself, resigned the mansion-house to her son Wildgoose and his lady; where they now live together with as much felicity as this life is capable of; yet no more than what every contented unambitious couple may be sure of obtaining, who study to make each other happy; and whose expectations are not disappointed by the vain hopes of complete happiness in this world, or who do not fatigue themselves in the constant pursuit of violent and immoderate pleasures, in a state of existence where ease and tranquillity are the highest enjoyment allotted them.

Mr Wildgoose keeps as much of his estate in his hands as will employ a pair of horses and two servants and heartily concurs with Mr Powel, both by his example and persuasion, to countenance industry and sobriety in the parish, as his lady does in visiting the sick and afflicted.

He has also prevailed upon Mr Powel to lay aside his *argumentum bacculinum*, or crabtree conviction, with the lower and less docile part of his parish, and to endeavour to gain their love by the milder arts of soft persuasion; having convinced him of the truth conveyed in those beautiful lines of Dryden (alluding to the fable of the Sun and the North-wind:)

> To threats the stubborn sinner oft is hard,
> Wrapt in his crimes, against the storm prepar'd;
> But when the milder beams of mercy play,
> He melts, and throws his cumbrous cloak away.

Soon after he was married, Mr Wildgoose received a visit from his friend Rivers, who was just got into orders, and was going with his family to live with his kinsman, Mr Gregory Griskin, and to assist him in the care of his parish (as Wildgoose had hinted,) with a very handsome stipend, the presentation of the living after his cousin's death, and a promise of the perpetuity: so that Rivers also was now as happy as he could wish. And we may draw the same *moral*, or rather the same *religious maxim*, from each story:

That where we do not obstinately oppose its benevolent intentions, nor presumptuously persist in a wrong course of life, Providence frequently makes use of our passions, our errors, and even our youthful follies, to promote our welfare, and conduct us to happiness.